BEYOND
THIS
BROKEN SKY

BOOKS BY SIOBHAN CURHAM

An American in Paris

Sweet FA
Frankie Says Relapse
The Scene Stealers

NON-FICTION
Antenatal & Postnatal Depression
Dare to Dream
Dare to Write a Novel
Something More: A Spiritual Misfit's Search for Meaning

BEYOND THIS BROKEN SKY

SIOBHAN CURHAM

bookouture

Published by Bookouture in 2021

An imprint of Storyfire Ltd.
Carmelite House
50 Victoria Embankment
London EC4Y 0DZ

www.bookouture.com

ISBN: 978-1-80019-402-1
eBook ISBN: 978-1-80019-401-4

For Michael Curham and Jack Curham, with all my love

PROLOGUE

He's been watching her for days now, from the cover of the garden in the middle of the square. Others complain about the blackout – about the way it renders you almost blind, barely able to see a foot in front of you – but not him. He likes the way it makes everyone vulnerable – even the officious ARP wardens in their tin helmets and mock military uniforms. Their squeaking whistles and feeble torches are no match for the fathomless darkness. They're no match for *him* – a proper soldier. After all, none of them have spotted him when they've been out on their nightly patrols, barking at people to take cover as the air-raid siren wails. He likes the way the darkness wraps itself around him like a cloak, making him the perfect hunter stalking its prey, knowing that, at any moment, he could step from the shadows and finish it. Finish her. Finish *them*.

Tonight, after the bombers finally left and the wail of the all-clear sounded, sending people scurrying like startled rats from the shelter, they returned to the house together. It took every sinew in his body not to reach for his gun and finish it right there, especially when they had the brass neck to stand on the front doorstep and kiss. Rage rises inside him at the memory, tightening his chest and blurring his vision. How dare they make a fool of him like that? But he isn't the fool, he reminds himself. He's the clever one. Because he knows how this story is going to end. And he will decide exactly when.

The first of the dawn light bruises the night sky purple and blue, and the birds in the skeletal trees begin to sing. It's time for him to go, lay low, while a Blitz-weary London rouses itself from sleep. But he'll be back again soon. He feels for the comforting presence of his revolver on his belt beneath his coat. Yes, he'll be back again soon to finish things.

CHAPTER ONE

September 1940

Of all the times to hold a séance, Ruby thought to herself as she drew the thick velvet curtains over the blackout blinds, the eighty-degree heat of a late-summer afternoon was by far the most stupid. It was only the third time she'd had one of her soirees, as she liked to call them. She'd held the previous two in the evening, but tonight she had a dinner date with a dashing but slightly dull lieutenant colonel at the Savoy, so she'd brought the time forward. A decision she was now deeply regretting as she felt a bead of sweat roll down the back of her neck.

'Shall I light the candles?' Kitty asked, hurrying into the room holding a book of matches. She reminded Ruby of a faded pencil sketch of a person, with her pale blonde hair scraped back into a ponytail and her dreary lilac housecoat and flesh-coloured nylons.

'Why not?' Ruby exclaimed. 'May as well hasten my demise from this cursed heat. I can just see the headline in tomorrow's *Express* – "*She Evaded the Hun but Was Done for by the Sun*". Or perhaps, "*Dazzling Doyenne Dies of Dehydration*". Editors seem so obsessed with alliteration these days.'

'I'll only light a few then,' Kitty murmured, her thin eyebrows raised.

Even in this heat, Kitty was still as white as a ghost, not to mention skinny as a rake. Ruby had tried fattening her up with various meats, cheeses and chocolates from the Fortnum & Mason food hall but to no avail. Anything the poor girl ate seemed to be burned off as soon as it passed her lips. Ruby couldn't help smiling as she pictured Kitty's brain chugging away like a piston, burning up calories as it churned out anxious thoughts.

As Kitty began lighting the cluster of white candles at the centre of the table, Ruby took a sip of her lemon and honey. Since the war had begun, a year previously, finding a lemon had become akin to spotting a unicorn, but thanks to her contacts on the black market, she'd managed to procure one. Good job too, or she wasn't sure her throat would be up to another séance.

The doubts she'd experienced prior to her previous soirees began flooding her mind: would she be able to convince her guests that they were receiving messages from their dearly departed? Or would she be exposed as a fraud? Would she burn in hell, if such a place existed, for deceiving people?

She swatted the doubts away by reminding herself why she'd begun holding séances in the first place – to reassure people and try to bring them some comfort in what was a deeply unsettling time. Perhaps today she'd finally receive a genuine message from the other side. It certainly wouldn't be for the lack of trying. And it wasn't as if she was charging people money to come. She was doing it purely from a place of compassion.

She thought back to the first séance she'd attended as a teenager, after her beloved father was killed in the Great War. Her father had been the person she loved the most in the entire world. The thought of him never returning home again, never waltzing her around the parlour again, never regaling her with tales of his life as a West End theatre star again, had left her catatonic with grief. Hearing her father speak to her once more – albeit through a rather intimidating pot-bellied, hairy-warted medium named Madame Blavosky – and telling her that she must get on with her life and 'live it with gusto!' had changed everything. It had enabled her to feel a tentative glimmer of hope again, and gave her permission to live life to the full – a gift that had sadly been denied her poor mother.

Ruby glanced at the sepia portrait of her mother hanging over the mantelpiece. The photograph had been taken five years previously – three years before her mother's death. She'd spent so long grief-stricken by that point that her mouth had actually reset itself into a permanent droop. The contrast with the beaming, twinkly-eyed bride in her wedding day portrait was shocking. Ruby couldn't help shivering in spite of the heat. Her mother's fate was something she'd spent years trying to avoid at all costs.

She took a notepad, quill and bottle of ink from the sideboard and placed them on the table. A spot of automatic writing might be the easiest option in this weather. She would have to play it by ear, of course, and read her audience. This was a tip she'd learned from her father. 'Every audience is different,' he'd once told her, when talking about his acting career. 'You have to read their energy and play to it accordingly.' She hadn't really known what he'd meant at the time, but now his advice was serving her well.

The doorbell rang, wrenching her from her memories.

'Your first guest,' Kitty mumbled.

Kitty had a knack of stating the obvious, but Ruby tried not to hold it against her. Ever since the timid young woman had become her tenant, moving into the flat above hers at the start of the war, Ruby had made it her mission to try to bring her out of her shell. Enlisting her help with the séances was part of this grand plan, although Kitty still barely said a word.

Ruby finished her lemon and honey infusion and sat down. Her heart was pounding. *You're only trying to help people,* she reminded herself.

'I am ready to receive them,' she boomed, slipping into her medium's voice. The truth was, she didn't feel ready at all. 'Please help me, Papa,' she whispered, praying that spirits actually did exist and that her father was watching over her.

Kitty returned to the room with a middle-aged man wearing a crimson polka dot bow tie with a matching band around his trilby hat. The heat had obviously got to him too as he'd already removed his jacket and patches of sweat darkened his shirt beneath the armpits.

'This is Mr Blackwell, Miss Glenville,' Kitty mumbled.

Mr Blackwell was the first 'member of the public' to attend one of Ruby's séances, having responded to a discreet advertisement she'd placed on a noticeboard in the British Library. At the time, she'd thought it might be easier trying to receive or create messages for people she didn't know at all, but now she wasn't so sure and her stomach clenched.

'Good afternoon, Mr Blackwell, please take a seat,' Ruby said, gesturing at the chair to her right. She looked at Kitty pointedly.

'Oh, uh, yes, would you like me to take your hat, sir?' Kitty stammered.

'Thank you.' Mr Blackwell sat down and took a handkerchief from his pocket and began dabbing at his brow, his eyes darting this way and that.

While he was scanning the room, Ruby scanned him, searching for clues. Men tended to be harder to read than women as they wore less accoutrements. She looked at his face, at the shadows beneath his eyes, at the nick on his jaw where he'd clearly cut himself shaving. She glanced down at his stubby fingers resting on the table. No wedding ring. Perhaps he was a widower.

'Have you travelled far to get here, Mr Blackwell?' she asked.

'Only from Clapham,' he replied. His voice was soft and he sounded educated. Ruby estimated that he was around fifty. Perhaps he'd lost a son to the fighting in France.

The doorbell rang again and Kitty hurried out, returning moments later with Mary Scott. Mary had been to every one of Ruby's soirees. She used to be her mother's charwoman and she came to receive messages from her husband, Bill, who'd been killed three months previously in the Battle of Dunkirk. Ruby decided to begin proceedings with a message for her, as a way of winning Mr Blackwell's confidence.

''Ello, Miss Glenville.' Mary bustled her portly frame over to the table and sat down with a sigh. 'Lumme, it's hot enough to fry an egg on the street!'

'It really is quite frightful,' Ruby agreed.

As Mary took off her jacket and hat, Ruby observed that her blouse had been buttoned unevenly and the roots of her grey hair were dark with grease. The poor woman looked ravaged by grief. She made a mental note to deliver an extra-comforting message from Bill.

The doorbell rang again and Kitty returned with the two remaining guests – a former flapper dancer named Charlotte, whom Ruby had befriended during a hazy night of cocktails at the Florida Club, and her elderly Aunt Maud, who, according to Charlotte, was desperate to receive a message from her brother Roger, who'd been lost to cancer a few months ago. Ruby was very grateful when her guests were indiscreet about their losses – it made her job so much easier.

She exchanged a few pleasantries with the women, noting Maud's hawklike stare and seating her in the chair furthest from her. Kitty took the women's hats and jackets and left the room. Ruby cleared her throat.

'Good afternoon, everyone,' she said. 'And welcome to our soiree, during which we shall hopefully be joined by some very special souls, dear to your hearts. If I could ask you to please place your hands on the table, like so.' She placed her hands palms down on the table, praying that this time they wouldn't be trembling from nerves. 'And move them so that the tip of your little finger is touching the tip of the little fingers of those either side of you so we may form a circle. Then I'd like you all to close your eyes as I offer up a prayer for protection.' She checked that everyone had closed their eyes. 'May the light of the Lord shine over us,' Ruby began, adding a silent prayer that, if there really was a God, He would be as forgiving as He claimed. 'May the presence of the Lord protect us from evil…' She felt Mr Blackwell's finger twitching against hers. 'And may those of us we long to hear from visit with us today. Amen.'

A murmur of amens rippled around the table.

'Is there anybody there?' Ruby asked, lowering the tone of her voice even further. She waited for a moment, trying to clear her mind, just in case a spirit was trying to communicate with her. 'Please make your presence known.' Mr Blackwell's finger twitched again. Sweat beaded on Ruby's forehead. 'Speak to us so that we may relieve your burden!' she cried. But it was no good. All she could hear was the ticking of the grandfather clock in the corner, louder and louder. There was nothing else for it; she would have to pretend again. She inhaled deeply through her nose and raised the back of her tongue to the roof of her mouth. She tightened her stomach muscles and slightly parted her lips. 'Over here,' she said, projecting her voice to the other side of the room.

'Ooh!' Maud shrieked, causing Mr Blackwell to jump.

'I'm sensing a very strong presence,' Ruby whispered. 'Please, let's hold hands so that we can maintain the connection.' Mary and Mr Blackwell took hold of her hands. His was hot and clammy. 'To whom do you wish to speak?' Ruby asked. She dropped her head slightly to make it look as if she'd gone into a trance. Then she prepared to throw her voice again. 'To Mary,' her voice echoed from the other side of the room.

'Aw, it's my Bill again,' Mary said. ''Ello, Bill, duck. How are you doing?'

Ruby breathed a sigh of relief. Words beginning with M, like Mary, were notoriously hard to pull off when it came to throwing one's voice. But she'd learned the art of projection at the knee of one of the world's most successful ventriloquists – her grandfather, the Fantastic Frederick Rose. She inhaled deeply through her nose before projecting again. 'When you're sad, I'm sad.'

'Oh, Bill.' She heard Mary sniff.

'I want you to be happy.' Ruby rocked back and forth, as if in a trancelike state.

'I'm sorry, Bill,' Mary said. 'I've been so down in the dumps lately, but I promise I'll cheer up.'

Ruby inhaled again. 'I love you, duck.'

'I love you too, Bill.'

Ruby opened her eyes and glanced sideways at Mary. She was relieved to see a smile on her face, which instantly warmed her heart.

'He must have been watching over me,' Mary said. 'I've had a right bad week this week.'

'He's always watching over you,' Ruby said with a smile. Her throat was really sore again from the projecting. She glanced down at the notepad and started to twitch her arms. 'I'm picking up the presence of another soul. But this one wants to write through me.' She let go of Mary and Mr Blackwell's hands and picked up the pen. Her head was pounding. Damn this heat.

Just as she was about to pretend to go into another trance, there came a high-pitched wail from outside.

'Bloody sirens,' Charlotte muttered. 'Bound to be another false alarm.'

Ruby paused for a moment. They were supposed to take shelter as soon as they heard the air-raid warning, but, so far, London had been pretty much untouched by the German bombs. They only seemed interested in bombing the airfields on the outskirts of the city. 'What would you like to do?' she asked the group. Normally she was loath to obey the siren's command, but this could be the perfect excuse to end the séance early.

'I say carry on,' Mary said. 'We'll be all right, we've got my Bill watching over us.'

Ruby looked around at the others. To her disappointment, they were all nodding, even the twitchy Mr Blackwell. 'All right, let's continue.' She closed her eyes. 'Are you still there, friend? To whom do you wish to speak?' Trying to tune out the wail of the siren, Ruby began rocking back and forth. 'I'm sensing the spirit of a young man.' She bowed her head so they wouldn't see her open her eyes, and gave Mr Blackwell a quick sideways glance. He suddenly seemed very alert.

'Wh-what does the young man look like?' he stammered.

'He's of average height.' Ruby glanced sideways again. Mr Blackwell's face was blank. A bead of sweat trickled down the side of her face. 'Actually, I'm sensing that he was slightly shorter than average.'

Mr Blackwell began to nod.

'I think he might be the son of someone present,' Ruby said.

Mr Blackwell frowned and looked disappointed. Damn it. If the young man wasn't his son, then who was he to Mr Blackwell? Nephew perhaps.

'Or maybe he's someone's nephew.'

Again, there was no response from Mr Blackwell.

The tension in Ruby's head intensified. This heat was dulling her wits. Then she thought of the dandyish manner in which Mr Blackwell dressed and something dawned upon her. She began to write, using her right hand instead of her customary left.

WE SHARE A VERY SPECIAL KIND OF LOVE, she wrote, in jagged letters.

Mr Blackwell gasped.

Phew, third time lucky. Ruby thought of her friend Teddy, from her New York days. He'd been that way inclined too. Unlike the prim and proper disapprovers, Ruby didn't give a hoot who people fell in love with. But she knew that men like Teddy endured a terrible time, trying to keep their love secret. Her heart panged for poor Mr Blackwell.

She uttered a gasp for effect and began to write again. *OURS IS THE BRAVEST KIND OF LOVE, ONE THAT DEFIES TIME AND SPACE AND THE HATRED OF OTHERS.* She heard Mr Blackwell give a low sob. *WHEN YOU ARE SAD, THINK OF OUR SPECIAL TIME,* she wrote, reasoning that every couple must have had at least one time together that they classed as special.

Sure enough, Mr Blackwell began nodding enthusiastically.

Satisfied that he would now leave more content than when he'd arrived, Ruby turned her attention to Maud. But just as she was about to channel a message from Roger, a strange humming sound filled the humid air.

'What the heck's that?' Mary said.

Ruby chose to ignore it. If she moved swiftly, she could have the whole thing over and done with in a few more minutes. But the humming grew louder and louder, as if the air outside had filled with angry hornets.

'What the dickens?' Mr Blackwell muttered.

Ruby opened her eyes to see that the rest of the circle were all looking apprehensively towards the window. 'Let me just check,' she said. She went over and peered through a chink in the blackout blinds. 'Oh my!' she exclaimed. A weird gloom had fallen over the square as if a cloud was passing over the sun.

'What is it?' Charlotte asked.

Ruby looked up at the sky. It was filled with what looked like hundreds of black birds, all flying in neat V-shaped formations.

There was a knock on the parlour door and Kitty burst in, her pale face for once flushed. 'I – I'm sorry to interrupt, Miss Glenville, but – but – the Germans are here!'

CHAPTER TWO

September 1940

Joseph looked out of his window, his heart thudding. When he'd heard the siren begin to wail, he'd assumed it was yet another false alarm. But now the sky was filled with German bombers like a swarm of giant black moths. What were so many of them doing flying over London? Was this the start of the long-dreaded invasion? His stomach churned at the thought of the fascist Nazi wave that had conquered so much of Europe sweeping over Britain's shores. People assumed that because he was a conscientious objector he didn't care about such things. But nothing could have been further from the truth. Joseph hated the Nazis and their brutal regime. That was why he was a conscientious objector after all – he abhorred all killing.

He grabbed an old tobacco tin from the mantelpiece and stuffed it in his trouser pocket. It contained a couple of photographs of his parents and his brother's dog tag. It was the only thing he now deemed worth saving in the event of an emergency and he couldn't quite decide if this fact was tragic or liberating.

He glanced around the room, praying that he wasn't looking at it for the last time, then, shunning the lift, he hurried out of the back door of his flat and raced down the stairs. As he reached the entrance hall, with its huge chandelier and black and white chequered floor, the door to the ground-floor flat flew open, causing his heart to sink. Ever since he'd moved to Pendragon

Square almost a year previously, Joseph had done all he could to avoid his landlady. She was everything he hated: vain, pampered and privileged. How else could you describe a young woman who'd inherited such a huge house in one of the most fashionable parts of London and, by all accounts, hadn't had to work a day in her life?

But instead of his landlady, a rather flustered-looking man wearing a red bow tie appeared. Upon seeing Joseph, he tipped his hat and hurried across the hall. As he opened the front door, the hum from outside grew louder. Three women came hurrying out of the flat behind him. Joseph sighed. Ruby must have been holding one of her 'séances' again. When Kitty had told him about Ruby's decision to start holding séances, it had made his blood boil. The nerve of the woman, taking advantage of people when they were stricken with grief. It wasn't as if she needed the money; apparently her mother's side of the family owned half of Scotland, so she had to be doing it out of greed, boredom or cruelty, or a mixture of all three.

'All right, duck?' one of Ruby's poor victims said, spotting him on the stairs. 'Looks like Jerry's arrived.'

Joseph nodded.

As he followed the women to the front door, Kitty came flying out of the flat, looking panic-stricken. Joseph liked Kitty, even though she barely said a word. He was hardly surprised she was timid as a mouse. Living above her flat, he'd heard the sharp bark of her husband's yells piercing the floorboards late at night, followed by Kitty's soft sobs. He wondered if Kitty had been as relieved as he was when her husband had enlisted and had been stationed down on the south coast.

As Joseph reached the front door, he heard the distant rap-rap-rap of anti-aircraft fire. But would it make any difference against this German show of force?

'Well, Hitler sure knows how to ruin a sunny Saturday!'

Joseph instantly tensed at the sound of Ruby's jaunty voice from behind him. How could she joke about it? If all of those planes were about to unleash their bombs, hundreds of people could be about to lose their lives.

'They'd just better not scupper my supper plans,' Ruby continued, following him out onto the steps and locking the front door. As always, she was dressed to the nines, in a figure-hugging black dress and a pair of bright green heeled shoes. A huge emerald sparkled on her ring finger, although as far as Joseph knew there wasn't a husband on the scene, which didn't surprise him. The woman was intolerable, worrying about her supper plans when the Germans could be about to invade. It annoyed Joseph even further that she was so beautiful. With her wavy raven hair and rosebud lips, she looked as if she'd sprung straight from the pages of a fairy tale, like some kind of enchanted princess. If there was any justice in the world, she'd have been born stooped and gnarled. But there was no justice in the world; Joseph had learned that long ago.

Ignoring Ruby, he hurried over to the tree-lined garden at the centre of the square. A shelter had been built there for the residents at the start of the war. Thankfully there'd been no need for its protection yet.

'They're heading east,' Ruby continued, gazing at the planes crowding the sky and clearly unable to take a hint. 'Why do you think they're heading east?'

'The docks maybe,' Joseph replied bluntly.

When they reached the entrance to the shelter, he somehow mustered the good grace to stand back and let her inside first.

'For what we are about to receive…' Ruby said dramatically, before heading down the concrete steps.

As Joseph followed her, it took a moment for his eyes to adjust to the gloom after the brightness outside. The shelter was long and narrow, more like a tunnel than a room, and the walls were lined with corrugated iron. As his eyes adjusted, he saw rows of frightened faces, all tilted upwards, listening and waiting.

Joseph had hoped he'd be able to escape Ruby, but as the shelter was almost full to capacity he had no choice but to sit down opposite her. Feeling the tobacco tin in his trouser pocket cutting into his leg, he took it out and examined its contents, and not just for comfort. If he looked otherwise occupied, it might stop Ruby from speaking to him. He felt for the round leather dog tag. In the gloom of the shelter, he wasn't able to see the blood staining the bottom just beneath his brother's name. Liam had only just turned eighteen when he'd been slaughtered in Ypres. His life, like so many others, taken before it had even begun. In effect, his dad's life had been taken too. To his lasting shame, Joseph hadn't even recognised the emaciated, lice-ridden figure who returned from the trenches, appearing one day in their backyard in Blackpool and causing Joseph to drop his football in fright. Gone was the fun-loving man he remembered from his earlier childhood, and all that was left was a haunted shell.

'Ooh, if you're having a smoke could you be a doll and roll me one?' Ruby said, nodding at the tin.

'It isn't tobacco,' Joseph replied.

'Then what is it?'

Joseph sighed. 'Some personal belongings.'

Ruby laughed. 'I wish I could pack all of my worldly goods into a tobacco box.'

Kitty giggled beside her, then shot Joseph an apologetic look.

Joseph's cheeks burned. 'Well, maybe the world would be a better place if people didn't insist on having so many things.'

'I say…' Ruby leaned forward and lowered her voice to a whisper. 'Are you a communist?'

'No, I am not,' he snapped.

'I wouldn't mind if you were, it's just that, what with your views on the war…' Ruby glanced at the Peace Pledge Union badge on his jacket lapel. 'I thought—'

'Well, you thought wrong.'

There was a distant thudding sound, vibrating through the ground.

'What was that? Have they started bombing?' Kitty exclaimed, turning to Ruby. She looked terrified.

'Don't worry. We're safe down here. Isn't that right, Mr O'Toole?' Ruby looked at Joseph.

'Absolutely,' he agreed, although with every thud that reverberated through his spine, his fear increased. Would they be safe inside this shelter if they suffered a direct hit? Or were they waiting to be buried alive inside a corrugated metal tomb?

CHAPTER THREE

September 2019

I should have known Marty and I were doomed the moment he turned to me and said, 'I could never marry a woman who earns more than me.' But he'd said it on our second date and I was drunk on wine and possibility, so I chose to ignore it. I never for one moment thought he was delivering a curse that would come back to haunt me.

I stand on the pavement and look up at my new, post-marital-break-up home: 22 St George's Square, Pimlico. An elegant Georgian townhouse in a pretty little pocket of London, tucked away behind Victoria and a stone's throw from the river. I want to feel happy to be here. I want to feel grateful that I earn enough to be able to buy such a swanky apartment. I want to feel proud that I've made it so far from the Manchester sink estate I was born into. But all I feel is numb.

I take my keys from my bag. They're still attached to the estate agent's fob, which promises '*Your home is where our heart is.*' Something about this statement conjures the unsettling image of an estate agent's heart pulsing away on my new mantelpiece and I make a mental note to remove the key fob as soon as possible.

I'm just going up the wide stone steps to the front door when the ground-floor sash window slides open and a head bearing a long mane of poker-straight silver hair appears.

'Not today, thank you,' a haughty voice booms.

'I'm sorry?' I reply.

'I take it you're from that hideous double-glazing company, trying to persuade me to change my windows. Well, I might look like a daft old bat, but I can assure you I'm still in firm possession of every single one of my marbles and these sashes are staying. This is a listed building, you know!'

'I'm not—'

'And what's more, if your company sends one more person out to harass me, I shall be forced to take legal counsel and we shall eviscerate you in the law courts.'

I bite my lip to stop myself from laughing. The thought of this tiny, birdlike old woman 'eviscerating' anyone is amusing, to say the least. But I mustn't laugh; this silver-haired spitfire is clearly one of my new neighbours.

''Ello, 'ello, what's going on here then?'

I turn to see a man behind me at the bottom of the steps grinning up at me. His salt-and-pepper hair is immaculately styled and his skin glows with a deep tan. He's wearing well-cut black jeans and a grey camo shirt from Tom Ford's latest collection. I know this because one of the perks of being the newly appointed editor-in-chief of *Blaze* magazine means I get an invite to all the shows.

'Are you doing your pitbull routine again, Pearl darling?' the man continues, looking at the woman.

'It's another of those slimy sales slugs, sweetheart,' the woman replies, and this time I can't help laughing out loud.

'I'm not a slimy sales slug,' I say. 'I'm your new neighbour. I just bought the top-floor flat.'

'No way!' The man runs up the steps and extends a well-manicured hand. 'Welcome to the madhouse, darling.'

'Well, you could have said something,' Pearl huffs as the man and I shake hands, before withdrawing inside and sliding her window down with a crash.

'Oh dear,' I laugh. 'Looks like I haven't got off to the best of starts.'

'Don't worry about Pearl,' the man says. Now he's close, I catch a waft of his aftershave. It smells as expensive as his clothes. 'Her bark's a lot worse than her bite. I'm Heath. I live in the first-floor flat with my husband, Guy.'

'Lovely to meet you. I'm Edi.'

'Welcome to St George's Square, Edi.' He beams at me, revealing a row of perfect white teeth. 'You'll have to come for drinks so we can properly toast your arrival, once you've settled in of course.'

The faintest tinge of warmth prickles through my numbness as I imagine a new life in London peppered with drinks with my lovely new neighbours, well, some of them, at least.

I follow Heath up the stone steps and through the grand front door. The entrance hall made me instantly fall in love with the property when I first came to view it. With its black and white tiled floor, ornate chandelier and old-fashioned sliding gate elevator, it felt like stepping back in time to a London of calling cards and carriages, or so I imagined. History has never been my strong point.

Heath pulls the latticed iron gate of the lift open and stands back to let me enter. But just as I'm about to step inside, the front door to the ground-floor flat flies open and Pearl appears. She's wearing a black shirt dress and bright coral trainers, which is so out of keeping with how I'd imagined someone of her age to be dressed I can't keep my mouth from gaping open.

'Where are you rushing off to?' she asks.

'Oh, I'm sorry, I thought I'd annoyed you.'

'Why would you think that?' Pearl comes into the middle of the hall and looks me up and down. I feel a pang of regret that I didn't wear something more stylish, but I'd dressed for the journey from Manchester and a day of unpacking, opting for the comfort of a tracksuit. 'So, do you have a name?' she asks.

'Yes, sorry, it's Edi.' I go over to her and hold out my hand. Thankfully, she takes it. Her hand might be tiny but her grip is strong. There's a huge oval moonstone set in silver on her ring finger. It doesn't look like a traditional wedding ring, but I'm already sensing that there's nothing traditional about Pearl.

'And what do you do for a living, Edi?'

Heath chuckles. 'Maybe you could let her get moved in first, sweetheart, before you start the inquisition.'

Pearl frowns at him. 'I'm just trying to ascertain her character. You can tell a lot about a person from their profession.'

'I'm amazed you give me the time of day then, darling.' Heath grins at me. 'I'm a hairdresser.'

'There are a lot worse things one could do.' Pearl purses her lips. 'And besides, you're not just any old hairdresser, are you?' She returns her hawklike gaze to me. 'Well?'

'I'm a magazine editor.'

'Ooh, exciting!' Heath exclaims.

'We don't know what kind of magazine yet,' Pearl interjects. 'Please tell me it isn't one of those ghastly things you find by the checkouts in supermarkets. The ones with all the ridiculous real-life stories.' She sighs. 'I saw one the other day that claimed a woman's dead husband had reincarnated as a goldfish named Splosh.'

'No, it's OK. I'm the editor of a lifestyle magazine called *Blaze*.'

'Hmm.' Pearl doesn't look overly impressed.

'Right, enough with the questions,' Heath says. 'I'm sure Edi is dying to get up to her new home. We'll have some welcome drinks for her in a week or so and then you can ask her all you want – if that's OK with you?' He looks at me.

I nod. 'Of course.'

'Right you are then. I'll be seeing you soon,' Pearl says, slightly menacingly, before disappearing back into her flat.

'Don't worry, she's an absolute sweetheart once you get to know her,' Heath says as we get into the lift and he pulls the grille gate shut.

'Glad to hear it,' I laugh.

After Heath has left the lift at the first floor, I continue on alone, trying to process what just happened. At first glance, my new neighbours are everything I could have hoped for in my new London life – hip, quirky, fun – well, Heath seems fun at least. Pearl seems more formidable – but I like formidable women, they give me something to aspire to. The lift arrives with a judder at the second and final floor, right at the door to my apartment, which was another huge selling point to me – being able to pretend that I live in a penthouse suite.

I unlock the door and step inside. When I'd viewed the property, months before, it had still been occupied and furnished. Now it's stripped bare and I can't help feeling a pang of concern at the starkness of the white walls and the bare floorboards. I think back to the places Marty and I moved into during our ten years together. The sight of a new, vacant property had always been cause for excitement and celebration, but now all it seems to do is reflect back the emptiness I'm feeling inside.

I go into what will be my bedroom and my eyes are drawn to the fireplace. According to the estate agent, the fireplaces in the property all date back to when the houses were built in the nineteenth century. I think of all the people who must have sat around this fire over the years. All of the lives played out between these walls.

'I hope you've been a happy place,' I whisper, looking around. I'm not really a woo-woo person, but I do have a theory that properties can become imprinted with the energy of those who've lived in them. I take a deep breath and look around. The room is at the front of the house, overlooking the garden in the middle of the square, and the windows are filled with the green of the treetops. I think of the previous inhabitants gazing out at the very same trees over the years. Despite being in the heart of London, it feels incredibly peaceful. Yes, I nod, trying desperately to convince myself, this *will* be a happy and healing place.

CHAPTER FOUR

September 1940

Ruby closed her eyes and focused on her breathing – another tip her father had passed on to her, back when she'd been twelve and crawling with nerves ahead of her first ever piano recital. 'Breathe in for as long as it takes you to say the word onomatopoeia in your mind,' he'd told her. 'And breathe out for the length of higgledy-piggledy.' *Onomatopoeia… higgledy-piggledy,* she thought to herself now and, in spite of the hellish sounds that had been coming from outside, and the stuffy, musty smell coming from inside, it brought a smile to her face.

'How much longer do you think it will go on?' Kitty asked.

Onomatopoeia… higgledy-piggledy… Ruby tried to calm her thoughts before replying. In the hour they'd been in the shelter, she'd tried her best to lift Kitty's spirits, wittering on about fashion and music and other such frippery to try to distract her, but to no real avail; she could still feel the poor girl trembling beside her. 'I'm sure it will be over soon,' she said. 'It better had, my supper date's at eight!'

Across from her, Joseph gave a pointed cough and frowned. Ruby really didn't know what his problem was. Ever since he'd started renting the top-floor flat, she'd bent over backwards to try to make him feel welcome, but he continued to look at her as if she were an irritating gnat. You'd have thought that, given the way most people viewed conscientious objectors, or conchies as they'd become known, he would have welcomed all the camaraderie he could get.

She sighed. After her mother died and she inherited the house in Pendragon Square, she'd thought that converting the top two floors into flats would provide a welcome opportunity for new friendships and high jinks. But so far her tenants hadn't been nearly as much fun as she would have hoped – in spite of the fact that she'd lowered the rents drastically in light of the war.

'Who are you dining with?' Kitty asked.

'Lieutenant Colonel Rupert Butterworth,' Ruby replied, loudly enough for Joseph to hear over the chatter in the shelter. Maybe if he realised she was the type to fraternise with army officers, he might show her a little more respect. Joseph wasn't to know that Rupert was the son of a family friend and an insufferable bore, and she'd only accepted his invitation as it meant the opportunity to dine at the infamous Savoy Grill. With food starting to be rationed, she was more than happy to be wined and dined in exchange for an attentive smile and a few well-placed nods and oohs and ahs of appreciation.

'Sounds like some poor souls out there have had their last meal,' Joseph said in his thick northern accent.

Ruby had always been a fan of the northern accent. It conjured images of hard-working factory folk with solid names like Ted and Bob, and swarthy miners with coal-streaked faces, and the dramatic struggles of the working classes. But it seemed as if sourpuss Joseph was intent on ruining her romantic notions of life beyond Watford. To make matters worse, he had the piercing blue eyes, dark hair and broad frame she favoured in her romantic heroes too. But if he carried on at this rate, she would have to take down the framed photograph of Clark Gable hanging over her bath.

'Yup,' he continued. 'I'd say hundreds will have lost their lives. And for what?'

Heavens to Betsy! What was the matter with him? Was he trying to send Kitty mad with fear? 'I'm sure they've only been bombing the docks,' Ruby responded, trying to shoot Joseph a warning stare, but in the gloom of the shelter she wasn't sure if he could see it.

'Do you really think hundreds have been killed?' Kitty asked. 'Do you think the Germans have started their invasion?'

The tension in Ruby's head reached bursting point. 'Of course not! How could they possibly invade with the might of the RAF against them? We will win the Battle of Britain.'

'What, just like we won in Dunkirk?' Joseph muttered.

'Anyone would think that you want Hitler to win,' Ruby hissed.

'Of course I don't want him to win,' he spat back. 'I'm just tired of all this pointless bloodshed.'

But how can it be pointless if it's shed in the pursuit of beating Hitler, Ruby wanted to ask, but her head was pounding and she was starting to feel an acute case of claustrophobia, trapped in this underground hellhole with her misery guts of a tenant.

Then, as if in answer to her prayers, a single continuous note sounded from outside – the all-clear! In her attempt to get up quickly, she came over dizzy and, reaching out blindly to steady herself, she grabbed on to Joseph's arm. He pulled it away as if he'd been scalded. Good God, the man had the manners of a grumpy old goat.

'Come on,' she said, grabbing Kitty's arm. 'Let's see what's happened.'

They emerged, blinking, from the shelter. Thankfully, all of the houses in Pendragon Square were still standing. Ruby had already concluded as much, given that the thuds of the bombs had sounded so far away, but it was reassuring nonetheless to discover that she and her tenants still had a home.

'There you are, see, there was nothing to worry about,' she said, giving Kitty's arm a comforting squeeze.

'Hmm,' Joseph muttered. 'I wouldn't be so sure.'

Ruby followed his gaze over to the east, where a black cloud had gathered on the horizon. Ruby shivered. For so long the war had felt at arm's length – something that was happening across the Channel in the rest of Europe. What if the RAF wasn't as impenetrable as Churchill would have people believe? She pushed the thought away. Clearly she'd been spending too long with doubter Joseph.

'Come on,' she said to Kitty. 'I have a supper to get to.'

'Are you still going out?' Kitty asked, wide-eyed, as they hurried across the garden.

'Of course. You heard the all-clear. Our boys must have sent them packing.'

Ruby unlocked the front door and looked over her shoulder to see if Joseph was behind them, but he was standing by the entrance to the garden looking deep in thought. What a strange and difficult character he was. But what could she expect from someone too cowardly to go to war? Her father could have taken the coward's way out during the Great War, but he didn't. He was brave enough to go and fight for his country. He was brave enough to sacrifice his life.

She opened the door and marched inside. From this moment forward, she wasn't going to spend a single ounce of energy trying to befriend Joseph. He really wasn't worth the effort.

*

Joseph looked back into the garden at the people emerging from the shelter, blinking in the daylight like startled rabbits. Then he looked at the cloud of smoke over to the east. The compulsion to go and help burned inside of him. It was the same compulsion that had caused him to set up a charity to help feed and clothe the down-and-outs back in Blackpool. A compulsion he'd been born with, it seemed. Even when he was a young lad, he was always trying to heal injured birds or house stray dogs. To the point where his mam had begun to despair. 'I've barely enough money to feed us humans,' she'd said once, when he brought home a three-legged mongrel he'd found on the seafront. But twelve-year-old Joseph had been undeterred. He'd gone down to the pier and started performing card tricks for the passers-by and soon he was earning enough money to feed all of them. He felt a pang of sorrow as he thought of his mam, but at least she was safe from the German bombs up north.

He strode to the end of the square, where the River Thames glimmered and coiled like a dark serpent, and turned and headed east.

*

Ruby sat at her dressing table, powdering her nose. According to the news on the wireless, the East End of London had taken quite a pounding from the Germans, but the raid was over now, so surely it would be safe to go out. It would be a distraction, if nothing else. She had a feeling that if she stayed home with just her thoughts for company, she'd end up a nervous wreck, like poor Kitty.

She applied a coat of scarlet lipstick, then used a lip-brush to add some volume to her upper lip. According to all the magazines, a full pout was just the thing needed to lift the nation's spirits at this critical point in history. As Ruby looked in the mirror at her perfectly curled black hair and painted lips, she felt a rush of satisfaction. She wasn't going to let Hitler and those pesky Germans lower her morale. No siree, Bob! She gave herself a generous spritz of Je Reviens and put on a string of pearls and she could practically hear the spirit of her father whispering, 'Atta girl!' She would live her life to the fullest, even if it killed her.

Normally, it was easy to hail a taxicab at the bottom of the square, but today there didn't seem to be one in sight, so Ruby hopped on a bus and took a seat at the front of the top deck. On board, all talk was of the bombing raid.

Ruby gazed out of the window. In the distance, the sky glowed amber, streaked with black. She wanted so badly for it to be a storm cloud, but she knew deep down that it had to be smoke. She took out her compact and checked her lipstick. The tension she'd been feeling before returned with a vengeance. *Onomatopoeia… higgledy-piggledy,* she repeated in her head, trying to drown out the nervous chatter of the passengers around her.

As the bus followed the river through Westminster, she was relieved to see the majestic Houses of Parliament still standing, along with all of the other iconic London landmarks. Hitler stood no chance against the might of the British, Ruby reminded herself. At the back of the bus, a chap who'd clearly had one too many stouts began singing a round of 'Roll Out the Barrel', but no one else joined in.

Ruby got off the bus on the Strand. As was the norm for a summery Saturday evening, the street bustled with people. But in addition to the usual theatre- and restaurant-goers, there seemed to be a predominance of rather scruffy-looking people clutching suitcases and bags. She made her way over to the grand silver canopied entrance of the hotel.

'Good evening, Miss Glenville,' the doorman greeted her, tipping his hat. It was Tom, a cheery Scotsman with a round, ruddy face and a wonderfully wry sense of humour, and her favourite of all the Savoy staff.

'Good evening, Tom. How's the knee?'

'Still giving me bother, miss, but ach, mustn't grumble. There's people dealing with a lot worse at the moment.'

'Indeed, but I do hope it gets better soon.'

Tom ushered her into the revolving door. The glass panels had all been painted dark blue when the blackout began, making the splendour of the Savoy lobby a delightful surprise when one whirled one's way inside. Not that Ruby didn't know what to expect, of course. She had spent, or rather *misspent*, a large portion of her early twenties here, before embarking on her world travels, and the Savoy felt as familiar and comforting as home.

She followed the tinkling of piano music through the lobby and saw the broad outline of Rupert standing at the bar, clad in his army uniform. Despite his ability to annoy her to the point of combustion, she felt a wave of reassurance at his familiarity. Rupert was the son of her mother's best friend and, both being only children, Rupert and Ruby had grown up together, agreeing at the ages of seven and five respectively to be one another's honorary sibling. Ruby knew her mother had always harboured a secret desire for them to marry, but as far as Ruby was concerned this prospect felt as wrong as marrying an actual brother – and an insufferably pompous brother at that.

'Good evening, Roops,' she called gaily, tapping him on the shoulder.

'Glenners!' he exclaimed, turning to greet her. 'I wasn't sure you'd make it, given what's happened.'

'What *has* happened?' Ruby took off her jacket and put it on a bar stool.

Rupert ran his hand over his Brylcreemed hair. 'Apparently the East End's taken quite a drubbing. Drink?'

'Scotch on the rocks, please.'

Rupert ordered her drink and lit them both a cigarette.

'What do you think's happening?' Ruby asked, trying to maintain an air of nonchalance. 'Do you think they're going to try to invade?'

Rupert shook his head. 'No! I think Goering's having a temper tantrum after we bombed Berlin last week, but they'll never be able to take us like they took France. We're the British!'

As Rupert started delivering a soliloquy about the might of the British Empire, Ruby took a sip of her whisky, but instead of relaxing her it made her feel even more hot and bothered. The Nazis had spread like wildfire through the rest of Europe. She'd never believed them capable of taking France, but they did, and without much of a fight even. When they'd marched into her beloved Paris unhindered, she'd felt utterly bereft. Who was to say that they couldn't do the same to London?

'Shall we go and dine?' Rupert asked. 'I'm famished.'

'Absolutely.' Ruby picked up her coat and drink, but as she followed him downstairs into the new, supposedly bombproof restaurant, her appetite seemed to have deserted her and her stomach churned. What if one day soon the Savoy would be overrun with the grey uniforms and black jackboots of the Nazis, just as they'd invaded the Paris Ritz?

'So what are you up to these days, old girl?' Rupert asked as the maître d' showed them to a table.

'Less of the old if you please,' Ruby retorted.

'Hmm, I'd say thirty-four is positively ancient.'

'You're thirty-six!'

'Yes, but it's different for us chaps. We improve with age.'

'And women don't?' Ruby glared at him. As far as she was concerned, she'd improved enormously as she'd grown older. She'd travelled the world, meeting all kinds of interesting people from all walks of life, and she'd educated herself in the world's finest theatres, museums and galleries – not to mention drinking dens. Surely that made her a far more interesting prospect than the naïve debutante she'd been at eighteen.

A waiter arrived at their table, glancing around the place and shifting nervously from foot to foot. Ruby wondered if the bombing raid had rattled him too. They ordered their meals and Rupert asked for a bottle of Burgundy without even consulting Ruby. If he had taken the time to ask her opinion, she would have gladly informed him that he'd picked a very poor vintage. And if her head hadn't been pounding, she would have taken great pleasure in sharing her extensive knowledge of French vineyards with him.

'I say, have you finally accepted some poor fool's proposal?' Rupert nodded at the emerald glinting on her ring finger.

She shook her head. 'Good heavens, no! This ring was a gift to myself.'

He looked at her as if she were deranged. 'Why on earth would you buy yourself an engagement ring?'

'It isn't an engagement ring; it's a freedom ring.'

'Freedom from what?'

'Being propositioned by undesirables and insufferable bores.'

He laughed and shook his head. 'I don't think I'll ever understand you.'

'Excellent.' She raised her glass of Scotch. 'I live for being misunderstood by simpletons.'

'Bloody cheek!' He grinned and chinked his glass to hers. 'Great to see you again, old girl, especially as it looks as if my leave is about to be cancelled, thanks to Jerry.'

Ruby lit a fresh cigarette and studied Rupert. Beneath his grinning façade, she could see shadows under his eyes and worry lines creasing the centre of his brow. 'How is it going?' she asked. 'And I don't want a Ministry of Information-style spiel, I want the truth.'

'Not great. I—' But before he could say another word, the howl of the air-raid siren sounded. 'Drat!' Rupert exclaimed. 'Why did it have to go off before our steak arrived?'

A hush fell upon the restaurant and all eyes turned to the maître d'.

'I am terribly sorry, ladies and gentlemen,' he called, 'but I'm afraid we will need to vacate the restaurant and take shelter.'

'Don't worry,' Rupert said. 'I'm staying here tonight, so we can go down to the guest shelter. Wait till you see it, it's top-notch.' He grabbed the arm of a passing waiter. 'I say, old chap, could you send our food downstairs when it's ready?'

'Of course, sir,' the waiter replied.

Ruby followed Rupert through the throng of people and down another flight of stairs.

'Well, this is certainly an adventure,' she said as they made their way through a door surrounded by teetering piles of sandbags.

'Wait till you see inside,' Rupert replied. 'Even Hitler can't ruin the Savoy style.'

As Ruby followed him into the shelter, she instantly saw what he meant. In sharp contrast to the dark, dank shelter in Pendragon Square, the Savoy shelter was positively sumptuous. It was so large, there was even room for a dance floor! Over on the other side were rows of perfectly made-up beds, in the traditional green, pink and blue Savoy bed linen. Some even had curtains around them that could be pulled for privacy.

A maid in a crisp black and white uniform hurried over to greet them and after Rupert told her his room number, she led them to one of the beds.

'Don't go getting any funny ideas, Roops,' Ruby quipped as she perched on the end of the mattress.

'But what if this were our last night alive?' he said mock-earnestly.

'Do you think I'd want to ruin it by seeing your naked body?'

He let out one of his loud guffaws. 'I can see you haven't changed at all.'

Ruby laughed, but inside she felt a pang of sorrow. What if this were their last night on earth? Would she really want to spend it trading insults with Rupert? Was this all she had to show for her thirty-four years on the planet? Was this all her existence boiled down to?

'How about you?' she asked, trying to ignore her budding existential crisis. 'Have you changed at all?'

His smile faded. 'Dunkirk was pretty dicey. But we got out. Well, most of us, anyway.'

'Did you lose some of your boys?'

He nodded. 'But let's not talk about that. It's Saturday night, we're at the Savoy. Let's have a party!'

*

As the siren began to wail again, Joseph's heart sank. The East End was still reeling from the earlier raid, with fires burning all around, and the sky was filled with an acrid black smoke. Surely there wasn't going to be another attack so soon. When he'd got to the East End a couple of hours earlier, he'd ended up helping a family who'd had their house bombed try to retrieve some of their personal possessions. Then he'd helped an air-raid warden dig out a family who'd become trapped beneath the rubble of what used to be their home. Thankfully they'd succeeded, but the whole business had left him feeling shaken.

'Let's head west,' a portly man called out to a large group of people behind him. Most of them were clutching suitcases and one of them had a wheelbarrow filled with belongings. But surely they'd be safer taking shelter here than heading west.

Joseph looked up and down the street for any sign with the red letter S, signalling a public shelter, but there was none to be found. The fierce rattle of anti-aircraft fire rang out above, sending sparks like shooting stars across the darkening sky and causing the windows of a nearby pie shop to tremor. Joseph needed to take shelter, but where? He turned a corner and saw Whitechapel Underground station up ahead. An air-raid warden was standing at the entrance talking to a thin young woman with three children clutching at her legs like limpets to a rock. She was holding a perambulator filled with clothes and toys.

'You can't shelter down there, love, it's against the rules,' Joseph heard the warden say as he approached them. 'You need to go to a proper shelter.'

'They're not sheltering,' Joseph said, hurrying over. 'We're taking a train, aren't we, pet?' He gave the woman a knowing look.

'But I don't have the money to—' she stammered.

'I told you I'd pay for the tickets,' he cut in.

The air-raid warden sighed. 'All right then.'

'Come, quick.' Joseph ushered the woman inside the station, helping her carry the perambulator down the steps to the ticket hall, where he bought them all tickets. 'Stay down here on one of the platforms until the all-clear sounds,' he told her.

'Thank you, sir.' Tears spilled from the woman's eyes and down her soot-streaked cheeks.

'No problem.' Joseph cleared his throat. Crying women always made him feel slightly awkward. 'I'll be off then. You take care.'

He made his way to a platform, which was already crowded with people sitting on the floor. A train rattled in and the doors opened. A handful of people got off, staring in bemusement at the growing crowd sprawled on the floor in front of them. Joseph walked to the far end of the platform and sat down. Up above, he heard the distant thud of bombs. He felt in his pocket for the tobacco tin and clutched it tightly to his chest.

CHAPTER FIVE

September 2019

As I make my way onto St George's Square, the tension from deadline week at work that had turned my muscles into knots starts to ease. The sight of the beautiful old church at the top of the square bathed in the golden glow of twilight conjures an instant feeling of peace and the amber-trimmed leaves of the trees remind me that we're coming into my favourite season – autumn. Maybe it's because I still associate it with a new school year, but September has always felt like a far better time to start afresh than grim, barren January.

I trudge up the steps to number 22 and unlock the front door. I'm midway through my first week as an official London resident and I'm already shattered. All I can think of is a glass of Cabernet and plummeting head first down a Netflix rabbit-hole. But as soon as I step into the hallway, Pearl's door flies open. My heart sinks. I've managed to avoid my spitfire of a neighbour for the past few days thanks to my insanely long shifts at the office; I'm not sure I've got the energy for another encounter.

'About time,' Pearl says, by way of a greeting. She's wearing a crimson kimono and black biker boots and her eyes are lined in thick dark kohl. Her silver hair is piled on top of her head in a loose bun, held in place by what looks suspiciously like one of those pencils with an eraser on the end.

'I'm sorry, have you been waiting for me?' I stare at her, confused.

'Yes!' Pearl replies impatiently.

My brain is so foggy from exhaustion that for a horrible moment I think she might have invited me to something I've completely forgotten. But my welcome drinks at Heath and Guy's aren't until next week and there definitely aren't any other house get-togethers that I'm aware of.

'I need your help with that.' Pearl points to a large brown cardboard box on the floor beside her door. 'The imbecile of a delivery man just left it there when I buzzed him in and flew off like a bat out of hell before I had a chance to get out here. How am I expected to carry that in on my own? I'm almost eighty. *And* I'm predisposed to brittle bones.'

'Of course, no problem at all,' I reply, hugely relieved that I hadn't forgotten anything and grateful for an opportunity to try to get in Pearl's good graces. I bend to pick up the box and notice from the label that her surname is Steele. The appropriateness isn't lost on me. As I lift the box, I almost buckle beneath the weight. 'Wow, what's in here?'

'Books.' Pearl turns and heads back inside her flat.

'OK then,' I mutter. Using the wall as support, I somehow manage to hoist the box up and follow Pearl inside. 'Wow,' I gasp as she leads me off a long hallway into a stunning living room. With its grand piano, grandfather clock and elegant chaise longue, I feel as if I've stepped onto the set of a period drama. A large antique bureau has pride of place in the bay window, housing a vintage typewriter and piles of notebooks and papers. Clearly Pearl spends a lot of time at the desk as it's also littered with coffee cups and an open box of chocolates. The window overlooks the square, which explains why Pearl saw me come in – it's the perfect observation post.

'Well, don't just stand there,' she says with a frown. 'Put them down before you do yourself a mischief.'

'Yes, sorry. Where would you like them?'

Pearl points to an oak coffee table in front of the chaise longue. It's also covered in notebooks and an open box of after-dinner mints. 'Would you care to join me for a Scotch?' she asks as I put the box down.

'Oh, uh—' I'm so tired, the thought of spending more time in Pearl's company isn't exactly appealing, but if I say no it will probably make things even more awkward between us.

'Or any other beverage. I have a full selection.' She points to a glass-fronted drinks cabinet in the corner.

Maybe she's trying to make amends for us getting off on the wrong foot. 'Do you have any wine?'

Pearl gives me a withering stare. 'Does a bear shit in the woods? Red or white?'

Or maybe I was wrong. But it's too late to back out now. 'Oh – er – red, please.'

As Pearl goes over to the cabinet and pours us both a drink, I take a proper look around the room. 'I assume you're a book lover then,' I say, nodding at the heaving bookshelves lining the alcoves either side of the fireplace.

'Books are my life blood,' Pearl replies dramatically.

'I love reading too,' I say, trying to find some common ground.

'I bought your magazine.' She nods to a copy of *Blaze* lying open on a leather-bound armchair.

'Oh, that's great. I hope you enjoyed it.' I think back to the scathing attack she made on women's weeklies and hold my breath.

'I thought it was good.' She passes me my wine in a beautiful crystal glass. 'I particularly liked the interview with the Bedouin tribal queen. It made a refreshing change from all of the celebrity guff one normally has to plough through.'

I can't help feeling a small flush of pride. Having features on fascinating, but non-famous people was one of the changes I implemented when I took over as editor-in-chief. I'm still waiting to see if my gamble pays off in terms of sales figures, so to have Pearl's endorsement gives me a much-needed boost.

'Well, don't just stand there, take a seat.' She gestures to one of the armchairs and sits down on the chaise longue. 'I have to say, it's good to have another woman in the building. What with the boys upstairs and that godawful cosmetic surgeon who used to live in your apartment, it was starting to feel like a bit of a sausage fest.'

Hearing the phrase 'sausage fest' come from Pearl's mouth almost causes me to spit my wine all over my lap.

'So, how long have you been editor of *Blaze*?' she asks.

'Three months, but I edited the culture section for years before, when I lived in Manchester.'

'I see. And how are you finding life in the Big Smoke?' She stares at me intently.

'I love it. I love that there's so much going on here. Or I would, if I wasn't having to work such long hours.'

Pearl nods and, for the first time, I sense a slight thawing in her expression. 'Yes, it's certainly impossible to be bored here, that's for sure. So, tell me, what is it that you want to do with your one wild and precious life, to paraphrase Mary Oliver?'

The fact that Pearl has just quoted from my all-time favourite poem further endears her to me, although her question has me a little stumped. 'I don't know. I suppose I'm already doing it. Being the editor of a magazine has been my dream ever since I went into journalism.'

'How old are you?' she asks.

'Thirty-five.'

Pearl snorts. 'A mere babe in arms! To give up dreaming now would be criminal. I'm seventy-seven and I still have grand ambitions.'

'Oh really, what are they?' I'm genuinely intrigued.

'Well, for a start I'd like to walk the Inca trail and I'm determined to learn to play the harp before I pop my clogs.'

'The harp? Wow, where would you put it?' I look around the crowded room.

She frowns at me. 'What do you mean?'

'Well, harps are a little on the large side. They sound beautiful though,' I add quickly, not wanting her to think me a killjoy.

'I'm talking about the blues harp – the *harmonica*,' she says, with extra emphasis, as though explaining to a toddler. 'Sonny Boy Williamson is my hero – or one of them, anyway.'

'Oh.' I really have no idea what to say to this revelation.

'That's just a couple of my dreams though. I have hundreds.' Pearl glances at one of the notepads on the coffee table and I picture it bursting with a list of her grand ambitions.

When I grow up I want to be just like you, I think, looking at Pearl in her crimson kimono, her pale blue eyes sparkling with life.

For the next half an hour, Pearl asks me all about my childhood and the places I've travelled to and the pros and cons of my job. It's so refreshing to have a conversation with someone who seems genuinely interested in me, by the time I finish my wine I feel totally invigorated.

'Right, I'd better get going,' she announces, getting to her feet. 'My life drawing class begins in twenty minutes.'

'Oh, is painting one of your dreams too?' I ask.

She shakes her head. 'No, darling, I'm the nude model.'

Of course you are, I think, trying to stifle a grin.

As I get up to leave, I look at the desk. 'Do you still work?'

'Of course! Retirement is for wimps!'

Again, I have to fight the urge to laugh. 'What is it that you do?'

'I'm a writer, darling – a writer of books.'

And so, as soon as I get up to my own apartment, I head to my laptop and google Pearl's name. It turns out she's an author of

'cosy crime'. It's a genre I'd never heard of before, but according
to Goodreads, it's a sub-genre of crime fiction where any sex or
violence takes place 'off camera' and, more often than not, the
setting is somewhere quaint, like a picturesque village. I look Pearl
up on Amazon and I'm amazed to see a whole host of titles – all
of which have garnered hundreds of reviews, hovering around the
four- to five-star mark. I keep scrolling and reading the blurbs
until I reach what appears to be Pearl's first ever book, a historical
novel titled *Beneath a Bomber's Moon*, which was published in
1982. The cover is very different to the others, which all seem to
feature thatched cottages and other cutesy rural tropes. Instead,
it shows a huge moon suspended over the London skyline, peppered with the outlines of old-style fighter planes. Beneath the
moon, the darkened silhouettes of a man and a woman embrace,
but another figure is lurking in the shadows, watching with a
gun drawn. I'm instantly intrigued and click on the blurb. It's
short and sweet: *A tragic tale of love and revenge set during the
London Blitz.* As the book was published so long ago, there's no
Kindle version available, but I do find a second-hand copy of the
paperback and order it immediately. My eccentric downstairs
neighbour just became even more intriguing.

CHAPTER SIX

September 1940

As Ruby hurried past the church at the top of Pendragon Square, she felt a wistful pang. Normally at this time on a Sunday morning, the church bells would be pealing loudly – a sound she always loved, despite not being a church-goer. But as soon as the war started, the government ruled that all church bells across the land should fall silent – only to be rung in the event of a German invasion. Ruby shuddered at the thought. Could an invasion now be imminent? She and Rupert and the other Savoy guests had ended up putting on a brave face and partying the night away in their shelter, but now her headache had returned and her mouth was dry from too much liquor.

As she reached home, she saw Joseph at the top of the steps fumbling in his pocket, no doubt for his key. He was also wearing the same clothes as yesterday, but they were crumpled and his face was streaked with dirt. Where on earth had he been? Ruby's curiosity overrode her desire to avoid him at all costs and she hurried up the steps.

'Allow me,' she said, brandishing her key.

Joseph turned to face her with an expression that could best be described as abject dismay.

'So, where have you been until this time in the morning?' Ruby asked, determined not to let his insolence ruin her morning.

'The East End,' he muttered, following her inside.

'What? But why?' She stared at him, shocked. The East End had borne the brunt of last night's bombing. Why on earth would Joseph, of all people, knowingly put himself in danger?

'Because I wanted to help.'

'Help who?' Ruby asked, but he was already at the lift, pulling the grille gate open.

'The poor people who got bombed out of their homes,' he replied.

'Their homes? But I thought it was the docks the Germans were targeting.'

Joseph stepped into the lift and pulled the gate shut behind him. 'You thought wrong,' he muttered as the lift began its juddering ascent, but not so fast that she didn't see him look her up and down in disgust.

She glanced at her fur wrap, hanging open over her figure-hugging dress, nylons and heels. *I was caught in the raid too*, she wanted to yell after him. But dancing the night away to Glenn Miller tunes and drinking Scotch didn't exactly feel like a hardship.

She sighed and let herself into her apartment. Why should she care what that misery guts Joseph thought? She went into her bedroom and collapsed onto the bed. As she gazed up at the chandelier hanging above her, she knew she should feel fortunate to still have her home, and such an opulent one at that, but the nagging unease that had plagued her the day before seemed to be curdling into a much sharper feeling of despair. Seeing Rupert again had thrown a harsh and unforgiving spotlight upon her life. She felt so alone and with so little to show for her thirty-four years on the planet. Perhaps she should have given in to her mother's wishes and allowed herself to be married off at an early age to someone with a suitable pedigree and an inherited title. But the trouble was, Ruby wasn't a thoroughbred – she was 'her father's daughter', as her mother had reminded her at every opportunity.

She'd always taken this as a compliment – she found her father's bohemian side of the family wildly exciting compared to the highly starched lords and ladies on her mother's side. But had inheriting his free-spirited nature actually been a curse? Oh, if only she could have been born with the insipid personality of a blancmange! How much easier life would have been!

She rolled onto her side and gazed forlornly at the framed photograph of her father on the nightstand. Unlike the countless staged professional pictures taken during his theatre days, this was a far more candid shot of him holding the five-year-old Ruby on his lap and whispering something into her ear. Ruby couldn't remember what he'd been telling her, but from the delighted expression on her face it had clearly been entertaining.

'I miss you, Papa,' she whispered. 'I wish you were still here.' She closed her eyes and prayed that sleep would come quickly to save her from her misery.

Ruby woke a couple of hours later feeling slightly more positive. *Enough of this mooching about feeling sorry for yourself*, she told herself sternly, *if you want something to show for your life, you have to show up for it.* She grinned at her clever turn of phrase. Perhaps she ought to seek employment at the Ministry of Information. Lord knows they could do with some help with their clumsy attempts at trying to galvanise the nation's spirit. She decided that once she'd freshened up, she would check on Kitty and then go out for the day. Even better, she would take Kitty out for the day, try to lift both their spirits.

She went through to the bathroom and began drawing a bath, gazing at the framed picture of Clark Gable on the wall. The handsome devil always improved her mood and today was no exception. Thankfully, any resemblance to Joseph had failed to dampen her ardour. Ruby took the pink and black packet of

Radox from the shelf. The writing on the side claimed that the bath salts 'radiated oxygen', so hopefully they, along with Clark, would make her feel tickety-boo. She threw an extra handful under the running water, just to be sure.

Once she'd had a soak and reapplied her make-up, Ruby put on a pink satin blouse and a pair of slacks – far more practical than a frock if they got caught in another air raid. Then she took the lift up to the second floor and knocked on Kitty's door.

'Are you there, Kitty-Cat?' she called.

The door opened almost immediately and a petrified-looking Kitty stared out, her eyes ringed with dark shadows. 'Oh, Ruby, I've been so worried about you.'

'Why on earth would you be worried about me?'

'When you didn't come home last night, I thought you'd been caught in the second raid.'

'Oh, darling girl, there was no need to worry. I was snug as a bug in a rug in the shelter at the Savoy.'

'Oh.' Kitty gave a sigh of relief.

Seeing her concern made Ruby want to grab her in an embrace, but she managed to restrain herself. The one time she'd attempted to hug Kitty before – after Ruby had won the princely sum of almost two hundred pounds playing poker – the poor girl had flinched as if it physically hurt. 'How about you?' Ruby asked now instead. 'Did you go to the garden shelter?'

'Yes. I didn't get a wink of sleep. But Freddy from the butcher's was there and he kept me company.'

'Oh, you poor thing.' Ruby peered beyond Kitty into the apartment. The blackout blinds were still drawn, but she could make out an old milk bottle containing a sprig of freshly cut flowers in the middle of the kitchen table. It was a sight that gladdened Ruby's heart, as Kitty wasn't normally one for any kind of adornments. It took every fibre in Ruby's being not to bring an ornament with her every time she called. 'I was wondering if you fancied a spot of lunch. My treat. We could go to the West End.'

Kitty frowned. 'But what if the Germans come back?'

'I'm sure they won't. Not after last night. They won't have any bombs left, by the sounds of it.'

'I think I'd rather stay here, if you don't mind. My Reg is supposed to be ringing me today.'

'Oh.' Ruby bit her lip. She hated Kitty's husband Reg with a vengeance. He was a horrible, weasel-faced man who seemed to have created a sport out of bullying his wife. Hearing the way he spoke to Kitty – or rather yelled – through the ceiling had done a lot to reaffirm Ruby's belief that marriage, for a woman at least, was akin to a prison sentence. She'd done a jig for joy when Reg had enlisted a few months previously and had been posted to Newhaven down on the south coast. 'Well, if you're sure I can't persuade you…'

'I'm sorry.' Kitty glanced down at her threadbare slippers. 'He gets really mad if I'm not here when he phones.'

'Of course. I understand.'

Ruby bade her farewell and got back into the lift. The lift sank in perfect synchronicity with her spirits and her feeling of loneliness returned with a vengeance. At least Kitty had someone to call her, someone to turn to in this hour of need, even if he was a weasel.

Sighing, Ruby realised there was only one thing for it – she had to go and see her father.

'I don't know what's wrong with me, Papa,' Ruby said, an hour later. 'Hitler and his blasted Nazis seem to have got under my skin and I can't stop worrying about everything.'

Her father looked back at her vacantly. *Don't let them get to you, poppet*, she imagined him saying. Of course, she had to imagine him saying this because the figure of Oscar Glenville standing in front of her was actually a waxwork dummy. Her father had been forever immortalised in wax at Madame Tussauds shortly after he was killed in the First World War. When she'd first come to visit the waxwork with her mother at the age of thirteen, the whole experience had left her deeply disturbed. The dummy's lifeless expression and waxy skin only emphasised the fact that her effervescent father was dead and gone. But as she'd grown older and the pain of his death had faded slightly, she'd taken great solace from the fact that if she wanted to see a life-sized likeness of her father at any time, she could hop on a bus and come and talk to him.

'What should I do, Papa?' she asked. 'Should I stay in London or should I go back to New York where it's safe?'

At some point, you have to stop running, a voice whispered in her mind, causing her to feel an instant flush of shame at her cowardice. Her father hadn't run away at the start of the Great War. He'd readily enlisted and faced the enemy. Ruby had left her apartment in Paris as soon as it became clear that the French government were about to capitulate to Hitler, but she wouldn't run again. She would stay and confront the enemy, just as her father had done. But how? What exactly did she have to offer when it came to fighting the Nazis? Thanks to her family's wealth, she'd never had to work. She'd spent her twenties flitting like a butterfly from one exciting adventure to another. And yes, she'd experienced a lot, but she hadn't exactly acquired any skills that would come in useful in the context of war. But her father had had no military experience when he enlisted. And she was undoubtedly a fast learner – as the Moldovan prince who'd taught her how to play poker and then promptly lost two hundred pounds to her had discovered to his cost.

'What should I do, Papa?' She gazed at the waxwork.

You can do anything you put your mind to, she imagined him replying.

Madame Tussauds had been a lot quieter than usual, probably due to the previous day's bombing raid, but now a couple came into the room, giggling at the waxwork of Charlie Chaplin. But it was all right; Ruby had found the solace she'd come for.

'Goodbye, Papa, I'll see you again soon,' she whispered before turning to leave.

*

Joseph woke to the sound of laughter drifting up from the street outside and for a blissful moment he forgot all about the war and the latest deadly developments. In his dreamlike state, he was back home in Blackpool, having an ale with the lads after football. But then memories from the night before came slamming into him.

He fumbled for his wristwatch on the bedside cabinet and squinted at the hands. It was almost four in the afternoon.

'Oh heck!' He sat up and rubbed his eyes.

The laughter from outside wafted up again and this time he recognised it as belonging to Ruby. How typical that she should be giggling away after one of the worst nights in London's history. Clearly nothing troubled that woman's conscience – even in the midst of a deadly war, to her, life was one big party. He'd smelled her stale perfume and the liquor on her breath this morning. While she'd been living it up in the West End, the poor people in the east of the city were having their lives decimated.

He went over to the window and looked out into the square. A couple of children were playing ball in the garden. It was so rare to see children playing on London streets these days following the mass evacuation, it warmed his heart. But then he thought of the woman he'd helped down into the station the night before and how her children had clung to her, terrified, and he wanted to whisk the children as far from London as possible.

Ruby's laugh rang out again and he spotted her standing at the foot of the steps talking to the coal man. Clearly a good judge of character, the coalman's horse gave an impatient whinny, but Ruby carried on chatting away ten to the dozen.

Joseph sighed and went over to the washbasin and splashed his face with water. Then he sat down on his bed and recalled everything that had happened the previous day. He had to do something to help, but what? He took his peace pledge card from his pocket and re-read the words printed on it. *'I RENOUNCE WAR and never again, directly or indirectly, will I support or sanction another.'* Some conscientious objectors refused to help out in any way as they saw it as a form of indirect support for the war, but there was no way Joseph could sit back and do nothing while so many innocent people were in danger. He was a conscientious objector because he believed in saving lives not taking them. It was time for him to step up and offer his services. But before he could do any more, the air-raid siren began to wail.

CHAPTER SEVEN

September 1940

Ruby spread the newspaper on top of the piles of books and gramophone records littering the kitchen table and peered at the headline through bleary eyes. *BLITZ BOMBING OF LONDON GOES ON ALL NIGHT.*

'*Goering restarted his great blitzkrieg on London last night, promptly at blackout time,*' the article began. '*Half an hour before that time, he made a gloating, boasting speech to the German people: "A terrific attack is going on against London. Adolf Hitler has entrusted me with the task of attacking the heart of the British Empire."*'

Ruby felt a chill to her very soul. Her worst fears had been confirmed – the bombing raids on Saturday and Sunday were part of a concerted campaign that could end in an invasion.

The smell of something burning tore her from her gloom and she leapt to her feet. The timer on the Toastmaster had failed to work again and smoke was coiling from the slots in the top. She turned the machine off and forced the bread out. It was black as charcoal. For some irritating reason, it was a sight that drove her to tears. She wasn't sure why; it wasn't as if bread had been rationed – not yet at least.

She was about to scrape the charred surface of the bread into the sink when there was a loud rapping on her door. She wiped her eyes and opened the door to see Kitty standing in the hallway, looking ashen-faced as usual.

'Oh, Ruby, have you heard the news?'

'About Goering? I was just reading his speech in the paper.' She gestured at Kitty to come in. 'Have you had any breakfast? I have burned toast if you'd like some. I know it isn't the most appealing offer, but I can—'

'Not about Goering, about Madame Tussauds,' Kitty interrupted as she followed Ruby into the kitchen. 'The Germans bombed it late last night. It took a direct hit.'

'What?' Ruby felt a jolt of fear so strong she had to hold on to the table to steady herself. 'Why would they bomb Madame Tussauds? I don't understand.'

'I don't think they care where they bomb,' Kitty said with a sigh.

'I have to go there. I have to check on my father.'

'That's what I thought. That's why I came down as soon as I heard. Would you like me to come with you?'

Ruby nodded, once again feeling dangerously close to tears.

They rode the bus to Baker Street in near silence, Ruby unable to speak out of fear. What with its cinema and galleries, Madame Tussauds was a large building; surely the Germans wouldn't have destroyed it all. Hopefully her father's waxwork would have been spared.

By the time they arrived, a crowd of onlookers had already gathered. The street was littered with debris from nearby buildings that had had their roofs blown clean off.

'Oh my, the cinema is destroyed!' Kitty exclaimed, clamping her hand to her mouth in horror.

A terrible dread descended upon Ruby as she stared at the ruins of the building, the like of which she hadn't felt since the day the telegram boy arrived at their house during the Great War and delivered the news that brought her mother to her knees, yowling like a dying animal.

A strange compulsion took over her body, so strong she couldn't resist. Without saying a word to Kitty, she raced towards the entrance of the waxwork museum. She heard the shrill blast of a whistle behind her, followed by a man's voice, a warden no doubt.

'Miss, miss, you can't go in there, it isn't safe.'

But Ruby ignored him. Another woman was at the entrance of the museum, wearing a tin helmet over her tightly curled hair and holding a notepad and pen.

'I'm from the *Daily Express*,' she was saying to someone inside. 'I've come to report on the bombing.' Just as she was about to go in, Ruby grabbed on to her sleeve and pulled her back.

'Please, can you take me in with you?' she whispered.

The woman frowned. 'I'm not a tour guide, you know, I'm a journalist.'

'I don't want a tour,' Ruby snapped. 'I need to find out if my father's all right.'

'Your father? Goodness me, does he work here? Are you afraid he's been injured?'

Ruby nodded. It was only a partial lie.

'All right,' the woman said. 'I'll say you're my assistant, as long as I can have a quote from you about your father, especially if he's been, you know, hurt in some way.'

'Yes, yes, of course.' Ruby followed the journalist inside, her heart pounding. The stench of burning grew even stronger and the only sound she could hear was the drip-drip of water coming from somewhere deep within the gloom.

While the journalist went over to a member of the Tussauds staff, Ruby slipped along the corridor to the gallery housing the stars of stage and screen. As she entered, she felt a sharp breeze and her heart sank. A gaping hole had been blown clean through the exterior wall and the sun was pouring through and onto the shattered remains, causing the dust particles in the air to glimmer. The podium that had once housed her father's waxwork was empty.

What remained of his dummy lay on the floor in front of it, the clothes tattered and scorched and the head completely missing.

Ruby looked around in despair. She saw Charlie Chaplin's hat and cane on the floor and then she spotted a shock of dark hair. She went over and nervously prodded the object with her foot. It rolled over to reveal half of her father's waxwork head. The other half had been blasted to tiny fragments all over the floor. Ruby retched and if her stomach hadn't been empty, she was certain she would have been sick. Her father had been killed by an artillery wound to the head in the First World War. Was this what his corpse had looked like? She'd spent years trying not to think of what had happened to him, cramming her mind full of books and adventures and people and parties so she wouldn't have to think of the horrors of his final moments, but now – staring down at the remains of his waxwork head – there was no escape. The parallels were too horrifying to bear.

'So here's where you vanished off to,' the journalist said, appearing in the doorway. 'Are you all right?' She came and stood by Ruby. 'I see Charlie Chaplin got it. Unfortunately the waxwork of Hitler's still intact. It's as if the Luftwaffe knew exactly where to bomb.'

Ruby's throat tightened.

'Was that Oscar Glenville?' the journalist asked, looking at the remains of the head at Ruby's feet.

'No, he was my father,' Ruby replied, a sob catching in the back of her throat.

*

Joseph left the house and headed along the square towards the river. During the previous night's raid, Freddy, the local butcher and an ARP warden, had told him they were looking for volunteers at the first-aid post in Neptune Square just around the corner. The thought of offering his services was the only thing keeping him positive in the light of the news that the Nazis were now targeting London as part of their blitzkrieg or 'lightning war'.

Neptune Square was a newly built apartment complex comprising of several large, red-bricked blocks of flats built around a courtyard. Apparently it was the largest of its kind in all of Europe. At the start of the war, when many of the wealthy occupants of Neptune Square had evacuated themselves to greener, safer pastures, the government had turned the underground car park into an ambulance station and set up a hospital in the gymnasium of one of the buildings. Unlike Pendragon Square with its communal garden, Neptune Square was completely private, the only access coming via three arched gateways.

Joseph approached a warden who was stationed at one of the gates. He was about sixty, with the kind of mottled purple cheeks that signified a lifelong love of one too many stouts.

'Yes, sir. Can I help you?' As the warden noticed Joseph's Peace Pledge Union badge his smile soured to a frown, but Joseph didn't let that put him off.

'I'd like to volunteer my services.'

'Oh yeah?' Again, the warden looked pointedly at his badge.

'Yes. I understand you're looking for first-aiders and ambulance crew.'

As if on cue, an ambulance pulled up on the road outside. The warden stepped aside to let it through the gate.

'I live on Pendragon Square, just next door,' Joseph continued.

'Very nice indeed,' the warden practically sneered.

Joseph gritted his teeth. 'Well, if you don't need my help,' he said, turning to leave.

'I didn't say that.' The warden fumbled in his jacket pocket and pulled out a leaflet. 'As it happens, they're having a meeting here for new volunteers at two o'clock this afternoon.'

'Thank you.' Joseph took the leaflet. But as he made his way home, he couldn't help feeling down-hearted. The seed of doubt that had haunted him all year began to grow. Should he have enlisted for the armed forces instead of registering as a conscientious objector? He'd paid such a high price for his conscience – *but not as high as the lads who've paid the ultimate price losing their lives fighting*, he reminded himself, feeling a hot wave of shame.

Just as he was reaching the house, he saw Kitty and Ruby approaching from the opposite direction. Great. Why did Ruby always appear when he least wanted to see her?

'Hello, Joseph,' Kitty said, as they met on the steps. She seemed even more subdued than ever.

'Hello.'

'We've just been to Madame Tussauds,' she continued.

Typical. She'd been dragged there by Ruby no doubt. While the rest of London burned, all she wanted to do was go and stare at a load of dummies. Clearly he hadn't been able to keep the disdain from his expression as suddenly Ruby was glaring back at him.

'What?' she said sharply. She didn't look quite as polished as usual, he noticed. The make-up around her eyes was slightly smudged.

'What do you mean, what?' Joseph opened the front door and stepped inside.

'Why were you staring at me like that?'

'Like what?'

'Like you're disgusted by me.'

Joseph considered lying, but why should he? Maybe if someone had given Ruby a talking-to when she was a child she wouldn't have turned into such a spoiled and shallow princess. 'I just think it's a bit rich to go gadding about town looking at waxworks, when half of London has been bombed.'

'Oh no, it wasn't—' Kitty began, but Ruby cut her off.

'Gadding about?' she practically shrieked.

Joseph squirmed. He really didn't want to get in a full-blown altercation, but she was leaving him no choice. 'Yes. For your information, a lot of people died this weekend. Way more than they're reporting in the papers.'

'I know!' Ruby yelled. 'And for your information, I haven't been gadding about. I've been retrieving the remains of my father, who was blown to smithereens in the raid last night.'

'What?' Joseph stared at her, aghast. He was sure Kitty had told him Ruby's parents were dead. Perhaps he'd misheard.

Ruby shook the bag she was holding in front of him. 'Yes. And for your information, I have them right here.'

Joseph glanced down into the bag and gasped in horror as he caught a glimpse of what looked like half a head. 'I – I – I'm very sorry.'

'So you should be,' Ruby retorted. 'I've been nothing but nice to you since you moved in here, but you've been nothing but mean. Well, I've had it with you, do you hear? As far as I'm concerned you no longer exist! But obviously you do exist when it comes to paying the rent,' she added quickly.

Joseph stared back at the bag. Did she really have half of her dead father's head inside it? He'd heard some terrible tales in the shelter last night about people discovering body parts on the East London streets. The thought of picking up a body part and bringing it home in a bag, even if it did belong to your father, well, it was gruesome, to say the least. Ruby was clearly traumatised and not thinking straight.

'Are you all right?' Kitty asked him. 'You look as if you've seen a ghost.' Then she gasped. 'Oh no, you don't think that's Ruby's father's actual remains, do you?'

'She said… I saw the head…' Joseph stammered.

There was a terrible silence, then, to his amazement, Ruby began to grin. 'Oh my goodness. Did you think I had my father's actual head in here?' She waved the bag at him.

Joseph nodded, too shocked and confused to speak.

'It's his waxwork head, you fool.'

This really didn't make things any clearer.

Ruby and Kitty looked at each other and burst out laughing. Joseph's face flushed. What the heck was going on?

Ruby stopped laughing and clutched her side. 'Even though you are the most miserable person I've ever met, not to mention something of an ignoramus, I must thank you. Making me laugh like that was just the tonic I needed.'

Joseph frowned.

'Her father was the actor Oscar Glenville,' Kitty explained. 'He had a waxwork in Madame Tussauds and it was bombed last night.'

'So I wasn't gadding about looking at waxworks,' Ruby said. 'I was worried. I wanted to see what had happened to him.' Her face fell. 'He was killed in the Great War. Had his head blown off then too,' she muttered.

In that instant it was as if the lens through which Joseph had been viewing Ruby fell away, and instead of seeing haughtiness and privilege, all he saw was pain and loss.

'I'm really sorry,' he said. 'I had no right to say those things to you.'

'No,' Ruby agreed. 'But then you also made me laugh at a time when all I wanted to do was throw myself to the floor and weep, so I suppose I shall forgive you.'

Joseph bit on his lip to stop himself delivering a sarcastic retort. 'Thanks.'

'Perhaps now we can have a truce.' Ruby cocked her head to one side and fixed him with a stare.

'Perhaps.' He turned to Kitty. 'I've just been round to Neptune Square to find out more about what Freddy was saying in the shelter last night. I don't know if you're interested, but they've got a meeting for new volunteers this afternoon.' He handed her the leaflet.

'Oh yes, thank you,' Kitty replied.

'What about me?' Ruby asked.

'What about you?'

'Well, is anyone invited to this volunteers' shindig, or just Kitty?'

'Anyone can come, I – I just didn't think you'd be interested.'

'Why?' Ruby's gaze sharpened again.

Good grief, this woman was difficult.

'I don't know. I mean, it will be a lot of hard work.'

Ruby put her hands on her hips. 'Are you saying I'm not capable of hard work?'

'Oh dear,' Kitty muttered.

But Joseph kept his cool. He wasn't going to let Ruby get one over on him again. 'I don't know. Are you?'

'Of course!' Ruby snatched the leaflet from Kitty. 'Right, let's meet here at just before two. We can all go together. It will be fun, like going on a house expedition.'

Kitty nodded enthusiastically.

Joseph supressed the urge to shudder. How had this gone so horribly wrong? Both women were looking at him, clearly expecting a response.

'Great,' he muttered.

'Great,' Ruby replied, with a smile that didn't quite reach her eyes. Then, clutching the bag containing the remains of her father's head, she turned on her heel and let herself into her apartment.

CHAPTER EIGHT

September 1940

Ruby went into the kitchen and plonked what remained of her father's waxen head on top of the gramophone on the table. She wasn't sure what had possessed her to bring the head home with her, but the journalist from the *Express* had told her that the Madame Tussauds bombing had destroyed over three hundred head moulds. Chances were, her father's had been among them, so he'd never be immortalised in wax again. In that moment, she'd felt a desperate need to keep the remains, but now it seemed foolish, not to mention macabre. Although it had been worth it to see that imbecile Joseph almost pass out from shock. Ruby smirked. He really was one of the most obnoxious men she'd ever met, and she'd met a few. If only she'd realised the day he came to see her about renting the top-floor apartment; it was unlike her to be such a bad judge of character.

She thought back to that day, at the beginning of the year. It was a couple of months after Britain had entered the war and everyone and everything seemed to be buzzing with a strange kind of nervous energy. Joseph hadn't had any references, but he had offered to pay six months' rent in advance, so Ruby hadn't quibbled. Besides, his eyes had sparkled when he smiled and she'd always been a firm believer that the eyes were the window to a person's soul – Kitty's Reg's tiny weasel eyes being a perfect case in point. But maybe her theory had been misguided. Joseph had done barely any smiling since he'd moved in and now whenever he looked at her, his eyes were icy cold.

Ruby frowned. How dare he accuse her of being work-shy? She'd show him. She looked at the leaflet. 'YOUR COUNTRY NEEDS YOU', the heading read, above a plea for first-aiders, stretcher-bearers and ambulance crew. Ambulance crew, now there was an idea. She'd learned how to drive the summer she turned thirteen when she and her mother had been staying at her uncle Horace's country estate. Horace was one of those wonderful adults who believed that children should be seen *and* heard, and as soon as Ruby asked him what it was like to drive a car, he'd taken her out to his Aston Martin and thrown her the keys. Unlike the other girls in her school, Ruby had never seen the appeal of horse riding, but the moment she turned the key in the car's ignition and heard the roar of the engine, she realised that this was the kind of speed and power she craved. She spent many a happy hour that summer driving around the narrow, twisting roads on Horace's estate. It had been a baptism of fire, but she'd loved it and, according to Horace, she'd been an absolute natural, or, as he put it, 'top-notch, especially for a female.'

Throughout her adult life she'd often had a car and the thought of driving an ambulance around London's streets filled her with excitement. It was the type of job never normally available to a woman, but maybe now the war had reached Britain's shores they'd make an exception. Women were working in factories and on farms and manning the anti-aircraft searchlights, after all. She shoved her father's half-head into the oven, hoping that, as she viewed cooking as a crime against her very will to live, it would now be out of sight, out of mind. She set off to her bedroom, wondering what an aspiring ambulance driver about town ought to wear to an audition.

At ten minutes before two, Ruby emerged into the hallway of the house clad in a tweed hunting jacket and trousers, a red velvet flat cap and a pair of men's boots she'd acquired from an old lover named Gus. Gus was a gamekeeper from Dorset who'd taught her two things. One: the legend about men with small feet isn't true, and two: you should never get involved with a grown man who calls his hunting rifle Doris. Ruby had viewed stealing his boots the day she left as appropriate compensation.

Kitty and Joseph were waiting for her by the front door, both of them gaping at her attire. She was pretty sure Kitty's was a gaze of admiration, but as for Joseph…

'I didn't realise it was the start of grouse season,' the rat said with a smirk.

'It was the most appropriate attire I could find for the job I wish to volunteer for,' Ruby replied, trying and failing to prevent her face from flushing. Damn Joseph and his insolence.

'And what job's that?' Joseph asked as he opened the front door. 'Churchill's head gamekeeper?'

'So much for our truce,' Ruby muttered, raising her eyebrows at Kitty as they followed him outside.

As they went down the steps, Freddy the butcher came walking up the pavement towards them in his black ARP uniform. Freddy had been born with one leg significantly shorter than the other, causing him to walk with quite a pronounced limp. Ruby pondered the irony of something he must have viewed as a curse now being a blessing as it meant he'd been able to avoid the call-up. He stopped and tipped his helmet, grinning pointedly at Kitty, Ruby couldn't help noting.

'Good afternoon, Kitty. How were those sausages I got you?' he asked.

'Very good, Freddy, thank you,' Kitty replied, her pale cheeks flushing.

Well, this was an interesting development, Ruby thought to herself. Yes, it was nice that Freddy had got Kitty some sausages, but why was she blushing as if he'd just declared his undying love for her? As they continued on their way, she glanced over her shoulder and saw that Freddy was standing watching them – or rather, watching Kitty, with a huge smile upon his face.

'He's a lovely chap, isn't he?' she said to Kitty.

'I suppose,' she mumbled, her face flushing even redder.

Ruby made a mental note to investigate further at the earliest opportunity, then turned her attention to Joseph, who was striding towards the end of the square, a couple of yards in front of them.

'What job will you be volunteering for?' Kitty asked, glancing at Ruby's hunting gear.

'Ambulance driver,' Ruby replied confidently.

'Driver?' Kitty's mouth hung open. 'But – can you drive?'

'Of course.' Ruby quickened her pace to keep up with Joseph as they rounded the corner. She had to admit that part of the attraction of coming to this volunteers' meeting – as well as providing her with a sense of purpose and a way of fighting back against the Germans – was to sneak a peek inside Neptune Square. It was one of the most exclusive addresses in London, or at least it had been before the war. It would be good to see what all the fuss was about.

She, Joseph and Kitty introduced themselves to the warden on duty at the entrance and they made their way inside. With its enclosed courtyard, it reminded Ruby of the apartment buildings in Paris – although the blocks here were red-brick instead of white. All of the buildings had names to do with seafaring, in keeping with the Neptune theme.

They'd been sent to Ocean House, where the volunteer recruitment was taking place inside the residents' gymnasium that had been requisitioned for the war effort. As she watched Joseph give his name and address to a female warden behind the reception desk, she couldn't help feeling surprised that he was volunteering his services. A lot of conchies refused to do anything to help with the war effort – some of them had even gone to prison over it. If Joseph wasn't so annoying, he'd be quite an enigma. But before she could muse on Joseph's enigmatic qualities any further, it was her turn to give her details to the warden.

'Please take a seat,' the woman told them once she'd taken Ruby and Kitty's names, gesturing at some rows of chairs at the other end of the gymnasium. 'Bill is about to give a talk about the volunteers' training.'

'Let's sit here,' said Ruby, grabbing Kitty's elbow and steering her away from where Joseph was sitting.

As they sat down, she glanced around. There were about thirty people present, a motley mixture of ages and class, judging by the drab clothing worn by some of the attendees. She felt a pang of doubt. Was she doing the right thing coming here? Did she look ludicrously out of place? Damn Joseph for planting seeds of doubt in her mind. She had just as much right to be here as he did! She glanced across the aisle and glared at him. At exactly the same moment, he looked over at her, instantly returning her glare.

Ruby sighed and moved her gaze to her lap. *Please help me to stay strong like you, Papa*, she silently prayed.

Bill turned out to be a ruddy-faced cockney with the kind of cheery disposition that Ruby instantly warmed to.

'Right then, ladies and gents,' he began. 'I'm sure it hasn't escaped your attention that old Hitler is stepping up his attacks on Blighty. As Churchill said at the weekend…' He glanced at a newspaper cutting in his hand and began to read, '"Each to our part, each to our station. We must guard the streets, succour the wounded, uplift the downcast and honour the brave."' Bill looked back at his audience. 'We are here today to succour the wounded – although, to be honest with you, I ain't exactly familiar with the term *succour*, but you know what Churchill's like with his fancy words.' He gave a hearty chuckle.

'It means to give aid and comfort to,' Ruby called out.

Everyone turned to look at her.

'Well, does it now?' Bill replied. 'Thank you for explaining, madam, I'd never have worked that out without you.' He said it with a twinkle in his eye, but Ruby couldn't help cringing as everyone started to laugh. She hadn't meant to sound patronising; she was only trying to help.

She glanced across the aisle and, sure enough, Joseph was beaming with delight at her misfortune. She pictured herself going home and packing her possessions into trunks and booking her passage on the next steamer to America. But instantly an image of her father loomed into her mind. *You need to stop running*, she heard him whisper.

'So, our station has been asked to recruit more first-aiders, stretcher-bearers and ambulance crew,' Bill continued. 'You would be expected to work shifts and—'

Before he could continue, the siren outside began to wail.

'Not again,' Kitty cried.

'Right, everyone, let's decamp to the basement shelter,' Bill instructed.

The hall filled with the sound of chairs scraping on the floor as people got to their feet and started hurrying over to the door. As they followed Bill out of the gymnasium and down a stairwell, Ruby's heart sank. Part of her had been hoping that the German blitz of London had just been a one-off weekend thing, like Rupert had said, a tit for tat for the British bombing of Berlin. But if the bombers were on their way back, at least this time she wouldn't be stuck in a shelter twiddling her thumbs; this time she would be doing something constructive.

As Ruby entered the basement of Ocean House, she tried to focus on the positives. With its concrete floor and network of pipes running along the ceiling, it might not have been as plush as the shelter at the Savoy, but at least it wasn't as cramped and damp as the shelter in the Pendragon Square garden. The surreal nature of the situation struck her for a moment. Were Londoners doomed to live some kind of subterranean existence from now on? Scurrying like rats from one underground shelter to another while the Luftwaffe rained their bombs down upon them. The prospect filled her with dread. Ever since the war had begun, it felt as if her life was shrinking smaller and smaller. But not if she was able to become an ambulance driver, she reminded herself.

'All right, folks, let's try to get organised,' Bill called above the chatter. 'Can anyone with driving experience wanting to join the ambulance crew come over here please and could those of you wanting to be first-aiders go to the other end of the shelter and see Gladys.'

A melee ensued as they all rearranged themselves in the gloom. Kitty joined the queue for the first-aiders and Ruby joined the smaller line for the ambulance service. She turned to look behind her – and there was Joseph.

'This is the line for the ambulance crew,' he said.

'I know,' she replied.

'You have to be able to drive,' he said, as if talking to a child.

'I am.' She turned her back on him. What an ignorant swine, assuming that just because she was a woman she wasn't able to drive. She had just as much a right to be there as he did, and anyway, what *was* he doing there? Surely driving an ambulance around the streets of London while bombs fell from the sky required a level of courage he didn't possess. She clenched her hands into fists. She'd show him she had what it took.

Finally, she reached the front of the queue.

'Oh, hello again.' Bill looked her up and down with a grin.

'I'd like to volunteer to be an ambulance driver please,' she said firmly.

'Driver?' He raised his bushy grey eyebrows.

'Yes.'

'And do you know how to drive?'

'Of course. I wouldn't be here if I didn't,' she said, loudly enough for Joseph to hear. 'It would be like – like turning up at a funeral without a coffin – if you were the deceased, of course.'

'Quite.' Bill's smile grew. 'And do you have a driver's licence?'

'I do.'

'Right, well, we'll need to send you for a test to see how you get on with a larger vehicle.'

'If you insist.'

'I'm afraid that the government insists, madam.'

'Very well.' Ruby wrote her details on Bill's clipboard, then stepped aside and watched as Joseph introduced himself.

'Hello, I'm Joseph O'Toole.'

'Hello, Joseph – oh…' Bill fell silent and stared at the pacifist badge on Joseph's jacket lapel. 'One of them, are you?'

Ruby tensed as she watched and waited for Joseph to respond. Much as she didn't like him, she didn't appreciate Bill's sneering tone either.

'Yes, I'm a conscientious objector,' Joseph replied, his voice calm and even, as if he'd dealt with this question a thousand times before, which Ruby guessed he must have. 'I'd like to volunteer for the ambulance crew.'

'I thought your sort didn't believe in helping out,' Bill said sharply.

'I did six weeks' training for the Friends Ambulance Unit up in Birmingham when the war started,' Joseph continued, ignoring Bill's dig.

'And what's the Friends Ambulance Unit when it's at home?' Bill replied.

'It's a volunteer service that was founded by the Quakers at the beginning of the First World War,' Joseph replied. 'It was started up again last year – for people who want to save lives rather than take them,' he muttered.

'Right, well, you'll have to go and take a test, to make sure you've got what it takes.' Bill looked at Joseph as if he were examining a slug, all of his earlier warmth gone.

'Of course.'

Bill passed his clipboard to Joseph. 'Name and address please,' he said curtly.

As Ruby watched Joseph write down his details, she couldn't help feeling a certain admiration for the way he'd handled himself in the face of Bill's rudeness. *But Joseph can be equally rude*, she reminded herself, looking around the shelter for Kitty. She spied her chatting away to the woman who was organising the first-aiders. It was so good to see Kitty looking vaguely happy for once, Ruby decided to leave her to it and took a seat. She half wanted Joseph to come and sit next to her so she could ask him about the voluntary ambulance service he'd trained for, but he walked straight past her and sat down in the opposite corner of the room.

*

Joseph leaned against the cold stone wall of the basement and sighed. His heart was pounding so hard he could hear the blood pulsing in his eardrums. He knew that the best thing to do when folk like Bill sneered at him was to turn the other cheek, but sometimes it was so bloody hard. Sometimes, he wanted to grab the person concerned and shove them up against the wall and yell at them until he was blue in the face. It was an urge that instantly made him feel ashamed. He was meant to be a pacifist, against all violence, which he was pretty sure included refraining from shoving folk up against a wall. But when did it become so wrong to not want to kill another human being? Why couldn't people see that hatred and violence only ever spawned more hatred and violence? The papers had kept pretty quiet about it, but Goering's blitzkrieg on London had been a direct response to the RAF's bombing of Berlin the week before. An eye for an eye, a life for a life. Or in this case hundreds and probably thousands of lives.

Joseph closed his eyes. He thought of the terrible day his mam had received the telegram about his brother's death in Ypres. Joseph, who'd only been ten at the time, had found her standing motionless by the open doorway. At first he'd thought she was playing a strange version of the parlour game musical statues. But when he'd tugged on her arm, she'd turned to look at him with an expression so devoid of life it had terrified him.

'Come on, Mam,' he'd begged. 'Let's go to Ted's.'

Ted owned the sweetshop on the corner of their street and his mam had promised him some barley sugar for going a whole week without breaking anything with his football. He'd tried so hard all week, only knocking one ornament off the sideboard, which didn't break so it didn't count. When his mam ignored him and went up to her bedroom and climbed into bed, he felt so cheated. It was only when he went out to kick his ball – and frustration – against the wall at the end of the street and the kid next door, Arthur Bainbridge, called out, 'I hear yer brother's dead,' that he realised the full horror of what had happened. Despite the eight-year age difference, Joseph and Liam had been really close and Joseph had idolised his big brother. The thought of never seeing him again had been too much for his ten-year-old brain to cope with. So he'd pushed Arthur to the floor and fled indoors.

'Arthur's lying about Liam, Mam,' he'd cried, pulling the blanket from her. 'He's saying he's dead. He's not dead, Mam, is he?'

But instead of consoling him, she'd stared at him, her blank eyes shiny with tears, and in that moment it was as if something in Joseph had died too – his youth, his innocence, his trust that the world was essentially a benevolent place.

He gulped and opened his eyes. Ruby was sitting across from him, looking at him. As soon as he caught her gaze, she looked away. Joseph sighed. He bet she'd really enjoyed his humiliation at the hands of Bill. He still couldn't quite believe that she'd turned up to volunteer – and for the ambulance crew too. One thing he'd learned early doors about the rich was that they seemed to be born with a sense of entitlement that beggared belief. He bet she wouldn't pass the test. At least he'd had the training in Birmingham last year. It would be good to finally put it to use. And maybe if he got the job, he could start feeling something other than hopeless.

CHAPTER NINE

September 2019

I wake up on Sunday, hot and headachy from a dream about Marty. In the dream, he was a work colleague rather than my husband and he was barking criticisms of my editorial skills at me in front of a crowded office. Although the dream fades with every second I'm awake, one line from Marty remains, playing on a loop in my brain: 'If only we could all be as lucky as you.'

I rub my eyes and sigh. Marty always seemed to know exactly what to say to plant seeds of self-doubt in my mind. When I was offered the job of editor at *Blaze*, his first response was, 'And they say nepotism is dead?' When I asked him what he meant, he smirked and said, 'Your friendship with Jake. Clearly that's why you got the position.'

Jake is the founder and owner of *Blaze* and I've known him since we were little kids, when we were next-door neighbours on the same council estate. Even though Jake relocated to London once he went off to uni and I remained in Manchester, we stayed in touch and always had each other's backs when it came to our careers, proofing each other's articles when we were budding journos and then, when Jake founded *Blaze* seven years ago, he offered me a freelance gig editing the culture section. I'd assumed I'd got the editor-in-chief gig because I'd worked hard and proved my worth these past seven years, but as soon as Marty dropped the nepotism bomb, doubt set in. And it's a doubt that's nagged at me during my first few months in the role.

I roll onto my back and stare up at the loft hatch in the ceiling. Having a loft was another huge selling point for the flat as it's somewhere to store my vast collection of vinyl, currently gathering dust in the living room. I sit up, determined to start the day on a positive note. I'll put my records up in the loft this morning and then I'll go shopping for things to make the place feel more homely – some pictures and cushions and a throw maybe. I need to be busy, in spite of my exhaustion, and keep my mind distracted from thoughts of Marty.

I hear the front door downstairs shut and the sound of Heath's voice. I get up and go over to the window and see him and a man I assume must be Guy heading across the road to the garden in the centre of the square. They're both in workout gear and carrying exercise mats. A tentative glimmer of hope cuts through my early-morning gloom. I now live in a beautiful London square with its very own communal garden. The sun is shining, the sky is blue and the leaves are turning from green to gold. I'm not with Marty any more, and that's a good thing.

'It *is* a good thing,' I mutter out loud to convince myself.

I no longer have to put up with his barbed jibes, in my waking moments at least, and hopefully he'll soon stop haunting my dreams.

After I've showered and got dressed, I fetch the mop from the kitchen, stand on a chair beneath the loft hatch and start prodding it with the mop handle. It doesn't budge. I prod it again, harder this time, but again there's no sign of movement. *This is the kind of job you need a husband for*, a distinctly unenlightened part of me chides. *I don't need a husband*, I think furiously in response. *Why won't you open?* I silently implore, hitting the hatch cover harder and harder. *Why couldn't Marty have accepted my promotion? Why couldn't he have been happy for me and moved with me to London?*

On closer inspection, I see that the hatch has been painted over, but that doesn't deter me. I seem to have accidentally struck upon a well of anger inside me and the loft hatch is suffering the consequences.

'Why? Why? Why?' I cry with every bang of the mop.

Suddenly the hatch flies open and a ladder comes half sliding out. I stare at it in surprise, as if I'd forgotten my reason for bashing it in the first place.

I take a deep breath and pull the ladder down. *This will be a good day. I choose to be positive,* I silently affirm. But annoyingly I feel dangerously close to tears, and bone-achingly lonely. I turn on the torch on my phone and tentatively make my way up the ladder. I've always had a slight nervousness around heights, so I try not to look down. When I reach the hatch, I cast the torchlight around the interior. Judging by the stale smell and the way the hatch had been sealed, I'm guessing it hasn't been used for quite some time.

I climb inside, and promptly snag my bare foot on a slightly loose floorboard. *Damn it! Damn Marty! Why couldn't he have supported me? Why has he left me all alone to deal with crap like painted-over loft hatches and stupid loose floorboards?* I stamp on the board to try to push it back in place, but this only results in pushing it out further. I kneel down and catch a glimpse of something beneath the board in the beam of the torchlight. I move my phone closer. It looks like some kind of fabric. I pull up the board and reach inside, praying there aren't any spiders lurking. My fingers brush against a thick fabric. I take hold of it and start pulling it through the gap. A cuff appears and then a sleeve. I keep pulling until it's all out and examine it in the torchlight. It's a heavy-duty khaki shirt that looks as if it could be from a military uniform. I turn it over to examine the front and notice a dark stain over one of the breast pockets. Maybe it's damp from being up in the loft? Judging by the musty smell, it's clearly been up here a long time. But when I touch the stain, it feels stiff and dry. Then I notice a small ragged hole in the fabric at the centre of the stain. My heart rate quickens. Could it be blood?

I swallow hard and try to process this turn of events. Did the owner of this shirt die here? Were they killed here? Why else would the shirt be hidden? A shiver runs up my spine.

Trying to ignore the troubling stain, I carefully unbutton the breast pocket and feel inside. I find a small piece of card. It looks like some kind of ticket, but the writing is faded. I focus the torchlight on it and see that it's a really old train ticket. A single, second-class, from somewhere called Newhaven to London. The date is obscured but I can just make out the letters Dec and the year 1940.

I take a couple of breaths to try to slow my heart rate. I have no idea what to do, but my first instinct is to message Jake. He's an avid fan of true crime podcasts and documentaries. This discovery will be right up his street. I take photos of the shirt and the ticket to send to him, then hurry back over to the hatch. But in my haste to get out of the loft, I lose my footing on the ladder and suddenly I'm plummeting down. I try desperately to cling on to the ladder, but because I'm holding my phone in one hand, I'm not strong enough to support my body weight and I go crashing straight to the floor. My right foot takes the brunt of the fall and I feel something snap before I keel over backwards. A searing pain rushes up from my ankle, radiating throughout my body.

'Shit!' I exclaim, gasping for breath. I'd let go of my phone in the fall and it went flying across the floor, and is now lying by the window.

I haul myself into a seated position and almost retch at the sight of my foot bent at a crazy angle away from my leg. Once again, the harsh reality of my new life confronts me. I have no partner to come rushing in to take care of me. I'm all alone in a new city and the apartment I'd hoped would be a fun and peaceful haven could actually be some kind of crime scene, albeit from a long time ago.

I gaze into the gaping darkness of the loft hatch. I'd thought this would be the perfect place to start again, but what if I was wrong? What if the people who lived here before me weren't happy? What if one of them was killed here?

CHAPTER TEN

September 1940

As the train clanged and chugged its way out of Euston station, Ruby fixed her gaze firmly on the window. The glass was grimy and the overcast sky had turned the world outside into a palette of greys, but it was still preferable to looking at Joseph sitting opposite her. Ruby had been the one to suggest they travel to the ambulance driving test together. It seemed like the most neighbourly thing to do, and besides, it would avoid the embarrassment of encountering each other en route and having to feign delighted surprise. Not that she could ever imagine Joseph feigning delight at anything. Although he'd accepted her invitation, he hadn't uttered a word on the bus ride to the station, leaving Ruby to gape in horror at the scenes of devastation along the way. On almost every other street, there were vehicles lying on their sides beside huge craters and buildings with their fronts blown off and interiors exposed like giant dolls' houses. Normally, Ruby loved the opportunity to peek inside other people's homes, but today every glimpse of wallpaper, furniture and personal possessions felt like a violation. London had suffered five nights of bombing at the hands of the Germans now. Earlier that morning, Ruby had received a tearful telephone call from her friend Violet, delivering the devastating news that Burlington Arcade in Piccadilly had been bombed.

'All of the shopfronts have been blown to smithereens,' Violet had sobbed, 'and the walkway is nothing but rubble.'

Ruby had spent many a fun afternoon strolling along the glass-covered walkway of Burlington Arcade, stopping off to buy a silk scarf or a fine perfume, so this news had hit her hard. Now more than ever, the war felt like a personal affront to her freedom and she was determined to do whatever she could to fight back, even if it meant spending time with the ignoramus Joseph. The train ride to the test centre in Hertfordshire was meant to take an hour, but it was bound to be longer, given the delays to the trains since the war started. She decided to bite the bullet and try to engage him in conversation.

'So, where did you have your ambulance training before?' she asked. 'I couldn't help overhearing you talking to that imbecile Bill.' She hoped that by calling Bill an imbecile it would curry favour with Joseph and, judging by the slightest of smiles curling at the corners of his mouth, it appeared to have worked.

'For the Friends Ambulance Unit – it's a Quaker organisation,' he replied, taking off his hat and unbuttoning his jacket. 'They had a training camp in Birmingham at the start of the war.'

'I see. So are you a Quaker then?'

'Not quite, but I agree with a lot of their views.'

'I'm not religious, but if I was, I think I'd be a Quaker,' Ruby said, her curiosity piqued by this morsel of information from Joseph.

'Really.' Joseph yawned and stared out of the window, as if Ruby and everything she had to say made him wither with boredom. Ruby wasn't used to being treated like this, especially by men – it was both infuriating and strangely challenging.

'Yes, I once had a great meeting of minds with a Quaker,' she continued, undeterred. 'Obviously, it was a relationship that remained unconsummated, owing to his religious beliefs and my desire never to be enslaved by marriage, but it was a most passionate connection nonetheless. He was a member of the Cadbury family – you might have heard of them.' She bit her lip to stop herself from smirking. Everyone in Britain had heard of the Cadbury family; they were responsible for the most delicious chocolate that had ever been created – in Ruby's humble opinion at least.

'Of course I've heard of them.'

Ruby felt a warm burst of satisfaction. Her bombshell revelation had worked; Joseph was looking at her again and for once it was with what appeared to be interest.

'Yes,' she continued, 'I do like the notion that we all have the light of God within us – if God actually exists, that is. That's one thing that really frustrates me about religion; why can't we all agree that none of us know for sure how we all came to be?'

'There can be different ways of knowing,' Joseph said.

'What do you mean?'

But before he could reply, the door to their compartment opened and a couple of soldiers came in. They looked barely out of their teens and the sight of them in their slightly oversized uniforms caused Ruby's heart to contract. Who knew what horrors they would have to endure if the Germans invaded?

As the soldiers sat down beside them, Joseph turned slightly towards the window. As always, he was wearing his metal pacifist badge on his jacket lapel. Ruby wondered why he did that. Surely it would be so much easier for him if he didn't declare his anti-war stance in such a public way.

The soldiers began chatting away and Ruby soon deduced that they'd been home on leave and were on the way back to their barracks. Then she noticed the soldier next to Joseph looking at his badge.

''Ere, Ralf, take a look at—' he began saying.

'I say, chaps,' Ruby cut in, 'do either of you have a light?'

'Only if you have a smoke,' Ralf quipped.

'Of course.' Ruby took a pack of Craven A from her handbag and offered them to him. 'It's the least I could do to say thank you for the sacrifice you're making for our country.'

'You're very welcome, madam,' the soldier next to Joseph said, puffing up his chest.

For the rest of the journey, Ruby engaged the soldiers in a stream of chit-chat so boring she wished she had a pair of matchsticks to prop her eyelids open. She'd have much rather spent the journey finding out more about Joseph and his beliefs, but there was no way she wanted to witness him being harangued by the soldiers.

Finally, the train pulled into a station and Joseph stood up.

'This is it,' he muttered to her.

Ruby glanced out of the window. The signs on the platform had all been covered, as all stations signs had at the start of the war, to confuse the Germans in the event of an invasion. It would have confused Ruby too, if she hadn't had Joseph with her.

'Lovely to meet you, boys,' she called gaily to the soldiers as she left the carriage. 'Best of luck beating the Bosch!'

Joseph had clearly reverted to his normal silent and stony-faced self as they left the station, marching on ahead of her. Ruby sighed. It always seemed to be one step forward, three back with him – such an awkward dance. But she wasn't here to win Joseph's favour, she reminded herself. She was here to pass a driving test so she could do her bit to help beat the Nazis.

*

As Joseph waited to be called for his test, he glanced across the room at Ruby. She was clearly deep in concentration, sitting bolt upright, hands neatly folded in her lap, eyes closed. He really didn't know what to make of her. Earlier, on the train, when she'd started talking about Quakerism, he'd felt a glimmer of hope that maybe there was a brain buried beneath her shiny exterior, but then the soldiers had come into the carriage and she'd dissolved into a giggling fool. How she hoped to cut it as an ambulance driver, he really didn't know. At least she hadn't turned up to the test in her hunting get-up, opting instead for a pinstripe trouser suit and fedora, which wouldn't have looked out of place in a gangster flick.

'Right then.' An officious-looking man clad in dark blue overalls came striding into the room holding a folder. 'Miss Ruby Glenville?'

Ruby's eyes shot open. 'Goodness me, you made me jump. I was just meditating to help me get ready.'

'I beg your pardon.' The man frowned.

'I was meditating. Like they do in India.'

'I see.' The man gave her a withering look. Clearly he was experiencing similar misgivings to Joseph about Ruby's suitability. 'Can I just check that you are actually able to drive?'

'Of course,' Ruby replied. 'Why else would I be here? Time-wasting is my least favourite pastime – well, aside from croquet.' She gave a dramatic sigh. 'Has a duller game ever been invented?'

The man's frown deepened. 'Hmm, well, I hope you realise that it's one thing taking a Sunday afternoon tootle in your husband's Ford, but it's quite another trying to handle a crash gearbox.'

'Firstly, I don't have a husband,' Ruby replied, with an obvious sense of pride that made Joseph think of what she'd said on the train about having no desire to be enslaved by marriage. He had to admit that this intrigued him slightly. He'd always been under the impression that most women longed to be wed. 'And secondly, I'll have you know that I am gifted in the art of the double declutch.'

'Are you now?' The man looked at Joseph and raised his eyebrows.

'Yes.' Ruby sprang to her feet. 'So let's get to it, shall we?'

As Ruby left the room, followed by a very bemused-looking examiner, Joseph scratched his head. Was there more to Ruby after all – or was she about to make a complete fool of herself?

*

As Ruby followed the examiner across the courtyard to a line
of vehicles, she focused on her breathing to try to calm herself.
Onomatopoeia… higgledy-piggledy… The impertinence of the
man, talking to her like she was a witless child. Tootling about
in her husband's Ford indeed! Well, she'd show him a thing or
two about driving. She'd… Her train of thought came crashing
to a halt. The examiner had led her over to the hugest lorry she'd
ever seen. Surely there had to be some horrible mistake?

'I say, this is the audition for the ambulance drivers?' she asked.

'Audition?' he replied, raising an eyebrow.

'Yes, because that's the part I'm here to try out for.'

He frowned at her and shook his head. 'Madam, this isn't
some kind of theatrical performance. This is a very serious matter.'

'I know. I just don't see how this gargantuan beast of a vehicle
has anything in common with an ambulance.'

'This is a war, madam, and all kinds of ve-hic-les are being
requisitioned for use as ambulances. I thought I'd start you off
with one of the larger ve-hic-les you might encounter… if you
were to pass your… audition.'

'Right, I see.' And she did see, clear as crystal. He wanted
her to fail. Well, damn him and his stupid smirk and the way he
pronounced ve-*hic*-les as if he was suffering from an attack of the
hiccups. She'd show him!

Ruby clambered up into the cab. It was strange being so far
from the ground, simultaneously scary and exciting – like all of
the best things in life, she reassured herself.

'I say, does this seat come forward at all?'

The examiner leant over and fiddled with something and the
seat jolted forward.

'Thank you.' Now Ruby was able to reach the pedals, she
felt slightly more confident. Yes, the lorry was a lot bigger than

anything she'd ever driven before, but the set-up was exactly the same. *You can do this*, she imagined her papa whispering to her. *Remember, you have the Glenville spirit.*

'Whenever you're ready,' the examiner said, handing her the keys.

Ruby turned the key in the ignition. The engine spluttered and promptly cut out. She turned the key again. She wouldn't have put it past her examiner to give her a dud vehicle just to be able to fail her. She fought to stop her cheeks from flushing. *Stay calm, Ruby, don't let this imbecile get to you*, she told herself, glancing in the rear-view mirror.

'Chocks away!' she cried gaily as she tried again and this time the engine roared into life. She shifted the gearstick into neutral. It was so stiff and heavy. Ruby gave a silent prayer of thanks for the morning exercise routine the BBC had been broadcasting on the wireless every morning, as part of their initiative to keep the nation fit during the war. She turned to the examiner. 'Where to, kind sir?'

'I'd like you to reverse out and follow the road around to the left,' he told her.

Ruby pressed her foot on the gas, a little too enthusiastically as it turned out, and the truck shot backwards. 'Whoops!' she cried gaily. *Focus*, she told herself. She couldn't let this man fail her; it was a matter of principle. She reversed the truck and somehow managed to turn the lumbering beast out onto the road.

'Now you can pick up a bit of speed,' the examiner said.

'Yes, sir.' She pressed the clutch and shifted gears and started to relax a fraction. She could do this. She could drive the biggest ambulance the world had ever seen and help defeat the Nazis. She'd show Hitler. She'd...

'Whoa!' the examiner yelled. 'Watch out for that tractor!'

'What tractor? Oh!' Ruby slammed on the brakes as a tractor came chugging out of a dirt track in front of them. For an awful moment she thought they were going to crash, but thankfully they juddered to a halt just in time.

A red-faced farmer type leaned out of the cab tractor and hurled a stream of frightfully unimaginative and predominantly animal-themed insults at Ruby.

'There's really no need for such hostility,' Ruby called back, leaning from her window. 'I didn't actually hit you.'

'I think you need to reverse,' the examiner snapped.

'Why?' Ruby frowned at him. 'Clearly this imbecile pulled out without looking. He should be the one to go back, not me.'

'Reverse!' the examiner barked.

Good grief, why was everyone so angry? Ruby yanked the gearstick into reverse, or at least what she thought was reverse. As she put her foot on the gas, the lorry lurched forwards.

'Holy cow!' she exclaimed as the farmer unleashed another torrent of abuse.

What felt like several lifetimes later, Ruby returned to the test centre, just in time to see Joseph getting out of another, much smaller truck with another, much friendlier-looking examiner. She watched as the two men shook hands and the examiner patted Joseph on the back. He'd obviously passed, but had she? After the tractor incident, she'd managed to regain her composure and the rest of the test had passed without incident, and the tractor had barely been dented at all.

She switched off the engine and turned to her examiner.

'So, how did I do?'

'I'm afraid I won't be able to pass you,' he replied, 'due to the collision with the tractor.'

'But he was the one who wasn't looking where he was going,' Ruby exclaimed.

'That might be so, but you would be driving an ambulance at night in a blackout. Your reactions need to be razor-sharp and they weren't. If I hadn't yelled, you would have crashed into him the first time, let alone the second.'

Ruby was surprised at how crushed she felt. Once she'd got over the tractor incident, she'd started to quite enjoy driving The Beast, as she'd named the lorry.

'However, I shall be recommending you for the position of an attendant,' the examiner continued. 'An attendant accompanies the ambulance driver on their calls.'

Ruby sighed. An attendant didn't sound nearly as exciting as an ambulance driver. She hefted her door open and jumped down from the cab.

'I take it congratulations are in order,' she said to Joseph as the two examiners greeted each other.

'Yes, thanks. How about you?' For once Joseph was actually smiling, causing dimples to form either side of his mouth. He looked at the lorry behind her. 'Is that what you took your test in?'

'Yes,' she muttered.

'How did you get on?'

'I failed.' Ruby scuffed the toe of her shoe on the ground. She couldn't bring herself to look at him. No doubt he'd be gloating.

'Oh, sorry to hear that.'

Ruby glanced up at him and saw to her surprise that he actually looked concerned.

'But she'll make an excellent attendant,' her examiner called over, as if this poor attempt at a consolation prize was something to be coveted.

Ruby wanted to stamp her feet at the injustice of it all. But what good would that do? And she'd never been a bad loser.

'Why did she have to do her test in that thing?' Joseph asked Ruby's examiner, nodding at The Beast.

'I needed to see if she was cut out for every eventuality,' her examiner replied sniffily.

'But shouldn't we all be tested in vehicles of the same size?'

'It's the luck of the draw,' the examiner said with a shrug before heading off across the courtyard.

'I don't need you to fight my battles,' Ruby muttered to Joseph as they followed the examiners back over to the building, her pride smarting.

'I know,' he replied, looking straight ahead. 'I just don't like to see injustice… no matter who it happens to.'

'I see,' she said. 'Well, in that case, thank you… I think.'

'You're welcome… I think.' And he marched inside the building without holding the door for her.

CHAPTER ELEVEN

September 2019

'Hello, sweetheart, it's only me. Are you decent?'

The sound of Heath's voice jolts me from a woozy sleep. I try to shift upright and a bolt of pain shoots up my leg.

'Yes, come in, I'm in the bedroom,' I call, my voice cracking and my mouth dry. How long have I been asleep? What day is it? I check my phone and do a double-take. It's Monday morning, just before eight. A whole day since I fell out of the loft and broke my ankle.

Heath comes in holding a tray containing a pot of coffee, a jug of orange juice and a plate of toast. 'Breakfast is served,' he announces, putting the tray on the bedside table. 'You've got some mail too.' He places a brown package on the bed. 'How's the foot?'

'I'm not sure, but the painkillers they gave me at the hospital are awesome.'

'Every cloud, eh?' he chuckles.

'Right.' I grin. The real silver lining to have come from my loft disaster is that Heath and I have definitely bonded. As soon as I realised I'd broken my ankle, and overcome my resulting existential crisis, I phoned the emergency services. The sight of an ambulance arriving at the house brought all of the neighbours out into the hallway and as soon as he saw me being carried down by the paramedics, Heath offered to accompany me to A&E. We ended up being at the hospital for almost four hours

and he turned out to be the perfect companion, taking my mind
off the pain by regaling me with hilarious tales from his Bond
Street salon.

'Right, I need to go to work. Is there anything I can get you?'
he asks.

'No. As long as I have caffeine and toast, I'm all good,' I reply.

'Excellent, well you have my number if you need me and
Pearl's said she'll check in on you this afternoon. I can give her
the spare key you gave me yesterday, if that's OK?'

'Of course. Thank you so much – for everything.'

'You're welcome, sweetheart. I'm just so sorry you've had such
a traumatic start in your new home.' He glances at the loft hatch,
which is still open. 'Do you want me to shut that for you?'

I suddenly remember the shirt. Due to the brain fog caused by
the pain meds, it all feels like a bad dream, and one that I don't
want to revisit in a hurry. 'Yes please.'

Heath pushes the ladder back up inside and the hatch closes.
I breathe a sigh of relief. I contemplate telling him about my discovery, but he's in a rush to get to work and there's a good chance
I was overreacting and there's a perfectly innocent explanation.
For all I know, the shirt could have been a costume from a theatre
production. And even if it is evidence of something more sinister,
it's clearly been up there for years and has no bearing on me.

'Guy and I are getting pizza tonight,' Heath says, as he makes
his way to the bedroom door. 'Let me know if you want us to
order you one too.'

'Thank you.'

He leaves and I hear the lift clanging its way back downstairs.

I pick up my phone and check my emails. I'd sent a slightly
spaced-out message to my deputy editor last night, telling her
what had happened and that I wouldn't be in work for a while.
Thankfully she's sent me a really nice reply wishing me well and
telling me not to worry.

I put down my phone and notice the package Heath put on the bed. I open it and pull out a book, which causes a moment of confusion until I see Pearl's name on the front. I'd totally forgotten I'd ordered it. I turn it over and read the blurb on the back.

London, 1940. The Blitz has begun and plucky Londoners are rushing to do their bit, including the three residents of a London townhouse: Ruby, Kitty and Joseph. But as the bombs rain down, it isn't just the Nazis they have to fear. Someone harbouring a murderous intent is lurking a lot closer to home. A powerful love story with a tragic twist.

I turn the novel over and study the front cover. The menacing figure with the gun watching the couple embracing reminds me of the Agatha Christie novels I used to devour whenever I went to stay with my gran as a kid. It could be the perfect read for my convalescence, and knowing that it's written by Pearl gives it an extra layer of intrigue. I open the book and start to read...

CHAPTER TWELVE

September 1940

As the air-raid siren began to wail, Ruby felt like flinging her head back and joining in. It had been almost a week since the Germans started their relentless bombing campaign on London and, if anything, it was getting worse. They weren't just bombing during the blackout, they were bombing in broad daylight too. This was the second raid of the morning and it wasn't even eleven o'clock. Ruby was starting her first shift at the Neptune Square ambulance station this evening, and by the sounds of it, they were going to be really busy.

She put on her shoes and grabbed her bag, which now doubled as a shelter survival kit, from the table in the hall. She'd come up with the idea of creating her own personal survival kit after three consecutive nights in the Pendragon Square shelter. Other people might bring their gas masks and bibles, but Ruby was fast becoming dependent on romance novels to make it through the night. Prior to the war, she'd found romance novels to be rather irritating – the heroines were always so frightfully insipid. But prior to the war she'd thought that her neighbours were fine, upstanding people. It was amazing what spending a few hours cooped up together in an underground sardine tin revealed. The flatulence. The snoring. The drunken singing. The petty bickering. It really was insufferable.

The other night, in desperation, she'd asked Kitty if she could borrow the novel she'd just finished and, to Ruby's surprise, she was instantly hooked. It turned out that romances were the perfect antidote to the air raids – allowing Ruby to escape into a rose-tinted world where love reigned and no one belched or farted.

She grabbed her current tome, the rather dubiously titled *Dance for Me, Little Lady*, and hurried out into the hallway, where she found Kitty trudging down the stairs, looking distinctly green around the gills.

'I can't believe there's another raid already,' she said. 'I'm so tired.'

'Me too. But don't worry, I have some Kendal mint cake in my bag. If it can get people up mountains, it will hopefully power us through another few hours of Mr Jones snoring and dribbling.'

Ruby hooked her arm through Kitty's and they hurried to the garden and down into the shelter. It was already crowded, but there was no sign of Joseph. She hadn't seen him in the shelter since the first day of the Blitz. Not that Ruby was bothered. She was still smarting from her humiliation at the driving test.

'Are you enjoying it?' Kitty asked as Ruby took the book from her bag.

'Yes indeed,' Ruby replied. 'I've just got to the part where Robert gives her the roses.'

'It must be so lovely to have a man buy you roses,' Kitty sighed.

'Has no one ever bought you flowers before?' Ruby stared at her, aghast.

Kitty shook her head wistfully.

'Not even Reg?'

'Oh no. He doesn't approve of spending money on things like that.'

'Things like what? His wife?'

Kitty looked down into her lap. 'He shows his affection in other ways,' she muttered.

How, by yelling at you? Ruby wanted to say, but she stopped herself. Then she had a wonderful idea. *She* would buy some roses for Kitty.

The raid lasted for a couple of hours, by which time Ruby had read *Dance for Me, Little Lady* through to its frankly disappointing ending.

'I can't believe Nancy accepted Robert's proposal of marriage,' she said to Kitty as they made their way out of the shelter, blinking in the sunlight. The steady whine of the all-clear filled the air and the birds in the trees were singing, as if celebrating the end of the raid.

Kitty stared at her in shock. 'Of course she accepted it. Why on earth would she not?'

'He was a pompous cad,' Ruby retorted. 'If I met a man who called me "little lady", I'd have his guts for garters.'

'But he was so dashing and…' Kitty broke off and Ruby followed her gaze up the street. Freddy was hurrying towards them in his ARP uniform, his tin helmet tucked beneath his arm, his blonde curls still imprinted with its shape.

'Good afternoon, Freddy,' Ruby called.

'Hello, Miss Glenville.' Freddy looked at Kitty and Ruby noticed his ruddy cheeks become even redder. 'Hello, Kitty. Have you heard the news? The Germans just hit Buckingham Palace – the actual building this time.'

'Oh no!' Kitty clamped her hand to her mouth. 'Are the king and queen all right? And the princesses?'

'I think so. But it was a close shave all right.'

Ruby shivered. This was the third time in a week the Germans had targeted the palace. What if they killed the king? Surely then an invasion would be next. She quickly gave herself a stern talking-to. This was no time to waver. As of tonight, she would be doing her bit to fight back, and even if it was just as an ambulance attendant, it couldn't come a moment too soon.

'Are you all right, Kitty?' Freddy asked, his face flushing further still.

'Yes, thank you, Freddy. Just a bit worn out from all the sleepless nights.'

'Well, if you don't mind me saying, you look as lovely as ever.'

'Oh – I – uh—'

Ruby despaired at Kitty's stammering. What was wrong with the girl? Why was she acting so strangely? Then she noticed that Kitty was blushing too. Aha! So her hunch the other night had been correct. Not only was Freddy soft on Kitty, but it appeared she was soft on him too. This was a wonderful development, and her cunning plan to send Kitty roses burst with fresh new potential. She could leave a card with the flowers, saying they were from a secret admirer. It wouldn't be a total lie; after all it would appear that Kitty did indeed have a secret admirer and it would give the poor girl a boost. She couldn't believe that weasel Reg had never bought her flowers. Well, she could believe it, but still. Yes, she would deliver Kitty some flowers and make her think they were from Freddy. Ruby positively fizzed with joy at her ingenuity.

*

Joseph jumped from the bus and ran along the road to Neptune Square. It was just before blackout and he'd spent most of the day with some of his fellow Peace Pledge Union members helping in the East End, in a school hall that had been set up to feed some of the people made homeless by the Blitz. Due to the repeated bombing raids, they'd ended up spending a large portion of the day taking shelter in the school cellar, so who knew what his first shift as an ambulance driver would entail.

As he reached the arched entrance to Neptune Square, he showed his newly acquired papers to the warden on duty. The warden opened the gate and directed him to the underground car park, which now housed the ambulance station.

Joseph walked past the line of ambulances, an assortment of customised trucks and saloon cars, and into the makeshift staffroom at the end. When he saw Ruby sitting amongst the other volunteers, clad in her blue serge uniform, he almost didn't recognise her. Her hair was tied back and her face was free from make-up. Stripped of her usual finery, she actually looked more beautiful. It was an observation that immediately made Joseph uncomfortable as he really did not want to find this woman attractive in any way at all.

'Evening, O'Toole,' Bill said, coming into the room and handing him a uniform. 'Go and get changed, then I'll brief you on tonight's shift.'

As Joseph went through to the back room and got changed, he was struck by how similar his uniform looked to that of a soldier. The only difference was the colour. *You're doing this to save lives, not take them*, he reminded himself as he looked in the mirror. But as he saw his reflection, he couldn't help drawing a breath – he looked so much like his brother Liam in the photo of him in his army uniform before he was despatched to the front.

He hurried back into the staffroom and Bill began his briefing.

'As you all know, we've taken quite a pummelling today, so we're probably in for a rough night.' Bill looked at a piece of paper in his hand. 'I'm now going to assign you to your crews. Jenkins…' He turned to a formidable-looking middle-aged woman. 'Your attendant will be Smith, here.' He nodded at a mousy-haired younger woman. 'Price, you're with Simpson, and O'Toole, your attendant will be Glenville.'

'Oh,' Ruby said, looking as unimpressed as Joseph felt.

'Everything all right, Glenville?' Bill frowned at her. 'Or can we get on with the important business of helping the injured and saving lives?'

'Everything's just tickety-boo,' Ruby replied drily.

Joseph internally groaned. He'd been hoping against hope that he wouldn't be paired with Ruby. She was bound to be harbouring a grudge about the fact that he'd passed the driving test and she hadn't, which was sure to make her more disagreeable than ever.

A phone rang in the room next door and a few moments later a woman came hurrying through. 'A block of flats has been hit in Victoria,' she called. 'On the corner of Hirley Road and Howick Place. Several casualties reported and some trapped under the rubble. They hit a water mains too.'

'Right,' Bill said. 'O'Toole and Glenville, you just got your first call.' He took some keys from a row of hooks on the wall and threw them to Joseph. 'Take the ambulance in bay four.'

Joseph and Ruby grabbed their tin helmets and hurried out to their ambulance. It was a converted truck but significantly smaller than the one Ruby had had to do her test in, a fact which still made Joseph smart from the injustice, in spite of the fact that it had happened to his nemesis.

As they got into the cab, Joseph felt slightly awkward at their close proximity. He supposed he ought to say something to try to break the ice.

'So you came,' was all he could come up with.

'Of course.' She gave him an indignant stare. 'Don't worry, I'm still furious about the miscarriage of justice that took place on Tuesday, but my being here is what's known as taking the higher moral ground.'

'Oh.' Joseph supressed a sigh. This was looking like being a very long eight hours.

'Yes. I won't let one man's ignorance and bias thwart me. I shall accept my appointment as your attendant with dignity and grace, even though we both know I'm vastly overqualified for the role.'

'Hmm.' As Joseph put the truck into first, the gears ground.

'I rest my case,' Ruby declared, sighing and shaking her head.

Joseph grimaced. This was going to be a very long eight hours indeed.

CHAPTER THIRTEEN

September 1940

Ruby gripped the dashboard as Joseph turned the ambulance off Westminster Bridge. They were about four hours into their shift now and although it pained her to admit it, he was actually quite an accomplished driver. Before she'd left home to travel the world, Ruby had loved driving around London late at night, especially by the river, where the twinkling reflection of the lamplight on the water always looked so magical. But driving during blackout was a different thing entirely. It was like driving along the bottom of the deepest ocean, the pitch dark completely unnerving and disorientating. In the first few months of blackout, so many pedestrians had been killed by cars, the government had ordered white lines to be painted on the kerbs. Not that they made all that much difference.

'Which way now?' Joseph asked as they reached a crossroads, marked only by a pile of sandbags in the middle.

Ruby studied the map in her lap with her torch. 'It's right, then the next left.'

Planes hummed overhead, followed by the sharp rap-rap-rap of anti-aircraft fire. The sounds that were muffled in the shelters were louder than ever. Ruby knew she should feel scared, but she actually felt a weird kind of excitement. At least she was doing something, rather than being stuck like a sitting duck in a shelter, waiting to be buried alive. There was a strange sense of empowerment in being a moving target.

As they arrived at their destination, the smell of gas drifted into the cab. Little fires were blazing all over the street, giving the scene a surreal air.

'Must have hit a gas mains,' Joseph said, as they got out. 'Whatever you do, don't light a cigarette.'

'Oh you don't say,' Ruby retorted. 'How about my pipe?'

He looked at her and sighed. 'Come on.'

They made their way to the site of the bomb blast, a huge crater in the middle of a row of small houses.

A woman came running over and tugged on Ruby's sleeve. 'You have to save my son.' She pointed to the ruins of a house next to the crater. 'He's trapped down there. Please, please save him, miss.'

'Of course, don't worry.' Ruby began picking her way over the rubble in the direction the woman was pointing, her heart pounding. What if they weren't able to find the boy? What if they weren't able to save him?

'We need to wait for our rescue crew,' Joseph called.

'Why?' Ruby hissed. 'You heard her, her son's down there somewhere. Surely we should at least try to help her.' She took her torch from her pocket and shone it on the rubble. The beam shook as her fingers trembled.

An ARP warden came running over, blowing his whistle. 'What are you doing, miss?'

'I'm looking for this poor woman's son.'

'It isn't safe. The gas could blow at any minute,' the warden said.

'But…' Ruby looked back at the woman. She'd never seen a face so contorted by anguish. How could the warden not want to do something to help her? Then she heard a whimper from under the masonry. 'I think I hear him!' she cried. She grabbed Joseph's arm. 'Come on!'

Ruby crouched down and began tearing at the rubble with her hands.

'It's all right,' she called. 'We can hear you. We're going to save you.' She tugged at a wooden beam and as it came free, she shone her torch into the gap and saw a child's fingers. 'I see him!' She turned to the mother, who was standing on the pavement next to the warden, wringing her hands. 'What's his name?'

'Oh thank God,' the mother cried. 'It's Alfie.'

'All right, Alfie, we're coming to get you,' Ruby called, her fear morphing into determination as she pulled more bricks away. With Joseph's help, she was soon able to see Alfie's arm and then a mass of curly brown hair. 'It's all right, Alfie. Won't be long now. You're such a brave boy.'

Finally, they'd moved enough debris to be able to grip Alfie beneath his shoulders and, slowly and gently, they pulled him free. Ruby shone her torch on the child. His face was cut and he was moaning.

'Are you hurt?' she asked, stroking his hair.

Alfie nodded.

'Whereabouts?'

'Here,' he said, touching his leg.

'Could be broken,' Ruby whispered to Joseph and he nodded. She turned back to the boy. 'All right, Alfie, how would you like to come for a ride in our ambulance?'

In spite of his pain, the boy's face lit up. 'You have an ambulance?'

'We do indeed and you are going to be one of our very first passengers, so do you know what that means?'

His eyes widened as he shook his head.

'It means, you're going to be crowned our special Ambulance Prince.'

'Really?' He gave a weak smile.

The rattle of anti-aircraft fire filled the air and in the distance came the boom of another bomb falling.

'Yes.' Ruby heard the sound of voices and looked over her shoulder. Their rescue crew had arrived. 'And, as you are a very brave prince, we're going to carry you on a special stretcher.' She heard Joseph cough and looked up to see a bemused expression on his face. 'This is Joseph,' she said to Alfie. 'He's your servant and he's going to carry you to the ambulance.'

Joseph raised his eyebrows.

'Are you really my servant?' Alfie asked.

'I am indeed,' Joseph replied, much to Ruby's relief. She wasn't sure he'd be game enough to play along. 'We both are,' he added. 'Right then, fellow servant, shall we take Prince Alfred to his chariot?'

They carefully moved him onto a stretcher. His pyjama leg had been torn open, revealing a nasty gash on his calf.

'Alfie!' his mother exclaimed, ignoring the protestations of the warden and clambering over the rubble to them. Tears of relief were streaming down her face.

'We've renamed him Prince Alfred for being such a brave boy,' Ruby replied, as they carried him back to the road. 'And now he's going to come for a ride in our ambulance as a special treat.' She lowered her voice to a whisper. 'We think his leg might be broken so we need to take him to hospital.'

'Of course.' His mother leaned over and kissed Alfie on the forehead.

Ruby and Joseph carefully put the boy in the back of the ambulance with his mother, then got back in the cab.

'Prince Alfred,' Joseph muttered as he turned the ignition.

'I've found that life is a whole lot easier when one turns it into a game,' Ruby said.

'Hmm,' Joseph replied as he pulled out onto the road.

The following morning, Ruby lay in bed completely unable to sleep. She and Joseph had finished their shift at four, but she was too pumped full of adrenaline to rest. Her mind raced as she recapped the night's events. Yes, there had been some hairy moments, but overall it had felt so good to be doing something instead of hiding away like a frightened mouse in a shelter. She looked at the photo of her father beside her bed.

'I did something, Papa. I helped people,' she whispered. She wondered if her father had felt the same sense of purpose when he was fighting in the Great War. From what she'd read about life in the trenches, it was hard to imagine the experience being remotely uplifting. But then she would never have imagined that pulling injured children from the rubble of a bomb blast would be uplifting either. She thought of Alfie and the relief she'd felt when she'd heard his cry. Ruby had always loved children – in many ways, she found it easier to identify with them than she did with adults; they were so much more straightforward, and so much fun. Then she thought of Alfie's mother and the way she'd embraced Ruby when they arrived at the hospital.

'I'll never forget what you did for us,' she'd said, hugging her tightly. 'Not for as long as I live.'

The notion that Ruby could have made such a difference to a complete stranger was mind-boggling and now, as she recalled what had happened, she started to cry. But her tears felt cathartic. She, Ruby Glenville, had saved someone's life. If she died tomorrow, she could die happy, knowing she'd made a positive difference to two people's lives at least.

She closed her eyes and sighed, and finally succumbed to an exhausted sleep.

CHAPTER FOURTEEN

September 2019

I stop reading and rub my eyes. I hadn't known what to expect from a book written by Pearl, but I'm not disappointed. The detail about London during the Second World War is so vivid, it's as if Pearl lived through it. But, of course, that couldn't be possible, as she isn't old enough. It's funny how similar the house on Pendragon Square is to our house on St George's Square. Maybe Pearl used our building as inspiration. Although that would mean she's been living here since – I check the copyright page for the publication date – 1982.

I wince as I move my leg and a sharp burst of pain erupts in my ankle. But I refuse to feel sorry for myself. Reading about the young boy trapped beneath the rubble of his bombed home has really helped put my own problems into perspective.

Gingerly, I shift myself into an upright position and swing my legs out of the bed. Reaching for my crutches, I manage to pull myself upright and hobble through to the bathroom. By the time I've gone to the toilet and made it back to the bed, the pain is almost unbearable. I take another couple of painkillers and slump against the pillows.

Pride comes before a fall, I imagine Marty saying if he was able to see me now. He accused me of being arrogant several times after I started working at *Blaze*. The first was when I received a glowing email from a reader about a feature I'd written on women choosing not to have children. 'You've made me feel OK to be me again,' the woman had written. 'I can't thank you enough.'

'Isn't it lovely that something I wrote helped a complete stranger,' I said to Marty, as I showed him the email, feeling aglow with pride.

'Is that your reason for writing?' he'd asked in response. 'To boost your ego?'

I'd told him that of course it wasn't, but another seed of self-doubt had been planted. Was my career success turning me egotistical? I really hoped not, but from that moment on I never shared any positive feedback I received with Marty again, and my joy was always dampened slightly as a consequence.

I take a sip of water and wonder how Marty would have reacted if he'd received any praise for the novel he's been writing for the past five years. Surely he would have felt proud and wanted to celebrate. But, of course, we never got the chance to find out as the minute he received his first rejection from an agent, he refused to submit it again. The one time I tried to give him some constructive advice, he raised his eyebrows and shook his head and told me that I 'just didn't get it'.

Anger starts bubbling up inside of me, making the pain in my ankle worse. I can't remember whether I've taken one or two painkillers, so I down another one. I really am better off without Marty; I just wish I didn't feel so alone. And I wish I hadn't fallen out of the bloody loft. And I wish… I wish…

I close my eyes as the meds kick in.

In my dream I'm running late for work and riffling through my wardrobe, trying to find something to wear. But everything I pick is stained or has holes in. 'The ambulance has arrived,' a voice calls from somewhere in the distance. I look out of the window and see an old converted truck with AMBULANCE painted on the side. The square looks different too. The garden is full of huge craters and the sky is swarming with giant moths. 'The Germans are here…' someone whispers.

Then I'm at the magazine office, both my arms and legs in giant casts. 'I can still work,' I implore, but Jake, who for some reason is wearing an old-fashioned soldier's uniform, shakes his head.

'I see that pride has come before a fall,' he replies sombrely.

Then I notice a dark stain on his chest. It's growing.

'Are you OK?' I ask.

But he ignores me and the stain becomes bigger and bigger until it's reached the carpet.

I wake in a cold sweat. The sun that had been streaming in the window earlier has gone and the air feels chill. It was just a dream, I tell myself. But I can't get the image of the blood-stained Jake from my mind.

I glance up at the loft hatch. Maybe it's the drop in temperature or maybe it's the thought of what's up there, but I can't help shivering. Whatever happened to cause the stain on the shirt happened ages ago, I remind myself, remembering the ticket I'd found in the shirt pocket. What had the date been?

I shift upright and open the gallery on my phone, zooming in on the photo of the ticket. The date was 1940, almost eighty years ago. I glance at Pearl's novel lying beside me on the bed and re-read the blurb on the back. *London, 1940…*

Perhaps the person the shirt belonged to had sustained an injury in the war. But the hole in the shirt would indicate that they'd been shot or stabbed, and why would someone have been shot or stabbed in London during the Blitz? Before I can get myself even more confused, I hear the clang and whir of the lift and a few moments later there's a sharp rap on my front door.

'Come in,' I call.

'Hello, darling,' Pearl calls, letting herself in with my spare key. 'I thought I'd pop up and see how you're doing.'

'Oh!' I glance around the bedroom at the rumpled bedding and the pile of discarded clothes and the remains of my breakfast on the tray on the floor. This really isn't how I'd wanted Pearl to see me in my home environment, but it's too late now. I hurriedly smooth down my hair. 'I'm through here, in the bedroom.'

'Good afternoon.' Pearl appears in the doorway, a vision in black leather trousers, silk shirt and silver waistcoat. She's holding a gift bag and a plastic food container. Her effortless style only heightens my discomfort. It's been two days since I had a shower; I really hope I don't smell. 'I thought you might need a care package.' She comes over and places the gift bag on the bed.

'That's so kind of you, thank you.' I look into the bag, expecting to see a plant or some chocolates but to my surprise I find a bottle of tequila, two limes and a bag of tortilla chips.

'Did you know that tequila is the only alcoholic drink that doesn't give one a hangover,' Pearl says.

'I did not know that.'

She nods. 'It's because it's made from the agave plant. The Aztecs used to use the agave for all kinds of purposes. And we all know how wise they were.'

I laugh. 'Are you sure about the hangover bit? I seem to remember quite a few hangovers after doing tequila shots.'

Pearl gives me a withering stare. 'Well, of course you're going to have a hangover if you don't respect the process.'

'What process?'

'The drinking process. Tequila is a drink of the gods, it deserves to be treated with respect – sipped and not downed in shots. It also helps if you buy the real deal too.' She nods at the bag. 'I can assure you, there are no additives in that bottle.'

'Right.'

'Now, have you eaten? I don't want you drinking on an empty stomach.' She puts the container on the bed and I catch a waft of something delicious. 'I made a beef stew. You're not one of those pesky vegetarians, are you?'

'No,' I laugh.

'Excellent. Would you like some now? Shall I get you a plate?'

'That would be great. I'm starving.'

As Pearl heads off to the kitchen, I catch a glimpse of the corner of her novel sticking out from under my duvet. I quickly shove it down. Having to explain that I internet-stalked her would be all kinds of awkward.

Pearl comes back into the room with a plate and knife and fork. 'So, you fell out of the loft, did you?'

I nod. Maybe I ought to tell her what I found up there. She clearly knows a lot about the war, so she might be able to come up with some kind of explanation. 'I found something strange up there actually.'

'You did?' She opens the container and starts dishing me up a bowl of stew.

'Yes. I think it's been there a long time, possibly from the war.'

'Which one?'

'The Second World War, in 1940.'

She stops dishing up for a second but doesn't look at me. 'Oh really? What was it?'

'A shirt.'

'How do you know it was from the war?'

'It looks like it's from an old-fashioned soldier's uniform and I think whoever was wearing it might have been seriously injured – or worse.'

'What do you mean?'

'There's a stain on it, and I think it could be blood.'

There's a clatter as Pearl drops the spoon she'd been ladling the stew with onto the floorboards. She stares at me. 'Blood?'

'Yes, from some kind of—'

I'm interrupted by a rap on the door, which Pearl had clearly left open, as Heath's voice echoes through the flat. 'Hi, honey, I'm home!'

Pearl bends to pick up the spoon. Am I imagining things or does she look shaken by my revelation?

'Hello, ladies.' Heath bounds into the room, bringing a waft of his signature cologne. 'Mmm, that looks good.'

'I made some beef stew,' Pearl mutters. She definitely seems rattled.

'Very nice. How are you doing, lovely?' Heath asks me, perching on the edge of the bed.

'OK, thanks to the painkillers, and Pearl also brought me this.' I show him the tequila.

Heath throws his head back and laughs. 'Honestly, Pearl, what are you like?'

But instead of laughing along, Pearl takes an old-fashioned pocket watch from her waistcoat and frowns. 'Is that the time? I must dash. I have a martial arts class to go to.'

'Was it something I said?' Heath calls as she hurries from the room.

I grin, but I can't help wondering if it was something *I* said that caused Pearl's sudden exit.

'She's certainly one of a kind,' Heath says as we listen to the lift rattle its way back downstairs.

'So I'm discovering. Do you know how long she's lived here?' I ask nonchalantly.

'Oh, forever. She was here long before Guy and I moved in, and we've been here seven years. She's a writer, you know.'

'Yes, she told me the other night. Have you read anything by her?'

Heath shakes his head. 'No, Guy and I looked her up on Amazon, but her books aren't really my cup of tea. I'm more of a sci-fi man.'

I nod, deciding against telling him that not only have I looked Pearl up on Amazon but I've already started reading one of her books. I don't want him thinking I'm the kind of person who does background checks on her neighbours, even though, clearly, I am.

He stands up and checks his phone. 'OK, sweetheart, better go, Guy's looking for me. Can I get you anything? I take it you won't be needing any pizza.' He nods at the plate of stew.

'No, I'm all good thanks. And thank you for checking in.'

'No problem at all. You have my number if there are any emergencies.' He heads over to the door. 'Have a nice evening.'

'Thank you, you too.'

I pick up the stew and start to eat. But my appetite seems to have deserted me. All I can think of is Pearl and her strange reaction to my revelation about the shirt in the loft. Why did she drop the spoon? And why did she leave so hurriedly? It doesn't make sense. If only my brain wasn't so foggy from the pain meds.

I reach under the duvet for the novel, feeling the sudden compulsion to carry on reading, as if the answers I'm seeking might be hidden within its pages.

CHAPTER FIFTEEN

September 1940

Joseph woke with a start to the sound of a bell ringing outside and he was momentarily thrown into a panic. Was it the toll of the church bell? Had the Germans invaded?

He sat up and rubbed his eyes. The bell rang again and he heard someone call, 'Any old iron?' The rag-and-bone man! He sank back on the bed in relief. He'd been so tired when he returned from his first shift at the ambulance station, he'd fallen asleep fully dressed. He loosened the stiff serge collar on his shirt as memories from the night before came flooding back to him. Driving a truck around London during blackout and a bombing raid had been challenging, to say the least. And working with Ruby had tested his patience at times too. Although that was hardly a surprise. To give her credit where it was due, she had shown great courage saving Alfie from the rubble, but when she'd told him that life was so much easier when you turned it into a game, he'd felt like shaking her. *If only the rest of us had that luxury*, he'd wanted to say, and probably would have if they hadn't had the child to attend to. Yes, it must be easy to treat life as one big game when you never had to worry about keeping a roof over your head or where your next meal was coming from.

As if on cue, he heard the tinkle of Ruby's laugh echoing up from outside. He went over to the window and peered through a chink in the blackout blind. She was standing on the pavement chatting away to the rag-and-bone man, and holding a huge bouquet of red roses.

'I always wanted to be a rag-and-bone man when I was little,' he heard her say. 'I say, could I have a go on your bell?'

Joseph wondered where she'd got the flowers from. He'd never seen her have a gentleman visitor since he'd lived there – apart from the poor victims trooping in for one of her séances. And she'd made it abundantly clear that she wasn't interested in getting married. Not that he cared, of course. If Ruby had a suitor buying her flowers, then more fool them was all he could say.

He went over to his wardrobe and pulled out a change of clothes. Today he had way more important things to think about than Ruby. Today he was taking part in something that he hoped would be truly monumental.

*

Ruby sat at the drawing-room table and chewed on the end of her pen.

'To my dear Kitty…' she murmured thoughtfully. 'Please accept this token of my affection…' She frowned. The word 'dear' wasn't quite exciting enough – perhaps because it was too reminiscent of 'dreary'. 'To my *darling* Kitty…' she said, louder this time. 'In eager anticipation, from your secret admirer.' Yes, that was much better, far more enticing. She grinned as she pictured Kitty's face when she discovered the flowers waiting for her in the entrance hall. Would she think they were from Freddy? Would this make her more confident about talking to the poor smitten fellow? Ruby certainly hoped so. Before she knew it, she was picturing Freddy sweeping Kitty into his arms, offering her a lifetime of free pork chops and sausages from his butcher's shop, and promising to save her from her weasel of a husband.

At the thought of Reg, Ruby paused. Was what she was about to do morally wrong? Kitty was a married woman, after all.

Should she really be encouraging her to look elsewhere for love and affection, and assorted meat products? She thought back to the countless times she'd heard Reg yelling at Kitty through the ceiling before he'd mercifully enlisted. And she remembered the sound of poor Kitty's sobs late into the night. Her plan was morally righteous, she was certain of it. She was giving Kitty a taste of what it felt like to be loved and appreciated; how could that possibly be wrong?

Ruby put her pen in her right hand and began to write. If she used her usual elegant script, she'd instantly give the game away. She chuckled as she watched the clumsy letters form on the card. It looked exactly like the kind of writing belonging to a fellow like Freddy. Surely Kitty would think so too.

Once Ruby had finished writing the card, she attached it to the flowers and went to her front door and peered into the hallway. As soon as she'd checked the coast was clear, she tiptoed across the black and white chequered floor to the table for the post by the door. She placed the bouquet on the table, making sure that the card was clearly visible, then crept back inside, her skin tingling from a mission successfully accomplished.

*

As Joseph marched along the Strand, his heart thudded in his chest. When his friends in Stepney told him of the plan to storm the shelter at the Savoy, he'd thought it was a great idea. But as the silver canopy of the hotel came into view, he couldn't help wondering if it would all end in disaster.

A councillor from Stepney named Phil had organised the protest, and about fifty of them were now gathered outside, and some of them had brought their children. Bringing children had been Joseph's idea, inspired by the woman he'd seen on the first night of the Blitz, trying to get shelter for her and her kids at Whitechapel station. Surely if people knew what was happening to the children in East London, they would put pressure on the government to open more shelters for them.

'All right, brothers and sisters,' Phil yelled from the front of the procession. 'Are we ready?'

'Yes!' they all roared back, causing curious stares from passers-by.

As they marched up to the grand entrance of the Savoy, the doorman did such a dramatic double take it was almost comical. Joseph bet he'd never seen such a motley crew before.

A woman dressed to the nines who'd been talking to the doorman looked at them in horror before darting inside.

'We're here to protest the great injustice that's going on right now in London,' Phil bellowed to the doorman. 'While the rich up west are sheltering in luxury, the East End have nothing. Why should the poor be deprived of shelter from Hitler's bombs?'

To Joseph's surprise, and relief, the doorman stepped back to let them inside. As they marched through the revolving door and into the lobby, Joseph couldn't help gasping. A chandelier practically the size of a car hung above them, glimmering gold, and the crimson carpet was so plush it was like stepping onto a bed of cloud. It was so different from the world he grew up in, so different to the parts of London he was accustomed to, his jaw clenched at the inequality.

The staff behind the counter, clad in crisp black and white uniforms, looked on aghast as the protestors filled the foyer. One of the kids ran over to an ornamental fountain in the corner, laughing with joy as he splashed the water.

'What the blazes is going on?' An officious-looking man dressed in a black suit and white shirt came strutting out from behind the counter like an angry penguin.

'Come on, let's go to the restaurant,' Phil called.

They swarmed forwards, following the signs downstairs into an elegant restaurant with tables as shiny as conkers shimmering in the light of yet more chandeliers. The aroma of grilled steak filled the air. It was a smell that simultaneously made Joseph's mouth water and his skin prickle with indignation. So, while the poor in the East End were being bombed out of house and home and having to survive off scraps, the wealthy were still feasting as if nothing had happened.

'Don't let them in,' the angry penguin man bellowed to a waiter standing by the restaurant door.

'We're protesting at the lack of shelter for the poor in the East End,' Phil called, marching past the waiter into the centre of the restaurant. 'We mean you no harm, we just want to bring attention to our plight.'

'I'm a journalist from the *Daily Mirror*,' a man called from a table in the corner. He got up and went over to Phil. 'I'd love to know more about this.'

As they started talking, the penguin man practically blew a gasket. 'Call the manager,' he bellowed to a waitress.

'Yes, sir,' she replied before scurrying away.

'What on earth is going on?' an elderly woman dining at the table next to Joseph asked, peering up at him over her half-moon-shaped spectacles.

'We're protesting over the lack of support for the East End, madam,' Joseph replied, removing his hat and holding it to his chest. 'These poor folk have all lost their homes during the blitzkrieg and they're being denied shelter.'

'What do you mean, they're being denied shelter?' the woman's husband, a chubby-faced, pompous-looking fellow demanded.

'There are hardly any public shelters in the East End,' Joseph replied. 'Definitely not enough to meet demand, and the government won't even let them use the Underground stations.'

The man remained stony-faced, but the woman was watching a couple of the children, who had sat down and started playing on the restaurant floor. Their clothes were ragged and their faces streaked with dirt.

'That's a terrible pity,' she said.

'Yes, it is,' Joseph agreed.

'Which way is it to the shelter?' Phil asked one of the waiters.

To Joseph's surprise, the waiter readily gestured to a door at the back of the room. 'Through there and down the stairs, sir,' he muttered.

'What did you tell him for?' penguin man spluttered as the crowd surged towards the door.

They went down another flight of stairs and along a passageway until they reached a door surrounded by sandbags.

'I think this is it,' Phil called.

As soon as he got inside the shelter, any trepidation Joseph might have been feeling about their invasion of the Savoy vanished. As he looked around the huge room at the rows of neatly made-up beds, the ambient lamplight and the dance floor – *a chuffing dance floor!* – he gasped.

'Bloody Norah!' a man beside him exclaimed, taking off his flat cap and scratching his head. 'This is their bomb shelter?'

'It's as posh as a palace,' a woman gasped.

'That's right,' said Phil. 'And when the siren goes off, all they have to do is come down here and get tucked up in bed for the night. No roaming around in the cold for them. No trying to stay safe sheltering under a bleedin' table.'

At that point, penguin man reappeared, accompanied by a man in a dark grey suit and a paisley-print cravat.

'Good afternoon, everyone, I'm the manager of the Savoy,' he said, looking around with a bemused expression on his face.

Penguin man visibly cringed as some of the children clambered onto one of the beds and began bouncing around. 'Could you please control your offspring!' he exclaimed.

'So, what's this all about then?' the manager asked affably, clearly trying a more diplomatic approach.

'It's about the fact that while the East End is being bombed to smithereens, up west you're all sheltering in the lap of luxury,' Phil said.

And then, in a moment of timing so perfect it couldn't have been scripted, the air-raid siren began to wail.

The children immediately stopped bouncing on the bed.

'Are the Germans coming back again?' the little boy asked anxiously.

'Are we going to die?' the little girl said, her bottom lip quivering.

'It's all right, love, we're safe down here,' her father replied.

'Yes, we are,' Phil said, looking at the manager challengingly.

The door opened and Savoy guests started filing into the shelter. The expressions of shock on their faces as soon as they saw the protestors was priceless.

All eyes turned to the manager. Joseph held his breath. Surely he wouldn't send them out into the streets.

'Welcome, ladies and gents, today we have some extra guests,' the manager called jovially. He turned to one of the maids on duty with a smile. 'Perhaps you could fetch us all some tea, and some bread and butter for the children.'

*

As the siren began to wail, Ruby groaned. She wasn't sure she could bear another afternoon cooped up in the Pendragon Square shelter. And, even worse, she'd run out of reading material to distract herself with.

Sighing, she picked up her handbag and gas mask and left the flat. The flowers for Kitty were where she'd left them on the hall table. Kitty must have been on first aid duty, or else she'd been in such a rush to get to the shelter she hadn't noticed them. After making sure the card was still prominent, Ruby went outside. A handful of planes swooped by overhead, causing her heart to leap into her throat. Were they about to unload their deadly cargo right on top of her?

She raced over to the shelter, the harsh rattle of gunfire causing her head to ache. How much longer was this onslaught going to go on for? According to the Americans, the German invasion of Britain was probably going to happen this weekend. It was getting to the point where her nerves couldn't stand the not knowing.

Don't be so pathetic, Ruby scolded herself as she ran down into the shelter and took her place in the cold, dank corner.

The raid went on for a couple of hours, but for Ruby it felt like a couple of lifetimes. There'd been no sign of Kitty or Joseph, and old Mr Wilson from a house across the square had stationed himself opposite her and spent the entire time picking at various orifices on his body. By the time the single wail of the all-clear rang out, Ruby was on her feet and up those shelter steps so fast she almost knocked over a warden who was standing just outside.

'Where's the fire?' he joked.

'Everywhere!' she replied.

As she hurried up the front steps of the house, she heard the sound of raised voices coming from inside – or rather a man's raised voice and the plaintive pleading of a woman's.

'I wasn't born yesterday,' the man shouted. 'Of course you know who they're from.'

Ruby's heart plummeted as she realised that the voice belonged to Reg. He must have discovered the roses. But what the hell was he doing here?

She opened the door and stepped into the hallway. Kitty was standing by the lift and Reg was facing her, brandishing the bouquet.

'So, while I've been away risking my life for king and country, you've been getting yourself a secret admirer?' he spat.

'No, I haven't, I swear!' Kitty looked at Ruby desperately.

'I can explain,' Ruby said quickly. *Damn it, damn it, damn it!* How would she explain?

Reg spun around and glared at her. 'Oh yeah?'

'Yes. I actually left those flowers for Kitty.'

'You what?' His weaselly eyes grew so small as he frowned they practically disappeared into his face.

'Yes. It was all just a case of perfectly innocent jolly japes,' Ruby continued.

'I don't believe you,' he said defiantly. 'You're trying to cover for her.' He turned back to Kitty. 'Is she in on this? Does she know who this so-called secret admirer is?'

'I told you, it's me,' Ruby cried. 'I mean to say, I left the flowers. I'm not Kitty's secret admirer. Although, of course, I do admire her greatly.'

'I don't understand,' Kitty said, looking at Ruby.

'I was just trying to cheer you up,' Ruby replied.

'By making her think she had a secret admirer?' Reg hissed. 'She's a married woman.'

'I know but—'

'Something smells fishy to me,' Reg interrupted. 'For a start, this here handwriting. There's no way a lady wrote this.'

'I wrote it with my right hand!' Ruby exclaimed. 'I'm left-handed, you see.'

Reg frowned at her and shook his head. 'You two must think I was born yesterday.' He marched over to Kitty and grabbed her by the arm. 'Come on, let's go.'

'It really was me,' Ruby cried as Reg practically shoved Kitty into the lift, but her pleading was to no avail.

Reg slammed the lift gate shut and it began its juddering ascent.

'Drat!' Ruby exclaimed as she let herself into her flat. She paced up and down in the drawing room, not knowing what to do. If she went up to Kitty's flat, it would probably only inflame things further. Reg had clearly decided what he was going to believe. Ruby wanted to kick herself, she was so frustrated. She'd got the flowers to try to cheer Kitty up, but all she'd done was give Reg another excuse to make her life hell.

She went into her bedroom and flung herself on the bed. 'Oh, Papa, I've made a terrible mistake,' she cried to the photo on the nightstand. She heard the creak of floorboards from the flat above, followed by a crash and a thud so violent it caused the chandelier to tremble. Her mouth went dry. What if Reg was physically attacking Kitty? She heard a yell and a cry and then the rhythmic squeaking and thudding of something banging against the wall. Her stomach churned and she sat for a moment, frozen rigid. If she heard Kitty scream or yell, she'd run straight up there. But there was no other sound but the thud, thud, thudding. It was a sound that sickened her even more than the boom of Hitler's bombs.

CHAPTER SIXTEEN

September 2019

I put down the book and pull the duvet up to my shoulders, feeling sick to my stomach at the thought of what was happening to Kitty. *It's only fiction*, I remind myself. *It isn't real.* But the more I read of Pearl's novel, the more I'm struck by the strange similarities with the real world. There's the uncanny resemblance between Pendragon and St George's Square, and the house itself, which could obviously be explained by Pearl using her home as inspiration – if she was living here back in the early eighties, that is. But surely the fact that the ticket I found in the shirt pocket matches the year in which Pearl's book is set is a similarity too far? Could the shirt somehow be connected to Pearl? Is that why she reacted so weirdly when I told her about it? Could her novel be based on a true story? If only my head wasn't so woozy from the pain meds and I could think a bit straighter.

I pick up my phone and google 'Pendragon Square London.' There's no such address. I draw a similar blank searching for Neptune Square. Of course there's no such address, I tell myself. It's a work of fiction. And anyone would have been shocked at my revelation that I'd found a possibly blood-stained shirt in the loft; Pearl's reaction wasn't out of the ordinary. But still… I stare at the hatch in the ceiling and think of the shirt lying up there in the darkness and my scalp tightens.

In a bid to stop torturing myself with 'what if's, I fumble onto my crutches and hobble through to the bathroom. As soon as I see my reflection in the mirror on the wall, my spirits sink. I'm gaunt and pale and my hair is lank and greasy. When I'd dreamed of starting over in London, I'd pictured myself as a dynamic girl about town, breezing around in a range of sophisticated yet edgy 'office to bar' outfits, clutching the obligatory takeaway coffee to fuel my escapades. I'd imagined zooming around the Underground with all the ease of a native Londoner, glowing with green juice and supple from yoga. But, instead, I'm trapped in my new home, looking and feeling like crap, with a loft containing evidence from a potential deadly crime scene and a neighbour who might be in some way connected to it.

Wobbling on one leg, I clean my teeth and splash some water on my face. I bet Marty would love to see me now. But then I think back to the time I got really ill with food poisoning a few months after we started dating. He'd been so caring and atten-tive, holding my hair back when I was sick, rubbing my back to help me fall asleep, bringing me water whenever I needed it. It had been wonderful to feel so taken care of and his attentiveness had made me fall even more in love with him. Where did it go wrong? *Why* did it go wrong? What I wouldn't give to have that old Marty taking care of me now.

I hobble back into the bedroom and with every hop I feel a biting stab of pain. The question I've tried so hard to avoid looms large in my mind: did I do the right thing breaking up with Marty? He was never abusive, like Reg in Pearl's novel. He never physically hurt me, and he was so loving in the early days. It was only when my career took off that we started having issues. Of course, he never openly said he had a problem with my career, but that was definitely what caused the tension between us. And it all came to a head when I was offered the job in London. Commuting from Manchester long-term would have been too much, but Marty refused to relocate. Then he'd dropped the bombshell that he wanted us to have a child and he didn't want to wait. At the time, I'd thought this was deeply unfair of him, but was I wrong? Had I made a massive mistake, choosing my career over him? After all, what use was my high-flying job now, in my hour of need?

I grab my laptop from the chest of drawers and hop back into bed. I take another painkiller and open Facebook. Only last month I commissioned an article titled *How to Avoid Internet-Stalking your Ex* and the irony of that fact isn't lost on me. *But I'm not stalking Marty*, I tell myself as I search for his profile. I just want to see how he's doing. We were together for almost ten years. He was – *is* until the divorce comes through – my husband. It's hardly as if I'm spying on a stranger. But as his profile page loads, I see something that makes my breath catch in my throat. His most recent post is a photo of him with another woman. On closer inspection, I see that the woman – a pouty blonde named Amy Parsons – had tagged him in the photo, which is why it's on his wall. '*That moment when you just know…*' she's written in the caption. When you just know what? I think to myself. That you're draping yourself all over someone else's husband?

But he isn't your husband any more, a snide voice in my mind reminds me, *not really*. I study the way Amy Parsons is draping herself over Marty for any sign that it could be purely platonic. But judging by the way her chin is resting on his shoulder, I'd say that whatever she *just knows* about Marty, it's more than just friends. And so, down the stalker hole I go, clicking on the comments beneath the post. '*So happy for you babe*' someone named Sheryl has written. Why? I stare at the screen until the letters swim. Why are you so happy that this woman is draped all over my husband? My ankle is now throbbing with a red-hot pain, but the rest of me feels icy cold. Could he really have moved on so soon? It doesn't make sense. Only a few months ago he wanted us to start a family. How could he go from wanting to have children with his wife to being embraced by a woman named Amy effing Parsons so quickly? Who the hell is this woman?

I click on her profile. The work bio reads: 'Marketing Exec'. Marketing. Could she be a colleague of Marty's? I scan the page. There's no mention of who she actually works for – on Facebook at least… I open another window and do a search for her on LinkedIn. And, sure enough, the same blonde hair and pout appear. She works for the same company as Marty. My pulse quickens as I start constructing the backstory of what must have happened. I picture Marty coming into work the day after I decided to leave, clearly distraught.

'My career-obsessed wife's moving to London. She's leaving me for her job,' I imagine him telling Amy Parsons by the water cooler.

'Oh no, babe,' I imagine her cooing (she looks like the type of woman who coos and says babe, especially to men). 'I think you need a drink.'

And so they go to the pub after work and one drink leads to another and one thing leads to another and, before they know it, she's draping herself all over him in bed. In *our* bed.

It's the strangest thing. Even though my attraction to Marty was chipped away at with every little barbed remark he made about me and my career, the thought of him naked with another woman, of him doing those things he used to only do to me to another woman – and one as instantly annoying as Amy effing Parsons – makes me feel sick to my stomach. I feel Pearl's stew churning away inside me and taste the onions in the back of my throat.

A terrible thought looms in my mind. What if Marty and Amy Parsons had been draping themselves over each other for longer? What if he'd been sleeping with her before we broke up? A tickertape of memories starts playing in my head. Marty certainly went to a lot of conferences in the past year or so. Conferences that required overnight stays. He said it was all part of his bid to get promotion, but was it just a cover for him and this woman?

I click back onto her Facebook page with all the consumed focus of a sniffer dog on the hunt. Because she and I aren't friends I can only see each time she updated her profile pic. Luckily for me, she's one of those people who updates her picture just about every week. Most of them involve her signature pout and, more often than not, a generous amount of cleavage. The most recent profile pic was taken by the sea. Amy Parsons is strad- dling a cannon and gazing provocatively into the lens. I scan the comments. They're all from her friends and variations on the theme of *gorgeous, babes*. And then, right at the bottom, I see a comment from Marty. '*Top day*', he's written. I look at the date. It was taken just over a week ago – the day after I moved out of our flat and down to London. I think back to that last day in the flat together and how Marty had drifted around like a wounded swan, pointedly ignoring me. All the time I'd been feeling wracked with guilt at the pain I thought I was causing him, he had this 'top day' to the coast with Amy Parsons planned. He probably couldn't wait for me to leave.

I scroll further down the page like a woman possessed. I can't find any more comments from Marty on her profile pics and I'm about to give up when I click on one from Christmas last year, in which Amy Parsons is pouting in a 'sexy Santa' outfit. And there's Marty again, midway down the comments. '*I would*,' he'd written with a winking emoji.

I push the laptop away, fighting the urge to retch. Last Christ- mas we were still very much together. It was still five months before I was offered the London job, six months before Marty told me he wanted to start a family.

Like a voyeur at a car crash, I look back at the screen and see that Amy Parsons had replied to his comment. '*I know*,' she'd written, with a winking emoji *and* a red heart. I sit, frozen rigid. If she knows that he 'would', did that mean that he 'had'?

Anger starts burning its way through my shock. So, all that time he made me feel like a dreadful human being for daring to care about my job, he was having an affair with this – this...

I'd always thought the phrase 'seeing red' was poetic licence, but as I stare at their words, a red haze descends before my eyes like a filter. I think of all the times I cried and pleaded with Marty to understand – that just because I wanted a successful career it didn't mean I didn't want him, or us, or a family. And all the times he'd acted like the victim and cast me as the selfish one, who'd only got my job because of nepotism. But all the while he was actually cheating on me.

The pain in my ankle fades to a dull throb and my brain becomes foggy again. The meds are obviously kicking in. I want to do something, vent the rage building inside of me, but I feel too woozy. I snap my laptop shut and lean back against the pillows. Nothing feels real any more. One of the foundation stones of my life has been ripped out from under me.

Unable to bear thinking about it any longer, I grab Pearl's novel and continue to read.

CHAPTER SEVENTEEN

September 1940

Joseph scrambled into his ambulance uniform, stuffing a slice of stale bread into his mouth as he went. He'd stayed at the Savoy until the all-clear sounded, and due to bomb damage to the roads, he'd had to get off the bus and run half of the way back. Now the sirens were wailing again and he only had a few minutes before his shift at Neptune Square started.

For the first time since the war began, he felt something close to hope. Storming the Savoy had gone better than he ever could have expected. The journalists who'd been lunching there had made detailed notes and interviewed many of the protestors. He couldn't wait to see their write-ups in tomorrow's papers. Hopefully then the government would succumb to pressure and allow people to shelter in the Underground stations.

He put on his helmet and hurried out of the back door, opting to take the stairs rather than wait for the lift.

As he was running downstairs, he heard the back door to Kitty's flat open.

'Good evening, Kitty!' he called cheerily, but to his dismay, Kitty's husband Reg stepped into the stairwell.

Reg looked him up and down, his thin lips pursed in a frown.

'Evening,' Joseph said, but Reg didn't reply; he just carried on glaring.

Kitty appeared behind him, her head bowed.

'Hello, Kitty,' Joseph said. 'Are you heading to the first-aid station?'

Kitty shook her head but still didn't raise her face to look at him.

'Oh. All right.' The three of them stood there for a moment in awkward silence. 'I'd better get going then. My shift starts in a few minutes.'

'Bye,' Kitty murmured.

Joseph carried on running down the stairs. He heard Reg mutter something, but he couldn't hear what. He must be home on leave. Joseph hoped for Kitty's sake that he wouldn't be home for long.

Outside, the air smelled of smoke and long thin fingers of pearly white light searched the darkening sky, picking out planes swooping by overhead. It was strange how quickly this surreal sight had become normal.

When he reached Neptune Square, the warden waved him through the gates and he raced down into the underground car park. Ruby was already in the staffroom, sitting at the table smoking a cigarette and drinking a cup of tea. He was expecting one of her usual effusive greetings, but she just raised her eyebrows at him. She looked really tired.

'Nice of you to join us, O'Toole,' Bill commented, coming through from the office, bringing with him a wave of chatter from the operators and the shrill ring of the phones.

'Sorry, I got caught in the earlier raid on the other side of town.'

Bill nodded. 'Looks like we're in for a busy one all right.'

'Bill, you're needed on the telephone,' one of the women called from the office.

'See what I mean,' Bill sighed and hurried back through.

Joseph sat down at the table across from Ruby. He'd never really smoked much, but tonight her cigarette smelled so inviting he had half a mind to ask her if he could have one.

'So, how has your day been?' Ruby asked flatly.

'Excellent,' he replied.

She looked at him. 'Oh really? Do share. Right now, I'd give up three years of my prime to have one day I could describe as excellent.'

'Surely your prime has long gone.' Joseph couldn't resist the obvious dig.

Ruby took a drag on her cigarette and fixed him with a stare. 'My dear, I can assure you that my prime hasn't even begun.'

'If you say so.'

'So, go on then,' she said, wisps of smoke trailing from her mouth as she spoke. 'Pray tell.'

'I've been at the Savoy.'

Her mouth fell open in shock. 'You? But…'

'But what?' He stared at her defiantly.

'I didn't think…'

'What?'

'That the Savoy was your cup of tea. You should have told me you were going. I could murder a steak.'

Joseph sighed. 'I wasn't there to eat.'

'Oh. That doesn't matter. I could murder a cocktail too.'

'I wasn't there to drink either.'

'What were you there to do then?' Her face lit up. 'I say, were you having a liaison?'

'A what?'

'Were you there to meet one of the guests… in their room?' She gave him a knowing wink.

'No, I was not! I was there to storm the shelter, if you must know.'

'What?' Ruby cried, causing the other people in the room to look over.

But before Joseph could reply, Bill came hurrying through. 'Crew Four, got a job for you. Pub's been hit on Wilton Road, by Victoria station.'

*

'What do you mean you were storming the shelter?' Ruby asked, as she climbed into the ambulance cab. She was beginning to think that Joseph was the darkest horse she'd ever encountered. Just when she thought she had him all figured out, he'd pull another fascinating revelation from the hat.

'Exactly that,' Joseph replied, turning the key in the ignition.

As the engine rumbled into life, Ruby twisted in her seat to stare at him. 'But why?'

'I was part of a protest organised by a councillor in Stepney.'

'But Stepney's in the East End; why on earth would an East End councillor be protesting at the Savoy?'

They drove up the ramp and out onto the pitch-dark street. The hum of the planes above sounded louder than ever – as if they were flying lower than ever. Clearly the brutes were becoming more cocky in the light of their blitzkrieg success. Ruby prayed the brave RAF boys and the ack-ack gunners would send them packing.

'We were protesting about the lack of shelter in the East End,' Joseph replied.

'What do you mean? Surely they have shelters. Weren't shelters built all over London?'

'Most of their shelters are surface level – and there are barely enough of those. All they're good for is protecting from shrapnel, and the government won't even allow them to take shelter in the Underground.'

'But—'

'Did you know that at the Savoy shelter the guests all have beds made up for them? And maids to wait on them hand and foot.' Joseph turned left onto Vauxhall Bridge Road. 'While the poor are being left to fend for themselves, they're getting tea and biscuits brought to them on chuffing silver platters.'

Ruby felt a hot flush of shame as she remembered that first night of the Blitz and how she'd spent it partying in the Savoy shelter with Rupert. 'But surely it isn't all that bad…' she offered feebly.

'Isn't all that bad?' He took his eyes off the road to glare at her.

'Look out!' she cried, grabbing the wheel and pushing it to the right, narrowly avoiding a warden who'd stepped into the street. 'I told you I should be driving this thing,' she muttered.

'Thank you,' he retorted. 'But forgive me if I'm a little shocked at your ignorance.'

'My what?' Ruby's skin prickled with indignation.

High above, a plane swooped by, picked out for a moment by a sweeping searchlight. A loud burst of gunfire rang out, leaving an iridescent trail like a string of pearls. If it wasn't all so awful it would have been stunning.

'Do you really think that this war is some kind of great leveller?' Joseph said. 'Do you really think we're all in this together?'

'Well, yes of course. The Germans are bombing everyone, even the royal family.'

'Bloody hell!'

Even though it was pitch dark in the cab, she could tell he was rolling his eyes. 'What? It's true. That's why the queen said she was able to look the East End in the face – because Buckingham Palace got hit.'

'Right. So do you think the royal family are having to shelter above ground?'

'No, of course not.'

'Why of course not?'

'Because they're our royal family!' Ruby shook her head. Joseph really was being ridiculous. He'd be saying next that there shouldn't be a royal family.

'And why should their lives be any more precious than that of a docker's or a factory worker's? And why should some posho who happened to be born into enough money to be able to stay at the Savoy feast on steak and champagne while the rest of London is burning?'

Ruby couldn't help feeling his last remark was aimed at her and again her cheeks burned. 'Their lives aren't more precious, it's just that…' She paused.

'Yes?' he pressed.

'That's the way it's always been.' She was aware her answer was lame. Joseph clearly agreed, judging by the loud sigh he was giving. But before she could try to redeem herself, a loud whistling sound whooshed by them.

'What the heck was that?' Joseph exclaimed as they both instinctively hunched down in their seats.

'A bomb?' Ruby gasped, barely able to breathe.

Suddenly the gaping darkness beyond the windscreen exploded into colour – a blinding white flash followed by a flare of orange and, a split second later, a deafening boom, sending great tremors through the truck.

'Shit!' Joseph muttered, slamming on the brakes.

Ruby gripped the edge of her seat, her palms suddenly slick with sweat. If they had been just a few yards further along… If they had left the station just a few moments earlier… If Joseph had driven just a tiny bit faster…

They looked at each other, their faces frozen in shock.

'Don't you just hate it when that happens?' Ruby finally broke the silence, her voice wavering.

'Is everything a joke to you?' He grabbed the map from her lap and held it up to the orange glow.

As a fire truck went tearing past them, Ruby felt suddenly and annoyingly close to tears. Of course she didn't think the bomb was a laughing matter. She'd only been trying to alleviate the tension. Why couldn't Joseph see that?

He shoved the map back onto her lap and turned up a side road.

Ruby swallowed hard and gritted her teeth. She wouldn't let him make her cry. She couldn't!

When they finally got to the pub, they found the roof and side wall caved in as if they were made from cardboard and the air filled with dust. Through the dust, Ruby could just make out the bar inside. It had somehow managed to survive the blast and a couple of half-drunk glasses of beer still stood on top, giving the place a spooky, *Mary Celeste* feel. A team of stretcher-bearers was already at the scene.

Ruby leapt from the ambulance and picked her way along the rubble-strewn pavement, her legs wobbly from shock. The wail of the siren mingled with the sound of people moaning and crying.

'Got a couple for you to take to the hospital,' a warden told her, flicking his torchlight over two of the stretchers. One of the casualties, a young man with red hair, was clutching his arm and groaning. The other, a woman with sharply bobbed blonde hair wearing a dusky pink dress, was completely out for the count. If it weren't for the gash on her forehead it would have looked as if she was fast asleep.

Ruby and Joseph opened the back of the ambulance and helped the stretcher-bearers put them in the back.

'D-Daisy,' the man stammered, looking at the woman.

'Do you know her?' Ruby asked.

'She's my wife. Is she all right?'

'I'm going to ride in the back with them,' Ruby said to Joseph. He nodded brusquely.

She climbed in and he slammed the doors behind her. Ruby sighed. *At least our patients might actually appreciate my company,* she felt like yelling at him.

'I'm sure she'll be right as rain as soon as we get her to hospital,' Ruby said, giving the man a reassuring smile. She felt the woman's neck for a pulse. It was so faint she could barely detect it. 'Step on it!' she called through the partition to Joseph and the engine rumbled into life.

'We've only been married a couple of weeks,' the man mumbled.

'Congratulations!' Ruby tried to sound jolly, but her voice came out high-pitched and strained.

'I don't know what I'd do if…' He broke off.

'She's going to be fine. Aren't you, Daisy?' Ruby turned to the woman and stroked her hair. *Please, please be fine. Please, please don't die.* She took hold of her hand and gave it a gentle squeeze. Daisy's skin was cold as ice. Ruby grabbed one of the army-issue blankets from the corner of the ambulance and tucked it around her tightly.

The roar of the planes and the rattle of the gunfire outside grew louder. What if a bomb were to land on top of them? Surely they wouldn't be able to cheat death twice in such short succession. God damn the Germans! God damn that noise! If only they had a wireless in the back of the ambulance, she could play music to try to drown it out.

'Daisy, Daisy, give me your answer do,' she started singing. 'I'm half crazy, all for the love of you.' She turned to the man. 'Come on, let's sing to her.'

'It won't be a stylish marriage,' the man sang gruffly. 'I can't afford a carriage.'

'But you'll look sweet,' Ruby continued, 'on the seat, of an ambulance built for two.'

The man chuckled and Ruby felt the slightest squeeze of her hand. 'I think she can hear us!' she exclaimed. 'Daisy, can you hear us? Keep singing!'

She and the man sang louder and louder, repeating the chorus over and over again. But all the while, Ruby was singing a different, silent chorus in her mind. *Daisy, Daisy, please don't die! Please don't die!*

The ambulance lurched round a corner, causing Ruby to topple to the side. As she regained her balance, a terrifying boom rang out, reverberating through the road and causing the floor of the vehicle to shudder. Ruby closed her eyes tight. *Please, keep us all safe!*

CHAPTER EIGHTEEN

September 1940

Joseph pulled up outside the hospital, his heart pounding from a mixture of adrenaline and anger. While he'd been trying to negotiate the pitch-dark London streets and ignore the terrifying sight of German bombers swooping like vultures overhead, Ruby had decided to throw some kind of impromptu party in the back of the ambulance with their casualties. She really didn't have a clue; the way she'd been so shocked earlier about the storming of the Savoy. The way she'd practically said that the rich deserved better shelter than the poor because that was the way it had always been. The flippant way in which she'd made a joke about the bomb almost landing on them. Her ignorance was breathtaking.

He leapt from the cab and marched round to open the back doors. Ruby was still singing that bloody Daisy, Daisy song. He'd never liked it before, but now he loathed it. He wrenched the doors open, half expecting to find Ruby dancing a jig. But, to his surprise, she was hunched over the injured woman.

'We're here,' Joseph said curtly.

'Oh thank God.' Ruby looked up at him. 'We need to get her inside immediately.'

'Daisy,' the injured man groaned.

'I'll go and fetch someone.' Joseph ran over to the hospital entrance, but there were no staff to be seen.

'Where are they?' Ruby yelled from the ambulance.

He ran back across to the ambulance. 'They must all be busy.'

'Help me carry her,' Ruby said.

Joseph picked up one end of the stretcher and they carefully lowered her out of the ambulance.

'Daisy!' the man called.

'Don't worry,' Ruby replied. 'We're just taking her to a doctor. We'll be back for you in just a sec.'

When they got into the light of the hospital, Joseph could see that Ruby's face was etched with worry. 'Daisy, Daisy,' she kept singing as they hurried along the corridor. Joseph didn't know why she was singing, but clearly it wasn't because she was in good cheer.

'Where are the doctors?' Ruby asked a flustered-looking nurse who was hurrying by. 'This woman needs help.'

'They're all busy,' she replied. 'We've had a lot of casualties this evening.'

'Don't worry, Daisy, we're going to find someone,' Ruby said. She looked at Joseph. 'Come on.'

They hurried around the corner into some kind of waiting room. Patients were sprawled all over the floor with makeshift bandages made from towels and pillowcases on their heads, arms and legs. It was like something out of a war zone, Joseph thought to himself before realising that that was exactly what it was. Thanks to the blitzkrieg, London had now become the front.

'We need a doctor!' Ruby yelled.

'Don't we all, love,' an older man muttered from the corner, where he was nursing a bloody arm wrapped in a scarf.

A man in a white doctor's coat with a stethoscope around his neck came into the room. 'Mrs Atwood?' he called.

'Come on,' Ruby said to Joseph and they hurried over to him. 'This woman needs urgent attention,' she said to the doctor, nodding at the stretcher.

'I'm afraid you'll have to wait,' he replied.

'She can't afford to wait,' Ruby yelled. 'Her pulse is fading. You need to do something. She only got married last week. Please!' she implored.

'All right. Take her in there.' The doctor gestured to a side room.

They went in and gently placed the stretcher onto a bed. Ruby felt for the woman's pulse. 'Oh no,' she said. 'No, no, Daisy, wake up!'

The doctor and a nurse appeared. 'We can take over from here,' he said.

'It's too late,' Ruby whispered.

Joseph saw a tear running down her cheek. 'Ruby.'

She pushed past him into the corridor.

Joseph watched as the doctor checked for a pulse. He looked at the nurse and shook his head, then he turned to Joseph. 'I'm sorry.'

For the first time since they'd got there, Joseph properly looked at the woman on the stretcher. She appeared to be no older than twenty. He swallowed hard. Damn this bloody war.

He walked out of the room and found Ruby crouching against the wall, her helmet on the floor beside her. Strands of her dark hair had broken free from her ponytail and were sticking to her tear-streaked face. He bent down beside her.

'Her husband – we have to tell her husband,' she stammered.

'It's all right. I'll see to him.'

'I tried.' Her voice was shrill. 'I tried to keep her alive. I tried to sing to her. I thought she could hear me. She squeezed my hand.'

'It's all right.' Joseph placed his hand on her shoulder. 'You did a great job. Come on, let's go.'

They walked back through the chaos of the corridor, cocooned in a bubble of stunned silence.

When they got back outside, Joseph saw two orderlies taking the man from the back of the ambulance. When he noticed Joseph and Ruby approaching, he sat up slightly.

'Daisy?' he asked. 'How is she?'

'I'm so sorry,' Ruby said. 'We lost her.'

'No!' The man collapsed back on the stretcher.

'I'm so sorry,' Ruby murmured.

As the orderlies carried the man inside, the sound of his sobs filled the air.

'Are you all right? Do you need a smoke?' Joseph asked.

Ruby shook her head. 'No,' she muttered. 'I don't need anything.'

*

As they got back into the cab the all-clear sounded. It was normally a sound that filled Ruby with giddy relief – like the sound of a champagne cork popping – but not tonight. Tonight, all she felt was a horrible numbness.

'There was nothing more you could have done,' Joseph said, before turning the key in the ignition.

'I thought that if I sang to her, I'd make her wake up.'

Joseph nodded.

But Ruby felt foolish. 'It was a stupid idea.'

'No it wasn't. And for all you know it might have given her some comfort, in her final moments.'

'She squeezed my hand. I'm sure of it.' Ruby looked at him hopefully.

'There you go then.'

'Her husband said it was her favourite song. He sang it to her when he proposed. Her name was Daisy, you see.' Ruby was aware that she was starting to chatter inanely, but she couldn't help it. Her body was suddenly awash with nervous energy and the only outlet for it seemed to be her mouth.

'Ah, I see.'

'I thought it might bring to mind memories of her happiest day on earth and that would pull her back into the land of the living. I mean, that's what would have happened in one of Kitty's romance novels, isn't it? The heroine would never die with her husband singing her favourite song to her. She'd cling to life and valiantly battle back to consciousness and then, years later, she'd tell their grandchildren all about the night she almost died but didn't because of the power of their love and his singing and…' She broke off, dangerously close to tears.

'That's the trouble with life,' Joseph said after a moment. 'Not everyone gets a happily ever after.'

There would have been a time when Ruby would have argued with him. She'd lived her entire adult life as if she were the heroine in a story of her own creation. Flitting about the globe from adventure to adventure, never allowing other people to knock her off course. And if things ever did start to go wrong, she'd simply up and leave and begin a new chapter. She thought of Daisy and her husband and the story they must have planned for themselves. Damn Hitler for turning up like some evil editor with a poison pen, determined to turn love stories into tragedies.

Thankfully, the rest of their shift passed without incident and by the time four o'clock came round the all-clear had sounded. Ruby and Joseph made their way back to Pendragon Square in silence. When they got to the house, Ruby stopped and gazed up at the sky. Now it was free from the bombers, she could see the stars again. Ruby had always loved gazing up into the night sky. Her father made her see it as a place of wonder and mystery, teaching her all about the different constellations and the legends behind them. Now the Germans had made it something to be terrified of and Ruby felt the urgent desire to reclaim it somehow, along with an equally urgent need for a drink. She wondered if Joseph was feeling the same; she had a couple of bottles of beer inside. But he was so earnest about everything, he probably abstained from alcohol.

'Are you one of those temperance movement people?' she asked as she opened the front door.

He looked at her, puzzled. 'No. What makes you say that?'

Somehow Ruby managed to refrain from replying that he seemed like such a killjoy. 'I don't know, I just thought that maybe… Would you care to join me for a beer?'

'Oh.'

Joseph looked so unimpressed by this proposition she instantly regretted offering, and the last thing she wanted was to give him the opportunity to be rude to her once again.

'Don't worry. I'm sure you must be exhausted. I'll see you tomorrow then.' She quickly slipped inside her flat, shutting the door behind her. What a stupid idea. What a terrible night.

She went through to the kitchen and took a bottle of beer from the pantry. Then she waited a moment until she was sure Joseph would be up in his flat and let herself back outside. She made her way to the centre of the garden and sat down on the grass, tilting her head back and taking a few deep breaths of the cool air. Tonight she had narrowly escaped death and had witnessed someone else dying. It all felt too much, too huge for her brain to process.

She noticed a star directly above her, burning brightly, and she thought of Daisy. Ruby had never seen a person die before today. She wondered what happened. Had Daisy's soul slipped out of her body in that hospital corridor while she wasn't looking? Had it floated up to heaven? Was that her soul burning so brightly in the sky above?

She took a sip of her beer. She'd so longed to receive word from the spirit world during her handful of séances, but to no avail. She thought of Daisy's poor husband and the sound of his guttural sobs as he was taken into the hospital. The thought of welcoming him to one of her soirees and making up messages from his dearly departed wife felt horrible. She made a vow there and then to never hold a séance again.

A tear rolled down her face. She brushed it away and took another swig of beer. Then she looked back at the house. She

thought of Kitty, trapped behind the blackout blinds on the
first floor with her horrible weasel of a husband. Their encounter
over the flowers felt like another lifetime ago. She glanced up
at the top-floor windows. For a second she thought she saw a
figure looking down at her, but her eyes must have been playing
tricks because when she blinked and looked again, all she saw
was darkness.

*

Joseph stepped back from the window and sighed. Seeing Ruby
sitting out in the middle of the garden had made him wish he'd
just said yes when she offered him the beer. But he'd been so
shocked by the question, it had left him momentarily lost for
words. Seeing her sitting out there gazing up at the sky reminded
him of when he was a kid and he used to sit in the backyard and
dream of being able to fly right up into outer space. Some nights,
when his dad was suffering badly from shell shock and yelling
in his sleep, Joseph would creep into the yard with his blanket.
The night sky was so infinite it always helped put his problems
into perspective. He wondered if it was doing the same for Ruby.

Once again she'd surprised him. He'd felt terrible when he
realised that her singing was her unique way of trying to rally a
dying patient. And her reaction to Daisy's death had gone a long
way to dispelling his belief that she had no feelings.

He peered through the crack in the blackout blind. Ruby was
lying down now, gazing up at the sky. Yes, it would appear that
he'd got her very wrong indeed.

CHAPTER NINETEEN

September 2019

I wake in a cold sweat, my head resting on Pearl's book. I'd been dreaming that it was the Second World War and I'd been living in Pendragon Square with Marty. In the dream, I'd discovered that Marty had been cheating on me with Ruby. I'd seen them kissing in the moonlight in the garden.

For a moment I forget about my broken ankle and attempt to get out of bed. A sharp bolt of pain courses up my leg. I fumble around on the bedside cabinet to check the time on my phone. It's just gone three in the morning. And then it all comes flooding back to me. I hadn't just dreamed that Marty cheated on me; it's my new reality. My head feels heavy and my mouth is dry.

I grab my crutches and hoist myself up and hobble over to the window. The garden is bathed in moonlight and I see a scrawny fox sniffing about by one of the bins. I remember the last thing I read before falling asleep and I picture Ruby lying exhausted on the grass gazing up at the stars, trying desperately to reclaim the night sky from the Germans. It's hard to imagine the terror Londoners must have felt, having bombs raining down on them morning, noon and night. How did they get through it? Whenever I've seen shows or read articles about the Blitz, they've always focused on the Blitz spirit and what a great leveller it was, as people from all classes came together to help with the war effort. I'd never heard of the Savoy being stormed, or the government refusing to let people use the Underground as a shelter. Maybe Pearl was using poetic licence.

I hobble back to the bed and open my laptop. The window is still open on Amy Parsons' Facebook page. I force myself to close it and open a fresh one. Hopefully, googling the Blitz will give me a welcome diversion from my internet stalking. I do a search for 'Savoy shelter World War 2' and discover that the protest did happen, although there are only a couple of eyewitness accounts of it. Maybe Pearl knew someone who'd been involved in the protest.

I pick up the novel and study the cover. Who are the couple kissing beneath the moon, and who is the shadowy figure watching them, gun drawn? Chloe, the beauty editor at *Blaze*, always reads the first and final chapters before deciding whether to buy a book. But the notion of skipping ahead to find out how a story ends is complete anathema to me.

I look back at my laptop and wonder if anyone else has commented on Marty's picture with Amy. Maybe there are more clues lurking on Facebook about how long they've been seeing each other. I push the laptop away and pick up the novel. It's just gone three in the morning and, to make matters even worse, there's a full moon. It's officially the crazy hour, when otherwise sane women become possessed by regret and fear and should not be trusted with social media. I take a sip of water and a deep breath. I am not going to be that woman. I open Pearl's novel and continue reading.

CHAPTER TWENTY

September 1940

Ruby woke up stiff and cold to the sound of the air-raid siren.

'No!' she cried. 'Not again.'

She opened her eyes to discover that she was still clad in her ambulance service uniform. Then, like the pieces of a most disappointing jigsaw puzzle, the events from the night before began falling into place in her mind. The near miss with the bomb. Joseph's obvious disdain for her. The roar of planes and incessant rattle of the guns. The man crying. Her singing 'Daisy, Daisy'. Daisy dying, right there on the stretcher in front of her.

Ruby shivered. Outside, she heard a warden shouting for everyone to take shelter, but she remained in bed. It was a peculiar thing, this thing called life. One was taught to treasure it, to stave off dying at all costs. But why? If the Americans were right and the Germans were about to invade, what did she really have to live for? And if this were to be her last day on earth, she would far rather spend it beneath the comfort of her satin counterpane than cramped in that dank tin coffin-in-waiting in the garden.

Thinking of the shelter brought to mind another memory from the day before, of Joseph storming the Savoy shelter. Could it really be true that the East End didn't have any adequate shelters? If Ruby was totally honest, she quite liked the idea of the Savoy being stormed. She would have found it most entertaining if she'd been dining there when it happened.

She heard the creak of floorboards from the flat above and her heart sank. In all of the drama of last night she'd forgotten about Kitty. She sat up and listened intently for any sound of Reg's voice. A few moments later she heard the front door slam shut and she hurried over to the window, just in time to see Reg skulking off across the square, wearing his khaki army uniform.

Ruby shuddered. She couldn't think of a man less deserving of that uniform. He was nothing but a coward, the way he picked on Kitty. She looked up at the ceiling. Where was Kitty? All was deathly quiet above. A terrible thought occurred to Ruby. What if Reg had done something awful to her? Lord knows, in all of the commotion of last night's bombing raids it would have been perfectly easy to get away with murder.

Telling herself off for being so melodramatic, she decided to go and check on her neighbour, just to be on the safe side.

She hurried up the stairs to Kitty's flat and knocked on the door. There was no answer, so she knocked again – harder this time. Kitty was probably in the shelter already, tucked up in the corner with one of her books.

Ruby was about to go back downstairs when she heard a noise from inside the flat.

'Who is it?' Kitty called.

'It's me, Ruby. Are you all right?'

'Yes thank you.' There was something strange about Kitty's voice. It sounded a little too high-pitched.

'Are you sure?'

'Yes.'

'Are you going down to the shelter?' Ruby asked.

'You go. I'll be down soon.'

Ruby frowned. Something was definitely wrong. Kitty was normally the first to take shelter. She had to get her thinking cap on quick smart and come up with a way to make Kitty open her door.

'Oh my goodness!' she shrieked, pounding on the door. 'Mouse! Mouse! You have to let me in!'

Thankfully, her cunning plan worked and the door opened a crack.

'I just saw a mouse,' Ruby exclaimed, barging her way in. 'It just scuttled past me on the stairs cool as you please.' The truth was, she was actually rather fond of mice, but it was the first thing that had sprung to mind. 'Are you all right?' she asked.

It was so dark it was impossible to see Kitty clearly.

'Yes, I – I just—'

'I'm so sorry about the flowers,' Ruby said, walking past Kitty into the small kitchen. The blackout blinds were still drawn but a lamp was flickering on the table. Ruby glanced around. The remains of a plate lay smashed in the sink and she could see the stems of the roses sticking out of the bin. The room smelled of cold, stale cooking oil.

'Was it really you who left the roses there for me?' Kitty stood in the doorway, hugging her stomach as if she were in pain.

'I'm afraid so.' Ruby looked at her remorsefully. 'I was just trying to cheer you up. After you said you'd never been bought flowers.'

'But why did you sign the card from a secret admirer?'

'I was hoping you'd think they were from Freddy.' Ruby glanced around nervously. 'I saw Reg going out just now – is he coming back soon?'

Kitty shook her head. 'He only had one day's leave.'

Ruby breathed a sigh of relief.

'Why did you want me to think they were from Freddy?'

'Because he really is your secret admirer.'

'What?' Her tone softened.

'It was foolish of me. I should never have got involved. I'm like that meddling friend in the book you lent me, *Three's a Crowd*.'

Kitty stepped into the room and in the flickering lamplight Ruby saw that one of her eyes was swollen and bruised.

'Your eye!' she gasped.

'Reg thinks I've been unfaithful to him.'

'Oh, Kitty.' Ruby hurried over and gave her a hug. Kitty flinched. 'Are you all right?' Ruby stepped back and stared at her. 'What did that brute do to you?'

Kitty gazed at the sink. She looked so detached it was as if her spirit had left her body. She reminded Ruby of Daisy, lying lifeless on the stretcher.

'I'm so sorry, I feel dreadful for wanting you to experience the joy of being desired.' Ruby touched her gently on the arm. 'Sometimes being born with a compassionate heart can be such a curse.'

Kitty looked at her strangely.

'But Reg has gone now, back to his barracks?' Ruby asked.

Kitty nodded.

'Good.' But Ruby realised it was only a temporary relief. What would happen when he was next home on leave? An idea began forming in her mind, but, given that her last great idea concerning Kitty had ended so badly, she decided to run it by her first. 'May I ask you a question?'

'Of course.'

'Do you love him?' Ruby half expected Kitty to answer yes to this, as she'd always seemed so meek and compliant wherever Reg was concerned, but to her surprise Kitty shook her head.

'No,' she replied in a tight little voice. 'I hate him and I wish he was dead.'

*

Joseph lay on his bed listening to the howl of the air-raid siren. He knew he should get down to the shelter, but he was so bone-tired after a week of barely any sleep, his body refused to comply.

The one good thing about the hellish sound of the siren was that it was drowning out any sound from the flat below. The night before, when he'd gone to bed after watching Ruby stargazing in the garden, he heard the endless rumble of Reg's voice, clearly berating poor Kitty about something. Joseph wondered how long he was back for. Hopefully not long. Kitty had slowly been coming out of her shell these past few weeks; it would be horrible to see her return to the shadow of a woman she'd been when he first moved in.

He heard a low hum coming from outside and his heart sank. He'd been hoping the siren might have been a false alarm. He hurried over to the window and peered through the crack in the blinds. A plane flew over the square, black against the paper white sky. Then there was another and another, filling the sky like blots on an ink pad. His heart sank further. Would today be the day it would all be over? The day that freedom left Britain and fascism swept in? He imagined rows of German soldiers marching along the mall. The brutal black stamp of the swastika flying above Buckingham Palace and the Houses of Parliament. He pictured them marching down Millbank, along the river and into Pendragon Square. He would no doubt be executed on sight for his pacifist beliefs.

He took his tobacco tin from his trouser pocket and opened it. There was no way he wanted the Nazis getting their hands on his beloved keepsakes. He looked around the room for somewhere to hide them and his gaze fell upon the loft hatch.

Joseph went through to the kitchen and got the stepladder, then climbed up and pushed the loft hatch open. Outside, the roar of the planes grew louder, intensifying his desire to hide the tin. He climbed up into the loft and looked around. Stupidly he'd forgotten to bring his torch. He felt around on the floor by the hatch and found a loose board. He pulled it up and tucked the tin beneath it and was about to climb back down when the ladder slipped. Joseph clung to the hatch as the ladder went crashing to the floor.

'Damn!' he cursed as he pulled himself back up inside the loft. It was too high to jump from without risking spraining his ankle at the very least. He heard the roar of more planes over head, so loud it was as if he was in one of them. He held his breath. If they unleashed their deadly cargo now, he'd be a goner for sure. What on earth had possessed him to climb up there? Surely it would have been easier to hide the tin inside the fireplace.

Just as he was about to settle in for the duration of the raid, he heard a hammering on his door.

'I say, are you all right?' he heard Ruby call in a gap between the roar of the planes and the artillery fire.

'I need help!' he yelled back.

'Did you say help?' Ruby called.

'Yes! Help!' he yelled again.

'Wait right there,' she shouted.

Well, where else was he going to go? He crouched by the hatch and waited. A couple of minutes later, he heard the door to his flat open.

'I hope you don't mind, but I used the spare key,' Ruby called from the hallway.

'I don't mind at all as long as you get me down from here,' he replied.

'Where the devil are you?' Ruby asked.

'Maybe he's in the kitchen,' he heard Kitty say.

Oh great, two people to witness his humiliation.

'I'm up here,' he called.

'So that was what made the almighty crash!' Ruby exclaimed, hurrying into the bedroom and looking at the ladder on the floor. She was still wearing her ambulance uniform. He wasn't sure if this was because she hadn't changed out of it, or if she'd got ready extra early for their next shift. Judging from her dishevelled hair, he reckoned it was the former. Joseph waited until she lifted her gaze. 'Oh dear,' she said, clearly trying to conceal a smirk.

'Oh dear indeed,' he replied. 'Now if you don't mind.' He nodded at the ladder.

'Of course.'

'Where is he?' Kitty said, coming into the room. To Joseph's horror, he saw a huge bruise around her eye.

'Up there.' Ruby nodded to the loft hatch and she picked the ladder off the floor. 'What in the blazes are you doing up there anyway? Did you not hear the sirens? We're supposed to be sheltering underground, not getting as close to those beastly planes as we can.'

'I needed to put something up here.'

'Hmm.' Ruby pursed her lips and frowned. 'Very suspicious behaviour if you ask me. You haven't been looting bombed-out shops, have you? You're not storing away your stash? My friend Gwendoline told me there's been a spate of looting over in Victoria.'

'No, I have not!' Hell's bells, there was no end to this woman's ability to annoy. All the goodwill he'd been feeling towards her the previous night began rapidly fading. Thankfully, she put the ladder back in position.

'Don't worry, I'll hold it for you,' she said as if she was talking to an infant – and a stupid infant at that.

'Thank you,' he muttered.

'You're most welcome,' she replied, again with a poorly disguised smirk.

'Are you all right?' Kitty asked, sympathetically.

'Yes, thank you. Are you?' He looked at her bruised face and she immediately turned away.

'Yes, yes, I'm fine.'

Ruby gave a dramatic sigh.

'I am,' Kitty said tersely.

'So, why aren't you two sheltering?' Joseph asked them.

'Have you ever had a moment in your life when you've questioned everything?' Ruby replied.

Joseph frowned. 'I'm not sure I—'

'And then you realise that the answer to your question isn't at all what you'd supposed it would be.'

Now Joseph was even more confused.

'The Americans say the Germans are going to invade this weekend,' Ruby continued. 'So I asked myself the question, would I like to spend my last day of freedom burrowed underground like a mole, inhaling Mr Jones from number seven's flatulence, and dying from despair at the plotline of one of Kitty's novels.' She broke off and turned to Kitty. 'I'm sorry, my dear, but they really can be very dispiriting.' She turned back to the bemused Joseph. 'And the answer to that question was an emphatic no.'

'I see,' Joseph replied, not really seeing at all.

'So, if you have no further need for my help I must go and live today as if it's my last.' She linked arms with Kitty and frogmarched her over to the door. 'And if it isn't my last,' she called back over her shoulder to Joseph, 'I'll see you tonight at Neptune Square.'

'I'll look forward to it,' Joseph muttered, to the sound of his door closing.

CHAPTER TWENTY-ONE

September 1940

'Are you sure this is a good idea?' Kitty asked Ruby as they headed up Vauxhall Bridge Road towards Victoria.

'Of course,' Ruby replied confidently, although in all honesty, she wasn't exactly sure that her plan to take Kitty on an afternoon stroll around London while planes were battling above them was the wisest endeavour she'd ever embarked upon. But she was determined to undertake one final act of defiance before Hitler invaded. And afternoon tea at Claridge's seemed like a fitting epitaph to her London adventures. It would be good to get some caffeine and sugar inside Kitty too. She'd thankfully managed to tone down the horrific bruise on the poor girl's eye with the help of some Max Factor and they were both now dressed in Ruby's finest glad rags. Ruby considered it a major achievement that she'd managed to persuade Kitty to wear both a fitted dress *and* heels.

As they walked past a coffee stand, a plane roared by overhead, followed by the rat-a-tat-tat of gunfire. The two women stopped and looked up. Another German bomber appeared in the sky above, swiftly followed by a smaller plane. Or was it being *chased* by the smaller plane?

'Oh my!' Ruby exclaimed as she watched it gain on the larger plane, closer and closer until…

'Goodness me!' Kitty exclaimed, clamping her hand to her mouth as the smaller plane clipped into the bomber, knocking off its tail with its wing. The German bomber began diving nose first towards the earth, making a dreadful squealing sound.

'Oh no, it's heading right for the station!' Ruby gasped.

'Looks like the other one's in trouble too,' Kitty said.

Ruby looked back into the sky to see the RAF plane spiralling out of control. Just in the nick of time, a small figure came parachuting out.

'Oh please God, let him survive,' Kitty cried.

A terrific bang rang out from the direction of the station, accompanied by a flash of light.

Ruby looked back at the parachuting pilot. He was approaching the rooftops to their left at a frightening speed.

'Come on,' she said, grabbing Kitty's hand. 'Let's see if we can rescue the poor fellow.'

They ran around the corner onto Buckingham Palace Road. A group of boys had gathered in front of a three-storey house chattering excitedly.

'Look! There he is!' Kitty exclaimed.

Ruby peered across the road and, sure enough, a young man was dangling from the guttering of the house by his parachute.

'Come on, let's see if he needs our assistance.' Ruby grabbed Kitty's hand and they ran across the road. 'Stand back, first-aid operatives coming through,' Ruby boomed.

The boys stepped back and looked them up and down.

'You don't look like no first-aider,' one of them said.

'Does that little pipsqueak Hitler look like he could conquer most of Europe?' Ruby retorted.

The boys stared at her, confused.

'Appearances can be deceptive, my dear boy.' She turned her attention to the pilot, who barely looked out of his teens himself. 'Good afternoon,' she said, extending a gloved hand.

'Good afternoon,' he replied with a bemused grin.

'Very good show you put on up there,' Ruby said.

'Thank you.'

'It was so brave of you to knock your plane into his,' Kitty added.

'I had no choice, miss. I'd run out of ammo and he was headed for the palace.'

'Phew!' Ruby shook her head. 'Well, I hope they give you some kind of medal for your efforts.'

'Right now I'd be happy with a cup of tea,' the pilot joked.

'But of course,' Ruby replied. 'Tea is the answer to everything, isn't it? It was actually first used for medicinal purposes, you know. In China. Yes, those Chinese knew what they were doing. They really were—'

The pilot coughed.

'Anyway, enough of this chitter-chatter, let's get you down from there.'

A shrill whistle pierced the air.

Ruby looked round to see a barrel-bellied warden hurrying over.

'Stand back, stand back, this ain't a bleeding tourist attraction.' He glared at her.

'I can assure you, my good man, my colleague and I are far from tourists,' Ruby retorted. 'We are residents of this fine city and members of the medical profession to boot.'

'Oh really?' He eyed them up and down. 'Interesting uniforms you're wearing.'

'We are actually currently off duty, but, as you know, the war effort never sleeps, and as soon as we saw this heroic pilot in distress we hurried to his aid.'

'I'm sure you did.' The warden shook his head. 'Right, well I'll take over now.'

'Glad to hear it,' Ruby replied. 'The poor man needs to be disentangled post-haste, not listen to you give us a lecture.'

'Well I never!' the warden exclaimed.

'Come on, Kitty, let's see where else we're needed.' Ruby flashed a grin at the pilot. 'It was an honour to assist you, sir.'

'The honour was all mine,' he replied with a grin.

Ruby linked arms with Kitty and they carried on along the road. 'Well, I don't know about you, but that was just the tonic I needed,' she said. 'Now let's get to Claridge's. All that talk of tea has got me thirsty.'

As soon as they were settled in Claridge's with a pot of tea and a silver stand of cakes, Kitty cleared her throat and looked at Ruby nervously.

'Can I ask you a question?' she said quietly.

'Of course.'

Kitty's cheeks flushed slightly. 'How do you – how do you find it so easy – to get along with men?'

'Oh, I don't know.' Ruby thought for a moment. 'Maybe it's because I got on so well with my papa. And then I had to deal with the insufferable Rupert throughout my entire childhood – my honorary brother,' she explained. Ruby looked at Kitty curiously. 'Why do you ask? Is it something you wish you could do?'

'Oh no – no, no, no,' Kitty stammered. But Ruby couldn't help thinking she was protesting too much.

'Not all men are like Reg, you know,' she said gently.

They fell silent for a moment and Ruby topped up Kitty's cup of tea.

'I never knew my dad,' Kitty said softly. 'He left when I was just a baby. Reg is the only man I've ever been with. We met in school.'

Ruby had to fight to stop herself from gasping at the horror of Kitty's predicament. She fortified herself with a mouthful of scone before responding. 'Oh, my dear, that's like confining yourself to eating gruel when there's a whole smorgasbord of exotic meats on offer.'

'A what board?'

'Smorgasbord. It's Swedish,' Ruby explained. 'It means a buffet of delicious treats. Just like this cake stand.' She picked up the silver tongs and plonked a scone onto Kitty's plate. 'Just because he's the only man you've ever been with it doesn't mean it has to stay that way.'

'But he's my husband.'

'He's a bully.' Ruby looked at Kitty anxiously. She hadn't meant to speak so harshly about Reg, the word had just blurted out.

But rather than looking upset, Kitty nodded. 'I know,' she said, picking at the hem of the tablecloth.

'I've heard how he talks to you,' Ruby said, deciding to bite the bullet. 'I mean, I don't hear exactly what he says, but I hear his shouting through my ceiling.'

Kitty's face flushed red. 'I'm sorry.'

'Why on earth are you apologising?' Ruby exclaimed. 'You have nothing to be sorry for.'

'But I'm the one who makes him so angry.'

Ruby stared at her. 'Is that what he tells you? Does he blame his temper on you?'

'Well, yes. I am the one he's getting angry with after all.'

'But only because he's such a brute!' Ruby paused to draw breath. 'I'm sorry, but he is.' She took a sip of her tea and added another spoonful of sugar. 'Anyway, I have a plan I wanted to discuss with you.'

Kitty's eyes widened. 'What kind of plan?'

'A plan to free you from his clutches.'

*

As Joseph made his way along the Charing Cross Road, he pictured columns of Nazis marching towards him, their arms flicking up and down in that chilling salute, and he broke out in a cold sweat. What would he do, if and when he was confronted by them? This was a question that had plagued him ever since the war began. Not just in his own mind but from others too. When he'd had his tribunal to prove his credentials as a conscientious objector, he'd had all kinds of variations on this question fired at him.

'Why would you not be willing to defend another's freedom?' one of the tribunal members, a clergyman no less, had asked him.

'I am,' Joseph had replied. 'I'm just not willing to take another's life.'

'What would you do if you witnessed a Nazi attacking a child?' another of the tribunal members had asked.

'And what if a Nazi raped your wife?' another, a retired soldier, had fired at him.

'I don't have a wife,' Joseph had replied, to which the soldier sniffed, as if to say, is it any wonder?

But then Joseph had told them what the Great War had done to his brother and father. He told them how, ever since returning from the front, his father had been trapped in a living hell, until finally it had all become too much and he hung himself. He told them how he'd come home from school to find his dad suspended from the parlour door frame by his belt. How he'd had to pull his lifeless body down before his mam came home. 'I don't dispute that Hitler is evil,' he concluded, 'but I truly believe that the only way we can overcome evil is by good means. Just as Jesus taught,' he added, looking pointedly at the clergyman. To his relief, he was granted a conditional exemption, meaning that he avoided conscription as long as he registered to work in an area of national importance, such as an ambulance unit.

It had been relatively easy to argue his case back then, before the bombing raids had begun, because the war still felt so far away. But now the prospect of him actually having to live the answers to the questions the tribunal had posed loomed large. What would he do if the Germans invaded and he saw them attacking a child? He would step in and try to save the child, obviously, but without using force. He could imagine the likes of Reg sneering at him for this response. But Reg routinely bullied his wife, Joseph reminded himself. He was hardly the epitome of bravery.

Joseph picked his way past a bombed-out bookshop. The window was now in smithereens on the floor. 'MORE OPEN THAN USUAL' a handmade sign by the door read. Joseph wondered what would happen to London's bookshops once the Nazis arrived. Would they burn the books and replace them with their own fascist tomes, just as they'd done in Germany and Austria? He shuddered at the thought.

As he reached Trafalgar Square, the air-raid siren went off again. The few people out and about on the street began hurrying towards the red S sign for the public shelter. Joseph joined the queue, behind an old man with long, unkempt grey hair and shabby clothes. When the man reached the entrance to the shelter, the warden on duty put his hand up to stop him.

'Sorry, sir, I can't let you in.'

'Why not?' the man asked, his voice wavering and feeble.

'No vagrants allowed, I'm afraid.'

The man began trudging off, muttering under his breath.

'Stink the place out, they do,' the warden said to Joseph with a knowing grin.

But Joseph felt sick. The old man was clearly down on his luck. Why should he be left to the mercy of the German bombers out on the street, just because he didn't look or smell a certain way? Surely if anyone deserved compassion it was him. He turned to follow the man.

''Ere, mate, where are you off to?' the warden shouted after him. 'It's all right for you to come in.'

But Joseph ignored him. This was what sickened him the most about life. It was like a game where the dice was loaded in the favour of the privileged few and the rest had no hope of winning. He hurried after the vagrant and tapped him on the shoulder.

The old man turned round and stared at him. His face was so lined and weather-beaten it reminded him of a walnut.

'Come with me,' Joseph said. 'I know somewhere you can shelter.'

As the roar of the planes grew louder, he took the man's arm and guided him down Villiers Street to the arches beneath the bridge beside Charing Cross station. It wasn't as good as being underground, but at least it would protect him from any shrapnel.

'Thank you, son,' the old man replied.

'You're welcome.' Joseph felt in his pocket and pulled out the sandwich he'd made for himself before leaving the house. 'Are you hungry?' he asked, offering it to him.

The man's pale green eyes filled with tears. 'I'm famished. Thank you.'

'Come. Let's sit down.'

They sat on the floor and the man began biting into the sandwich with an urgency that implied he may not have eaten for days. Every so often, he'd pause and mumble, 'thank you'.

'Where do you live?' Joseph asked once the sandwich was finished. The ground tremored from a nearby bomb blast.

'I'm currently of no fixed abode,' the man replied, looking visibly more energised from having some food. 'Lost my home after I came back from the war – the first one. Lived on the streets ever since. Never really minded until now though.' He looked upwards as the sound of gunfire echoed all around. 'Now I can't get no peace. Bloody Germans.'

Joseph frowned. The Great War had left a lot of veterans who were suffering from shell shock homeless. They'd been a common sight in his home town of Blackpool and there were even more in London. But who was taking care of them now the bombs were falling?

'Someone has to take care of them,' he said, speaking his thoughts out loud.

'Bloody Hitler,' the old man muttered.

CHAPTER TWENTY-TWO

September 1940

As Ruby reached the junction of Coventry Street and Rupert Street in Piccadilly, she popped some letters to her pals into the bright red postbox before heading inside the Lyons' Corner House. She was happy to see that, in spite of almost two weeks' bombing, it was as bustling as ever, with the black-clad Nippies, as the waitresses were known, nipping around between the tables with impressive speed.

She spied her friend Agatha at her normal table by the window, gazing into a mother-of-pearl compact as she touched up her lipstick. She was immaculately dressed as always, more so if anything, in a lime green dress and a red fox pelt, complete with head and tail, draped around her shoulders. It reminded Ruby of her mother's fox pelt, which Ruby had named Loxy and adopted as a family pet, forbidding her mother from ever wearing it again.

'Good morning, my dear,' she said cheerily as she approached the table.

'Ruby!' Agatha's smile faltered as Ruby sat down. 'Goodness me, are you all right? You look frightfully…' She broke off.

'What?'

'Well, exhausted. Have you been eating properly?' Agatha sighed and shook her head. 'These rations will be the death of me. You should come and dine with Walter and me at the club. There's no shortage of meat there.'

'I've actually been working,' Ruby replied proudly.

'Working?' Instead of looking impressed as Ruby had hoped, Agatha looked horrified. 'What on earth doing? Please don't tell me you've become one of those land girls. I'm sorry, I know a lot of men are away fighting, but I really do think that some jobs are best left to the boys, and farming is definitely one of them. So uncouth.'

Ruby fought the urge to frown. She'd accepted Agatha's invitation to go for tea as a welcome reminder of how things used to be. She'd thought it would be a taster of the good old days, not leave her with a bitter taste in her mouth within seconds. 'No, my dear, I haven't become a farmer. I've become a volunteer at my local ambulance station. I am now a proud member of an ambulance crew.'

'What?' Agatha's freshly painted lips fell open. 'You're driving an ambulance?' Once again, she looked more horrified than impressed.

'Yes, well, no. I wanted to drive an ambulance, but there was a terrible miscarriage of justice involving a tractor, which I won't get into right now as I'm afraid it will ruin my appetite, but I am part of an ambulance crew nonetheless.'

Agatha picked up the menu and began fanning herself with it furiously. 'But I don't understand. What on earth possessed you?'

'I wanted to do my bit,' Ruby replied, her skin prickling. In her desire to recreate some nostalgia for the good old days, she'd conveniently forgotten how shallow Agatha could be. She was great fun to go dancing or shopping with, but, it would seem, not so great in a time of national crisis. Never mind. At least they were at Lyons and she could console herself with a piece of her favourite Peek Freans shortcake.

'But isn't driving about in an ambulance frightfully dangerous?'

'Isn't everything frightfully dangerous these days? If I'm going to die, I'd rather die doing something than waiting like a sitting duck.' *Atta girl!* Ruby imagined her papa whispering in her ear and she grinned proudly.

'Well, rather you than me,' Agatha replied sniffily.

At this point one of the Nippies arrived at their table, pad in hand and pencil poised. 'Good morning, ladies, are you ready to order?' she asked with a smile.

'I do so love your uniforms,' Ruby said. 'Especially these.' She pointed to the double row of tiny pearl buttons that ran from the collar to the waist of the black dress.

'Thank you, madam.' The girl beamed.

They ordered a pot of tea and two rounds of shortbread. As soon as the Nippy had gone, Agatha looked at Ruby and shook her head.

'What?' Ruby frowned.

'I think this war business might be making you go all peculiar.'

'What on earth makes you say that?'

'Driving an ambulance. Swooning over a Nippy's uniform as if she's clad in Chanel. Coming out to tea with no lipstick on.'

'Oh, I must have forgotten.' *For pity's sake,* Ruby thought to herself, did it really matter that she wasn't wearing lipstick?

'Exactly. All of this war business is making you go strange.'

And it's making you even more pompous, Ruby felt like saying, but she managed to bite her tongue. Agatha had been born into wealth and married into even greater wealth. She had been cosseted from the hardships around her, just as Ruby had, albeit to a slightly lesser extent. It was only thanks to the perpetually annoying Joseph that she'd been made aware of her privilege compared to others. Perhaps she ought to pass the favour on to Agatha.

'Did you know that the East Enders have hardly any underground shelters?' she said.

Agatha stared at her blankly. 'Of course they have shelters.'

'Not proper ones and not enough.'

Agatha sighed. 'What's that got to do with us?'

'But don't you think they ought to have the same kind of shelters as we do? Think of their children.'

Agatha leaned forward conspiratorially, as if she was about to impart some kind of government-level secret. 'They're not the same as you and I,' she whispered.

'What do you mean?'

'I mean, they don't have the same kind of attitudes when it comes to their children.' She leaned even closer. 'They live like animals,' she hissed. 'Walter told me that in some of their hovels they live eight to a room and the children are like wild dogs, there's no discipline.'

Ruby thought of Alfie's mother. She'd clearly been dirt poor but the love and concern she'd shown for her son was greater than any Ruby had ever witnessed. It was all very well for Agatha to condemn those forced to live in two-up two-down houses; Walter owned a country estate, as well as their sprawling mansion in Hampstead. It must be easy to maintain a civilised façade when one could dispatch one's offspring to an entirely different wing of the house, along with their nannies and governess.

Ruby glanced out into the street at the people hurrying by. She thought of the conversation she'd had with Kitty the other day over tea, and how it had felt so much more nourishing than this. Perhaps Agatha was right, and the war was changing her, but was that really such a bad thing?

'Anyway,' Agatha said, sitting upright and playing with the pearls around her neck, 'did you hear the terrible news?'

'Which terrible news?' Ruby replied.

'About Selfridges? It was bombed yesterday. All of the windows were blown out and the roof garden…' Agatha broke off to fetch a neatly pressed handkerchief from her handbag, which she used to dab at her eyes. 'The roof gardens have been completely destroyed.'

'Oh goodness. Was anyone killed?'

'What? I'm not sure.' Agatha dabbed at her eyes again. 'Those beautiful gardens, reduced to rubble.'

Ruby frowned. There would have been a time when the destruction of the Selfridges roof garden might have elicited a similar response in her, but her experiences in the ambulance had somehow changed her perspective, making her realise that she'd previously viewed life through quite a myopic lens. But now the blinkers were off and she was able to see everything, including the self-absorption of her so-called friend.

*

Joseph returned to Pendragon Square with the glad heart of a man who'd spent his day living to his fullest potential. As soon as he had this thought, he couldn't help laughing. Clearly, all the time he'd been spending cooped up in an ambulance with Ruby and her fancy way of talking was rubbing off on him. They'd had the past couple of days off and he'd taken advantage of the spare time to call a meeting of his friends in the local PPU to discuss setting up an organisation to help London's down-and-outs. After his encounter with the homeless old man, he'd suggested the archway beneath the Hungerford Bridge as a location. One of the PPU members was going to have a word with Westminster council about it.

Joseph remembered the despair he'd felt the other day, when he thought the Germans were about to invade. Now that despair had been replaced by a steely determination. He wasn't going to sit back and do nothing. He was actively choosing to do good rather than evil.

The spring in his step was momentarily halted when he saw a burly-looking man by the front door of the house. His first thought was that it was Reg, but then he saw that the man was dressed in civvies rather than an army uniform, and he appeared to be doing something to the door.

'Can I help you?' Joseph asked, striding up the front steps.

'Afternoon,' the man replied in a strong East End accent. 'I'm just changing the locks.'

'What? But I live here. Nobody told me the locks were being changed.'

'Oh dear,' the man chortled. 'Fallen out with your other half, 'ave yer?'

'What?'

'Your missus?' The man wiped his brow with the back of his hand, leaving a black streak of grease on his skin. 'Miss Glenville. She asked me to change the lock.'

'She isn't my wife.' Joseph shuddered at the thought. 'She's my landlady.'

'What's up, ain't you paid the rent?'

'Yes, I—'

Before Joseph could say any more, the downstairs window flew open and Ruby's head appeared.

'I thought I could hear a hullabaloo,' she exclaimed. 'Oh, my poor dear Joseph, I'm so sorry. I meant to leave a note for you, to inform you of *the plan*.'

'What plan?'

'The plan to lock you out, mate,' the locksmith chortled.

'Oh Harry, you are terrible!' Ruby exclaimed. 'Let him in this instant. Come and see me, Joseph, and I shall furnish you with all the details.'

'Thanks,' Joseph muttered, as Harry stepped aside to let him in.

As soon as he set foot in the hallway, Ruby's door flew open. 'Come in, come in,' she cried. 'We're having rabbit pie from this dear little place in Elephant and Castle, it really is top-notch.'

Joseph had never been inside Ruby's flat before. He'd always assumed it would be dripping in opulence, but, to his surprise, it seemed more like the kind of apartment he'd imagine belonging to an intrepid explorer. Well, the hallway did at least. The walls were covered in all kinds of unusual artefacts, from a framed map of the world, to wooden tribal masks and various theatre posters, in different languages.

'Come into the kitchen,' Ruby said, ushering him through a door.

If she hadn't told him it was the kitchen, it would have taken a while to work out. The cooker and sink and other normal kitchen accoutrements were barely visible beneath the weird and wonderful accumulation of things littering every surface. Joseph's gaze travelled over a well-worn trunk covered in shipping stickers, a guitar with a broken string, a long blonde wig, what looked like a trumpet case and a model of the Eiffel Tower, finally coming to rest on Kitty and Freddy, who were sitting at a table by the window. The table was piled high with books and gramophone records. The only available space was filled with plates containing steaming pies. A waft of the pies caught Joseph's nose, causing his stomach to rumble.

'Would you care to join us for some pie?' Ruby offered. 'Dear Freddy here bicycled over to get them for us.'

'It was so kind of you, Freddy,' Kitty murmured.

'It – it was nothing,' Freddy stammered.

'Are you sure you have enough?' Joseph said, his mouth watering.

'Of course.' Ruby ushered him over to a seat at the table. 'Oh, I do beg your pardon.' She quickly swept some nylon stockings from the back of the chair. 'I was trying to dry them.'

She picked up a brown paper bag shiny with grease and plopped a pie out onto a plate for him.

'Would you care for a gin, seeing as we're celebrating?' she asked, rather confusingly nodding towards a teapot perched on top of a pile of books.

'Oh, er, yes please.'

Ruby passed him a delicate china teacup decorated with a purple pansy. She tipped the pot and, sure enough, a clear liquid smelling very much like gin came pouring out.

'All of my glasses are dirty,' she said by way of an explanation. 'I was going to wash them, but then I thought, what japes it would be to serve gin like tea.'

Freddy chuckled. 'You really are one of a kind, Miss Ruby.'

'And for that I bet Joseph is truly grateful,' Ruby quipped, meeting Joseph's gaze.

'I wouldn't go that far,' Joseph retorted. 'But thank you.' He put the cup to his lips and took a sip.

'No, I must thank you,' Ruby said, sitting opposite him. There was something different about her, a freshness Joseph couldn't quite put his finger on, and then he realised that she wasn't wearing any make-up again.

'Why's that?' he asked, before taking a mouthful of pie. She was right, it was delicious.

'You have shown me a new perspective on things.'

He frowned. Was this all just the build-up for one of her digs? 'How so?'

'All of your moaning about social injustice. All of your incessant griping about the ways of the world. I truly believe that knowing you has made me a better person and for that I am truly grateful.'

'Er, thanks.'

'Now, let me tell you about *the plan*,' Ruby continued.

Kitty shifted uncomfortably in her seat.

'We are changing the lock on the front door to keep a certain undesirable out.'

'Who?' Joseph asked.

'Kitty's beast of a husband.'

'You're locking him out?' Joseph mumbled through a mouthful of pie.

'Yes! We're changing the lock on Kitty's flat too. And from now on Kitty is officially the sole tenant of the aforementioned flat,' Ruby added. 'As the captain of this ship, I decide who stays aboard – and who walks the plank,' she added with one of her throaty laughs.

'I'm not sure a ship's captain makes anyone walk the plank,' Joseph said.

'They do if it's a pirate ship.' Ruby clapped her hands together gleefully. 'I always wanted to be a pirate, sailing the seven seas, drinking grog, searching for treasure with my one-legged parrot.'

Somehow this revelation didn't surprise Joseph in the slightest.

'But I won't be able to afford the rent without Reg,' Kitty said anxiously.

'Did you not hear a word I said?' Ruby frowned at her. 'I am the captain of this here ship and I also decide how much people pay for rent. So for now you can just pay what you can afford. Hell, you can pay me in romance novels if need be.'

'Oh no, I don't want any special favours,' Kitty replied. 'It wouldn't be fair.'

'To who?'

'To you – and to Joseph.'

'I'm sure Joseph won't mind, after all, he's such a man of character and principle and he abhors violence of any kind, don't you, Joseph?' She looked pointedly at his PPU badge.

'Yes, of course.'

'So I'm sure he will fully support any plan that abolishes violence from these premises.'

'I certainly do.' Joseph nodded in agreement.

'Really?' Kitty stared at him and her eyes filled with tears. 'That's so kind of you both. Thank you.'

'And I'm always here for you too,' Freddy mumbled.

'What was that?' Ruby asked.

'I'm always here for you too,' Freddy repeated, louder, his cheeks flushing bright red.

'Thank you.' Kitty smiled at him, then looked down into her lap.

'See, you are not alone,' Ruby said, clasping Kitty's hand. 'And, fear not, Joseph, I shall be providing you with a new front door key as soon as Harry has finished.'

Joseph nodded.

'But what will we do if Reg comes back?' Kitty asked. 'He's going to go crazy when he realises the locks are changed.'

'We'll cross that bridge when we come to it,' Ruby replied breezily. 'Or should I say, we'll sail under that bridge in our pirate ship.' She squeezed Kitty's hand. 'Don't worry, my dear, he won't be due home on leave again for an age, and if there's any justice in this world, in the meantime he'll be posted somewhere far away overseas.' Ruby raised her cup of gin. 'To new beginnings,' she toasted.

'New beginnings,' the others echoed.

Although he was loath to admit it, Joseph couldn't help feeling buoyed up by this unexpected development. Ruby might be irritating as hell at times, but there was no denying she'd just done Kitty a huge favour. And he for one would be very glad to see the back of Reg.

CHAPTER TWENTY-THREE

September 1940

As Ruby set off for the ambulance depot on Sunday, she found it hard to believe that the relentless Blitz had only been going for two weeks. Time no longer seemed to be the long flat line it used to be. Now it concertinaed in sharp, dramatic bursts. Thankfully, after sixty German planes had been shot down the day she and Kitty had discovered the pilot in the guttering, as they now referred to him, the Nazis had eased off on their daytime raids. But every night they returned, wreaking havoc. London had become like the magical snow globe her father had brought her after a theatre tour to Vienna. Every night, the city was shaken to its core. But every day, once the dust had settled, it reappeared, a little battered and bruised but still standing, with the grand dome of St Paul's looking down like a proud father, urging Londoners to keep their chin up.

As Ruby turned the corner, she saw a couple huddled by the entrance to Neptune Square. Due to the pitch dark of the blackout, it wasn't until she was upon them that she realised it was Kitty and Freddy.

'Well, hello!' she declared. 'What's going on here then?'

'I just walked Kitty round to her shift at the first aid post,' Freddy explained and even though it was pitch dark Ruby just knew he was blushing.

'Did you now?' she replied.

'I – I'd better get inside,' Kitty stammered, and Ruby knew that she was blushing too.

'Good luck, ladies,' Freddy said. 'Here's hoping it's a quiet night for once.'

'Yes, indeed,' Ruby replied.

As she and Kitty made their way past the warden on duty and into the square, Ruby linked arms with her.

'Well?' she said.

'Well, what?'

'What was going on with Freddy just then? You appeared to be very close.'

'We were just talking,' Kitty said defensively.

'Really?'

'Yes.' Kitty stopped suddenly. 'Oh, Ruby, he told me this evening that he can't stop thinking about me.'

'Well, I think that much is obvious. Even a blind old dear in a blackout could have told you that.'

'Really?'

'Of course. And don't sound so surprised.'

'But no one's ever told me anything like that before.'

'The boy is crazy about you. The question is, how do you feel about him?'

'I don't know. I mean, I'm married.'

'On paper maybe, but how about in here?' Ruby put her hand to her chest, forgetting that it was too dark for Kitty to see.

'In where?'

'In your heart, where it counts. Listen, I'd better get down to the ambulance station. I don't want to be late and give that smart alec Joseph any reason to have one over on me. But this conversation is to be continued, understand?'

'All right. Stay safe.'

'Thank you, my dear. And you.'

Ruby hurried off down the ramp to the ambulance station, just as the air-raid siren began to wail.

'Drat!' she muttered.

When she got down to the staffroom, she found Bill and Joseph standing by the door.

'About time too,' Bill muttered, looking at the clock on the wall. She was one minute late. She thought about telling Bill she'd been attending to an urgent matter of the heart, but thought better of it. The only hearts Bill probably thought about were those belonging to sheep that he had for breakfast! 'You have a call to attend to,' he continued.

'Already?'

'Yes. A bus has crashed head first into a crater over on Regent Street. Some of the passengers are injured. Your rescue crew just left.'

'Well, what are we waiting for?' Ruby said, turning on her heel before she could hear Bill's tut of indignation.

'So, how are you?' Joseph asked as they got into the ambulance.

'I beg your pardon?'

'How are you?' He turned the key in the ignition and shifted the gearstick.

'Well, I'll be damned. I do believe that's the very first time you've enquired as to my well-being,' Ruby replied. 'I'll have to serve you gin in a teacup more often.'

'It was a pretty tasty afternoon tea,' he replied, and although it was too dark to be sure, she could have sworn he was actually smiling.

'You seem remarkably chipper for one who is normally so…' She broke off, worried she might ruin the moment.

'Normally so…?'

'Sombre,' she replied. 'Not that there's anything wrong with being sombre, especially given the current state of affairs. Lord

knows, I'd be sombre too if I hadn't been born with this inexhaust-
ible sunny spirit. My father used to call me Ruby-Ra. Ra was the
Egyptian sun god, you know.'

'Yes, I know.'

'Oh, you do?'

'Yes, even us sombre folk can be interested in history. When
we're not wailing at the injustice of the world, that is.'

Was he poking fun at himself? Would wonders never cease?
Ruby settled back in her seat. This was shaping up to be a fun
shift – as long as no one died on them, of course.

'May I ask what has caused this upturn in your spirits?' She
wondered if Joseph might have fallen in love but instantly decided
against it. She couldn't imagine him showing passion for anything
other than a cause.

'You may,' he answered, turning the truck onto the main road.

'Well? Don't keep a girl in suspense, it's bad for the complexion.'

'What?'

'It is. According to *Woman's Own* magazine, too much stress
gives a gal wrinkles.'

Joseph muttered something under his breath that sounded a
lot like 'give me strength'.

'What's happened?' Ruby pressed.

'Some friends and I have got the all-clear to set up a charity to
help the down-and-outs who are being refused access to the shelters.'

Ruby stared at him in shock. 'But I don't understand. Why is
anyone being refused access to shelters?'

'For being undesirable, apparently.'

'That's awful.'

'I know. But they'll soon have the Hungerford Club to take
care of them.'

'Hungerford?'

'Yes, we've been given permission to build a shelter under the
arches of Hungerford Bridge by Charing Cross station.'

'That's incredible! Congratulations!'

'Well, it wasn't all my doing. I just suggested it to some of my colleagues in the Peace Pledge Union.'

Ruby nodded. 'Can I ask—'

'Not another question?' Joseph cut in, but again it seemed to be in good humour.

'What made you become a conscientious objector?'

He cleared his throat. 'I saw first-hand the futility of war,' he said softly.

'Did you lose someone in the Great War too?'

'Yes.'

She waited for him to proffer more information but he didn't and she didn't want to push it. This was the furthest she'd ever got in a conversation with Joseph and she didn't want to blow it. 'I'm sorry,' she offered instead.

'Thank you.'

*

By the time Joseph pulled up at the scene of the accident, two stretcher-bearers were already waiting with an injured passenger.

'Good grief!' Ruby exclaimed as they jumped down from the cab and surveyed the tail end of a red double-decker bus poking out from a jagged crater. 'Good job Fortnum & Mason taped up their windows.'

Joseph stared at her in disbelief. Was this really her priority when people could be injured and possibly dying in the wreckage of the bus? Just when he'd been starting to think she had a little more depth to her, but no, she was more concerned with the well-being of some windows in a fancy, overpriced store.

A plane roared by overhead and the sky lit up with a silvery trail of anti-aircraft fire.

'Don't you think they look just like shooting stars?' Ruby said, gazing up at the lights.

'No,' he snapped. 'Don't you think we ought to be getting on with our job?'

'Oh, yes, of course, I was just trying to...'

Another plane drowned out the end of her sentence.

Joseph strode over to the stretcher-bearers.

'Evening,' one of them said. 'We've got a lady here with a suspected broken arm. She's in a bit of shock too,' he added quietly.

Joseph looked down to see an elderly woman with grey hair set in neat curls. She was clutching her arm and muttering to herself.

'Hello,' Ruby said to the woman, crouching down beside her. 'What's your name?'

'Ethel,' the woman muttered. 'I'm on my way to my brother Stanley's. He's making me some tea. I said I wouldn't be late. Am I going to be late?'

Another plane roared over and a couple of seconds later there was a strange whistling sound.

Joseph looked at Ruby across the stretcher and he saw fear flicker into her eyes. The next second, there was a huge boom and the ground shook violently.

'Right, Ethel, let's get you to safety and then we can see about your Stanley,' Ruby said.

The stretcher-bearers quickly loaded her into the ambulance and Joseph and Ruby hurried into the cab.

'Little too close for comfort tonight,' Ruby said as Joseph turned the key in the ignition.

'I know.' As he started off up Regent Street, he had a horrible thought: what if he was driving straight into the path of another bomb? He tried to push the thought from his mind. The reality was, every day in London now was like this. Every choice made and action taken loaded with the prospect that it could lead to your death or your survival. Even staying in bed could potentially kill you these days.

The sky up ahead of them was now ablaze with searchlights, tracer bullets and parachute flares and, every so often, the blinding flash of white light as a bomb exploded. It was like a surreal storm in a surreal nightmare that just wouldn't end. All of the joy Joseph had been feeling at the success of the Hungerford Club was now draining away, replaced with a growing dread at how many more lives were going to be lost that night.

'Don't worry, Ethel,' Ruby called through the partition into the back of the ambulance. 'We'll soon have you safe and sound.'

Another huge boom echoed through the night air. Joseph noticed that Ruby was gripping the dashboard as tightly as he was gripping the steering wheel.

Somehow he managed to negotiate his way through the London backstreets and they finally reached the hospital. They jumped out of the cab and fetched Ethel from the back.

'We're going to get a nice doctor to check that arm for you,' Ruby explained.

'But what about Stanley?' Ethel cried.

'You'll be able to see him as soon as your arm is seen to. Does he have a telephone? I could try calling him to let him know where you are.'

Ethel gave Ruby the number and while she hurried over to the hospital pay phone, Joseph helped Ethel into the emergency room, which was already crowded with people.

'Busy night,' he muttered to one of the hospital porters.

'Got that right,' the porter replied. 'And looks like we're set for a lot more. Apparently Pimlico just took a pounding.'

'Oh no!' Joseph's heart sank.

Ruby came hurrying over.

'Yep. A high explosive just hit Neptune Square,' the porter continued.

'Neptune Square?' Joseph echoed.

'Kitty!' Ruby exclaimed.

CHAPTER TWENTY-FOUR

September 1940

Ruby and Joseph didn't utter a word all the way back to Pimlico. Not out loud at least. But inside her head, Ruby was yelling one sentence over and over again: *Please, please, please let Kitty be all right.*

As they tore along Millbank, the horizon burned gold, giving the bizarre appearance of a setting midnight sun. The ambulance bumped and jolted on the potholes in the road, but Ruby was numb to it. Just as she was numb to the shriek of the siren and the roar of the planes. It was only now she was faced with the prospect of never seeing her pale face again, of never hearing the soft lilt of her voice, that she realised how she had come to love dear Kitty. And in a moment of clarity as lightning bright as a parachute flare, she realised that Kitty was the embodiment of the younger sister she had so longed for as an only child.

'She can't be dead,' Ruby murmured.

'Did you say something?' Joseph asked, slowing down as they approached Neptune Square. The entrance was blocked by a fire engine.

'Kitty. She has to be all right,' Ruby said gravely.

Joseph nodded. 'I'm sure she's all right. They'll have gone down to the shelter at the first sign of trouble, the minute the siren sounded.'

Ruby nodded, but she couldn't shake a terrible sense of foreboding.

The fire engine drove through the gates to the square and Joseph followed in behind it. The courtyard was teeming with wardens and rescue teams. And then Ruby saw a sight that made her heart almost stop beating – a thick cloud of dust billowing from Ocean House, the building where the first-aid post was stationed.

Joseph wound down his window and called to a passing ARP warden. 'What's happened, pal?'

'Ocean House took a direct hit,' the warden replied. 'High-explosive bomb too, went right down to the shelter.'

'It hit the shelter?' Ruby called, leaning across Joseph.

'Yes. There's a lot of folk trapped down there as they'd all piled in as soon as the siren sounded.'

'Oh no!' Ruby slumped back in her seat.

'We're trying to dig them out now,' the warden called before hurrying off.

Joseph drove down into the underground car park. It too was crowded with people, some of them lying on stretchers on the ground.

As Joseph parked up, Bill came hurrying over.

'The first-aid post has taken a hit,' he informed them as they got out of the cab. 'We've got a lot of our staff trapped in there, so it's all hands on deck. We need to treat the injured as soon as they're brought out.'

'I – I need to find someone,' Ruby stammered.

She strode up the car park, scanning the faces of any women she saw.

'Kitty!' she cried. 'Kitty, where are you?'

'Are you looking for Kitty Price?' a matronly woman in a nurse's uniform asked.

'Yes!' Ruby exclaimed. 'Have you seen her? Is she here?'

The woman shook her head. 'She was in the shelter when it got bombed. Still no sign of her, I'm afraid.'

'Oh no!' Ruby felt sick to her stomach. Kitty couldn't perish. Not now she was finally free of Reg and had acquired a secret admirer to boot. She wouldn't allow it. She started running back along the car park towards the entrance.

'Where are you going?' Joseph called after her.

'I'm going to find Kitty,' she replied over her shoulder.

As she emerged into the cool air of the courtyard, a plane roared by overhead and seconds later there was an almighty bang.

'Go to hell!' she yelled, shaking her fist at the sky before racing over to Ocean House. A gaping hole had been torn down the side of the building and the entrance was blocked by a mound of rubble. 'I want to help and I won't take no for an answer,' Ruby announced, grabbing the shoulder of a warden who was holding a couple of shovels. As he turned round, she saw that it was Freddy.

'Miss Ruby!' he cried. 'Have you seen Kitty?'

Ruby shook her head. 'I just spoke to one of her colleagues. Apparently she's trapped in the shelter.'

'We have to get her out!' Freddy exclaimed; the poor man looked utterly bereft.

'Come on.' Ruby grabbed one of the shovels and they ran over to join the team of people digging away at the rubble.

'We have to save her,' Ruby muttered as she dug. 'We have to save her.' Even though the digging was warming work, she couldn't stop her teeth from chattering. What if it was too late? What if the people sheltering had already perished? The fact that those sheltering had been first-aid workers and their patients made the whole thing even more horrifying.

Don't worry, Kitty, we're coming to get you, Ruby said in her mind, praying there was some way her message would reach her. She began tearing at the rubble with her bare hands, oblivious to the pain as her skin tore on the jagged edges.

'We're through!' a man called from the remains of the entrance. 'OK, let's get down there. We'll need stretchers at the ready.'

'Stretchers at the ready!' Ruby called over her shoulder. She heard another plane roaring by overhead. What if it was coming back to finish what it had started? What if they were all about to be buried alive beneath another bomb blast? There was no way the building would withstand it. 'Help me, Papa,' she whispered.

Mercifully, she heard the calm, clipped tones of her father whispering to her in her mind. *Onomatopoeia... higgledy-piggledy...* and she slowed her breathing in time.

Slowly but surely, they made their way along the passageway, the thin, dust-filled beams from their torches providing the only light in the pitch darkness.

'Hello!' Bill called. 'Can anyone hear me?'

There was a second's silence and then a faint voice echoed back. It was impossible to know what they were saying, but it was a sign of life.

'We're coming to get you, Kitty!' Ruby cried. 'Hang on in there, my dear!'

Finally, they made it to the stairwell at the end of the passageway leading to the shelter. The man at the front of the procession opened the door and shone his torch down. Ruby peered over his shoulder and saw frightened eyes glinting up at them in the dark. She almost passed out from the relief.

'Is everyone OK?' the man asked.

'We have a few casualties,' another man called back. 'Some of them serious.'

Please, please, please don't let one of them be Kitty, Ruby silently implored.

'All right, let's get the most serious casualties out first,' the man in front of Ruby said. He and another man went down into the shelter and re-emerged carrying a man whose hair was matted with blood and was barely conscious.

Ruby's heart pounded as she and Freddy made their way into the shelter. 'Kitty! Are you there?' she called into the darkness.

There was a terrible moment's silence. Ruby and Freddy stared at each other.

'Ruby? Is that you?' Kitty's voice was as weak as a kitten's meow.

'Oh Kitty, thank goodness!' Ruby exclaimed, moving through the people in the direction of Kitty's voice. 'Yes, it's me. And Freddy's here too. We've come to save you!'

They found Kitty in a corner of the shelter, cradling an injured man who appeared to be unconscious. Ruby shone her torch on Kitty's face. It was streaked with dirt and shiny with tears. 'Are you all right?'

Kitty nodded. 'But I'm afraid he isn't.' She nodded at the man.

Ruby's stomach lurched. 'Is he...?'

Kitty nodded. 'We were treating him for injuries when the siren went off. We brought him down here but he didn't make it. He – he—'

Ruby crouched down and put her arm around Kitty's thin shoulders. 'It's all right,' she said, suddenly finding an inner calm she had no idea existed. 'We'll take care of it, won't we, Freddy?'

'Yes, of course,' Freddy agreed, placing a comforting hand on Kitty's shoulder.

Then, slowly and carefully, Ruby and Freddy picked up the man's body and carried him up the rubble-strewn stairs. *Just pretend you're carrying a shop mannequin*, Ruby told herself. *Kitty's alive. Focus on the positive.*

But as they emerged from the building into the night, it was very hard to focus on the positive. They weren't carrying a mannequin. They were carrying someone's son. And someone's husband, judging by the ring on his wedding finger. Ruby gulped as she thought of poor Kitty having to watch the man die, helpless. She could remember only too well how terrible she'd felt when Daisy had died on her. Poor Kitty was going to be devastated.

'I'm afraid this one's for the morgue,' she said to a warden holding a stretcher.

As they carefully placed the body on the stretcher, the warden tipped his helmet. 'Poor sod.'

'Indeed.' Ruby turned and saw Kitty emerging, blinking, from the building. But before she could run over and embrace her, Freddy stepped forward and, a second later, Kitty was in his arms. Completely unexpectedly, Ruby's eyes filled with tears. It was so hard to make sense of everything that was happening, the wanton destruction and devastation. But by the same token, it seemed that the more violence the Germans inflicted upon London, the more acts of love it inspired. A line from one of her favourite Dickens novels came to her mind: '*It was the best of times, it was the worst of times.*' He really could have been writing about the Blitz.

'Ruby, are you all right?'

She jumped at the sound of Joseph's voice behind her.

'Yes, yes, I'm fine. We found Kitty.' She started to laugh, but tears kept spilling from her eyes. 'She's alive.'

'That's great. But don't you think you should get those hands seen to.'

'What hands?' She looked down and saw that her hands were covered in cuts and scratches from where she'd been digging at the rubble. 'Oh dear, my manicurist is going to have my guts for garters.'

'Never mind about that, let's just get them cleaned up.' Joseph gently placed his hand beneath her elbow and guided her back across the rubble. It was such a small gesture and yet it felt so full of kindness.

She gazed back at the sky as another plane roared by. *You'll never defeat us,* she thought to herself with a burst of defiance. *We have kindness on our side.*

CHAPTER TWENTY-FIVE

October 1940

'Stop fidgeting,' Ruby muttered through a mouthful of hairpins as she coiled Kitty's pale blonde hair into a large knot.

'I can't help it, I'm nervous,' Kitty replied, shifting in her seat at Ruby's kitchen table.

It was three weeks since the bomb blast at Neptune Square and in that time Ruby had spent every opportunity she could with Kitty. She'd feared that the trauma might have made Kitty even more anxious than before, but, surprisingly, it seemed to have had the opposite effect. If anything, she had a new, quiet resolve about her. This could of course have something to do with the amount of time she'd been spending with a certain young butcher.

'Do you have any idea at all where Freddy might be taking you for lunch?' Ruby asked, applying the final pin to Kitty's hair.

'No, he's being very secretive. But I really would appreciate it if you didn't make a big song and dance about it. There's nothing going on, we're only friends.'

'Me! Make a big song and dance about something?' Ruby came to stand in front of Kitty with a grin on her face. 'How dare you even suggest such a thing!'

Kitty smiled. 'Well, it has been known…'

'That was my former, pre-war self. I'm now the epitome of the understated woman. A woman humbled by the trials and tribulations of war. A woman—'

'All right, all right, I get the message,' Kitty interrupted, giggling.

'Anyway, your chignon is complete. Chignon is from the French phrase *chignon du cou*,' Ruby added. 'It means nape of the neck. Perhaps you could drop that little nugget into your conversation with Freddy. Make it look as if you're a well-travelled woman of the world.'

'I don't think Freddy is the type to be all that impressed by French hairstyles,' Kitty said with a smile.

'Good point.' Ruby nodded thoughtfully. 'If you like, I could furnish you with my vast knowledge of French sausages. That might be more up his street. In Toulouse they make a delight-ful—'

'It really is all right,' Kitty interrupted. 'I told you, we're only going out for a quick lunch, and it's bound to be made even quicker by an air raid.'

'But think how romantic that could be,' Ruby said dreamily. 'Both of you seeking shelter from the Germans. And you seeking shelter in Freddy's strong butcher's arms.'

'I think I'd rather take my chances over ground,' Kitty replied, her smile fading.

'Of course. I'm sorry, that was insensitive of me.' Ruby sat down beside her. 'Are you still having the nightmares?'

Kitty nodded. 'I'm sure they'll stop eventually. I just wish there'd be some let-up in the bombing.'

'Me too.' Ruby took hold of her hand and gave it a squeeze.

'So, where is it you're going with Joseph today?' Kitty asked.

'He's taking me to his club,' Ruby replied.

'He's a member of a club?' Kitty's eyes widened.

'Yes, but not the kind you're thinking of. I'm afraid there will be no leather armchairs and smoking jackets and waiters catering to your every whim at this establishment.'

'What kind of club is it then?'

Ruby put the kettle on the stove and lit the gas. She'd better fortify herself while she still could. She'd invited herself along to the club on the premise of helping out but really it was out of curiosity. She was desperate to see what Joseph had been up to but she had no idea what she'd be walking into. 'It's a club for down-and-outs and vagabonds, those poor lost souls cast adrift by society.'

Kitty raised her thin eyebrows.

'It's under the arches of Hungerford Bridge by Charing Cross. Joseph helped set it up.' Ruby couldn't help feeling a stab of pride as she said this. In the past few weeks working with Joseph, she'd begun to feel a strange kind of bond forming with him. It was the unlikeliest of developments, but she guessed that this was another of the unexpected by-products of war. Witnessing death and destruction with another human being on a daily basis was bound to bring you closer.

'Joseph is so interesting,' Kitty said, taking a compact from her bag and applying a coat of rose-pink lipstick.

'Yes, I suppose he is.' Ruby scooped some tea leaves from the caddy and put them in the pot.

'He can do some amazing card tricks.'

'What?' Ruby practically dropped the teapot in shock. She loved a good card trick; they were so much fun – and so unlike the distinctly un-fun Joseph!

'Yes, when he was a child back in Blackpool, he used to do them on the pier to make some extra money to help out his mum – when his father returned from the Great War and wasn't able to work due to the shell shock.'

Ruby frowned. 'How do you know all of this?'

'He told Freddy and me one day, when we were in the garden shelter.'

'Oh.' Ruby felt a twinge of something weirdly close to jealousy. Joseph had always been so closed off with her. Whenever she'd tried to find out more about him, he'd shut the conversation down. She'd assumed he was generally antisocial. But clearly not. Clearly when he was with Kitty and Freddy he poured forth personal anecdotes like milk from a jug.

'He does a really funny trick with the King of Diamonds,' Kitty continued.

Oh, this really was too much! 'Why have you never told me this before?' Ruby asked, staring at Kitty indignantly.

'I assumed he'd have told you, seeing as you spend so much time together in the ambulance.'

'Well, you assumed wrong.' Ruby plonked the sugar bowl down on the table in front of Kitty, trying to ignore the twinges of hurt she was feeling.

*

As Joseph led Ruby down Villiers Street, he prayed he hadn't made a huge mistake in bringing her to the Hungerford Club. They might have been getting on a lot better recently but she was still Ruby. 'Now, you do realise that the folk you're about to meet aren't your usual silver spoon brigade?'

'Silver spoon brigade?' Ruby frowned up at him.

'Yup, you know, born with a silver spoon in their mouths. These folk have nothing.'

'I am aware of that, yes.' Ruby's scowl deepened. 'But I can assure you that I have mixed with all manner of people over the course of my life – from princes to paupers.'

'Paupers?' He looked pointedly at her fur coat and hat.

'Yes. Why, when I was in Sri Lanka, I—'

'You've been to Sri Lanka?' he interrupted, shocked.

'Absolutely. You're not the only man of mystery, you know. Well, actually, you are the only *man* of mystery present, obviously, but you're not the only *person* of mystery. I'll have you know, I have a thing or two up my sleeve too, if you'll excuse the pun.'

He shook his head. What the heck was she talking about?

'Yes, I spent a very enjoyable six months in Dimbula picking tea with the natives, and I can assure you, there wasn't a silver spoon to be seen.'

'*You* were picking tea?'

'Yes, that's what I said, wasn't it? Has all of this bombing turned you deaf?'

'No, I just… I didn't imagine you being—'

'Well, as I said, you're not the only one with a trick or two up his sleeve.'

Why did she keep saying that? Joseph frowned. Had she found out about his fondness for a card trick? Perhaps Kitty had told her. But before he could enquire further, they arrived at the Hungerford Club. The shelter was still being constructed, but the outer walls were complete, offering much-needed protection from the increasingly cold weather. He led Ruby inside. The main entrance room was pretty full already and two of his pals from the Peace Pledge Union were standing behind a trestle table, ladling soup from a large pot into tin cups.

'Oh I say,' Ruby murmured, looking around.

Again Joseph hoped he hadn't made an error of judgement bringing her with him. He wasn't entirely sure what the others were going to make of her airs and graces either, not to mention her attire.

'So, these poor people aren't allowed into the public shelters,' Ruby said quietly.

'That's right.'

'That's awful.'

Joseph was heartened to see what looked like real concern on her face.

'Right then, what do you want me to do?' she asked, rubbing her hands together.

'Well, I was wondering if maybe you could help with the lasses that come here.'

'The lasses?'

'Yes, you know, the *ladies*.' He nodded to a couple of women sitting at a table in the corner. 'We've got some washing facilities set up round the back; maybe you could help them get cleaned up a bit.' Joseph studied Ruby's face for any adverse reaction. He knew he could have given her an easier first task, but he wanted to test her mettle, see if she was all mouth and no trousers – or in her case, no fur coat.

'Of course, I would be delighted to,' she replied with a defiant air, as if she knew she was being tested.

Joseph watched as she strode over to the women.

'Good afternoon,' she said, extending her hand to the older woman, whose hair was lank and greasy and her cheeks a deep mottled red. 'I'm Ruby Glenville and I'm here to help you lasses get clean.'

Oh God. Joseph could hardly bear to look as the woman ignored Ruby's hand and let out a loud belch.

'Did you know that in some cultures it's considered the height of good manners to burp,' Ruby continued, clearly undeterred. 'Yes, in Arabic countries, a good hearty belch is one's way of conveying one's compliments to the chef. I take it the soup was good.'

'I ain't had no soup,' the woman snapped.

'Well, that won't do,' said Ruby. 'Would you like me to fetch you some?'

The woman stared at her for a moment, then nodded.

'And how about you, madam?' Ruby asked the younger woman.

'Yes please,' she muttered.

'Very good.' Ruby came back over to Joseph, taking off her coat. 'This is great,' she exclaimed. 'I always harboured a secret desire to be a Nippy and now my dream has finally come true.' She shoved the coat into his hands. 'Put this somewhere, would you.'

'What the heck's a Nippy?' Joseph mumbled. But Ruby had already gone, hurrying over to the soup station.

*

As Ruby gently washed the grime from the stick-like arms of a young woman named Polly, she came to a startling realisation. Her afternoon at the Hungerford Club had made her feel more contented than she'd been in ages. In her work for the ambulance service she often felt no more than a glorified taxi driver, or rather a taxi driver's assistant, ferrying people to hospital with minimal interaction. But here she was able to talk to people to her heart's content and discover their stories, and the whole enterprise was fascinating.

'Do you mind if I ask how you ended up here?' she said to Polly, as she lathered her thin arms with soap.

'Me mate Mabel told me about it,' the girl answered in a strong East London accent.

'No, I don't mean how you got to the club. I mean, how did you end up in a position to need to come here?'

'Oh.' Her face fell.

'You don't have to tell me if you don't want to,' Ruby said hurriedly.

'There was trouble at home,' Polly murmured. 'I couldn't stay there. Me mum had taken up with this fella she met down at the docks. Awful violent, he was. Liked to knock me about. So I decided I'd take me chances out on the street.'

'I'm very sorry to hear that.' Ruby looked at the tangled mass of hair sticking out from beneath Polly's shabby hat. 'Would you like me to brush your hair?'

'Oh, I don't know, I…'

Ruby looked around the room for a brush, but there was no sign of one. There was no talcum powder either, just a few bars of orange coal tar soap. She'd have to have a word with Joseph about the lack of toiletries. The ladies – or lasses, as he called them – deserved better than this. She opened her handbag and pulled out her own brush, a beautiful specimen with an ivory handle she'd bought in Manhattan. Polly's eyes lit up as soon as she saw it.

'Please, allow me,' Ruby said, removing her hat.

Unlike Kitty's hair, which had been so smooth and silky to the touch when she'd styled it earlier, Polly's mousy brown hair was rough as a straw. Very slowly and very carefully, Ruby began the painstaking work of untangling it.

Polly closed her eyes and sighed and her shoulders slumped as, finally, she appeared to relax. Ruby thought of the salons she'd been to in New York, Paris and London, and how relaxed she'd always felt when having her hair done. This poor girl had probably never set foot in a salon and it was an injustice that made Ruby burn with indignation.

Just as she'd got rid of the last of the tangles, Joseph poked his head around the door and promptly did a double take when he saw what Ruby was doing.

'We need to get going,' he mouthed, pointing to his watch.

Ruby nodded and gently tapped Polly on the shoulder.

She opened her eyes and gave her a sleepy smile. 'That was the nicest thing ever,' she murmured. 'Thanks, miss.'

'You are very welcome.' Ruby held the brush out to her. 'I have to go now, but I'd like you to have this, as a gift.'

The girl's eyes widened. 'Oh, but I can't. It looks so expensive.'

'It's yours. I insist.' Ruby pressed it into her hands.

To her horror, Polly's eyes filled with tears and, for an awful moment, Ruby thought she'd made a dreadful faux pas. Was it inappropriate of her to give the girl a gift? Was it insensitive? And to make matters even worse, Joseph was still loitering in the doorway, watching, no doubt already composing his next lecture to her.

'Thank you so much,' Polly sobbed, cradling the brush to her chest. 'This is the nicest thing anyone's ever done for me.'

'Really?' Ruby stared at her.

She nodded.

'Oh, you poor dear,' Ruby gasped. 'I'm so sorry you've been so cruelly battered by life's storms – not to mention brutish stepfathers – I do so hope that—'

'All right, all right, time for us to go,' Joseph said from the doorway.

Ruby grasped Polly's arms. 'I'll be back,' she said. 'As soon as I can. And I'm going to bring the contents of my dressing table with me.'

She hurried over to Joseph, who was holding out her coat. She didn't know why he was so anxious to go; surely there was ample time before they had to start their shift at the ambulance station. But as they left the shelter, she saw that it was almost dark already.

'Oh goodness, what time is it?'

'A quarter past seven,' Joseph replied.

'How on earth did that happen?' She hurried after him along the street.

'Time flies when you're having fun,' he replied.

'Yes.' They stopped as they reached the bus stop and she smiled. 'It really does.'

CHAPTER TWENTY-SIX

October 1940

'We've got a bomber's moon tonight, folks,' Bill said as he gave his briefing to Ruby and Joseph's shift. 'So I reckon the Bosch will be keeping us busy.'

As the staffroom filled with murmured agreements and nodding heads, Ruby mused on how quickly the surreal could become normal. If anyone had told her a year ago that a beautiful full moon would come to signify a night of heavy bombing, she would have thought them crazy. But now here they were, all nodding over cups of tea like it was the most natural thing in the world. The war had turned everything on its head. There were some changes she'd found favourable though, and her visit to the Hungerford Club was most definitely one of them.

'Here we go,' said Bill as the siren outside began to wail. 'No rest for the wicked.' He hurried through to the office next door.

Ruby watched as Joseph took a copy of the *Daily Express* from the table and began to read.

'Isn't it great?' he said from behind the paper.

'What?'

'The government changing their policy on allowing people to shelter in the Underground.'

'They've changed it?'

Joseph lowered the paper. There was a beaming smile on his face, causing his dimples to appear. It was a sight that happened so infrequently Ruby had started thinking of Joseph's dimples as a rare planetary constellation, only visible to the naked eye once in a blue moon.

'Yep,' he replied. 'The Home Secretary has announced that Londoners can now take shelter in the stations, and he's also opened up some disused stations and lines to the public.'

'That's fantastic!' Ruby exclaimed. 'And I bet it's all down to you storming the Savoy.'

'Well, I don't know about that,' Joseph said. 'But it can't have hurt. It certainly caused the government embarrassment.'

'You should feel very proud,' Ruby said.

Joseph's cheeks flushed and his smile faded. 'I really don't think so,' he retorted before disappearing back behind the paper.

'So, what do you say to my wonderful idea?' she asked, deciding it was probably best to change the subject as she'd clearly upset him again, although she had no idea why.

He peered at her over the paper. 'I wasn't aware that you'd had one.'

'Yes you are. My wonderful idea about offering my hairdressing skills to the poor dear women cast asunder by this cruel world. I always wanted to be a hairdresser.'

'I thought you always wanted to be a zippy.'

She stared at him blankly. 'Oh, you mean a Nippy!'

'Do I?' He raised his eyebrows.

'Yes, you know, the waitresses in the Lyons coffee houses.' She gazed dreamily. 'I do so love those mother-of-pearl buttons.'

He shook his head.

'I know you think I'm the world's biggest imbecile…' She waited a moment for him to correct her, but he annoyingly remained silent. 'But, anyway, doing those poor women's hair really is a wonderful idea.'

He put the paper down. 'Go on then, convince me.'

'Well, for a start, everyone knows that having one's hair brushed is one of the most pleasurable things known to mankind. Why, it's almost as good as…' She broke off and her face flushed.

'As good as?' He looked at her questioningly.

'As good as Cadbury's chocolate,' she hastily responded.

'I had no idea,' he replied wryly.

'I'll show you if you don't believe me,' she retorted, instantly regretting it. The thought of having to brush Joseph's hair made her feel all uncomfortable and peculiar, despite its thick waves and rich dark lustre.

'It's all right, I'll take your word for it.' Clearly he found the prospect equally distasteful.

'And secondly,' she continued. 'It will help their chances of being accepted into the public shelters. I've studied the craft of hair care at the finest salons in Paris. I know how to make a woman feel desirable.'

Joseph raised his eyebrows. 'Was this before or after you were picking tea in Sri Lanka?'

Ruby's skin prickled with indignation. Was he implying she was some kind of fantasist? 'It was after, and when I say studied, I don't mean to say that I was an actual hairdresser, but I was such a frequent patron of Parisian salons, I'm bound to have absorbed their methods. Like osmosis,' she added in an attempt to add some kind of scientific weight to her argument. Thankfully, before Joseph had time to make yet another condescending remark, Bill rushed into the room.

'Crew Four, got a job for you over in Soho. Restaurant been hit on Wardour Street.'

Ruby's heart sank. Soho was her most favourite part of London. 'Oh, please don't let it be Giuseppe's!' she exclaimed.

'Someone you know?' Joseph asked, as they got to their feet.

Ruby shook her head. 'I don't know him personally, but they do the best seafood stew in all of London.'

Joseph gave her a withering stare and she realised that, yet again, she'd lost favour with him.

'Obviously, I'm worried about the people who might have been injured too,' she called as she ran behind him to the ambulance.

'Obviously,' he replied drily.

*

It took several hours to get all of the people injured in the restaurant bombing free from the rubble and safely despatched to the hospital. As Joseph approached Piccadilly, en route from their final drop-off at the hospital, he felt drunk with exhaustion. Thankfully, the restaurant staff had brought everyone down to shelter in the cellar when the air-raid siren had gone off, but the bomb had reduced the building to rubble and burst a water main, making the rescue work all the more treacherous.

'Thank goodness no one died,' Ruby said for about the tenth time.

Joseph wasn't entirely sure why she kept saying it, but he had a hunch it was her way of trying to make amends for initially showing more concern for the fish stew.

'Do you think that's it for the night?' he asked, peering through the grimy windscreen at the sky above. The huge full moon was casting its silvery light all around and while it made driving in the blackout less treacherous, it also made life way easier for the German bombers.

'Hopefully. I haven't heard a plane for a— Oh no...' Ruby broke off as the black silhouette of a bomber arced across the moon. It was heading straight towards them.

Instinctively, Joseph put the truck into reverse and pressed down on the gas.

'Onomatopoeia... higgledy-piggledy...' Ruby started chanting beside him as the plane grew closer and closer and lower and lower, or at least that's how it sounded.

Joseph frowned; either he was going deaf or she was going crazy.

'It's one of theirs, isn't it?' she asked, her voice a squeak.

'Yup.' Joseph gripped the steering wheel, his knuckles white and his palms sweating.

The screech of the plane's engine grew so loud, he thought his eardrums might burst.

'Are we going to die?' Ruby asked.

He held his breath as the plane roared ever closer, filling the top half of the windscreen. Then came the whistling sound.

'Oh no,' Ruby gasped.

Joseph stopped the ambulance and closed his eyes, waiting for the deafening boom. He felt Ruby's hand on top of his and, instinctively, he gripped it.

'I just want you to know that I forgive you,' Ruby shouted in his ear.

What the hell? He opened his eyes and stared at her. 'What for?' he yelled back.

'All of the times you've—'

But before she could say any more, there was an almighty boom. The ambulance jolted forwards. Joseph glanced into the rear-view mirror. A cloud of dust was rolling down the street towards them.

'Shrapnel, get down!' he yelled, launching himself on top of her.

The ambulance rattled and rocked as shrapnel rained down upon it.

After several seconds, in which neither of them seemed to breathe, it stopped and they disentangled themselves.

'You – you saved me,' Ruby stammered.

'I was actually trying to save my ears from your incessant chatter,' he quipped, his heart still pounding.

Ruby gazed at him. 'It was just like one of Kitty's books,' she murmured. 'Where the hero bravely throws himself into harm's way to save the beautiful but slightly sappy heroine. Obviously I'm not sappy, but other than that it was exactly the same.'

'Jesus!' Joseph groaned. He checked the mirror again. The dust was starting to settle. 'Come on, let's see if anyone needs our help.'

He opened the door and jumped down from the cab. The road was covered in tiny pieces of broken glass from the blown-out windows of the shops lining the street. It shimmered like crystal in the moonlight.

Ruby got out of her side and came to join him, her feet crunching on the glass. 'I feel as if I'm on the set of a film,' she gasped. 'A really sinister film.'

Joseph couldn't help agreeing. As the cloud of dust continued to thin, the silhouette of a church appeared at the end of the deserted street, or what remained of the church at least. Half of the roof appeared to be missing.

'Should we check for casualties?' Ruby asked. 'I can't imagine anyone was in there at this time of night, but just in case.'

Joseph nodded.

As they made their way up the empty street, his heart rate slowly returned to something close to normal. That was the closest shave yet and he couldn't help wondering if one day soon his number would finally be up.

Ruby ran on ahead of him and over to the church. The bomb had landed smack bang in the centre of the building so only the steeple at one end remained fully intact.

'Hello?' Ruby called. 'Is anyone there?' She turned back to Joseph. 'Why would the Germans bomb a church?'

'Why would anyone bomb anything?' he replied.

A chill wind swept up the street and he pulled up the collar on his jacket.

'But it's so heartless,' Ruby continued. 'It…' Her mouth fell open as she looked up at the sky. 'Oh no!'

Joseph spun round to see another plane heading straight for them. 'Quick,' he said, grabbing her arm. As the roar of the engine grew louder, they raced back onto the street and into a shop doorway.

'Onomatopoeia… higgledy-piggledy…' Ruby began chanting again as she crouched down beside him. 'Onomatopoeia… higgledy-piggledy…'

The plane swooped over and for a moment Joseph thought they'd been spared, but then came the whistling sound that had come to chill him to the marrow.

'Onomatopoeia… higgledy-piggledy…' Ruby chanted louder.

'Why do you keep saying that?' he yelled.

'I don't want to die!' she yelled back as the whistling grew louder.

'Neither do I,' he yelled back. 'Even with you chanting gibberish in my—' But before he could say any more, she was leaning towards him and her cold hands were cradling his face.

'Kiss me!' she commanded before planting her lips on his.

Time suddenly seemed to stand still and all he was aware of were her lips on his, warm and soft and full, and something sparking into life deep in the pit of his stomach. A longing, the like of which he'd never felt before. Then the whistling stopped. Silence. The certain knowledge that he was about to die engulfed him. But instead of an ear-splitting boom, there was a thud. A thud. He was still alive. And Ruby was still kissing him. There was no sound, only silence. And her lips were still on his.

They broke apart, and the strange trance he'd been under lifted.

'What happened?' Ruby asked. 'Did we die? Is this heaven?'

I sincerely hope not, Joseph thought. He scrambled to his feet and cautiously peered out of the shop doorway. 'Bloody hell!'

'What is it?' Ruby leaned forward. 'Oh my goodness!'

A huge, unexploded bomb had landed on the street just a few yards away from them.

They looked at each other, stunned. Then Ruby started laughing.

'I thought we were dead. I thought we'd gone to heaven. You kissed me,' she spluttered.

'Er, I think you'll find that you kissed me,' he replied. 'And I think we ought to get out of here quick smart before we really do end up kicking the bucket.' He grabbed her hand and helped her up. And as she squeezed his hand tightly, he got that same strange feeling in the pit of his stomach. But now was definitely not the time to think of such things.

The bomb was now blocking their route back to the ambulance so they headed up the road in the opposite direction, half running, half stumbling and finally emerging onto a deserted Piccadilly Circus. The lights on the billboards had all been turned off in the blackout, but the moon was so bright Joseph could still see the advertisements. GUINNESS IS GOOD FOR YOU, one of them read, and for some strange reason this suddenly became one of the funniest things he had ever seen. He stopped running and started to laugh, louder and louder, clutching his side.

'What's so funny?' Ruby asked, panting from running.

'That.' Joseph pointed to the advert. 'This.' He cast his arm around the deserted streets. 'All of it.'

Ruby started laughing too. 'Look,' she said, pointing to a tailor's shop behind them. The front had been blown out and the suited dummies that had been in the window were now lying spread-eagled on the pavement. She ran over and picked one of them up. 'I say, old chap, would you care for this dance?' She started waltzing the mannequin up the pavement towards Joseph. Just as she reached him, the dummy's head fell off and rolled into the street. 'Oh no, not another casualty.' Ruby put the dummy down and gazed up at Joseph. Her eyes were burning brightly. 'How about you?'

'Me?'

'Would you like to dance?'

'But there's no music.'

'We don't need music.' And with that she took off her helmet and shook out her hair.

Again, Joseph felt a stirring deep within him. Ordinarily he would have told himself not to be so crazy and he would have reminded himself that it was the intensely annoying Ruby standing in front of him. But this was no ordinary night. The bomb that dropped beside them should have killed them. But it didn't. In some bizarre twist of fate, it had failed to detonate. And he'd gone from feeling like his number was up to some kind of strange invincibility.

'Well?' Ruby said, holding out her hands.

'Yes,' he replied. 'I'll dance with you.'

And there, in a deserted Piccadilly Circus, beneath a bright bomber's moon, he took her in his arms and they began to waltz.

CHAPTER TWENTY-SEVEN

October 1940

As Joseph pulled her closer, Ruby felt a very strange sensation sweep through her body, from the hairs on her head to the tips of her toes. It was as if she was no longer solid but now made entirely from vapour. A feathery mist in female form. Perhaps it was the fact that they'd had not one, but two dices with death. Perhaps it was the magical intensity of the moonlight. Perhaps it was the fact that everything had become so fantastical – that here she was, in the middle of the night, in the middle of Piccadilly Circus, in the arms of her arch-nemesis. Maybe they had died after all. But surely if heaven existed, it wouldn't involve dancing for an eternity with Joseph. Wouldn't that be hell? She'd certainly have thought so previously, but now he was holding her, she had to admit that it wasn't quite as unpleasant as she might have supposed. He was surprisingly strong for a start. And the tighter he held her, the more she seemed to dissolve.

She hadn't planned on kissing him in the shop doorway. It was just that she'd been so utterly certain that they were about to die, she wanted her final moment on this earth to have meant something. But what exactly did it mean? If she'd been in a shop doorway with another man, Freddy for instance, she was certain she wouldn't have grabbed him in an embrace. She wondered what Joseph had made of it. At least he'd accepted her invitation to dance, and now he was humming something. She could feel the vibration of his voice move through her, the breeze of his breath upon her ear. And it all felt so wonderful. Because this moment and every moment to come were moments she shouldn't really be experiencing. If that bomb had gone off, they would have been obliterated. What if they'd been saved for a reason? she wondered. She vowed there and then to make sure that this second chance she'd been given would mean something, that from this moment forth, she would dedicate whatever life she had left to making a positive difference.

Joseph stopped humming and they came to a standstill. He was still holding her though and, in spite of the fact that they didn't really get along, she didn't want him to let her go. Perhaps it would be better to address the elephant in the room while she couldn't actually see his face.

'I suppose you're wondering why I kissed you,' she muttered into his chest.

'Oh – uh – yes,' he replied.

'You have to understand that I thought we were about to die.'

'Right.' She felt his body tense slightly and his hold on her loosen.

'Although, having said that, I wouldn't have kissed just anyone I was about to die with. Kitty's husband Reg, for example, I would have preferred to have spat upon him.'

'I feel honoured.' Joseph let her go and took a step back. 'Shall we start heading home?'

Damn, she'd hurt his feelings. But she really couldn't under-stand why. He'd made it perfectly clear over the months she'd known him that he found her downright irritating.

She ran to catch up with him as he started striding off along the street.

'The truth is, you're the only fellow I could imagine wanting to kiss just before being blown to smithereens.'

'Oh yeah?' He looked down at her. 'What about the fellow who bought you flowers?'

'What fellow? What flowers?' Why was he being so strange?

'I saw you with some roses a few weeks ago,' he muttered, walking even faster, as if he wanted to get away from her. 'I assume they were from an admirer.'

'What? Oh no! They weren't for me, they were for Kitty!' Damn those stupid roses. She was starting to think they were cursed.

'Kitty?' Joseph frowned at her.

'Yes. I wanted her to think she had a secret admirer.'

Joseph slowed his pace. 'Why the heck would you want to do that?'

'To cheer her up. Did you know, the poor girl has never had a man buy her flowers before. Ever!'

'Tragic,' Joseph muttered.

'But it all went horribly wrong, so I'd really rather not talk about it.'

'Fine by me.' He picked up his pace again.

All of the joy Ruby had been feeling sucked from her like an ebbing tide, to be replaced by utter indignation. She had not escaped death twice in one night to be treated in this manner. 'Why are you being like this?' she said, coming to a halt.

'Like what?' Joseph stopped and turned.

'So beastly. I just told you that you're the only man I'd want to kiss if I was about to be vaporised by a Nazi bomb. Doesn't that count for anything?' As her words echoed up the empty street, she was struck by how ludicrous they sounded. Even the dialogue in one of Kitty's novels was better crafted. And suddenly, the urge to laugh took hold of her again, but as she let out a chortle, her eyes filled with tears. It was all so exhausting. The more Joseph stared at her, the more she laughed, until she actually snorted like a pig. 'Stop staring at me, you're making me worse.'

'Why are you laughing?' he asked, taking a step towards her. Thankfully, his voice was softer.

'I don't know.' The tears that had been threatening came spilling down her face. 'We almost died,' she gasped. 'Twice. We almost died.'

'I know.' And now he was standing right in front of her again. 'I know.' He put his hands on her shoulders.

'I didn't mean to offend you. I know you think I'm deplorable and silly and vain but—'

'I don't think you're deplorable,' he cut in.

She looked up and saw him grinning through her tears. 'Thank you. Well, I know you think I'm silly and vain, but I just want you to know that I really don't dislike you nearly as much as I did. I don't even hold the fact that you're a conchie against you. Now I've seen you at work, in the ambulance and at the Hungerford Club, I can see that you're a really good person and you're not a coward at all. In fact, I would go so far as to say that—' But before she could say any more, his hands were cupping her face and he was staring into her eyes.

'Can you please, please shut up for a second?'

'Oh – I—'

He tilted her face to his and leaned forward and kissed her lips. Then his strong arms wrapped round her and he pulled her in tighter and their mouths began exploring each other with such an intense hunger she thought she might collapse if he hadn't been holding her. He moved one of his hands to her hair, clutching a handful of it, moaning softly, and even though she was a woman of the world and had kissed more than her fair share of men, nothing had ever felt like this. The way their tongues danced together, the way their lips fit together. All she knew was that she never wanted it to end.

Finally, they came up for air.

'Well I never!' she exclaimed.

'What?' he said. He looked different somehow, lighter, brighter, as if their kiss had been some magical, youth-giving elixir.

She was about to launch into an impassioned speech about how she'd never have guessed that a man like him would kiss with such intensity, but she bit her lip. 'I've come to the realisation that whenever I say something to you, it always seems to be the wrong thing,' she finally said.

He laughed. 'Very well deduced, Sherlock.'

'So perhaps it would be better if I refrained from commenting on our kiss. And perhaps it would be better if you just did it again.'

'Oh really?' He grinned.

'Yes.'

'I don't think you're silly and vain,' he murmured as he wiped her tears from her face. 'Not any more.' And he kissed her again.

By the time they'd walked all the way back to the ambulance station and told Bill what had happened, Ruby felt light-headed with tiredness. She also felt strangely bereft at the thought of having to part company with Joseph. As they walked back home to Pendragon Square, she felt more down-hearted at the prospect with every step.

'You've gone very quiet,' he said as they went up the front steps.

'I thought you preferred me like that,' she quipped.

'Hmm, so did I, but it's quite unnerving.' He took his keys from his pocket, then stopped. 'It's been a very strange night all right.'

'Yes,' she agreed. *Please, please tell me that you don't want it to end either.*

'With some very strange happenings,' he added.

Again she nodded and held her breath.

'I'm glad that…' He broke off at the sound of someone hurrying past them in the dark and unlocked the door.

'Glad that what?' she asked, following him into the hallway.

'That we didn't die,' he said with a smile.

They stood there for a moment in a silence that swiftly moved from companionable to awkward.

'Well, I suppose we should get our beauty sleep,' she said gaily, pulling her key from her bag. Damn, why had she said that? Why hadn't she waited for him to speak?

'Yes, absolutely.' He stepped towards the lift. 'Goodnight then.'

'Goodnight.' A crushing sorrow fell upon her. Somehow she managed to get her key in the lock and she slipped inside, closing the door behind her and sliding down to the floor. Clearly they'd both been under some kind of spell earlier, cast by the shock of the bombing. But now they were back to cold reality and it felt so lonely.

She began crying freely. It had felt so nice to be held, to be kissed like she'd never been kissed. The thought of going back to their old awkward prickly dance was too dreadful to contemplate. Ruby waited for the sound of the lift, but it remained silent. He must have taken the stairs instead. She thought of Joseph going up to his own cold, empty flat. Of them both lying there in the dark, so close and yet so far apart, and she couldn't physically bear it. Just as when they'd kissed earlier, she felt a force take hold of her body, a need so strong she couldn't control it. She would go upstairs and knock on his door and she would pray that he was feeling the same as her and he'd pull her into his flat and into his arms and—

There was a knock on her door, so gentle she thought she'd imagined it at first. But then it came again, a little louder.

She wiped the tears from her face and smoothed down her hair and she opened the door. Joseph was standing there.

'I don't want to leave you,' he whispered.

She grabbed his hand and pulled him in.

CHAPTER TWENTY-EIGHT

September 2019

'Edi. Edi. I brought you some breakfast.'

The dream I'd been having morphs like a kaleidoscope being turned, and one of the darkened figures that had been dancing beneath a huge, blood-red moon looks over their shoulder and stares at me.

'Edi,' the voice says again. 'I've brought you some breakfast.'

The dreamscape fades to darkness.

'Edi.'

I open my eyes and my vision blurs. A figure wearing black looms over me and I instinctively put up my hands to protect myself.

'I didn't mean to startle you. I thought you might be hungry,' the voice says. *Pearl* says.

My mind floods with anxious thoughts. Pearl is in my bedroom. The book. The loft. The shirt.

I blink and my vision clears. She's standing right by the bed, but she's looking up at the loft hatch. Shit! I scramble into a seated position.

'Ow!' Pain shoots through my leg.

'I've toasted you some crumpets,' Pearl says, looking back at me.

'Thank you.'

'And made some coffee.'

I see a tray on my bedside table containing a plate of crumpets, a jar of jam and a cafetière. How did she get in without me hearing? I shouldn't have taken so many painkillers; they must have knocked me out for the count.

'I was just wondering,' Pearl says, her bright blue eyes darting this way and that around the room.

'Yes?'

'About the shirt you found.'

'Yes?' My mouth goes dry.

'You said you thought it might be from the war.'

I nod.

'And that it might have blood on it?'

She *does* know something about it. I pull the duvet up higher around me.

'What makes you think that it's blood?' She asks the question with a casual tone, but there's nothing casual about the way she's staring at me.

I stay silent for a moment, trying to gather my thoughts. I fell asleep midway through reading Pearl's book, but I know there was something I read that made me more convinced that Pearl's connected to the shirt, but what was it? Shit! I glance around the bed, but there's no sign of the novel. Hopefully it's under the duvet.

'There's a hole in the shirt, in the middle of the stain, as if whoever was wearing it was stabbed – or shot.' I watch her face.

She visibly gulps. 'Are you sure it—'

But before she can say any more, there's a loud knock on my front door.

'Morning, sweetheart, are you decent?' Heath calls.

I breathe a sigh of relief.

'Yes, through here,' I call back.

He comes in holding a tray. As soon as he sees Pearl and the breakfast already beside the bed, he roars with laughter. 'Pearl! I told you I was doing the breakfast shift. Ah, well, at least you won't be going hungry, Edi.' He plonks his tray down on the end of the bed. 'How's the ankle, sweetheart?'

'Not quite as sore as yesterday, but that could be because I've doped myself up to the eyeballs on the pain meds.'

He laughs, then claps his hands together. 'Right, I'd better get off to the salon. Got a reality TV star and a minor royal coming in today.'

'Good luck.' I clear my throat. 'Actually, I'd better call my deputy ed at the magazine.' I give Pearl a pointed stare. There's no way I want to be left on my own with her. I need copious amounts of coffee to try to figure out how she and the shirt are in some way connected. And then I remember what I read before crashing out – Joseph had hidden his tin beneath a floorboard in his loft right by the hatch. An identical hiding place to the shirt!

'Come on, sweetheart, let's leave her in peace.' To my huge relief, Heath starts steering Pearl towards the door.

'But I…' she stammers.

'I'll see you later,' I say firmly.

I wait for the sound of the lift going down, then I fumble onto my crutches and hobble to the front door, glancing into the other rooms as I go, just to make sure Pearl has really left. I double-lock the door and breathe a sigh of relief. Then I hop back into the bedroom and see a sight that makes my heart practically stop beating. Pearl's book is lying on the floor beside the bed. I must have dropped it when I fell asleep. It's right next to the bedside cabinet where she left my breakfast. There's no way she wouldn't have seen it.

I collapse down onto the bed, my face burning with embarrassment, and try to make sense of things. On paper at least, Pearl has done nothing wrong. She came to bring me breakfast. She asked a few simple questions about the shirt, questions anyone might have asked, but I still can't shake a growing sense of unease. Why did she seem so rattled? How did I not hear her come in? Surely she would have knocked on the door, like she did the day before. And surely that would have woken me.

My skin prickles with goosebumps. Did she creep in unannounced? Was she looking for the shirt? Why didn't she tell me she'd seen her book on my floor? And if she knows I'm reading the book and it is somehow linked to the shirt, she'll know that I'm on to her. I take a deep breath and try to rein in my fear. Pearl isn't out to get me; she's just being a concerned neighbour. But one thing's for certain, I have to finish her novel.

CHAPTER TWENTY-NINE

October 1940

Joseph woke to the sound of rain tapping against the windowpane and a tickling feeling on his chin. He blearily opened one eye.

'Oh thank goodness!' Ruby exclaimed.

Ruby!

He opened the other eye, thinking for a moment that he had to be dreaming. But no, there she was, lying in his arms, her hair tickling his jawline.

'I was starting to think you were never going to wake,' she continued. 'I was starting to think that I was doomed to lie here motionless forever, for fear of waking you, unable to breathe, unable to speak…'

'Now that would be a tragedy,' Joseph muttered with a grin.

She gave him a playful nudge. 'It's all right, you don't have to pretend any more.'

'Pretend what?'

'That you don't have feelings for me, of course. It all makes sense now.' She leaned out of the bed and took a pack of cigarettes from the nightstand.

'It does?' He shifted up onto his elbow. This he had to hear.

As she lit her cigarette, the flare from the match illuminated the room and he glimpsed what looked worryingly like a deer's head on the wall.

'Is that a deer?' he muttered, rubbing his eyes.

'Did you just call me dear? How lovely!' Before putting the match out, she used it to light a candle by the bed.

'No, I was asking if that was a deer?' He nodded at the head on the wall.

'That's Al Jolson,' she replied nonchalantly, as if having a deer's head named after a singer nailed to your bedroom wall was a totally run-of-the-mill thing. 'He's a family heirloom, shot by my mother's father on the grounds of Balmoral. Anyway, as I was saying, it all makes perfect sense now.'

'What does?' Perhaps he was dreaming after all.

'This. Us.' As she sat up straighter, he saw that she was completely naked and memories from the night before came rushing back to him. The softness of her mouth, the silkiness of her skin, the tangle of their limbs, and once again he was filled with the strangest, sweetest tingling feeling. 'What I thought was mutual dislike was actually animal magnetism.' She turned to him and laughed, the waves of her dark hair cascading around her face. 'Isn't it just the most delightful surprise?'

'Hmm.' He began tracing his finger along the curve of her spine. 'It's a shock all right.'

'It's just like one of Kitty's novels, but with the bonus of having a heroine who actually has her wits about her and a hero who subverts all of the rules of romantic fiction.'

'What are you talking about?' he chuckled.

'You! Mills & Boon would never have a conscientious objector as a hero. You would have to be a soldier.'

Joseph frowned. 'Right.'

'But this is so much better.' She leaned into him and offered him the cigarette. 'Smoke?'

He took it from her and inhaled deeply. Had he made a huge mistake? Was this, whatever *this* was, a terrible error of judgement?

They'd both been nervous wrecks last night. They'd both had a brush with death. They probably hadn't been thinking straight.

Ruby leaned across and took a framed photo from her nightstand. 'This is my papa,' she said, showing him the picture. 'And that's me, on his knee.'

'It's a great snap,' Joseph said, and it was. The look of love between Ruby and her father was palpable. 'Nice to see his head on his body too,' he added, almost instantly regretting it. He'd been referring to the waxwork, but hadn't Ruby said he'd suffered from a fatal head injury in the Great War? He hoped he hadn't upset her. To his relief, she burst out laughing.

'Your face that day was a picture. I can't believe you thought I'd got his actual head in my bag.'

'Yeah, well, it's not everyone who has a waxwork dummy of their dad.'

'I had to put it in the oven,' Ruby said, snuggling back into him.

'What? Why?'

'Out of sight, out of mind.'

'I see,' said Joseph, although he didn't really see at all.

'It was too distressing.'

'But don't you see it every time you want to cook something?'

'Oh, I never cook. I made a pledge long ago to not waste a second of my life doing anything that makes my soul weep. I don't sew either. The government are going to have a hard time getting me to make do and mend.' She turned slightly and gazed up at him. 'So when did you realise that you had such intense feelings towards me?'

Joseph squirmed. 'Oh – I – uh—'

'I think I felt the first stirrings when you threw yourself on top of me in the ambulance.'

'I didn't throw myself on top of—'

'And then, when I felt certain we were about to perish beneath a German bomb, and you kissed me.'

'Er, I think you'll find that you kissed me.'

'Tomayto, tomahto,' Ruby replied with a shrug.

There was a blissful moment's silence, filled only by the pitter-patter of rain on the window.

'I really like you,' she said, so quietly he barely heard. 'And I never really like men.'

'What do you mean, you never really like men?'

'They all seem so tedious and full of themselves. But not you, and it's ironic really because you, of anyone, should have a reason to be proud.'

He swallowed hard. 'Why's that?'

She looked up at him and he saw that her eyes were glassy with tears. 'Because you have a good heart, just like my dear papa did. You genuinely care about other people.'

Joseph gulped. It had been so long since someone had said anything nice about him, since someone had shown him affection and respect rather than scorn, he wasn't sure what to do with it.

'If you're struggling to find the words to express your appreciation for me you could always show me with one of your kisses,' Ruby suggested.

He let out a laugh and pulled her close. 'Is that so?'

'Yes. In fact, I'd be quite happy if you expressed yourself in kisses forever and an eternity.'

He leaned down and planted a kiss on her lips.

*

'What do you mean, you spent the night with Joseph?' Kitty stared across the kitchen table at Ruby, her eyes saucer-wide.

'Exactly that.' Ruby leaned back in her chair and gave a contented sigh. 'It really was the strangest thing. I mean to say, normally when I make love with a man it's been the climax of an intense attraction, not an intense loathing.'

'You and Joseph made love?' Kitty's jaw almost hit the floor.

'Oh yes, and it was so wonderful. He was so strong yet gentle and passionate yet…' She broke off. 'Good grief, I'm sounding just like one of your novels.' She looked at Kitty earnestly. 'But he really was all of those things.'

'Well I never.' Kitty shook her head in disbelief.

'But enough about me and my night of passion; how was your lunch with Freddy?'

Kitty's face instantly flushed.

'Did something happen? Did you make love too? Oh, Kitty, I think there was magic in the air last night. Maybe it was that incredible moon. I've always believed that the moon—'

'No, we did not!' Kitty interrupted.

'Oh.' Ruby sighed. It would have been so wonderful if Kitty had experienced just some of what she had last night.

'But he did – he did…' Kitty looked down into her lap.

'He did what?' Ruby stared at her. 'Don't keep me on tenter-hooks!'

'He told me that he had feelings for me.' Kitty continued staring into her lap, her face now ablaze.

'What kind of feelings?' Ruby practically shrieked. Honestly, it was like getting blood from a stone!

'Romantic feelings.'

'Oh Kitty, this is the most wonderful news.'

'Is it?' Kitty finally looked at her. 'I'm still married to Reg.'

'Only on paper,' Ruby replied. 'Unless… You don't still have feelings for him, do you?'

'Of course not!' Kitty exclaimed.

Ruby refilled their cups from the teapot. 'And how do you feel about Freddy?'

Kitty was silent for a moment and Ruby wondered whether she ought to change the subject, the poor girl looked so tormented. But then Kitty looked up and Ruby saw that her eyes were shiny with tears. 'I really like him,' she whispered. 'He makes me feel – he makes me feel as if I'm worth something.'

'Of course you're worth something!' Ruby got up and came round to Kitty's side of the table. 'You're good and kind and patient and calm. In fact, I would go so far as to say that you are one of the most decent people I've ever met.'

Kitty stared at her in shock. 'Really?'

'Absolutely. And you deserve to be loved by someone just as good as you – someone just like Freddy.'

Kitty began to smile. 'He is such a nice man.'

'He is indeed.' Ruby sat in the chair next to Kitty. 'So, what was your response when he told you of his feelings?'

'I told him I needed time to think about things.'

'You didn't tell him that you had feelings for him too?' Ruby asked, dismayed.

Kitty shook her head. 'I'm married. And before you say on paper only, it's not strictly true. My husband still exists.'

More's the pity, thought Ruby.

'And at some point he's going to come home on leave again,' Kitty continued. 'He's going to go crazy when he finds out the locks have been changed. I'm frightened of what he might do.'

'To you?' Ruby asked, her heart sinking as she thought of the awful sounds she'd heard when Reg had been home on leave.

'No, to Freddy,' Kitty replied. 'I think I should wait until I'm able to sort things out with Reg, once the war's over.'

'But who knows when that might be?' Ruby exclaimed. She thought of how she'd felt after her brush with death the night before, and the intensity with which she'd wanted to soak up every moment of life she could get. 'And who knows if we'll make it to the end of the war?'

'Don't say that,' said Kitty, looking alarmed.

'But that doesn't have to be a bad thing,' Ruby replied. 'In fact, if we choose to, we can make it a very good thing.'

'How?'

'The fact that we could die at any moment should be the greatest incentive to live our lives fully.' Ruby stood up, aware that the monologue she was about to deliver would be made all the more powerful with some dramatic pacing. She started walking around the table, her hands clasped in front of her. 'Last night, a bomb dropped right by where Joseph and I were sheltering in a shop doorway.'

Kitty gasped. 'But how…?'

'How are we still alive?'

Kitty nodded.

'It failed to detonate. But for a few moments I truly believed I was a goner, and do you know what, for the first time in my life I saw things completely clearly.'

'What do you mean?'

Ruby paced back towards Kitty. 'I mean that, when faced with death, all I wanted to do was kiss Joseph.'

'I'm not sure that—'

'What I'm trying to say, dear Kitty, is that I never felt more alive than I did in that moment. And as soon as I realised that my number wasn't up after all, I felt this fierce desire to live every moment to its fullest. To dance beneath the moon. To kiss Joseph. To make love to Joseph. We're alive for a reason, Kitty.' Ruby crouched down beside her. 'You and I and everybody. We're here for a reason and yet we waste so much of our existence putting things off until tomorrow. But what if there isn't a tomorrow?'

Kitty frowned.

'What if, God forbid, you or Freddy perish today? What if one of the bombs that falls from the sky has your name upon it? Would you really want to spend your last day on earth telling the man you love to wait? Would you really rather waste your last precious moments thinking rather than doing?' Ruby stood up again and took a breath. 'Or would you rather spend it following your heart?' She glanced down at Kitty. As far as she was concerned, her speech had been quite Churchillian in terms of its rousing passion, but would it have had the desired effect?

Kitty started to nod. 'I'd rather follow my heart,' she murmured.

'Atta girl!' Ruby jumped up. 'Well, what are you waiting for? Go and follow your heart to the butcher's shop!'

Her own heart burst with joy as Kitty got to her feet and headed to the door.

CHAPTER THIRTY

November 1940

As Joseph made his way past a huge bomb crater in the corner of Trafalgar Square, the dread in the pit of his stomach grew. He really didn't know why he'd agreed to come here with Ruby. Perhaps it was something to do with the fact that she'd been naked when she'd invited him. Naked, and sitting at the end of his bed, her hair wild and tousled and her eyes sparkling in the candlelight. She'd made it sound pretty enticing too, in that way she had with words, that part baffled and part entranced him. 'You must come with me to one of the lunchtime recitals at the National Gallery,' she'd said. 'It will set your spirit free and remind you of all that is true and beautiful.' And then she'd kissed him and the rest, as they say, was history.

'Aren't you excited?' Ruby asked him now with all the exuberance of a child on Christmas Eve.

'I'm not sure,' Joseph muttered. He looked across the square, past the statues of the majestic lions surrounded by sandbags and the morale-boosting posters stuck to the base of Nelson's Column, to the dome of the National Gallery. A long queue was snaking out from the stone pillars at the entrance and down the steps. A long queue of the type of people who went to 'recitals' at lunchtime: posh folk, no doubt, who had nothing in common with him.

'What do you mean, you're not sure?' Ruby looked at him indignantly.

'I don't really know if it's my cup of tea.'

Ruby stopped walking and put her hands on her hips. 'How can beautiful music not be your cup of tea? Oh no, please tell me you're not a philistine?' She clapped her gloved hand to her mouth in horror. 'I should have known it was too good to be true. I should have known we were doomed. I—'

'I'm not a philistine!' Joseph interrupted before she could go any further. In the month that had passed since they'd become intimate, Ruby fearing they were doomed had happened on a regular basis. It was almost as if she was looking for a reason to end their relationship – if indeed it could be called a relation-ship; they'd never officially defined it. There'd been the time he confessed to liking jellied eels, and the time he told her he'd never heard of Josephine Baker or Barker or something like that, and she'd practically expired when he'd told her he'd never left the country. It wasn't as if he hadn't experienced some doubts of his own either. But somehow as soon as they kissed, the fact that they were 'doomed' seemed to fade into insignificance. 'I'll have you know I'm a great fan of music,' he continued, taking her hands in his. 'Just not this type of music.'

Ruby pursed her lips and looked at him thoughtfully. 'You poor, poor boy,' she said finally. 'I'm starting to realise why we were destined to meet.'

'Oh yeah, why's that then?' Joseph braced himself.

'Clearly, I was brought into your life to expand your horizons.'

'Is that so?'

'Yes.' She smiled up at him. 'And it will be my absolute pleasure.'

Bloody cheek! But before he could respond, she was planting a kiss on his lips.

'Now come along, we don't want to miss our chance of getting in. They can only admit about four hundred people now that they've had to move the concerts down to the basement.'

'Only four hundred?' Joseph said wryly. Clearly London's toffs had way too much time on their hands.

He instinctively prickled as he thought of the folk he was helping at the Hungerford Club. While they were sleeping rough on the streets in the growing cold of winter, just a few hundred yards away, the upper classes were gadding about going to concerts. But as they joined the queue outside the gallery, he saw, to his surprise, that the audience was very different to what he'd imagined. Yes, there were a few women dripping in jewellery and draped in furs, but the vast majority of people looked as ordinary as him. Some appeared to be office workers on their lunch breaks and there were a handful of off-duty wardens in their uniforms and a lot of retired folk. Joseph relaxed slightly.

'Isn't it wonderful?' Ruby gushed, looking at all the people. 'Wasn't Myra Hess a genius for coming up with such an inspired idea?'

'Who's Myra Hess?' Joseph asked, aware that such a question could very well prompt another 'we're doomed' speech from Ruby but deciding that honesty was probably the best policy. 'Her name does sound familiar,' he quickly added.

'Well, of course it does!' Ruby exclaimed. 'She's one of the greatest pianists who ever lived. It was her idea to have these lunchtime concerts when the war started. She thought it was vital for the spiritual well-being of us Londoners – a way of sticking it to Hitler and showing him that we wouldn't be beaten.'

For the sake of keeping the peace, Joseph nodded, but he couldn't exactly see Hitler quaking in his boots at the thought of a few Londoners listening to a spot of piano music on their lunch breaks. Ruby had that faraway look on her face now, the one that told him there was another monologue incoming.

'I came to the concert here on New Year's Day,' she said, linking her arm through his. 'It was just wonderful. Nine different pianists played musical chairs while they performed Schumann's "Carnaval". And some of the musicians played tiny toy instruments during Haydn's "Toy Symphony", and Myra Hess even appeared as a cuckoo!'

Joseph feigned what he hoped was an expression of delight, in spite of the fact that everything she'd just said sounded like double Dutch to him.

Ruby's smile faded. 'It was such a hopeful start to the year. I came skipping down these steps truly believing that we'd have beaten Hitler by the summer.'

Joseph pulled her closer and planted a kiss on top of her head.

'But then, if we had beaten him and the blitzkrieg hadn't started, I wouldn't have experienced my grand passion,' she continued.

'Your grand passion?'

'Yes. You.'

'Oh.' Joseph's cheeks warmed. He'd never been called anyone's grand passion before.

'I expect that you've never been anyone's grand passion before,' Ruby said, as if reading his mind.

'What makes you say that?' he retorted, feigning indignation. 'I'll have you know, I'm regularly referred to as a grand passion – at the baker's, down the pub, when I'm trying to buy a ticket at the station. It's getting a little tiring to be honest.'

'Oh you!' Ruby exclaimed, poking him in the ribs. She gazed up at him. 'It's all right, you don't have to say that I'm your grand passion too if you don't want to.'

Joseph breathed a sigh of relief. He really wasn't cut out for that kind of soppy talk.

'I can tell that I am anyway.' She grinned. 'Now I understand what you meant that time on the train when we were on our way to that travesty of a driving test.'

'What did I say?'

'That there are many different ways of knowing something. You were talking about God, but I think the same thing applies to us. I just know that I'm your grand passion without you needing to tell me. Is that what you meant about God too – that you just know that God exists because you feel it – in here?' She put her hand to her heart.

Yet again, Joseph felt completely and utterly baffled by her torrent of words, but he couldn't help feeling flattered that she'd actually been listening to what he'd said that day on the train. 'Yes, I suppose it is,' he replied.

'I knew it!' she cried, flinging her arms around him.

*

Ruby led Joseph into the gallery, her heart racing from a cocktail of nerves and excitement. She really hoped Joseph was going to enjoy the concert. He'd seemed so reluctant for a moment, out there in the square, and she'd worried she'd made a terrible mistake by inviting him. But if they were each other's grand passions, then surely they should feel some kind of affinity with each other's favourite pastimes. Yes, she nodded to herself, once the music started, he would have no choice but to feel moved by it.

'Why are all the frames empty?' Joseph asked, as they made their way through the first exhibition room.

'The paintings were all sent into hiding at the beginning of the war,' Ruby replied. 'It was terribly exciting.' She lowered her voice to a whisper. 'Apparently they're in Wales. I'm not sure why they chose Wales to be honest. Maybe they assumed the Germans wouldn't think there was anything worth bombing there. Clearly they haven't heard a Welsh male voice choir singing "Myfanwy", as day breaks over a pit village.'

Joseph made a spluttering sound.

'Are you all right?' Ruby asked.

He nodded, his face flushed, his coughing fit thankfully over before it had even begun.

Ruby glanced around the room at the empty frames. The first time she'd seen them hanging there, it had felt like a literal portrayal of the emptiness she felt inside at the thought of the war. But that was before the Blitz had begun. Now she felt nothing but relief that Hitler wouldn't be able to destroy the paintings. Now the emptiness of the frames felt like an act of defiance rather than defeat.

'Isn't life so wonderfully bizarre?' Ruby murmured.

'Oh, it's that all right,' Joseph agreed.

They followed the crowd down a flight of steps into the basement of the gallery. Ruby felt a wistful pang as she thought of the gallery in Room 36, where the lunchtime recitals had originally taken place. With its octagonal shape and glass domed ceiling, it really had been the perfect setting, and so much more comfortable than the draughty basement. But beggars couldn't be choosers, Ruby consoled herself, and at least the recitals were continuing.

By the time they reached the room, all the seats were taken, but Ruby didn't mind. She liked the fact that they were allowed to sit on the floor. It all just added to the informal atmosphere. She led Joseph over to the corner by the slightly raised platform where the musicians' chairs and music stands were all waiting, full of promise.

'Are we allowed to sit here?' Joseph asked as she sat down on the floor.

'Of course. Anything goes at these recitals.' Ruby pulled a brown paper package from her bag. 'Can I interest you in a corned beef sandwich?'

'Are we allowed to eat too?' Joseph's eyes widened.

'Of course. It's a *lunch*time recital.'

'I know but I thought…'

'What?'

He gave a sheepish grin. 'I thought it would be a lot snootier.'

'Aha! Is that why you came over all doubtful outside.'

'I wasn't being doubtful; I—'

'It's all right. I understand.'

'You do?'

'You were worried that it would be all la-di-da and prim and proper and no place for a gritty man of the people from oop north like you.' She laughed.

'Well, I wouldn't have put it in exactly those words, but yes.' Joseph looked around the crowded room and, to Ruby's relief, he started to smile.

'That's what I love the most about it,' Ruby said dreamily. 'I know you think the war hasn't been fair and that the working classes have been badly done by, but it hasn't been all bad. Thanks to Myra Hess, we've all been free to enjoy wonderful music for just a shilling every day.'

Joseph nodded.

A woman came into the room holding a clarinet and took a seat on the platform.

'Shhh!' Ruby said to Joseph.

'I didn't say anything!'

'Shhh!' she said again.

The rest of the room fell silent. Myra Hess herself had only played at a few of the concerts; Ruby wished with all of her heart that today would be one of those days. If Joseph experienced the beauty of her playing, then surely any reservations he had about classical music would instantly disappear.

One by one, the musicians filed in and took their seats, but none of them sat at the piano. Ruby held her breath and then, finally, the miracle happened; she spied that familiar dark hair pulled into a loose bun, the white silk blouse, the black velvet jacket and floor-length skirt.

'It's her!' Ruby gasped. 'It's Myra!'

As the crowd began to cheer, Joseph gave an indifferent shrug. *Just you wait until you hear her play*, Ruby thought to herself.

'Good day, everyone,' Myra said, standing by the piano stool. 'Thank you all so much for coming.' She smiled. 'Do you know, when I did the first of these recitals here, last year, I truly thought only about forty people would come – and that they would all be my friends and family,' she added with a laugh. 'But one thousand people turned up that first day and hundreds of you have kept coming ever since, in spite of the bombing. It is such an honour for us to be able to play for you in these circumstances. Now, more than ever, we need the power of music to heal and uplift.' The other musicians nodded. 'So, without further ado…' She sat down at the huge Steinway, her back ruler-straight, hands poised above the keys, eyes closed, as if summoning the spirit of music to come through her, Ruby thought to herself – although, unlike Ruby's séances, Myra really did appear to be channelling something. Then she started to play.

As the opening notes of Bach's 'Jesu, Joy of Man's Desiring' echoed around the room, it was as if all of Ruby's dreams had come true. Hess was famous for her arrangement of the piece, and it couldn't have been a better introduction to her music for Joseph. Ruby snuck a sideways glance at him. He was staring at Hess, his face completely expressionless. Ruby really hoped he was enjoying it. Ever since they'd spent that first night together, she'd fluctuated between feelings of utter bliss and abject terror when it came to Joseph, pulling at her like opposing tides. She'd never felt anything like it before. She'd never felt anything so intensely before. She'd always managed to keep her life and emotions on an even keel and it was most disconcerting.

The music drew to a close and the audience began clapping wildly, including Joseph, Ruby noted with a smile. Then Myra Hess began playing a new piece, and in an instant it was as if her body had been turned to ice. It was 'The Lord's My Shepherd', her papa's favourite hymn. Ever since it had been played at his memorial service, Ruby had spent her life trying to avoid it. But now she was trapped in the corner of the basement, memories she'd tried for so long to suppress began bombarding her. The smell of incense in the cold, damp church. Her mother weeping behind a black veil. The pews crowded with people who purportedly loved her father. But so many of them were strangers – fans rather than family. The gnarled hands of the old woman who'd clutched Ruby and told her, 'He's in a better place now.' But he wasn't. Her father was in the worst place imaginable. It was as if the hymn had become imprinted with the sorrow of that day, Ruby's heartbreak woven into every note. And now it was bringing with it an image she'd tried so hard to suppress, her father's shattered carcass, buried in a mass grave in a cold field miles and miles from home.

Then a terrible thought occurred to her. What if she were to lose Joseph too? Every day bombs were raining down upon them. What if she found herself at another memorial service, trying to erase the horrific image of his shattered remains from her mind? What if she had to somehow carry on without him, just as she'd had to somehow carry on without her papa?

She closed her eyes and focused on her breathing. *Onomatopoeia… higgledy-piggledy…* but the hymn kept drowning it out and, for once, her father's mantra failed to soothe her. For her entire adult life, she'd managed to avoid feeling like this, falling in love like this, so that she'd never have to experience the kind of loss she felt when her papa had died. But now, here she was, risking it all again – and during a war to boot, when the risk of loss was at its highest. What had she been thinking? Her throat tightened.

She opened her eyes and looked at the half-eaten corned beef sandwich on her lap. It made her stomach churn. Why had she told Joseph he was her grand passion? What was wrong with her?

After what seemed like an eternity, the musicians began playing another piece of music – thankfully the more upbeat

Mozart's 'Sonata Number 17'. Joseph was tapping his hand on his leg in time, but it was too late, the damage had been done. As he looked at her and smiled, she felt something iron-like slide into place around her heart. She couldn't let this continue. She had to protect herself. She had to end their relationship.

CHAPTER THIRTY-ONE

November 1940

As Joseph strode out into the crisp November afternoon, he felt like a man reborn, which he immediately realised was a very melodramatic Ruby way of putting things, but still. Sitting on the floor in that cold draughty basement eating corned beef sandwiches and listening to wave after wave of sounds so beautiful they swept all the tension from his body had been a transformative experience. And it hadn't just altered his physical state; his mind felt lifted too. There was something so wonderful about the random selection of people who had gathered there, in the face of so much horror, to remind themselves that beauty still existed.

He turned to Ruby and grabbed her hand.

'That was bloody magic!' He grinned at her and waited for a monologue on the wonders of music, but to his surprise her expression remained blank.

'Glad you enjoyed it,' she replied coolly. Her hand felt limp in his, so he instinctively let it go. Perhaps she'd been so moved by the experience it had left her stunned. He wouldn't put it past her.

'Are you hungry? Do you fancy getting a bite to eat?' For once they had the night off and he was keen to make the most of it.

'Actually, I'm meeting a friend,' she replied, gazing across Trafalgar Square.

'What, now?' Why hadn't she mentioned this before? A memory from that morning came back to him, of Ruby lying in his arms and murmuring, 'I'm so glad I've got you all to myself for an entire day and night.' They'd joked that having twenty-four hours off felt like a holiday. 'I thought we were spending the whole day together,' he said, as she started walking off.

'Don't we already spend enough time together?' she retorted, keeping her gaze fixed straight ahead.

'Hey, hold up.' He grabbed her arm and she came to a halt, but she still wouldn't look at him. 'Have I done something to upset you?'

'No!' she exclaimed, then cleared her throat. 'Of course not,' she added softly. 'I just thought I ought to make the most of the time off and catch up with an old friend.'

'I see.' Joseph's body tensed. He might not be as sophisticated and worldly-wise as Ruby and her society friends, but he knew when he was being brushed off. 'Will I see you later?'

She shook her head. 'I doubt it. I'm going to the Savoy, so it's bound to be a late night.'

'Right.' Anger smarted inside of him. He had no idea what could have caused Ruby to go from declaring him her grand passion to snubbing him so coldly in the space of a lunchtime, but he knew for sure that he didn't want to prolong the pain. 'Have a great time then, with your friend.' And then a terrible thought occurred to him. What if this 'friend' was another man? What if it was the same fellow she'd been going to meet that first night of the Blitz? The one she'd spent the night with in the Savoy? He felt sick. What a prize fool he'd been.

'You have a lovely night too,' Ruby called, but he'd already started marching across the square in the direction of Charing Cross. He'd spend the rest of the day helping out at the Hungerford Club. He needed to be around decent folk who didn't tie his feelings in knots.

*

As Ruby watched Joseph leave, she felt the strangest sensation. *Go after him! Tell him you didn't mean it!* her mind was pleading, but she'd become rooted to the spot, like Nelson's Column, and her body just wouldn't move. As Joseph crossed the road and disappeared behind a double-decker bus, a feeling of loss hit her like a punch to the stomach. *But better to lose him now, than later,* a voice said in her head. *Better to lose him while he's still alive.*

As if on cue, the air-raid siren began to wail. People began hurrying to the shelters, but Ruby walked away, in the direction of Leicester Square. She no longer cared about the stupid war and the stupid German bombs. *Do your worst!* she wanted to yell to the sky. *I no longer care!*

As the streets cleared of people, she started to relax slightly. The bombers would be arriving soon, no doubt, but for now there was space to breathe. She walked through Leicester Square, past the nightclubs and the picture houses and the hot potato stand. Oh, the fun she'd had in that square before the war, giggling with girlfriends or on the arm of a beau. But none of those men had made her feel the way Joseph did, she thought wistfully. *Yes, and you were so much better off for it,* another voice soothed. *At least you had nothing to fear.*

She walked up into Soho, another of her favourite haunts from her life before, crammed full of memories. In spite of the air-raid siren, a few hopeful prostitutes were still standing in the doorways, clad in their figure-hugging dresses and bare legs regardless of the cold. And why not? Ruby thought to herself. Surely it would be better to die in the arms of another – even if it was a stranger – than be buried alive alone in a shelter?

An image from that morning flashed into her mind, of her lying in Joseph's arms, feeling like the happiest woman on earth. She cringed as she remembered telling him how lucky she felt having twenty-four hours off with him. What must he think of her now? He must think her the most callous woman to have ever existed.

A piercing whistle rang up the street. She turned to see an ARP warden waving at her. 'You need to take shelter, madam,' he barked. 'There'll be a raid any minute.'

Ruby ignored him and kept walking. She wondered where Joseph was. She hoped he was taking shelter.

I didn't mean it, she said to him in her mind, like some kind of telepathic Morse code. *I didn't mean to hurt you.*

*

As Joseph returned to Pendragon Square, his body felt leaden with exhaustion, which was certainly not how he'd been expecting or hoping to feel on his one precious day off. But then nothing had gone as planned on this nightmarish day. For about the thousandth time, an image of Ruby popped into his mind, and for about the thousandth time, he pushed it away. Why should he wonder or worry about where she was or how she was doing? Being concerned only made him feel like more of a fool. Going to the Hungerford Club had helped, as it had forced him to focus on others who were a lot less fortunate than him. But on the long walk home, his worst fears had had free rein, tormenting him with images of Ruby sheltering in the Savoy, in the arms, and even the bed, of another, with maids bringing them tea on demand in silver pots. All the luxuries he could never give her. He'd been such a fool to have thought that she might be genuinely interested in him. Clearly she'd seen him as just another game for her to play, a toy to pick up and discard at will.

Joseph walked past the church and into the square. It was five in the morning and the all-clear had sounded over an hour ago, so the garden was steeped in silence and darkness, the ground underfoot crunchy with brittle fallen leaves. He took a moment to drink in the peace and quiet, then ran up the steps and into the house.

He glanced at Ruby's door, the door that had become as familiar as his own in recent weeks. But now he'd probably never go through it again. He stood there for a moment, remembering how he'd felt during the recital, what seemed like another lifetime ago. The certain sudden knowing that in spite of all the terrible things that mankind had done, people were essentially good, and life was essentially beautiful. What had happened to Ruby to make her feel so differently, to turn her so cold towards him? It didn't make sense.

He wondered if she was home. Perhaps she was lying there in the darkness thinking about him? What if he knocked on her door, just to see? He went over and raised his hand, poised to knock. But what if she'd brought her 'friend' back home? What if they were lying in there together, laughing at him?

He turned and marched over to the lift.

CHAPTER THIRTY-TWO

November 1940

As Ruby walked down the ramp into the ambulance station, she felt a thickening sense of dread. But it wasn't at the prospect of another night on the London streets in the middle of a bombing raid; it was at the thought of seeing Joseph. Ever since she'd been so cold to him the day before, she'd spent a great deal of energy persuading herself – and Kitty, once she'd told her – that it had been the right thing to do. But now she was about to spend eight hours cooped up in the staffroom or the ambulance with him, it was harder to see anything positive about her actions. This was going to make things even more awkward than they'd been before she and Joseph had become intimate.

When she reached the staffroom, she took a deep breath before going inside.

Bill was standing by the table chatting to a square-shoul-dered, flat-chested driver named Mildred, who worked the earlier shift.

'Evening all,' Ruby said, sitting down at the table. 'How was your shift, Mildred?'

Mildred, who didn't seem to have been blessed with the largest of vocabularies, shrugged. 'Dunno yet.'

'Mildred's taking over from Joseph,' Bill said casually, as if this should mean something to Ruby.

'Taking over from Joseph? But why?' Ruby's pulse quickened and she felt sick. Had Joseph been injured in the previous night's raid? 'What's happened?'

Bill frowned at her. 'He can't work nights any more. I thought you knew.'

Ruby shook her head.

The door opened and Joseph came in, alongside Heather, a pretty young thing who was Mildred's attendant. Or at least she had been. Ruby's face flushed as she realised what had happened.

'All right?' Joseph muttered, looking straight at Bill.

'How did that last call go?' Bill asked.

'It was great,' Heather replied with a toothy grin. 'Joseph did such a wonderful job on Lambeth Road. There are so many craters there, but he managed to avoid them all.'

'Thanks.' Joseph smiled back at her.

Ruby felt sick to her stomach. *I didn't mean to hurt you*, she wanted to yell at him. *I don't want you to work with her. I want you to work with me.*

Joseph took off his helmet and ran his hand through his hair. Why did he have to look so devilishly rugged and handsome? Why was he making things so difficult for her?

'I'll be getting off then,' he muttered, still refusing to look anywhere in the vicinity of Ruby.

'Would you mind walking me to the bus stop?' Heather simpered.

'Of course not.' Joseph opened the door for her and it was only when he was following Heather out that he looked back at Ruby. His expression was unreadable but definitely not good, somewhere between anger and disdain.

Ruby took a deep breath and tried to compose herself. But it was as if one of Kitty's favourite authors had taken up residency in her head and was typing away at a shocking new plot twist. She pictured Heather and Joseph waiting together at the bus stop, no doubt waiting an age because buses never came on time these days. And what could they do with that time other than talk? 'I can't believe we have so much in common,' she imagined Heather simpering – for clearly all she did when it came to Joseph was simper. 'I love jellied eels too!' she imagined her shrieking with delight. 'And I really can't bear classical music.'

By the time Bill had finished giving Ruby and Mildred and the rest of the shift their briefing, Ruby had married Joseph and Heather off and envisioned their future children – a handsome tall boy with dark hair and a simpering blonde girl who was scared of spiders and hated doing anything remotely adventurous.

'Come on then.' Mildred nudged Ruby in the ribs, breaking her from her nightmarish fantasy.

'What? Oh yes.' Damn, she hadn't been paying attention and had no clue where they were supposed to be going.

She ran to keep up with Mildred as she strode over to their ambulance.

'Well, I must say it's great to be working with another woman,' Ruby said as they got into the cab, determined to try to find some kind of silver lining in this grim turn of events.

Mildred grunted and started the engine.

'Isn't it great that us women are finally being given these kinds of opportunities?' Ruby continued. 'We never would have got to drive ambulances before. Or worked on the land or in factories. Before, we were doomed to a life of needlepoint and parlour music – if we were lucky. Or working in shops or as secretaries or domestics. And who on earth would ever want to be a domestic? What did you do before the war?'

Mildred turned and fixed Ruby with what could only be described as a murderous stare. 'I was a domestic.'

'Oh.' Drat! This was not going at all as Ruby would have planned – if she'd had time to plan – if Joseph hadn't dropped this bombshell upon her. 'Well, when I said domestic what I really meant was—'

'Let's just get one thing crystal before we get started,' Mildred cut in. 'I ain't got no time for idle chit-chat and if we're going to get along, then I suggest you button it.'

'Oh, I see.' Good grief, this was going to be even worse than working with Joseph. 'When you say idle chit-chat, what exactly do you mean?' Perhaps there was some hope. Perhaps Mildred would enjoy engaging in a hearty discourse about politics or religion.

'I mean, shut it.' Mildred turned the key in the ignition.

Well, how rude!

As Mildred drove up the ramp and out onto the road, Ruby slumped back in her seat and stared out of the window. A silvery fog was starting to curl in off the river, making visibility even harder. It seemed like the perfect metaphor for her life, Ruby realised with a heavy heart. Nothing seemed clear any more and the more she tried to do the right thing, the more lost she appeared to become.

*

Joseph took his torch from his pocket and focused the beam on the ground. The filmy mist that had been hanging over London for most of the day was thickening into an icy fog and it was impossible to see where he was going.

'Light out!' a disembodied voice called to him from somewhere in the ether.

He quickly flicked the torch off and promptly stumbled on a pothole in the pavement. Damn it!

Somewhere to his left, he heard the mumbled voice of a man. 'Go on, darling, no one will see us.' A woman's giggle echoed in the dark, followed by a moan.

Joseph pulled up the collar on his coat and sighed. No matter how hard he tried to wipe her from his mind, everything seemed to remind him of Ruby. The hurt on her face tonight at the station had really shocked him. He'd assumed she'd be happy to be working with someone else. He'd assumed that he'd be happier too, but working the shift with Heather had only heightened his feeling of loss. Ruby's incessant chatter might have annoyed him at times, but it was certainly never boring. All Heather seemed to want to talk about was her desire to have babies and her love of cats. She had a cutesy way of speaking that really irritated him too. He was aware that he was probably being unfair. She was probably a very nice lass. But she wasn't Ruby.

Some sandbags loomed into view and Joseph only just managed to swerve in time. He turned left onto what he hoped was the Strand and he heard the crunch of feet on glass from somewhere in front of him. There was the low mumble of a man's voice – 'Here, Bill, let's try this one' – followed by a scrambling sound. As Joseph drew closer, he saw the shadowy figures of two men carefully clambering through a blown-out shop window. His heart sank. Ever since the start of the Blitz, opportunist thieves had swarmed like locusts over the bombed carcasses of shops and houses, scavenging for treasure. Freddy had told him only the other day that he'd come across a couple of young lads pulling the wedding ring off a dead man's finger, in the middle of the street, bold as brass.

He contemplated trying to apprehend the men in the shop, but what was the point? There were two of them and for all he knew they could be armed with knives, so he carried on. Even though he was bone-tired, he'd decided to do a shift at the Hungerford Club as he knew it would be a sure-fire way to wrench him from his self-pity.

The construction work had been completed now and the shelter provided a welcome relief from the cold outside. Joseph entered to find several of the men huddled around a heater singing 'We'll Meet Again', slightly less tunefully than Vera Lynn, it had to be said.

''Ello, Joe, where's Ruby?' a woman named Doris asked, grabbing Joseph by the coat sleeve.

'She can't make it this evening. She's working.'

'Shame.' Doris sighed. 'I could really do with another of her beauty treatments.' She gave a throaty chuckle and flicked her tangled hair over her shoulder.

Ever since Ruby had been going to the Hungerford Club with Joseph, her beauty treatments, as she called them, had been a great hit with the women. Initially, Joseph had thought the whole thing frivolous, but the effect it had on the women was nothing short of miraculous.

Joseph frowned. He'd thought that no longer working with Ruby would help him forget about her, but she'd simply ended up haunting his memories instead.

The all-clear sounded outside.

'That's early,' Doris said.

'Must be the fog,' Joseph replied. He breathed a sigh of relief. At least Ruby would be safe out on the streets.

CHAPTER THIRTY-THREE

December 1940

'On the first day of Christmas,' Ruby sang cheerily, as she cut a sheet of newspaper into strips for home-made paper chains, 'my true love gave to me…'

'A partridge in a pear tree,' Kitty continued singing from the other side of the kitchen table, where she was painting a strip of paper green.

'Have you ever stopped to wonder about the logic of that song?' Ruby mused. 'I mean, what would you do if Freddy actually brought you a partridge in a pear tree? Wouldn't you think it rather odd?'

'As long as he brings the goose he's promised us for Christmas dinner, I don't mind,' Kitty replied with a grin.

'Yes, I have to say, having an amour who works in a butcher's shop really is the most wonderful gift.' Ruby smiled at Kitty. Ever since she and Freddy had started stepping out, Kitty had been positively glowing. The pallor had gone from her cheeks and her eyes shone. She'd even filled out a bit, thanks to Freddy's steady supply of rabbit pies and sausages.

Ruby picked up a fresh sheet of newspaper. The headline was about a soldier who'd come home on leave and found his wife with another man. He'd shot and killed his wife, but the judge had bound him over for two years, saying that his wife's behaviour had reduced him to such a condition that he didn't know what he was doing. Ruby quickly slid the sheet of paper under the table. There was no way she wanted Kitty seeing it. She didn't want anything ruining her newfound happiness.

'So, have you seen Joseph at all?' Kitty asked casually. She'd been asking this question on an almost daily basis in the month since the Trafalgar Square Tragedy, as Ruby now referred to it, and her answer was always the same.

'No, sadly he has sent me to Coventry – not literally, of course, although I bet he wishes he could have!' In recent weeks, the Germans had launched their blitzkrieg on other British cities as well as London, and Coventry had suffered terrible bomb damage.

'I'm sure he doesn't,' Kitty said. 'I saw him yesterday in the hallway and he looked ever so sad.'

Ruby felt a shiver of excitement at this latest detail. 'Are you sure he looked sad? He was probably just tired.' Ruby hadn't seen Joseph for weeks now. Thanks to their different shifts, they were like ships that passed in the night – or rather, ambulances that passed in a blackout – leaving a void that monosyllabic Mildred certainly wasn't able to fill.

'Yes, I'm sure,' Kitty said, painting a fresh strip of paper red. 'He sounded so dejected when I asked him how he was. And when I asked him if he was looking forward to Christmas, he said, "Not really." It's such a pity.'

Ruby felt a strange mixture of regret and relief at this news, but before she could analyse it further, her doorbell rang. She went through to the drawing room and peered through a chink in the blackout blinds. A man was standing on the front steps dressed in an army uniform. He had his back to her and for a horrible moment she thought it was Reg. But then the man turned and she saw that he was older and much higher ranking, judging by the stripes on his sleeve. As she peered out, another soldier joined him on the steps. The older one stepped forward and rang her bell again.

Ruby hurried back into the kitchen. 'It's a couple of soldiers – don't worry, it isn't him,' she added as Kitty's face fell. 'I'd better go and see what they want.'

'Do you – do you think something's happened to Reg?' Kitty asked.

'I don't know. I'll go and see. You wait here.'

As Ruby made her way to the door, she couldn't help wishing something had happened to Reg. Even though there'd been no sight or sound of him since his last visit, it was only a matter of time before he would be home on leave again and she knew this prospect was hanging over Kitty like a curse.

She opened the front door and the soldiers both tipped their hats in greeting.

'Good morning, madam,' the older one said. 'I'm Brigadier Johnson and this is Lieutenant Bristow.' He gestured at the younger soldier.

'How do you do?' Ruby replied.

'We're looking for a Mrs Kitty Price,' he continued. 'We understand she lives in the building, but there's no answer when we ring her bell.'

Ruby swallowed. Could something have happened to Reg after all? 'Aha, that will be because she's currently in my kitchen making paper chains for Christmas. We're having to make them out of old newspapers due to the paper shortage, but I actually think this is far more in keeping with the Christmas spirit, don't you? After all, Jesus was born in a stable.' She was aware that she was gabbling, but her nerves seemed to have got the better of her.

'Quite,' Brigadier Johnson replied curtly. 'Can we come in? We need to speak to her about her husband.'

'Of course.' As Ruby ushered them inside, she felt a fluttering in her stomach. Could Kitty be about to be delivered the news that would finally set her free? If Reg had died, she'd be able to marry Freddy. And a wartime marriage would be just the tonic they needed.

She led the men into the kitchen. Kitty was standing in the corner holding a paintbrush, looking like a frightened rabbit.

'Kitty, these lovely gentlemen are here to see you.'

Kitty turned as white as a sheet.

'Good morning, madam,' Brigadier Johnson said. 'We're here about your husband, Private Reginald Price. I was wondering if you could tell me when you last saw him.'

'Wh-when did I last see him?' Kitty stammered. 'Er, when he was home on leave, back in October.'

'Right.' The brigadier stared at her intently. 'And you haven't seen him since?'

Ruby frowned. Why would he be asking this if Reg had been injured or died?

'No, not at all,' Kitty replied. 'Why? What's happened?'

'Your husband has gone missing, Mrs Price, and we have reason to believe that he's deserted.' The brigadier looked around the kitchen, as if he was half expecting to find Reg hiding under the table.

'Deserted, but…' Kitty looked at Ruby anxiously.

'Are you sure he hasn't suffered some kind of tragic accident?' Ruby asked hopefully. 'Have there been any bombing raids down there? Could he have perished without anyone realising?'

The brigadier shook his head. 'No, certain items of his have also gone missing.'

'What items?' Kitty muttered.

'Personal items he had beside his bed in the barracks. And his revolver.'

Ruby's heart skipped a beat. 'When did this happen? When did he go missing?'

'The night before last. We think he did a moonlight flit. He left his post when his fellow soldier was otherwise engaged.'

'Having a slash,' the lieutenant offered helpfully.

'I see. And there's no chance he could have been abducted?' Ruby asked, her hope dwindling by the second.

The brigadier shook his head. 'The fact that his personal effects were missing from the barracks would indicate that it was pre-planned.'

'But why would he…?' Kitty broke off and Ruby could tell from her quivering lip that she was dangerously close to tears.

'Don't worry, I'm sure it will all come good in the end.' She hurried over and put her arm round Kitty's waist and gave her a comforting squeeze.

'Why would he desert his post?' Kitty asked.

'We were hoping you might be able to help us answer that question,' the brigadier replied. 'Is there any reason he would want to leave? Are there any issues at home? Is he under any pressure that you're aware of?'

'Not that I can think of.' Kitty gave Ruby another anxious glance.

Ruby frowned. As far as she was concerned, there was a major issue. Reg was a bully and now he was on the loose, and armed too. 'Well, he did seem a little agitated the last time he was on leave.'

'Really?' The brigadier turned his piercing stare on her. 'How so?'

'He was fine,' Kitty cut in before Ruby could speak. 'He was just worried about me being here alone during the Blitz.'

'I see. Well, in that case, it sounds as if he will probably make contact with you at some point, and if he does, we need you to let us know. Desertion is a very serious business, you know.'

'What will happen to him if he has deserted?' Ruby asked, feeling a glimmer of hope.

'He will have to face a court martial.'

'I see. And what's the punishment for such an offence?' Ruby held her breath.

'He would face a prison sentence.'

'Oh dear.' Ruby really hoped he couldn't detect the insincerity in her voice.

'Unfortunately we don't have the manpower to station someone here on the off-chance that your husband might return,' the brigadier continued. 'And chances are he wouldn't have the nerve to turn up here, knowing that we'll be looking for him, but there's every chance he'll find another way of contacting you. He may very well write or telephone, and if he does, you owe it to your country to let us know.'

'Oh don't worry, Brigadier,' Ruby said quickly, 'if there's so much of a whisper from him, we'll let you know, you have my word.'

'Thank you.' He turned to look back at Kitty.

'Yes of course – I'll tell you immediately,' she mumbled.

'Very good.' Brigadier Johnson took some cards from his pocket and handed one to Kitty and one to Ruby. 'Here are my details. Please do call me as soon as you hear anything.'

'Thank you,' the two women murmured.

'Before we go, would it be possible to take a look upstairs, at your flat?' he asked Kitty.

'What? Now?' Kitty stammered.

Ruby inwardly groaned. The poor girl looked so jumpy they probably thought she had Reg up there, stashed away in a cupboard.

'I think that's a very good idea,' Ruby said quickly. 'I can take you up there if you like. I actually own the property.'

Once the soldiers had checked the flat and were satisfied that Reg wasn't hiding with the preserves in the pantry, Ruby saw them to the front door.

'Here's hoping we solve this mystery as soon as possible,' she said as brightly as she could muster.

'Yes indeed,' the brigadier replied.

Both men tipped their hats, then got into a car parked outside and drove off.

Ruby glanced out into the garden. Twilight was falling and the sky was streaked a strange orangey purple. A figure appeared in the gloom, striding through the garden. Ruby's skin erupted in goosebumps, but as he drew closer, she saw that it was just one of the local wardens. She sighed. If only the soldiers had come to deliver the tragic news of Reg's demise. The thought of him out there on the loose, and with a gun to boot, made her feel distinctly uneasy. And if it was making her jittery, she dreaded to think what it was doing to poor Kitty.

She hurried back inside and found Kitty still rooted to the spot in the kitchen, visibly trembling.

'Oh, Kitty, don't fret.' As Ruby came closer, she saw a puddle on the floor by Kitty's feet. At first she thought she must have dropped the glass of water the paintbrushes were soaking in, but then she saw a dark stain in the crotch of Kitty's slacks. 'Oh, Kitty.' She came running over and hugged her tightly.

Kitty pulled away.

'Don't, your clothes will get soiled,' she whispered.

'I don't give a hoot about that.' Ruby hugged her even tighter. The thought that Reg could have this effect upon her was both appalling and heartbreaking.

'Wh-why do you think he's deserted? Wh-where do you think he is?' Kitty stammered.

Ruby took a step back, still gripping Kitty's arms tightly and staring at her intently. 'I don't know, but the good news is, if he does turn up here, he can't get in. We changed the locks, remember.'

'But he has a gun.' Kitty's eyes were wide with fear.

'I'm sure it will be fine. You heard what they said. He'll be too afraid of being caught to turn up here. He's not going to risk going to prison, is he? The worst he's going to do is send you a letter or phone you.'

Kitty shuddered. 'I knew it was too good to be true. I knew I shouldn't have got involved with Freddy.'

Ruby gently wiped the tears from her face. 'Please don't worry. I won't let anything happen to you.' She put her arm around her shoulder and started steering her towards the door. 'Let me draw you a nice warm bath.'

Kitty looked back at the puddle on the floor. 'I'm so sorry. It just happened. I couldn't help it.'

'Don't worry,' Ruby soothed. 'It's nothing that a quick mop can't fix.' But as she led Kitty from the room, her throat tightened. What horrors must Reg have inflicted upon Kitty to make her fear him so?

CHAPTER THIRTY-FOUR

December 1940

As Ruby hefted her suitcase along the Strand, her heart was gladdened by the sound of a choir singing 'Silent Night'. It was Christmas Eve, and so far, it *had* been a silent night, with no sign of a bombing raid. The raids on London had dropped off slightly recently, but Ruby knew it was no cause to relax. She'd read in the *Observer* only the other day that the Germans could have something else up their sleeve – like a Christmas invasion. She shuddered at the thought.

As she turned down the side street beside Charing Cross station, she decided that she must focus on the positives. Kitty was safely tucked up at home, there'd been no sign of Reg since the soldiers had come to the house a week ago, and with every day that passed, Ruby had become more convinced that he'd fled to pastures new. The man was the kind of coward who beat women – he'd clearly deserted at the thought of having to face a German invasion and he clearly didn't love Kitty, judging by the way he treated her, so Ruby very much doubted they'd see hide nor hair of him.

Approaching the Hungerford Club, Ruby's pulse quickened. She wasn't sure if Joseph would be there, but if he was, she would simply distribute her gifts and leave. She'd had the idea to buy gifts for the women at the shelter the other day, when she'd been shopping for presents for Kitty on Regent Street. Ever since she'd fallen out with Joseph, she'd missed going to the shelter almost as much as she'd missed him and she was determined to give the women a little Christmas cheer.

She pushed open the door and stepped inside. The delicious spicy aroma of freshly baked mince pies filled the air and it was so mouth-watering and so reminiscent of far happier Christmases that for a terrible moment Ruby thought she might burst into tears. Thankfully, she managed to stiffen her upper lip and she looked around. The shelter was crammed to the rafters. Ruby recognised a few familiar faces and was heartened when a couple of the women came over to greet her enthusiastically.

'Miss Ruby,' one of them named Doris exclaimed. 'Where have you been? We thought the Jerrys had got you.'

'As if!' Ruby replied. 'I've been very busy manning the ambulances but, fear not, I come bearing gifts.' She placed her trunk on the floor.

Within seconds, Doris had spread the word and Ruby was surrounded by a group of women. They looked tired and even thinner than when she'd last seen them, but they seemed so happy to see her, and again she was almost brought to tears. What an exhausting year it had been.

'Come on then,' Doris chided. 'Give us our gifts. We ain't got all day.'

The other women started giggling.

'Hmm, I bet Father Christmas doesn't have to tolerate such insolence,' Ruby said with a grin as she opened the case.

'They're proper gifts!' one of the women cried, as they all peered into the trunk.

'They look beautiful,' another one gasped.

Ruby and Kitty had spent all morning wrapping the gifts. They'd had to use old newspaper due to the shortages, but Ruby had found yards of red and gold ribbon in her mother's old sewing box, so each gift came wrapped in a bow. 'Of course they're proper gifts,' Ruby replied as she began handing them out. 'Nothing but the best for the Hungerford Ladies.' She breathed a sigh of relief as, one by one, they began opening the presents and, one by one, they gasped with joy. Inside each parcel was a beautiful silk scarf and a comb from Liberty's and a pink sugar mouse from Fortnum & Mason. Within seconds, the awed silence was broken by giggles and cheers as the women started modelling their scarves, some wrapping them around their necks, others twisting them into turbans around their heads.

'Bloody hell, what's going on here?'

Ruby froze at the sound of Joseph's voice.

'It's Miss Ruby,' Doris replied. 'She's brought us all gifts.'

Ruby turned. Joseph was standing behind her. His black hair was longer and curlier than ever and his chin was shaded with stubble. Ruby felt consumed by a longing that almost brought her to her knees.

'Has she now?' he replied. To Ruby's relief, she was pretty sure she could detect warmth in his eyes.

'Thank you, Miss Ruby!' a girl called Ethel exclaimed, and before Ruby could respond, the young woman had grabbed her in a hug. 'This is the nicest gift I've ever been given.'

'Oh, uh, you're welcome,' Ruby replied, and as she looked around at the warm smiles of the women, she yet again felt embarrassingly close to tears. 'Well, I really ought to be going,' she said, picking up her now empty trunk.

'No!' the women chorused.

'Stay and have a mince pie,' Doris said.

'Oh I'm not sure I—'

'Go on,' Joseph said. 'It is Christmas.'

Ruby glanced at him again. Why was being so warm towards her? Had he been drinking? Then a terrible thought occurred to her. What if he was so full of good cheer because he'd fallen madly in love with the simpering Heather? Someone had hung a sprig of mistletoe over the staffroom door at the ambulance station. She could just imagine Heather batting her eyelashes at him as they stood beneath it. 'Oh, Joseph, would you care to join me in a Christmas kiss,' she imagined her cooing. And then Joseph would take off his helmet and take her in his arms and—

'Well?' Joseph asked, bringing the deranged romance writer in her mind to a screeching halt. 'Will you stay?'

'Yes, I will, thank you.'

'You can even have a glass of brandy too,' he added.

Ruby followed him over to the drinks table and scanned the crowded room. Thankfully there was no sign of Heather. Perhaps it was the brandy that was making Joseph so convivial. She waited while he poured her a glass. Over in the corner by a slightly misshapen Christmas tree, a few of the Hungerford Club staff were tuning up some musical instruments. 'Well, I must say, this is all very festive,' Ruby said as Joseph handed her a drink. Despite the fact that it was served in a paper cup, the brandy was heavenly and instantly warming.

'We tried our best,' Joseph replied. 'Isn't it nice to see the smiles on their faces?'

Ruby nodded. The women now appeared to be carrying out some kind of fashion parade, marching up and down in their headscarves while the others cheered.

'It was very kind of you to bring them gifts.'

'It was the least I could do. I miss coming here.' Ruby took a deep breath. 'I miss you.'

But her words were drowned out by a sudden toot on the trumpet and the band launching into a jazzed-up version of 'Jingle Bells'.

'Get over here, Joseph,' one of them called. 'You're needed on the triangle.'

'Oh dear!' Joseph looked at Ruby and laughed. 'I'd better get up there.'

'Yes, the triangle solo in "Jingle Bells" is the highlight of the whole piece,' Ruby attempted to joke, but Joseph was already making his way through the crowd to the makeshift stage.

*

As the band hit the final note of the final encore of the Hungerford Club Christmas singalong, Joseph scanned the crowd for any sign of Ruby. He wasn't sure if it was the brandy warming him to his bones or the fact that there hadn't been a single air-raid warning, but as soon as he'd seen Ruby tonight, surrounded by the laughing, cheering women, something had shifted inside him. The wall that had gone up after she'd snubbed him in Trafalgar Square and had stayed up in the weeks since suddenly seemed to be crumbling.

He gave the room another scan, but there was still no sign of her. She must have gone home. He tried to ignore how disappointed this made him feel.

As the Hungerford Club members prepared to bed down for the night, he said his goodbyes and fetched his coat. Stepping out into the cool, crisp darkness, he decided to walk home along the river. It didn't look like the Germans were coming tonight – perhaps even they didn't have the stomach for yet more death and destruction on Christmas Eve. Just as he was making his way onto the footpath that ran alongside the water, he heard footsteps behind him and then a woman's voice.

'Hello.' He took his torch from his pocket and flicked it on. 'Ruby, is that you?'

She stepped into the torchlight, her body quivering and her teeth chattering.

'How long have you been out here?' he asked.

'I'm not sure.'

As he peered closer, he could see thin black streaks of make-up running from her eyes and down her cheeks. 'Are you all right?'

'I would love to possess the grit to be able to tell you that, yes, I am fine and dandy and perfectly in the pink, but alas, my stiff upper lip has become a wobbly blancmange.'

'What?' Was it his imagination or was she slurring her speech?

Ruby gave a dramatic sigh. 'The truth is, I am so far from all right that even if I was the proud owner of the most powerful telescope in the world, I wouldn't be able to detect it.'

Joseph had to bite his lip to stop himself from grinning. How he'd missed Ruby and her crazy figures of speech. 'Why? What's happened?'

'I have been the biggest fool who ever lived!' She crossed her arms in front of her chest. 'In fact, I'm of half a mind to contact the Oxford English Dictionary in the morning and tell them to file Ruby Glenville under their definition of imbecile.'

'Right. Well, I'm not sure there'll be anyone there in the morning, seeing as it's Christmas.'

'Oh yes, don't remind me. The time of year to come together with loved ones. To exchange gifts in front of a roaring fire. To laugh gaily at the discovery of the sixpence in the pudding. To kiss each other beneath the mistletoe.'

Joseph frowned. What the heck was she going on about?

'I suppose you kissed *her* beneath the mistletoe?' Ruby lurched forwards and suddenly their noses were almost touching and he could smell the brandy on her breath. 'I bet she hung it there in the first place, didn't she, to try to entice you into her lair.'

'Who? What are you talking about?'

'Heather. Or as I refer to her, Simperella.' Ruby guffawed with laughter. 'Simperella, Cinderella, get it?'

'Not really, no.'

'Because she simpers when she's with you.' Ruby gave a coy little giggle. 'Oh, Joseph, you're so handsome,' she said in a squeaky little voice. 'And you drive an ambulance so well. I don't think I've ever met anyone who negotiates a pothole with such panache, you really are my Prince Charming,'

'Er, thank you.'

'That wasn't me, silly, that was Heather. Simperella. Your romantic heroine.'

'What are you talking about?'

'You and Heather.' She swayed slightly and he grabbed hold of her elbow to steady her. 'But don't worry, I'm not bitter. Well, I am, but I know it's no one's fault but my own.'

'There is no me and Heather,' Joseph said.

Ruby stared at him for a moment, swaying from side to side. 'You mean you aren't madly in love with her?'

'No!'

'And she didn't kiss you under the mistletoe?'

'What mistletoe?'

'The mistletoe hanging in the staffroom.'

'No. I didn't even know there was any.'

Ruby gave a hearty sigh of relief, followed by a belch. 'Oh my goodness, please excuse me.'

Joseph looked at her and laughed. 'I think you might be in need of some coffee.'

'Oh, I need more than coffee!' Ruby exclaimed. 'I need to turn back the hands of time. I need to beg the goddess of star-crossed lovers for forgiveness. I need to—'

'Well, let's start with coffee, shall we?' Joseph interrupted. It was way too cold for one of Ruby's monologues. He linked his arm through hers and started guiding her back up towards the Strand.

*

As Ruby sat in Franco's all-night café in Soho, sipping on her bitter coffee, harsh reality began piercing her drunken haze like pinpricks of light through a blackout blind. Had she really said all of those things to Joseph? Had she really demanded to know whether he'd kissed Heather beneath the mistletoe? What had she been thinking? Why had she drunk so much brandy? She hiccupped and tried to cover it with a cough.

'Feeling any better?' Joseph grinned at her across the red Formica table. Oh, how he must be loving this!

'Yes, thank you. I think I partook in a little too much Christmas cheer.'

'I'll say.' His smile grew wider.

Damn his twinkly-eyed grin and his stupid dimples. Still, at least he'd been adamant that nothing was going on between him and Heather; that was one small mercy at least. Not that it mattered now that Ruby had ridiculed herself beyond all redemption.

'So, what was all that about then?' he asked.

'All what?'

'All that talk of you being the definition of an imbecile. And all that talk of me being so handsome and such a good driver.'

'I didn't say that, that was Heather.'

'Funny that, I could have sworn you were the one saying those words when you were swaying in front of me.'

'Oh no, was I swaying?'

''Fraid so. And then there was the belch.'

Ruby put her head in her hands in despair. 'Is it any wonder I was expelled from finishing school? Although, in truth, that was for refusing to walk around with a book on my head, rather than anything as fun as too much drinking.'

'Good to know. Why did they want you to walk around with a book on your head?'

'Deportment.'

Joseph stared at her blankly.

Ruby looked down at the table and started picking at a chip in the red Formica. 'I'm awfully sorry,' she murmured. 'I fear I have made a terrible fool of myself.'

'Well, I wouldn't say a *terrible* fool,' Joseph replied. 'Run-of-the-mill fool would do the trick.'

Ruby sighed and took another sip of her coffee. 'The truth is, I've missed you,' she said quietly, painfully aware that her cheeks had started flushing.

'I've missed you too,' Joseph replied.

'You have?' She looked at him hopefully.

He nodded. 'Although God knows why.'

'I didn't mean to do it,' she blurted out. 'I mean to say, I did mean to do it, in that obviously I was in full control of my bodily functions. It wasn't as if I'd become possessed by some kind of demonic spirit.'

'Right,' Joseph said slowly.

'It's just that I did it for all the wrong reasons.'

'Did what?'

'Treated you so cruelly in Trafalgar Square.'

'Ah.' He nodded.

'Pushed you away with all the iciness of a snow queen. Locked you from my heart and threw away the key.'

'All right, all right, I get the picture.'

'But it was only because I was so frightened of you dying.'

'Dying in Trafalgar Square?' He frowned at her.

'No, dying anywhere and at any time. And having to go to a memorial service for you and weeping my heart out to "The Lord's My Shepherd" and—'

'Wait a second.' Joseph put up his hand to stop her mid-flow. 'You did what you did because you were afraid of me dying?'

Ruby returned to picking at the Formica. 'Yes. Terrified actually.'

'So, the friend you were going to see at the Savoy wasn't another man.'

'What? No! Of course not! There was no friend. I didn't go to the Savoy. I just had to get away. I didn't know what else to say. Oh my goodness.' She brought her hands to her heart. 'You thought I was betraying you?'

'I didn't know what to think, to be honest.'

Ruby sighed. 'Losing my father the way I did, well, it had a profound effect on me. I always vowed that I'd never allow that to happen to me again that I – I'd never love anyone as much again. If it's any consolation, you're the first person I've let get that close since I was twelve.'

'So it's been over fifty years then.'

'No!' She frowned and he started to laugh. 'Oh, very funny.' She grabbed one of the menus leaning against the salt and pepper pots and swatted him with it.

Joseph's smile faded and, to her surprise and relief, he took hold of her hands. 'I understand.'

'You do?'

'I lost my brother in the war and I may as well have lost my dad. The things he saw and did on the front, well, they changed him forever. Destroyed him.'

Ruby squeezed his hands tightly. 'And that's why you're a conscientious objector?'

Joseph nodded. 'But I still don't understand why you did what you did, or when you did it at least. I thought everything was as right as rain when we went into that concert.'

'It was, but then they played "The Lord's My Shepherd". It was my father's favourite hymn. They played it at his memorial service.'

A look of realisation dawned on Joseph's face. 'And it brought it all back to you?'

She nodded, a lump forming in her throat. 'It was the strangest thing. All of a sudden I was twelve again and in that church, feeling all of those feelings, and I had the terrible thought that I might lose you too and I went into a complete panic.'

'You're not going to lose me.'

His words had the strange effect of making her heart sing for joy and wail with sorrow all at the same time.

'How do you know? In case you hadn't noticed, we're living in the middle of a war zone.'

'I had noticed, but can I tell you something?'

'Of course.'

'And you promise not to butt in and start delivering one of your monologues?'

'What mono— all right, I promise.' She bit down on her lip.

Joseph leaned back in his seat. 'When the war started, I thought I'd lost everything. The day I went to register at the Labour Exchange as a conscientious objector, half of my pals from school were there too – but they were signing up to join the army. COs had to go to a separate desk, so they all knew immediately that I wouldn't be going off to fight with them. These were lads I'd grown up with. Lads I'd played football with. Only now I was on a different team.' He let go of her hands and looked away. 'They saw me as a traitor, a coward. A couple of them said as much to my face and the rest of them ignored me. Within days, word had spread all around town. Then we got dog shit posted through the front door.'

Ruby gasped.

'I had to move away because my mam started getting hounded. So I went down to Birmingham...'

'Where you did the ambulance training?'

'Yes. Then I came down here. And by that point I'd given up.'

'On what?'

'On everything really. But then I got the job on the ambulances and I helped set up the Hungerford Club and I felt like my life was worth something again. That I was worth something—'

'Of course you're worth something,' Ruby interrupted.

'Er, what did I say?' He put his finger to his lip.

'Sorry.' She shut her mouth tight.

'And then I got to know you.'

'Yes…?' She held her breath.

'And you didn't just make me feel worth something, you made me feel alive, for the first time in my life. You made me feel that maybe life is good and people are good and that this is all worth it, in spite of everything.'

Ruby's eyes filled with tears. 'I did all that?' she whispered.

'Yes.'

'And then I pushed you away.'

He nodded.

'I'm so, so sorry.'

'Good.'

'Why is it good?' She stared at him.

''Cos it means you care.' He took hold of her hands again. 'Yes, I could die tomorrow, but so could any of us – even if there wasn't a war on. Any of us could be run over by a bus tomorrow. The question is…'

'What?'

'Do we ruin our lives worrying about what might happen or do we spend them enjoying what has happened, what *is* happening?'

'That's so beautiful!' Ruby gasped. 'It's just like a line from one of Kitty's books. It—'

'Never mind all that. What do you want to do?'

Ruby looked at him. She drank in his curly black hair, his blue eyes, his dimples, the lines on his brow and the stubble on his jaw. And she knew then that she loved every inch of him, and even though that was terrifying, it wasn't nearly as bad as the prospect of a life without him. 'I want to kiss you,' she replied, leaning across the table.

CHAPTER THIRTY-FIVE

December 1940

Joseph woke on Christmas morning to the sound of Ruby's jagged breathing and his mouth full of her hair. He wouldn't have wanted it any other way though. As far as he was concerned, last night's turn of events was the best Christmas present he could have ever been given. As he watched her sleep, he thought of what she'd told him the night before about the loss of her father and how it had affected her. It was yet another example of the terrible cost of war. He'd long ago realised that the traumas endured by soldiers rippled out beyond them to their loved ones, but he hadn't quite realised how far those ripples could spread, years and years down the line. He hugged Ruby to him and she stirred and opened her eyes.

'Am I dreaming?' she asked sleepily.

'I hope not,' he replied, kissing the top of her head.

'So last night wasn't a dream either?' she said, running her fingertips along his stomach.

'I don't know,' he replied, his skin tingling beneath her touch. 'Maybe we need to do it again to make sure?'

After they'd made love, Joseph finally managed to disentangle himself from Ruby's arms and get out of bed.

'Why oh why did you volunteer to do the Hungerford Club Christmas dinner?' Ruby moaned, wrapping a blanket around her.

'Well, at the time, I thought I'd be celebrating Christmas on my own in my room with only the spiders for company,' he retorted. He leaned down and kissed her. 'Don't worry, I'll be back in time for our feast with Kitty and Freddy.'

'You'd better be.' She stood up, causing the blanket to fall, and hugged him tightly.

*

'Isn't this just the most wonderful thing?' Ruby gushed as she and Kitty laid the table for Christmas dinner. 'Both of us spending Christmas with our true loves.'

Kitty smiled as she placed a decorative pine cone by each of the settings. Ruby had dipped the cones in an Epsom salt solution to give them a snowy effect, as recommended in an article on wartime Christmas decorations in *Woman's Own*. 'I'm so happy you and Joseph are back together.'

'Thank you.' Ruby gazed dreamily into the middle distance.

'Tell me the bit about how he declared undying love for you outside the Hungerford Club again,' Kitty said, sitting down in one of the chairs.

Ruby grinned. She may have slightly embellished upon the tale of her reunion with Joseph and conveniently omitted certain details pertaining to her drunkenness, but what did it matter? The outcome was the same. She and Joseph were reunited, and no longer star-crossed. 'Ah well, if you insist,' she sighed, preparing to sit down. But just then the doorbell rang.

'That'll be Freddy with the goose!' Kitty jumped to her feet. 'I did give him my key, but I suppose he's got his hands full!'

'Let him in!' Ruby exclaimed, her mouth watering at the prospect of freshly roasted goose.

As Kitty hurried from the room, Ruby set about putting the festive napkins in their holders. The napkins had belonged to her parents and hadn't been used since her childhood, but instead of feeling pain at the memories associated with them, Ruby felt a warm glow of nostalgia. She was starting to realise that she'd got it horribly wrong, trying to evade love for fear of loss. The truth was, loved ones never died. They lived on forever in your hearts and minds – if you let them.

'Ruby,' she heard Kitty say from behind her. 'Ruby.' There was something off about her voice. She sounded distraught.

As Ruby turned, it was as if everything slowed: her heartbeat, her breathing, the ticking of the grandfather clock. Kitty was standing in the doorway with a dishevelled and unshaven Reg right behind her, holding a gun to her head, his fingers streaked with grime.

'He – he says he's killed Freddy,' Kitty stammered.

'What?' Ruby's mouth fell open in shock.

'That's right,' Reg sneered. 'And now I'm going to do for you too. Both of you.'

'No, let her leave!' Kitty cried.

'What, after she made a fool of me, lying about them flowers, telling me she was your secret admirer? I don't think so.'

'There was no secret admirer,' Ruby exclaimed, her mind racing. Had Reg really killed Freddy? As he pushed Kitty into the room, her stomach lurched. It wasn't dirt on his hands; it was blood.

'You're lying,' Reg replied. 'I saw her kissing him on the doorstep last night.'

'But I didn't see him last night,' Kitty exclaimed before clamping her hand to her mouth.

Reg gave a sinister laugh. 'So, you finally admit it. While I've been off fighting for king and country, you've been whoring it up with any Tom, Dick or Harry who'll have you.'

'I wasn't aware there was any fighting going on down in Newhaven,' Ruby retorted, her mind racing. Why had Reg accused Kitty of kissing Freddy last night when she hadn't even seen him? Had he been trying to trap her? She would never have credited him with the intelligence to be that cunning. Then a terrible thought occurred to her. Had Reg seen her and Joseph when they returned home last night and thought that they were Kitty and Freddy? She remembered how Joseph had taken her into his arms at the top of the steps before opening the door. How he'd whispered that he loved everything about her – even her monologues. And how she'd responded with faux outrage until he'd silenced her with a kiss. What if Reg had been watching them from the inky depths of the blackout? She shuddered and glanced at the clock. Joseph was due home at any minute. If he walked into this, his life would be in danger too.

Right on cue, she heard the front door close. But what should she do? If she yelled a warning, Reg might shoot Kitty; the gun was pressed right to her temple.

'I really wish you'd put down that gun,' she said loudly, hoping Joseph would hear. 'There's really no need to resort to violence.'

'Keep your voice down or she gets it,' Reg hissed.

Time slowed again as the door opened… and Freddy walked in holding a huge box, no doubt containing their Christmas dinner.

'Hello, Ruby, I managed to get us some sausage-meat stuffing too— Oh…' His mouth fell open in shock as he came into the room and saw Reg and Kitty.

'Oh thank God!' Kitty cried.

'Who the hell's this?' Reg asked.

Freddy put the box on the table. 'What's going on?' He looked from Ruby to Kitty and back again, the colour draining from his face.

Ruby looked at the blood on Reg's hands. Then she looked at Freddy, completely free from injury. A terrible conclusion began forming in her mind. If Reg was claiming to have killed Freddy, whom he'd allegedly seen kissing Kitty on the steps last night, but Freddy was standing right in front of them alive and well and Joseph was the only man to have done any kissing on the steps last night, could Reg have killed him instead? Her blood ran cold.

'Who have you shot?' she cried, launching herself at Reg.

'Keep away or she gets it!' Reg yelled, taking a step back but still gripping on to Kitty.

'What have you done to him?' Ruby screamed.

'What's going on?' Freddy asked, looking completely bewildered.

'Who is this?' Reg said to Kitty, waving the gun at Freddy.

'He – he's just the local b-b-butcher, come to deliver us some food,' Kitty stammered.

'On Christmas Day?' Reg scowled.

'Please, Reg, let them go,' Kitty implored. 'They've done nothing wrong. Let's you and me go upstairs and talk about this.'

Reg tightened his grip on her. 'I don't think we've got anything left to say.'

'That's as may be, but if you hurt them, you're going to get yourself in even more trouble.'

Reg snorted. 'You think I ain't in enough trouble already? I deserted because of you. Do you know what they do to deserters? I've got nothing left to lose.'

'But it's Christmas!' Kitty twisted slightly to face Reg. 'Please, let's go upstairs and talk about this.'

While Reg stared at Kitty, Ruby's mind went into overdrive. Where was Joseph? What had happened to him? There was a sudden flash of movement as Freddy leapt at Reg, knocking him clear of Kitty. 'Run!' he yelled as the two men fell to the floor.

'Freddy, no!' Kitty cried.

'He's Freddy?' Reg spluttered as he grappled to free himself.

Ruby grabbed Kitty's arm and dragged her from the room.

'No!' Kitty screamed, as a shot rang out.

'Come on!' Ruby pulled her into the entrance hall and through the front door.

A small crowd of people had gathered in the garden, and they were all looking at the house, no doubt having heard the shot.

'Take cover!' Ruby cried. 'There's a gunman on the loose.'

She saw a local warden and Mr Jenkins, both their faces ashen and rigid with shock.

'You have to take cover!' Ruby cried again, running towards them. If Reg had killed Freddy, then at any moment he could emerge from the house and train his gun on them. 'Go down to the shelter,' she called. But as she drew level with the crowd, she saw a sight that made her heart stop. A man was lying on the ground in the middle of the crowd, blood pooling from his chest.

'Oh no!' Ruby took a step closer and fought the urge to retch. The man had black curly hair just like Joseph. He was wearing Joseph's coat. He was wearing Joseph's scuffed boots. 'No, no, no!' She collapsed to the cold floor and rolled the body over. 'Joseph, no! Wake up!' she cried, shaking his lifeless arm. Somewhere in the distance, she heard Kitty start to sob.

The warden placed a hand on her shoulder. 'I'm sorry, miss, I'm afraid it's too late.'

'No!'

'Freddy!' Kitty cried.

Ruby somehow managed to tear her gaze from Joseph to see Freddy standing on the steps of the house holding the gun. He started stumbling towards them, looking dazed.

'Did you kill him?' Kitty asked.

Freddy shook his head. 'He escaped.'

Ruby looked back at Joseph's body and began to wail.

EPILOGUE

The next few days felt like an out-of-body experience for Ruby. She was vaguely conscious of other people coming and going – the police, officers from Reg's regiment, Kitty, Freddy – and somehow she dragged herself from her cold bed and answered their questions. But all the while it felt as if her spirit had drifted off to another dimension, wafting around above it all, searching helplessly for Joseph. Part of her hoped that it was all a dream, that one day she would open her eyes and roll over and see his dark hair on the white pillow next to her. She no longer cared about air-raid warnings, in spite of Kitty's pleading with her to take shelter. How could she set foot in the garden again, now that it was where Joseph took his last breath? She longed for the Germans to drop one of their bombs on top of her, to put her out of her misery. But, to her disappointment, the Christmas lull in the bombing continued. And so she remained trapped in her own personal hell.

It wasn't until the fourth day after Christmas, the fourth day after Joseph's death, that the planes returned with a vengeance.

'Ruby, please,' Kitty begged, sitting on the end of her bed. 'Half of London is ablaze. You have to take shelter. Freddy reckons the bombers will be back soon to finish what they started.'

Much as it pained her to admit it, Ruby felt a sour bite of jealousy at the mention of Freddy's name. It was he who should have died, not Joseph. It was Kitty who should be mourning. Horrified that she should think such a thing, she shifted upright in the bed.

'Will you come to the shelter?' Kitty said eagerly.

'Yes.' It was the first word she'd uttered all day and her voice was dry and cracked. 'You go on ahead. I'll just get dressed.'

'All right.' Kitty stood up and looked at her anxiously. 'Promise you'll come?'

'I promise.'

As soon as Kitty had gone, Ruby hefted herself out of bed. Her limbs felt leaden and stiff. She pulled the first thing she could find from the wardrobe and put it on. She couldn't wait any longer for death to find her. She was going to find death.

Outside, the cold night air smelled of a strange mixture of gasoline and bonfire smoke and the sky to the north glowed like a piece of amber. Ruby felt a weird morbid excitement bubbling in the pit of her stomach. Something felt different about this night. She sensed a strange finality in the air. Without looking at the garden, she turned sharply in the direction of the river. The dark water glowed with an orange sheen, reflecting the sky above. All around the city, sirens were wailing and the ack-ack guns rattled. It was the perfect discordant soundtrack to the nightmarish setting. Ruby marched determinedly in the direction of the glow.

As soon as she drew near to Westminster Bridge, she saw the cause for the strange sky. Most of the City of London appeared to be on fire, with only the bald white dome of St Paul's Cathedral free from the flames licking hungrily at the buildings around it. This was the Germans' final assault before their invasion, Ruby felt certain of it. And she didn't care one bit.

She looked up at the sky and saw a V-shaped formation of bombers flying by. *Just like a flock of wild geese*, she mused to herself, and hot tears filled her eyes. How had it come to this? In a world full of such untamed beauty, how had mankind been able to create such horror? *It doesn't matter*, she told herself. *You are no longer going to be a part of it.* And she carried on walking towards the fire.

CHAPTER THIRTY-SIX

September 2019

'No!' I say out loud, staring at the book in shock. I check to see if any pages have been torn from the back, but that really was it. I'm not sure I've ever read a more dispiriting ending to a novel. I'm not a fan of the cheesy happy Hollywood ending by any stretch, but still… To let Reg commit murder and then escape. To kill off Joseph and then have Ruby walking to her own certain death.

I re-read the final pages. If the story really did happen and Pearl is in some way connected to the characters, could it have been Joseph's shirt that I found in the loft? Joseph did live in the top-floor flat in the book, and he had access to a loft. But that wouldn't make any sense. Why would anyone take the shirt from a murdered man's body and hide it in his loft? Could Ruby have done it in a fit of grief, the way she brought home her father's damaged waxwork head? I frown. One thing's for sure; I need more coffee before I try to make sense of all this.

I deliberately avoided taking any more painkillers since seeing Pearl this morning as I want to have my wits about me, so as I hop through to the kitchen on my crutches, the pain from my ankle is intense. I think about the shirt again to try to distract myself and I realise that it can't have been Joseph's, as the ambulance service uniform was dark blue rather than khaki. The only person who wore a khaki shirt in the novel was Reg. But Reg wasn't killed;

he escaped. I sigh. All of this thinking is making my head hurt nearly as much as my ankle.

I make the coffee and hop back into the bedroom. As soon as I see my laptop on the bed, I wonder if there have been any further updates on Marty's Facebook page. *Don't do it!* I plead with myself. *You know it will only make you feel worse.* But before I know it, I've opened the laptop, and Facebook, and Marty's page, adrenaline pumping through my body.

It's exactly the same as it was last night. I stare at his profile pic – a photo I took of him last year on his birthday. Only it wasn't his actual birthday as he'd had to go away for work that day. My stomach clenches. Had he been with her? Gazing at his photo is like looking at one of those optical illusions where an image can appear to be two completely different things depending on your perspective. One minute you think you're looking at a candlestick, but shift slightly and you realise it's two faces in profile. As I stare at the picture of Marty, he changes from being my husband to a total stranger. I thought I knew him better than anyone, but maybe I didn't really know him at all.

I think of Ruby and Joseph and the love they shared. In spite of all their difficulties, it felt real and raw and full of passion. I pick up the book and re-read the page where they dance beneath the bomber's moon in the middle of a deserted Piccadilly. In all of my ten years with Marty, I never experienced a moment of such intensity. *But that's because you didn't live through a war together,* I remind myself. And besides, Ruby and Joseph were fictional creations. Real-life relationships are never that romantic, are they? Any romance is soon diluted by the nitty-gritty of reality, like pants on the floor and arguments over who does the most cleaning – and of course, cheating.

I jump at the sound of the lift whirring into life and look around in fright. Then I remember with relief that I double-locked the front door. The lift falls silent and I hear the click of a key turning in the door. Shit! I pull the duvet up to my chin. I hear a gentle knocking on the door and ignore it.

After what feels like an eternity, the lift judders into life again and goes back downstairs. I count the seconds as it goes, and realise that it's returning to the ground floor, so it must have been Pearl. What did she want? And why did she try to get in without knocking at first?

I haul myself upright. This is crazy. I need to get a grip. But the only way I can put my jittery mind at ease is by getting to the bottom of the shirt mystery, so I decide to see if I can find any more clues linking the book to reality. I grab a notepad and pen from my bag and start compiling a list.

EVIDENCE THAT THE STORY IS TRUE
The book is set in Pimlico, in a VERY similar house
The square is identical too, with a church and a communal garden
The river is at the bottom of the square too
It's next door to Neptune Square, a first-aid post during the war
Neptune Square was bombed – was St George's Square bombed?
Joseph lived in the top-floor flat and he had access to the loft
He hid a tin under a floorboard in the loft, exactly where I found the shirt

I stop writing and open a new window on my laptop and search for St George's Square on Google Maps. Due to being so busy at work, I haven't had any time to explore the local area since I moved here, apart from the route to the station. I look at the map and see that there's a square right next door to St George's, called Dolphin Square. I do a quick search for Dolphin Square London, and gasp as an image pops up. It looks exactly as I'd imagined Neptune Square to look, with red-brick buildings and three arched gateways leading to a private courtyard. I scroll through the entries for Dolphin Square; most of them are from estate agents, but then I find a site for the square itself and on the About page I see a sentence that makes my heart skip a beat. '*The square became an ambulance station and first-aid post during the Blitz of World War 2.*'

I add *Neptune Square is very like the real Dolphin Square* to my list.

Neptune. Dolphin. I stare at the words, suddenly realising the ocean theme. I scan the rest of the list. *St George. Pendragon.* St George and the dragon! This can't be a coincidence. Pearl must have used this setting as her inspiration. But there's nothing sinister about a writer using a location they know as inspiration, I remind myself, taking a sip of coffee. The only thing that is strange about all of this is the shirt in the loft and where I found it and Pearl's strange reaction to it. Then a thought occurs to me. What if the novel is based on a true story and Pearl is connected to one of the characters? What if she's *related* to one of the characters? If that were the case, then surely it would have to be Ruby. They're both such strong women, with such eccentric personalities.

My phone starts to ring, wrenching me from my amateur sleuthing. It's an unknown number.

'Hello?'

There's a moment's silence and then a well-to-do woman's voice says, 'Hello, my dear.' For a surreal moment I think it's Ruby. 'It's me, Pearl,' she continues.

'Oh.' *Shit, shit, shit!*

'I'm sorry, I hope I didn't wake you.'

'It's OK, I'd just woken up.'

'I was just wondering if you'd like me to come and collect your breakfast dishes.'

I glance at the tray on the floor. 'Oh, uh, no, it's OK.'

'I need my cafetière,' she says, more firmly this time.

Crap.

'I, uh, was just going to try to have a wash actually.'

'Oh, would you like my help?'

'No!' I practically yell.

'Is everything all right?'

'Yes, sorry. I – I just found out that my husband has been cheating.' *What did I say that for? I'd wanted to change the subject, but really?!*

'Your husband?'

Actually, this might be a useful development. 'Yes, and he's coming down to see me today – very soon.'

'That's funny, I could have sworn Heath said you were divorcing already.'

Damn it!

There's another awkward silence and I toy with the idea of just hanging up.

'I couldn't help noticing…' Pearl says and then pauses.

'Yes?'

'…That you'd been reading my novel.'

I flush so hot that I break out in a clammy sweat. 'Oh, er, yes. Heath told me you were a writer and I was intrigued to read some of your work. It's not every day you move upstairs from a published author,' I gabble.

'Interesting that you should have picked that novel,' Pearl says. 'I wrote it so long ago, and it was such a small print run, I didn't think there were any copies left.'

'I found a second-hand copy.' Oh God, this is excruciating.

'You must have gone on quite the hunt.'

'No, not really, a seller had it on Amazon.'

'Right. And how far have you got with it?'

'I, uh, I've finished it.'

I get the strangest feeling that we're now engaged in some kind of verbal chess. But it's as if I've been blindfolded and at any point I could make a move that will lead to my downfall.

'So, you must have noticed some interesting parallels between St George's Square and the setting for the book,' Pearl continues.

'Yes, but I guess most writers use locations they're familiar with as their inspiration. I take it you were living here when you wrote it.'

'No, I wasn't as a matter of fact. I only moved here twelve years ago.'

'Oh.'

And now it feels as if we've reached checkmate. The problem is, I'm not sure who to.

'It really would be good to talk to you about this face to face,' she continues.

My mouth goes dry.

'As soon as possible,' she adds before I'm able to reply.

I hear the clang of the lift as it begins whirring its way up the building. 'In fact, I'm on my way up right now.'

My heart thuds as I listen to the lift come to a halt and there's a sharp rap on my door.

CHAPTER THIRTY-SEVEN

September 2019

I sit frozen to the spot before terminating the call. What should I do? If I didn't have a pesky broken ankle, I wouldn't feel nearly so jumpy, but being virtually incapacitated puts me at a distinct disadvantage, even against a seventy-something woman. And a seventy-something woman who does martial arts, as I recall. But I could use my crutches as a weapon if need be. All of a sudden, the absurdity of the situation hits me and I let out a nervous laugh. I need to get a grip.

There's another rap on the door. I hoist myself out of bed and onto my crutches, tucking my phone into my pyjama pocket just in case of an emergency. I hobble into the hallway and unlock the door. Pearl is standing in the lift, clutching a large brown envelope to her chest. *Well, at least it's not a weapon*, I think to myself, and again I'm struck by the absurdity of things.

'Come in,' I say, my mouth so dry from nerves I can barely speak.

'Thank you.'

I motion for her to go ahead of me, just in case, and follow her into the bedroom. Her novel is clearly visible on the bed, but I guess that doesn't really matter now.

'You're a bright woman,' Pearl begins, as I sit down on the edge of the bed and she perches on the armchair by the fireplace. 'So I won't insult your intelligence by failing to address the elephant in the room – or rather the shirt in the loft.'

We both look up at the hatch.

'Oh, OK.' My stomach flutters. Is she admitting that she and her novel are somehow connected to the shirt?

'Is there any way that I could see it?' she asks, glancing around the room.

'It's still up there,' I reply. 'But I did take a photo of it.'

'Oh. Well, could I see that then?'

'OK.' I take my phone from my pocket and she comes over and I show her the photo.

She gasps. 'And you say there was a hole in the fabric?'

'Yes, look.' I zoom in on the hole at the centre of the stain, keeping a firm grip on my phone just in case she tries to snatch it.

'Goodness me...' She breaks off and, to my surprise, I see that she looks close to tears.

'Do you – do you know something about this, and how it came to be up there?' I ask tentatively.

She nods.

'And is it somehow connected to your book?'

'Yes,' she says, her eyes glassy.

'Were those characters real? Did the story really happen?' Goosebumps erupt on my skin as she nods again.

'Well, most of it happened, anyhow.' She looks back at the photo. 'I had no idea about the shirt though... and to think it's been up there all this time.'

'There was a ticket in the pocket too.' I swipe onto the photo of the ticket and show it to her.

'Are you able to read the writing on it?' she asks, squinting at the screen.

'Sure.' I zoom in. 'It's from a place called Newhaven and dated December 1940. Hang on a minute, wasn't Newhaven where—'

'So it was his,' she whispers, cutting in.

'Whose?'

Tears spill from her eyes onto her face. 'Goodness, I'm sorry, I don't know what's come over me, it's just that seeing it...'

'Who did the shirt belong to?' I ask softly.

'It belonged to Arthur,' she replies. 'Or Reg, as he was known in the book.'

'But – does that mean that he died too?'

She hands the envelope she's holding to me. 'I want you to read this.'

'What is it?'

'The original ending to my novel. The real ending to the story.'

'But I don't understand.'

'You will, once you've read it.'

I look inside the envelope and pull out some yellowing pages of typewritten manuscript.

'Go ahead,' she says, heading back over to the armchair.

I turn the first page and start to read.

CHAPTER THIRTY-EIGHT

29 December 1940

As soon as Joseph woke up and opened his eyes, Ruby began to speak. This was becoming quite a regular occurrence. He was beginning to think that she lay there all night composing new monologues to regale him with the second he woke.

'I've come to the conclusion that this has been the best Christmas of my entire life,' Ruby said, propping herself onto her elbow and gazing down at Joseph. 'Even Christmas 1927, which I spent with a mime troupe on Broadway, didn't come close. Nor did the Christmas I spent skiing in Oslo and—'

'Yeah, yeah, I get the picture,' Joseph interrupted.

'I wasn't being boastful,' Ruby said quickly. 'I was being nice. I was trying to say that there's no place in the world that compares to being in your arms.'

'Jesus, where'd you get that line from, one of Kitty's novels?'

'Shut up and hold me!'

He laughed and held her tighter.

'That was actually from one of her novels,' Ruby said. '*The Sheikh and the Scullery Maid*, but sadly it was the sheikh who told the scullery maid to shut up and hold him. They always give the best lines to the hero,' she sighed and planted a kiss on Joseph's chest.

'Yeah well, I think it's safe to say that you always have the best lines when it comes to us.'

'That is true,' she agreed. 'Although you shouldn't underestimate the power of your gruff northern parlance.'

'I'll try not to,' Joseph said wryly. He looked at his watch. 'I'm afraid I'm going to have to take my gruff northern parlance off to work.'

'Oh, it's so unfair,' Ruby wailed. 'I can't wait until Bill puts us back on the same crew.'

'Me too.' He kissed her on the tip of her nose.

'It seems so cruel that I should have an entire day off without you.'

'Yeah well, I'm sure you'll survive,' Joseph chuckled as he got out of bed. 'And we have spent the last three days together.'

'That's very true.' Ruby lay on her back and gazed up at the ceiling, one breast slightly exposed in a way that made Joseph want to get straight back into bed and never leave. 'What a truly magical Christmas this has been. Both of us overcoming our fears and abandoning ourselves to love, like two young salmon, leaping headfirst into a spring.'

'Right, I'm off,' Joseph said, pulling on his trousers and sweater. 'I'll be seeing you later, young salmon.'

'I shall be awaiting you, my sheikh, and in the meantime, my bosom shall be heaving with longing.'

'Bloody hell!' As Joseph opened the door to leave, he turned and looked back at Ruby. 'I love you,' he said quietly.

'Oh Joseph.' She brought her hands to her heart. 'I love you too.'

Ruby lay in bed for about an hour after Joseph left, basking in the warm afterglow of his words. 'Being brave really pays off, Papa,' she whispered to the photograph on her nightstand. 'Being in love is wonderful.' She heard the front door to the house close. *It must be Kitty on her way to see Freddy*, she thought to herself. It had been so nice spending Christmas Day with them both and witnessing such a sweet and heartfelt love developing between them. She heard the door close again. Kitty must have forgotten something.

Ruby sighed. She supposed she really ought to get up.

She put on her robe and went over to her wardrobe. Perhaps she would pay a visit to the Hungerford Club today, and see how the women were faring after Christmas. Yes, that's what she would do. She took some slacks from a hanger and was about to find a blouse when she heard the sound of something smashing. She wasn't sure if it was from outside or inside the building.

She went over to the window and peered through the crack in the blind. The square was deserted, the only living things in sight the bare winter trees, their spindly branches scratching at the pale sky. Perhaps Kitty had dropped something. She heard footsteps creaking on the floorboards above, a much heavier tread than Kitty's. Could it be Freddy? Ruby's eyes widened. Kitty had been adamant that, despite being in love with Freddy, she wouldn't allow things to become physically intimate until she'd divorced Reg. Had she finally capitulated? Had the love between her and Freddy become too intense to resist? Had…

She heard a thud and a muffled scream and her body went stiff with shock. 'Oh no…' she muttered. 'No, no…'

There was a crashing sound directly above her, so loud she thought the ceiling might collapse. And then she heard something that confirmed her very worst fears: the deep angry pitch of a man's voice – Reg's voice. Ruby thought of that terrible day the soldiers had visited and told them that Reg had gone AWOL. She thought of the moment she'd come back into the kitchen and seen Kitty cowering in the corner. And she thought of how different Kitty had been on Christmas Day when the four of them had feasted on goose and laughed and danced and sang. It had been so wonderful to see Kitty unfurl from her tight, anxious bud, blossoming in the light of Freddy's love. Anger blurred her vision, red and hot. How dare Reg come back to terrorise her again? The bully, the coward.

She heard a yelp from upstairs, and the heavy tread of footsteps on the floorboards. He must not be allowed to do this again. She wouldn't allow it. Ruby raced into the kitchen and grabbed the spare key to Kitty's flat from a jar on the shelf. Then she hurried out and into the hallway and up the stairs. When she got to Kitty's back door, she eased the key into the lock and opened it as slowly as she could. It was only at this point that it dawned on her that she had absolutely no idea how she was going to stop Reg. Perhaps she could pretend that she'd come to borrow something. Hopefully her unexpected arrival would be enough to make him stop whatever he was doing.

Ruby gasped as she peered inside. The kitchen floor was littered with broken crockery. She heard the angry bark of Reg's voice coming from the bedroom and she tiptoed through to the darkened hallway.

'Please,' she heard Kitty sob. 'Please don't.'

'I'm your husband,' Reg replied. 'I can do whatever I want.'

Ruby's skin prickled with a mixture of fear and indignation. *Help me, Papa,* she silently whispered. *Please give me courage.*

She crept along the narrow hallway, past the bathroom and the broom cupboard, until finally, she reached the bedroom. The door was slightly ajar and she heard a metallic clinking sound. Her throat tightened. It sounded like a belt being unfastened.

'Please,' she heard Kitty plead again.

'You can beg all you like,' Reg sneered. 'But it won't make no difference. And as soon as I've had you, I'm gonna kill you.'

'No!' Kitty cried, echoing Ruby's thoughts.

She peered through the crack in the door. Reg was kneeling on the bed with his back to her, Kitty's legs splayed either side of him, one shoe on and one shoe off. She heard the sound of fabric ripping and bile burned in her throat. She had to think and think fast. She pushed the door slightly and to her horror it

creaked. Thankfully Kitty's sobs must have drowned it out as Reg
didn't turn round. She peered further into the room.

'Did you really think you'd be able to leave me?' Reg said,
shifting himself on top of Kitty. 'Did you really think I'd let you?'

'I hadn't left you,' Kitty gasped.

'Don't lie to me!' Reg yelled. He raised his hand and struck
Kitty across the face with a sickening crack. 'I've seen him – your
not-so-secret admirer. I've seen you together, kissing on the
doorstep at night, bold as brass.'

'But we haven't…' Kitty broke off.

'Ha, so you admit it.' Reg leaned forward and Kitty yelped.
'Do you know what I'm gonna do, after I've finished with you?'

'What?' Kitty whimpered.

'I'm gonna wait for him to come back home and then I'm
gonna do for him too. And no one will blame me – no one, do
you hear? Because I'll be the poor soldier whose wife betrayed him
while he was away fighting for king and country, just like that
feller who got let off from killing his missus this month. There
ain't a court in the land who'd find me guilty after they find out
what you did to me.'

'H-how do you know where he lives?' Kitty gasped.

'He lives here, you stupid bitch. In the flat upstairs.'

'Oh no. Oh no!' Kitty sobbed.

'Shut up!' Reg yelled, raising his fist.

Ruby stood in the doorway, stunned, a terrible sequence of
realisations slotting together in her mind. Freddy didn't live here.
But Joseph did. And she and Joseph had kissed on the steps last
night when they'd come home from the Hungerford Club. Could
Reg have mistaken them for Kitty and her lover in the darkness
of the blackout?

'Betraying me with a bleedin' conchie,' Reg muttered. 'Yeah,
I'll have any judge and jury eating out of my hand when they
find out what you did to me.'

For a moment Ruby thought her legs might buckle beneath her. She leaned on the door frame to steady herself. Reg was going to kill Kitty and then, due to some terrible case of mistaken identity, he was going to kill Joseph. It couldn't happen. She couldn't let it.

She took a step into the room, and she saw something that nearly made her heart stop. There was a gun on the rug right next to the bed. Right next to Reg. Without stopping to think, she launched herself at it.

'What the hell?' Reg yelled as her hand wrapped around the cold metal. 'What are you doing here?'

Ruby took a few steps back, pointing the gun at him, her arms quivering like jelly. 'Get off her,' she said, her voice cracking.

'Ruby!' Kitty gasped.

Reg heaved himself off her and stumbled from the bed, hoisting up his trousers. He was wearing his military uniform, but it was barely recognisable it was so dirty and creased.

'You need to leave,' Ruby said in a voice that sounded more like a squeak.

Reg stared at her for a moment. The roots of his hair were thick with grease and his jaw was shaded with feeble patches of stubble. 'You ain't got the bottle,' he said, taking a step towards her. She caught a waft of his stale sweat and it made her want to gag. 'But now you're up here, maybe I could have a bit of fun with you too.' He looked at her robe.

'Get away from me,' Ruby said. Damn her arms! Why did they have to tremble so?

'I don't think so,' Reg replied, his voice low and chilling.

'Run, Ruby,' Kitty cried, sitting up in the bed. Her top had been torn off and her lip was cut and swollen, a thin trickle of blood staining the creamy lace of her brassiere.

'Give me the gun,' Reg said, taking another step towards Ruby.

Ruby took a step back. He mustn't get the gun from her. If he did, he would kill them both and then lie in wait to kill Joseph.

'Please, Ruby, just leave,' Kitty implored.

But there was no way Ruby could leave Kitty to this monster – leave her to die.

'I want you out of my house,' Ruby said, her heart racing.

'Who do you think you are, Miss High and Mighty? I think you need to be taken down a peg or two.' Reg took another step towards her.

Ruby stepped back into the doorway.

'Get away from me.' Her chest tightened.

'Yeah, I'm gonna teach you a lesson you won't forget,' he sneered, undoing the button on his trousers. 'You fucking uppity bi—'

Ruby closed her eyes. And she squeezed the trigger.

CHAPTER THIRTY-NINE

29 December 1940

'Is – is he dead?'

Kitty's voice pierced through the ringing in Ruby's ears.

'Is he dead? Ruby!'

Ruby opened her eyes. Kitty was standing in front of her. One of her eyes was as swollen and purple as a plum.

'Ruby!'

She felt Kitty's tiny hands gripping her arms. Ruby blinked and Kitty came back into focus.

'Ruby, I – I think Reg is dead.'

A jolt passed through Ruby's body. She looked down. The gun was lying on the floor in front of her. And so was Reg, a dark stain flowering on his chest.

'What happened? Did I…?' She felt dizzy and faint from shock.

'You saved me, Ruby.'

'Oh God.' Ruby sank to the floor, great shudders coursing through her body. 'Did I – have I killed him?'

Both women looked at Reg, lying lifeless on the rug.

'He – he was going to kill us – and Joseph,' Ruby stammered. 'He thought Joseph was Freddy.'

'I know.' Kitty crouched down and cautiously felt Reg's wrist. 'I can't feel a pulse.' Ruby watched numbly as Kitty placed her trembling fingers on Reg's neck. 'He's dead,' she whispered.

Ruby hugged her knees to her chest and began rocking back and forth. 'I didn't mean to kill him. I just didn't want him to kill you – or Joseph.'

'I know.' Kitty crouched beside her and hugged her. 'You saved our lives.'

'We – we need to call the police,' Ruby stammered. 'And those soldiers. The brigadier. He left a card…'

To her surprise, Kitty shook her head. 'We can't.'

'What? Why not?'

'You heard what he said. If they find out about me and Freddy, they'll say it was my fault – and you could be convicted of murder.'

'But…'

'Please!' Kitty had a wild look in her eyes. 'You saved my life. I'd never forgive myself if you ended up in prison. If you call the police, I'll tell them I killed him.'

'But then *you* might go to prison.' Ruby stared at Reg's body. 'And besides, if we didn't call the police, how would we – what would we do with him?'

Kitty started pacing up and down. 'I could ask Freddy to help. He has his butcher's van. Maybe – maybe he could take him somewhere.'

'But where? And then we'd be incriminating Freddy too.' Ruby's stomach churned. She had killed Reg. She had taken the life of another human being. The enormity of that fact opened up in front of her like an abyss.

Kitty stopped pacing and began wringing her hands. 'Freddy's expecting me. I was on my way to go and meet him when Reg…'

'What happened?'

'He was waiting just outside the front door. He had the gun. He made me bring him back inside. I thought I was going to die, Ruby, but you saved me.' Kitty was now shaking like a leaf. 'Freddy's going to be worried. I should have been at the shop by now. He's bound to come looking for me. Please, Ruby, let me tell him what's happened and see what he says at least.'

Ruby nodded numbly.

Just then the doorbell rang, causing both women to jump out of their skin.

Kitty ran over to the window and peered out. 'It's Freddy.' She grabbed a pullover from her chest of drawers and put it on. Then she helped Ruby up and ushered her from the room. 'You go down to your flat and wait there while I tell Freddy what happened.'

'But don't you want me there too?'

'No. You've done enough. Now it's my turn to help you.'

They hurried downstairs, Kitty guiding Ruby. When Ruby got to her door, she paused. 'Are you sure?'

'Yes,' Kitty replied firmly. 'Please, just go in and wait.'

Ruby went into her flat and shut the door. Her kitchen, which usually felt so welcoming, seemed distorted somehow. Too messy. Too chaotic. She stumbled through to her bedroom and lay down on the bed. *Please, please, please, let it all just have been a dream,* she silently implored. She pinched her arm twice, but it was no good. She was wide awake in some kind of nightmarish new reality.

She heard the tread of footsteps upstairs and then silence, followed by the sound of Kitty sobbing. Then she heard the deep low hum of a man's voice, gentle and consoling. She hugged a blanket around her, suddenly freezing cold and trembling violently. Oh, if only Joseph were there to hold her. But then a terrible thought occurred to her. She had taken a life. Even if it had been in self-defence, Joseph would never forgive her. He didn't even agree with killing Nazis. If he found out she'd killed Reg, he'd surely want nothing more to do with her. She pulled the blanket tighter around her and began to sob.

*

As Joseph arrived home from work, all he could think about was being reunited with Ruby. His shift had seemed to drag on forever, to the point where it even had him craving Ruby's crazy chatter about sheikhs and young salmon. But as he opened the front door, he saw a sight that stopped him dead. Kitty was sitting on the floor by the lift, her head in her hands, Freddy pacing the hallway in front of her.

'At last! You're back!' Kitty cried, stumbling to her feet. Her face was cut and bruised and he saw that her blouse was torn open beneath her cardigan.

Joseph's gut clenched. There was only one person he could think of who might inflict such harm upon Kitty. Had Reg returned? Had he somehow got into the house? 'What's happened?' he asked anxiously.

'We need your help,' Freddy said, hurrying over and grabbing Joseph by the arm.

Joseph glanced at Ruby's door. 'Where's Ruby?'

'She – she's fine. She's gone out for a walk,' Kitty stammered.

'Please.' Freddy's grip on Joseph's arm tightened. 'Can you come upstairs and help us?'

'Of course.'

Joseph followed them up the stairs and into Kitty's flat.

'What the heck's happened?' he exclaimed as they picked their way through the broken crockery littering the kitchen floor.

'He's through here,' Kitty murmured, leading them out of the kitchen and down the narrow hallway.

'Who is? What the…?' Joseph's heart pounded as he stared over Kitty's shoulder into the bedroom. Finally he managed to drag his gaze from Reg's body on the floor and glanced around the rest of the room. The crumpled, bloodstained bed sheets, Kitty's torn blouse and battered face and the gun on the floor beside Reg all told a terrible story.

'Did he – did he attack you?' he asked Kitty.

She nodded. 'He was going to kill me. He was going to kill you too.'

'Me?' Joseph frowned. 'Why?'

'He thought you were the man I was betraying him with. He thought you were Freddy. He said he was going to kill me and Ruby and then he was going to wait for you to come home so he could kill you too.' Kitty started sobbing.

'He said he was going to kill Ruby?' Joseph's skin prickled with fear.

'Yes.'

'Why?'

'She was here. She came to save me.' Tears flowed from Kitty's eyes. 'She saved you too.'

'Ruby did this?' Joseph's mouth went dry as he stared down at the corpse.

'She had no choice. He was going to kill us.' Kitty began to wail. Freddy put his arm around her shoulder.

'Where is she?' Joseph looked around the room wildly, his need to see Ruby so overpowering he could barely breathe.

'She was so shaken up,' Kitty replied between sobs. 'I told her to go out for a few hours and that I would fix everything.' Her voice grew higher. 'She can't go to jail. She saved our lives.'

'But why would she go to jail?' Joseph stammered. 'It was self-defence.'

'Reg was a soldier!' Kitty cried. 'They'll make it look as if we killed him so that I could be with Freddy. It'll be like that case where the soldier got away with killing his wife when he came home on leave because she'd been having an affair. They'll twist everything.'

Joseph felt sick to his stomach. He remembered reading about that case in the paper and how horrified he'd been that a judge had excused the murder.

'You have to help us, please,' Kitty pleaded. 'We have to protect Ruby.'

'It's all right, pet,' Freddy said, pulling her to him. He looked at Joseph over her shoulder. 'Will you help me get rid of it?' He glanced down at the body. 'I've got the van parked outside. I just need help carrying it.'

Joseph thought of Ruby coming up into the flat on her own, trying to save her friend, trying to save him, and his heart ached. All of his principles and beliefs about killing were muted by his love for her.

'Yes, I'll help you,' he replied softly.

*

Ruby hurried along Fleet Street, her hat pulled down against the cold. When Kitty had urged her to get out of the house and go for a walk, she'd jumped at the chance, longing to be as far away from Reg's body as possible. But no matter how far she walked, she couldn't escape the spectre of what she'd done. And now, as she walked past the newspaper offices lining Fleet Street, she felt fear engulf her. What if the truth came out? What if one day the journalists beavering away inside the buildings she was passing would be typing headlines declaring her a murderer? Or, even worse, announcing her execution. But she hadn't murdered Reg, she reminded herself. She'd been saving Kitty and herself and Joseph from being killed. But Reg had been a soldier away serving his country. His wife had fallen in love with another man. It would be so easy for the papers to twist the truth, to paint her as the villain and Reg as the innocent victim: the poor wronged soldier, murdered by an evil woman.

As Ruby reached St Bride's Church, she felt the strangest compulsion to go inside, and not only to escape from the cold. She pushed open the heavy wooden door. The church was totally dark, save for a few flickering candles lining the altar. Ruby slumped down on one of the pews and took a deep breath. The cool air smelled of incense and melting candle wax.

'Oh, Papa,' she whispered, 'I don't know what to do.'

She longed to hear her father's voice whispering some sage advice, but the church remained steeped in silence. She thought of all the people who must have sought refuge and comfort beneath the huge oak beams of the church before, praying to another unseen Father.

'I didn't mean to take his life,' she whispered. 'I only wanted to save Kitty and Joseph. Please forgive me.'

A sudden chill breeze swept through the empty church and Ruby's mind filled with an image of her father, in his army uniform in the trenches. And it occurred to her that during the years he'd spent fighting on the front, he must have taken many lives. It was a thought that had never dawned on her before; she'd always been so caught up in the pain of his death. But there had to be people in Germany mourning the loss of people her papa had killed too. How had he dealt with the guilt? One small consolation was that Reg had been an only child with no remaining family. According to Kitty, his mother had died of consumption when he was a child and his father had drunk himself into an early grave. By all accounts, no one would be mourning his loss.

Outside, the air-raid siren began to wail and Ruby felt an exhaustion that defied description. She'd been hoping that the lull in bombing over Christmas signified a change in tactic from the Germans. When would the death and destruction end? Hoping it was a false alarm, she stayed sitting there, head bowed.

'Please forgive me,' she whispered again.

Her mind filled with an image of Kitty immediately after the shooting: the finger-sized welts on the sides of her neck, her eye bruised and swollen, her lip bleeding. If Ruby hadn't shot Reg, Kitty would now be dead. If Reg hadn't attacked Kitty and threatened to kill them all, he would still be alive. He chose to come to the house that day. He chose to attack Kitty. He chose to threaten them, but Ruby hadn't chosen any of it. The only choice she'd made was to save her friend. How would she have been able to live with the guilt if she'd done nothing? If she'd stayed cocooned in the safety of her own flat, hearing the awful sound of Reg shouting, the thud, thud of the bed as he raped Kitty, and then the shot ringing out as he killed her? Ruby felt a strange kind of peace wash over her. Reg had been acting out of anger and hate. But she had been acting out of love for her friend. She took a moment to allow that thought to sink deep into her subconscious. She had been acting out of love.

'Thank you,' she whispered.

Then she heard the distant hum of a plane. Damn it. Clearly it wasn't a false alarm after all. She gathered her things and got to her feet.

'Thank you,' she whispered again, looking around the beautiful building.

The hum outside grew to a roar and she heard the strange plop, plop, plop of something being dropped. Plop, plop, the sound came again, as if the roof of the church was being pelted with stones. She hurried outside. A plane was swooping away, leaving a trail of white and green lights flaring on the rooftops in its wake. Incendiaries. Ruby's heart sank.

There was a rattling sound and a canister rolled from the roof of the church onto the pavement in front of her, catching light on impact.

'Oh no!' Ruby gasped, looking back at the roof of the church. Orange flames were beginning to lick at the wooden slats.

Another plane roared over. Ruby dived into a tobacconist's doorway as again there came the plop, plop, plopping sound as more incendiaries fell from the sky. As soon as the planes had passed, she decided to risk breaking cover and ran back towards the river. Just as she got there, a bus pulled up at a stop beside her and she jumped on board.

'Looks like the Bosch are back then,' the conductor said as he issued her a ticket.

'Yes, more's the pity.'

She took a seat at the back of the top deck and peered through the rear window. The night sky was now quite a spectacle, what with the white and green flares from the incendiaries, the sweep of the searchlights and the crackling, blazing trails of the artillery. Thankfully, as the bus made its way along the river in the direction of Pimlico, the sky became clear of planes. The Germans seemed to be focusing their attentions right in the heart of the city.

Ruby got off the bus outside the Tate Gallery and began meandering her way back towards Pendragon Square. For once she wouldn't mind going into the garden shelter; anything would be better than going back home. Having to see Joseph and tell him what she'd done was a moment she wanted to put off for as long as possible because she knew that once she told him it would all be over.

*

As Joseph helped Freddy carry Reg's body downstairs, his throat tightened and the palms of his hands became clammy.

'I'll just check the coast's clear,' Freddy said.

They lowered the body to the floor in the hallway and Freddy slipped outside. A couple of seconds later, he returned, giving Joseph a thumbs up. They picked up the body and hurried outside. Blackout wasn't as dark as normal, due to a strange tangerine glow on the horizon, but thankfully there wasn't a soul around as they put the body into the back of Freddy's van. They hurried round to the front and Freddy gave Joseph the keys. They'd agreed that he should drive as he was more used to driving during blackout. Thankfully Freddy's van was a lot smaller and easier to handle than the ambulance.

Joseph took a moment to try to slow his breathing, then headed out of the square and on to Millbank. He drove towards the glow on the horizon as if it were some kind of beacon. For the first time ever, he was grateful for a German bombing raid. Hopefully it would provide them with the distraction they needed.

'Where are we going to put it?' Freddy asked.

'We'll know when we see it,' Joseph replied.

The deeper they got into the heart of the city, the more the fires raged around them, creeping ever closer to the majestic dome of St Paul's Cathedral. Joseph spotted a huge building ablaze down a narrow side street and turned in towards it. There was no sign of a fire truck, which wasn't really a surprise – with so much of the city now alight, the fire services must have been stretched to breaking point.

'Wait here,' he said to Freddy as he parked up. As soon as he got out of the van, he was hit by a wall of heat. He saw from a sign on the building that it was a publisher's warehouse. No wonder it was going up like an inferno with all of that paper inside.

Joseph hurried down the alleyway until he reached a door. He tried the handle, but it was locked. Damn. He was on his way back to the van when he heard the sound of glass smashing. He turned to see that a window on the side of the building had exploded in the heat. He raced back to the van, beckoning wildly at Freddy to get out. Together they pulled Reg's body from the van and hurried down the alleyway.

Don't think about what you're doing, Joseph silently urged himself. *Just do it.* Before they'd left he'd changed Reg's body into some of his own clothes to try to help prevent identification. It was surreal now, seeing his sweater and trousers on Reg's corpse. How had it come to this? *Don't think about, just do it.*

'In here,' he yelled to Freddy over the roar of the fire, nodding towards the window. The heat was so intense he could barely breathe. They brought the body up to the window and hurled it inside. Joseph watched for a moment, as the flames began devouring it. Then he heard a terrible rumbling sound coming from deep within the warehouse.

'Run!' Freddy yelled.

They both raced back up the alleyway and into the van, Joseph driving off before they'd even had time to shut the doors. The rumbling turned to a roar. Joseph pulled out onto the main road and looked in his rear-view mirror. The building was collapsing like a deck of cards, completely consumed by the fire.

'Bloody hell, that was a close shave,' Freddy gasped.

'You're telling me.'

Joseph drove on in silence. All he could think of was Ruby.

*

Ruby sat in the middle of the garden, gazing up at the sky. The thin beams of the searchlights swept this way and that through the darkness, every so often picking out a plane. Then came the snap and pop of the tracer bullets, blazing through the air like comets. And presiding over it all was a huge moon, turned amber by the number of fires now blazing below. London was burning. After unloading their first round of incendiaries, the bombers had returned, the blazing city now a beacon to guide them in.

Perhaps this was it, Ruby thought as she listened to the whistle and boom of the bombs falling. Perhaps this was the night the Germans finally razed this great city to the ground. The lull over Christmas had clearly just been a case of them gathering themselves for an even more brutal assault.

The silhouette of a plane passed over the moon and there was a blinding flash of anti-aircraft fire, casting the garden in a brilliant white glow. And in that second she saw a figure standing by the gate looking at her. Joseph. She scrambled to her feet, but before she could take a step, he was there, right in front of her. His face was streaked with what looked like soot.

'It's done,' he murmured. 'He's gone.'

'Who's gone?'

'Reg.'

Ruby let out a gasp. 'You know?'

'Yes. Kitty told me. Freddy and I, we – we got rid of it.'

'The body?' Ruby whispered.

'Yes.'

'Did Kitty tell you that I…' She broke off, unable to utter the words that would condemn her.

'She told me that you saved her life,' he said softly. 'And that you saved mine too.'

'And you – you don't hate me for it?' she asked hopefully.

'Why would I hate you?'

'I took a life.'

'You saved three lives.' He took hold of her hands.

'Thank you,' she whispered.

'I love you,' he replied.

And there it was again, that one little word, but the strongest of anchors – love. He loved her, and she loved him, and she loved Kitty, and Kitty loved Freddy. And now that love would bind them together forever.

As Joseph pulled her into his arms and held her tight, she looked up at the sky, ablaze with the luminescent trails of anti-aircraft fire. A V-shaped formation of bombers flew across the amber moon, just like a flock of wild geese, Ruby mused. She'd never seen such terrible beauty, but she knew that beyond the brokenness the stars still burned and would continue to burn, long after this dreadful war was over, guiding people onward.

CHAPTER FORTY

September 2019

'Wow.' I put down the manuscript and look at Pearl. While I've been reading, she's shrunk further into the armchair, appearing even more diminutive than ever, and it strikes me as ludicrous that I should have ever been afraid of her. 'So, is this what actually happened, in real life, I mean?'

She nods.

'Why didn't you put this ending in the book?'

'I was afraid to.'

'In case someone worked out it was a true story?'

'Exactly.' She gives a sad laugh. 'But you worked it out anyway, thanks to the discovery of the shirt. They're all dead now though,' she adds defensively.

'Of course.' Pearl is clearly hugely emotionally invested in whoever these characters were based upon.

'Was she your mother?' I ask softly.

Pearl nods.

'I don't think she was wrong to kill him,' I offer as some form of consolation. 'If it went to court today, it would be an open and shut case of self-defence. I can't believe it wouldn't have been back then, to be honest.'

Pearl shakes her head. 'There were several cases of soldiers getting away with murdering their wives during the war, or having extremely lenient sentences. It was a terrible business. But in any case, Ruby wasn't my mother. My mother was Kitty.'

'What?' Of all the shock twists I've encountered today, this was one I really did not see coming. Pearl seems so like Ruby, and so unlike Kitty!

'Ruby was my godmother,' Pearl continues. 'And we were very close. She used to call me her honorary soul daughter.' She laughs. 'She always loved a flowery turn of phrase.'

'So, was Freddy your father?'

Pearl nods.

'But what happened to them all?' I move forward on the bed, so eager to hear more I barely notice the pain throbbing in my ankle.

'Ruby and Joseph moved to America at the start of 1941. I suppose they wanted to get as far away as possible, just in case the truth ever came out, but it never did. I'm guessing there was so little left of Reg's remains that it was impossible to identify him. They set up a shelter for the homeless in Brooklyn, which is still running to this day, and Ruby sold the top two flats and gave the ground-floor flat to my parents. I moved back in here after my parents died.'

'But doesn't it freak you out, knowing what happened here?'

She shakes her head. 'This was my childhood home. I had only fond memories of it. I had no idea what happened until Ruby told me when she was on her deathbed – she died of cancer back in 1980. Joseph had passed away a couple of years earlier so I'd gone out to take care of her. I think being faced with her own mortality brought it all back to her. I got the sense that by telling me she wanted me to absolve her somehow. And I think, or at least I hope, I did.' Pearl smiles. 'I pointed out that she hadn't just saved my mother's and Joseph's life that day, but she'd saved mine too. I think that really helped her.'

'I'm sure it did.' I sigh and shake my head, still trying to process everything.

'Tom – the real Joseph,' Pearl adds, 'must have hidden Arthur's shirt up in the loft before they got rid of the body.'

'I guess so.' I nod. 'So Joseph was called Tom and Reg was called Arthur. What was your mum's real name?' I ask.

'Mary.'

'And how about Ruby? What was she called?'

Pearl smiles. 'She was called Pearl.'

EPILOGUE

Pearl and I stand in the garden of St George's Square, looking up at the house. It's the end of October and my cast has been off for a week so we decided to go for a celebratory stroll in the golden autumn sunshine. In the six weeks since Pearl's big reveal, we've become firm friends. I guess bonding over a historical love story does that to people, and in the end it *was* a love story, rather than some of the terrifying alternatives I'd been imagining when I was out of my head on pain meds. When I'd told Pearl that at one point I thought she was going to kill me, rather than being mortified as I'd feared, she beamed with pride, telling me she'd always secretly wanted to be a Hollywood-style villain. As I link arms with her now, I can't imagine feeling anything other than affection for this eccentric woman I've come to call my friend.

'The shelter was just over there,' Pearl says, pointing to a circular flowerbed in the middle of the garden.

As I look at the copper-coloured leaves on the ground and the pale pink petals of the last of the roses, it's hard to imagine that this was once a place of refuge from German bombs. I picture the former residents of the square, huddling together in the underground shelter, or 'sardine tin', as Ruby referred to it, and a shiver runs up my spine.

'There's still evidence of the war everywhere in this city,' Pearl says. 'Gaps in between houses where bombs fell, shrapnel damage to the walls of buildings. If you look close enough, you'll find it.'

I nod and picture the ethereal figures of Joseph and Ruby hurrying from the house on their way to the ambulance station as an air-raid siren wails. All of those lives played out on this same stage, overlapping and entwining down through history, like the leaves coming and going on the trees. Perhaps the greatest gift of getting to know Pearl and her story is that it's left me with an acute awareness of the harsh beauty of life and the importance of love in helping us navigate our way through it. This last realisation has helped me enormously in moving on from the end of my marriage. That, and knowing that the love Ruby and Joseph shared was real after all. It's something I know I haven't experienced yet but I'm determined to hold out for, and the best reason ever for moving forward with hope.

A LETTER FROM SIOBHAN

Dear reader,

Thank you so much for choosing to read *Beyond This Broken Sky*. If you enjoyed it, and want to keep up to date with all of my latest releases, just sign up at the following link. Your email address will never be shared and you can unsubscribe at any time.

www.bookouture.com/siobhan-curham

Beyond This Broken Sky is my second World War Two novel. If you've come to it via my first historical novel, *An American in Paris*, I hope you enjoyed the new cast of characters and change of setting. As a Londoner, I've always been intrigued by the Blitz and what it must have been like to live in the city during that time. When I was a child, I loved listening to my grandma's tales of her life as a young woman, living and working in London during the war. One story that really stayed in my mind was how she and her friend decided to move to an apartment in Pimlico at the start of the war, as the rents had been dramatically reduced due to the bombing risks. When they were flat-hunting, they viewed two properties on adjacent squares. My grandma preferred a flat in St George's Square, but her friend wanted to move to one in Dolphin Square. Thankfully, my grandma got her way because the apartment they would have moved into in Dolphin Square was destroyed shortly after in a bombing raid. The fact that a previously inconsequential choice like deciding where to live could become a matter of life or death during the Blitz blew my mind, and it was something I really wanted to capture in the novel. I decided to use Pimlico as the central location as a tribute to my grandma and when I discovered that Dolphin Square had housed a first-aid centre and ambulance station during the war I couldn't think of a better place to set my story!

While I was planning the book, I paid a visit to St George's Square and spent some time in the garden there. It was a very strange and somewhat eerie experience, imagining my grandma and her friend walking along those same pavements, hurrying off to work, or to the communal air-raid shelter. Like so many of her generation, she'd always been very matter-of-fact when recounting her wartime experiences, but there can be no denying that it must have been a terrifying time, and putting myself in her shoes in order to write *Beyond This Broken Sky* was a very poignant experience.

One of my main aims with my historical fiction is to unearth and bring to light lesser known yet fascinating stories from history – stories like Madame Tussauds being bombed and the waxwork of Hitler remaining intact! On a more serious note, I was horrified to discover that during the war, several soldiers were let off with no or very little punishment for killing their wives. As soon as I started researching the Blitz, I was intrigued to discover that the famous 'Blitz spirit' wasn't quite all it was cracked up to be. I had no idea that the government had initially banned the use of the Underground as a public shelter and I'd never heard the story of the storming of the Savoy shelter to try to bring attention to the plight of the East Enders. Similarly, I wanted to subvert a common trope in World War Two fiction, where the hero is a soldier. I was really interested in exploring the experience of a conscientious objector and examining how there can be many different types of bravery.

I hope that reading *Beyond This Broken Sky* shone a slightly different light on the Blitz for you, and if you did enjoy it, it would mean the world to me if you would write a short online review. I'd love to hear what you think, and it will make such a difference when it comes to helping new readers discover the book, which is critical for me as a relatively new historical novelist!

I always love hearing from my readers so please feel free to get in touch via my Facebook page, Twitter, Goodreads, Instagram or my website.

Thanks so much,
Siobhan

Siobhan Curham Author

@SiobhanCurham

@SiobhanCurham

www.siobhancurham.com

ACKNOWLEDGEMENTS

Huge gratitude first and foremost to my lovely editor, Cara Chimirri. It's an absolute joy to work with you – thank you so much for all of the faith and support you give to me and my writing. Ditto all of the wonderful team at Bookouture: Sarah Hardy, Kim Nash, Noelle Holten, Natasha Hodgson, Alexandra Holmes and Alba Proko, to name but a few. Much love and thanks to Jane Willis at United Agents for being the best agent I could ever wish for. I'm also hugely indebted to all of the people who took the time to review my first historical novel, *An American in Paris*, on their blogs, Goodreads, Netgalley and Amazon. Reviews and recommendations make such a positive difference, especially when you're starting out in a brand-new genre as a writer, as I am. On a more personal note, your kind words about my writing have helped me so much during the challenges of the past year.

I read some wonderful books while researching for this novel. If you would like to find out more about life during the Blitz, I highly recommend *London Was Ours* by Amy Helen Bell, *The Secret History of the Blitz* by Joshua Levine, *Few Eggs and No Oranges* by Vere Hodgson and *The West End Front* by Matthew Sweet.

NAMASTE! to my dad, Michael Curham – if it weren't for you I would never have had the idea to write about a conscientious objector. Thank you for constantly guiding me towards love and simplicity, and for getting me to question everything, in your quintessential 'Awkward Bastard' way! Huge love and thanks also to my son, Jack Curham – there's not a day goes by when I'm not grateful for being your mum. And much love and gratitude to my own mum, Anne Cumming, for all of your help piecing together Grandma's life during the Blitz, which ended up inspiring the basis of this novel. Massive love and thanks to the rest of my family, Alice (aka the mysterious A, thank you for always being the first to read my books and for always being so encouraging), Luke, Bea, Danno, Katie, John, and all of my Irish and American cousins – with special thanks to Charles Delaney, Amy Fawcett, Lacey Jennen and Gina Ervin for being the best cheerleaders ever! And to Kayhan – thank you for everything, Khodafez, azizam!

There's a very good reason why so many of my novels end up being a celebration of friendship – because I've been blessed with some of the very best friends. I'm especially grateful to the following friends for always being so encouraging and supportive of my writing: Tina McKenzie, Sara Starbuck, Linda Lloyd, Sammie (and Edi) Venn, Pearl Bates, Stuart Berry, Charlotte Baldwin, Steve O'Toole, Lexie Bebbington, Marie Hermet, Mara Bergman and Thea Bennett. Huge thanks also to the wonderful writing community I've amassed over the years through my writing workshops and coaching: Gillian Holland, Tony Leonard, Michelle Porter, Liz Brooks, Miriam Thundercliffe, Dave Moonwood, Rachel Swabey, Jim Clammer, Ade Bott, Paul Gallagher, Meriel Rose and the rest of The Snowdroppers. Jan Silverman, Patricia Jacobs, Mike Davidson, Mavis Pachter, Phil Lawder, Julia Buckley, Gabriela Harding, David Stroud, Barbara Towell, Mike Deller, Pete 'Esso' Haynes, Lorna Read and the rest of the Harrow and Uxbridge Writers. Big love to Lara Kingsman, Lesley and John Strick, Pete Barber, 'Captain' Iain Scarlett, Anita, Gill July, Gillian Davies, Claire Gee-Gee, Linda Newman, Graham Stewart and Shirley Smith and the rest of the Nower Hill crew – you make Facebook so much more fun!

Made in United States
Orlando, FL
26 October 2022

23878606R00173